PRAISE FOR *REMN*   *Allnach*

Finalist, Science Fiction .... Awards

"Each of the three novellas is a beautifully crafted gem of a story." Douglas R. Cobb, Bestsellersworld.com

"Allnach's writing style can be described as smart, elegant, and addicting." San Francisco Book Review

"An interesting read. "Remnant", especially, is one story that all individuals should read and strive to understand." Amy Lignor, Feathered Quill

"Remnant: an anthology' will appeal to those who enjoy science fiction novels, particularly military science fiction. Allnach's intelligent writing style is quite appealing and I expect we will see more from him in the future." Kam Aures, Rebecca's Reads

"("Remnant") is a book well both the reading and the thinking that comes with the reading. If you're interested in a somewhat different tale of what's ahead, this is a 'Must Read'." Donn Gurney, BookReview.com

"Roland Allnach is destined to become recognized for his contributions in whatever genre of writing he may choose." Richard R. Blake, Reader Views

"With "Remnant", Roland Allnach presents three novellas that promise to haunt the reader long after the cover has been closed. A nearly perfect gem of sci-fi." Peter Dabbene, ForeWord Clarion

"With plenty to ponder and plenty to keep readers reading, "Remnant" is a fine assortment of thought, highly recommended." Willis M. Buhle, Midwest Book Review, Reviewer's Bookwatch

To Alicia,
Best of luck in
your publishing dreams!
Thanks,
M allm

Oddities & Entities

Roland Allnach

ALL THINGS

THAT MATTER

PRESS

ISBN: 978-0-9850066-4-8

Library of Congress Control Number: 2012934191

Cover design by All Things That Matter Press

Published in 2012 by All Things That Matter Press

"Shift/Change" first published in the June/July 2010 edition of Aphelion webzine

To all the little voices

Table of Contents

Before Allison knew the meaning of words or the context of visions, she knew the Curmudgeon. It was there, lodged in her earliest memories, the memories that imbed themselves deep in the psyche to shadow all future memories. When she lay in her crib as a pale and lumpy baby, she didn't know to cry when it came in her room, when it passed through her walls as if their existence were some unsubstantiated rumor rather than studs, slats, and plaster. And though at any greater age she might have cowered and screamed, in her unclouded infantile mind there was no reference for fear or judgment, only the absorbance of what was. Perhaps the Curmudgeon knew this but, then again, perhaps not. As the years passed, it was a matter of little importance.

She remembered her first years of school. She was different; this realization was as stark as the full moon visits of the Curmudgeon were fantastic. When other children clamored to play in the sun and warmth, she found herself possessed by an ever-present chill. She felt most comfortable wearing black, without perceiving any conscious decision to that end. She preferred to stay inside, or in places of deep shade or shadow, and gaze out at the light. It wasn't that she shunned the warm light of the Florida sun, but the glare seemed to scald her eyes with its white intensity. Her eyes were her source of distinction, after all. Vast for her narrow face, their luminous, sea green irises formed tidal pools about the tight black dots of her pupils. Her stare was one that few could bear for long. Children and teachers alike found her unblinking silence a most uncomfortable experience, and her mute distraction in school led to the inevitable conclusion that she wasn't very bright.

She had no friends. Her world, though, wasn't as lonesome as it may have seemed.

She lived with her grandmother, a reclusive widow of Creole descent, who wandered about their old manor house singing under her breath in her broken French dialect. Allison loved the old house, despite its state of disrepair and the ratty look of its worn exterior, with the few remaining patches of white paint peeling off the grayed wood clapboard. The oak floors creaked, but there was something timeless about the place, with its high ceilings, spacious rooms and front colonnade. The house was surrounded by ancient southern oaks; they were broad, stately trees, the likes of which one could only find in Florida. Their sinewy, gargantuan branches split off low from the trunk, with gray-green leaves poking out between dangling veils of Spanish moss. The trees shielded Allison from the sun, and provided a home for squirrels, chipmunks, and birds. The Curmudgeon would leave their cleaned skulls on her windowsill as gifts when the moon waxed in silvery twilight.

Her parents loved her—or so they claimed, when she would see them. They seemed more like friends than her elders. She often watched them with curious eyes, peering from her window at night as they frolicked about the front lawn. Her mother, very much a younger vision of her grandmother, had long dark hair, hair that would sway about her as she danced naked under the trees at night. Her father would be there with her, dancing naked as well, the strange designs tattooed down his back often blending with the swaying lengths of Spanish moss. They claimed to be moon cultists, though Allison had no idea what that meant. It was of no matter. Soon enough they became part of the night, passing to her dreams forever.

The memory of that change was the first emotional turmoil of her secluded little life. She was seven, and her parents had come out for the weekend. It was one of those times when her parents sat under the sprawling branches of the oaks, drinking and smoking throughout the day until they lay back on a blanket, their glazed eyes hidden behind their sunglasses. The hours drifted by, and the day faded to the lazy serenity of a Florida evening. Beneath long, golden rays of sunshine they began to stir, rising from their stupor to a restless sense of wanderlust. They came in the house after dinner, settling themselves at the table and exchanging small talk as Allison ate a bowl of vanilla ice cream with rainbow sprinkles. They smiled over Allison's drawings, complimenting her budding artistic skills, and talked to her grandmother about some plans for the next weekend. Even at her young age Allison could tell her grandmother humored them. Her parents didn't have a false bone in their body, but they were not reliable people. Free spirits, her grandmother would say.

Yet as those thoughts rolled about Allison's head her eyes seemed to blur, and she stared at her parents with that unnerving, unblinking gaze of hers. Her heart began to race, her skin tingled, and then it came to her: not a shadow, but a different kind of light than the sun, a light that seemed to seep from within her parents, until the tactile periphery of their bodies became a pale shadow over the ivory glow of their skeletons. She trembled in her seat as the sight gained clarity until she could see all their bones in all their minute detail, but then it changed, changed in a way that froze her blood in her veins. Black fracture lines spread across the smooth ivory like running rivers of ink, until every bone in their bodies was broken to jagged ruin.

Her grandmother called her name, snapping her out of her stupor. She blinked, then screamed and ran from the table to the living room. Her parents and grandmother came after her, but she buried her head under the couch pillows. Despite the pillows, the moment she opened her eyes she could see them, right through the pillows and couch, standing there in their shattered translucence. She ran for her room, scratching at her eyes, and that was when things changed. Her grandmother charged after her, following her to her room, and tore through every drawer until she found the small collection of skulls Allison kept—the tokens the Curmudgeon had left her. Her grandmother stuffed her in her closet, closed the door to her room, and sat outside the door. She could hear her grandmother's voice, even in the dark of the closet. She clamped her eyes shut; it was a desperate final measure to blot out the sight of her parents. She could see them, through the walls, through the floor, through the trees, as they hopped on her father's motorcycle and raced off.

She screamed for them to stop, but she was a child with a trifling voice, stuffed in a closet.

She cried herself to sleep.

***

She woke to the utter darkness of the closet, and refused to move. Her eyes slid open, and she saw nothing. Hesitant at first, she nevertheless uncoiled from her fetal ball to push open the closet door and look out on her bedroom. The Curmudgeon was there, gathering up the miniature skulls Allison's grandmother left scattered on the floor. It turned to Allison and offered the tokens, which she took and hid in a different drawer. When she glanced over her shoulder the Curmudgeon was watching her, the pale nimbus of blue light that sheathed its emaciated body providing a dim glow in the dark room. It tipped its head, turning when Allison looked to the door at the sound of her grandmother's voice. She was singing—or rather, she was chanting—her broken French coming in low, repetitive passages. Allison looked to the Curmudgeon, but the glowing, featureless orbs of its green eyes were incapable of any expression. It stepped toward the door and crouched, looking back at Allison as it waved the tapered claws of its fingers by the door. Allison shook her head and held up her hands, afraid that her grandmother would open the door and scare off her mischievous friend. The Curmudgeon stilled its claws, instead sweeping them over its bare skull to send several tendrils of bright blue light dancing through the air before they dissipated. Allison smiled and, for a moment, she remembered her innocence. She looked back to the Curmudgeon, but it was already floating toward the outside wall. It gave her a last wave before it disappeared.

She went to sleep. When she woke, her grandmother was waiting outside her bedroom door to tell her the news. Her parents had been hit by a bus and splattered across two lanes of traffic.

***

When Allison turned eighteen she started to work at the tattoo shop her father's brother owned. Walking Canvas was a bustling business adjoining a popular biker bar that her uncle owned as well. He took an interest in her after seeing some of her artwork, which had blossomed to works of exquisite excess. At the end of her senior year in high school she even won an award for a painting, oil on canvas, which she gave the title *Dispiritu Rex*. It depicted a naked man, pinned like a butterfly in a case of velvet. His body was opened with forensic precision, with his entrails pulled out and formed into letters that spelled a simple word: FALLEN.

Her name and picture appeared with the award in the senior yearbook, which she didn't buy, so she was oblivious to the recognition. It suited her, as nobody knew her, and the recognition was more like empty cognition as to who she was. Most students had passed her off as some Goth freak with her black clothes and the round, black sunglasses she wore to protect her eyes. On the other hand, nobody in the Goth crowd knew her, and she knew none of them. She had kept to herself; it was easier to be a loner. The less she saw of people, the less chance she had of seeing their bones. She even came up with a name for it: *boneview*. After her parents, there were two kids in her senior class that she saw, and then knew, what waited for them. She warned one of them; he punched her in the hallway and told her she was a freak. His neck snapped during a football game. The other boy had cancer; he died before graduation. She never said anything to him.

Her uncle took her under his wing, though. He set her up in the back of Walking Canvas with a drawing board, and let her work her craft. She was never one to put ink to skin; rather, she made designs for others to make one with customers' bodies. Given her nature, she rarely spoke with anyone, preferring her quiet corner. She knew better than to share too much conversation with people, knowing that sooner or later the boneview would come. Although in many cases she saw nothing more than the long deterioration of arthritis and old age waiting for people, there were those few other horrible premonitions she preferred not to see. She didn't entertain the luxury of empathy. Her only peace was at home, where her grandmother's singing would lull her to sleep, where she could lounge beneath the trees and their dangling moss and listen to the peaceful breeze, where the Curmudgeon would visit her on full moons and entertain her with its little slights of hand.

Until then, she had never questioned the Curmudgeon's presence in her life, or her boneview, for that matter. These were simply realities of her existence. She never wondered if anyone else had such things in their life, because she knew she wasn't like anyone else. All she had to do was

4

take off her black glasses and look in the mirror at her luminous sea-green eyes to know she was different.

She painted the Curmudgeon one night when she stayed late at Walking Canvas, after closing hours. She had a little too much to drink and, though the drink had nothing to do with her creative impulse, the moment came upon her. It wasn't much different than the stupor she felt during a phase of boneview, but it felt more productive, leaving her with something tangible to show for her trance other than some eccentric premonition nobody would understand. Nevertheless, when she was done she thought she captured the Curmudgeon's appearance in splendid detail, only for it to summon the one question she never asked.

She waited until the next full moon, fighting to stay awake as her grandmother fell into her Creole chant outside Allison's bedroom door, the way she did every full moon. Allison waited and, sometime after midnight, it came—the misanthrope diffusing through her wall to stand full before her. She studied the lanky length of its form to make sure she caught it right in her painting. It was tall and skeleton thin, though it was not a skeleton—instead sheathed in a tight veil of leathery skin, ivory pale and dimpled, like a plucked chicken. Scars, long and discolored, ran in uneven lines along its hide. There were the claws on its four fingers, broad where they grew out from the fingertips before tapering in tight curves to vicious points. The thin neck seemed frail, but showed no strain in supporting the head, a bare skull with a lipless sheath of skin covering the jaws. The eyes were featureless green orbs that glowed as they hovered in the cavernous eye sockets. Their color contrasted with the pale aura of blue light flickering along the creature's skin, the aura cresting atop its skull in wavering tendrils that resembled the undulating tongues of a fire.

It tipped its head as she stared at it, stared with her artist's stupor, and the question formed on her lips—silent but nevertheless asked.

Why do you come to me?

The Curmudgeon held up a hand, waving its claws. Its lipless mouth opened, revealing a cluster of needle like fangs that sat in tight rows, cramped within its mouth. They began to rustle against each other, emitting a low buzz that rose in volume to produce a raspy voice.

"Me wants, me wants what me wants, and me wants me not to be lonesome."

She put out her hand. "You chose me?"

It looked to her fingers, rattling its claws by its chest with a low clicking sound. It reached out, almost as if it was unsure to touch her, and caressed her palm with a claw.

"Me old, me old, and me only see what me see, and want to see more."

She touched its hand, her fingers recoiling at the bitter cold of the Curmudgeon's hide. It drew its hand back at once, hunching before her and retreating toward her window.

"Where are you going?"

"Girl wants me to stay, wants me to stay, but me not like bone people."

She glanced at the door as her grandmother's chant rose in volume. Her eyes drooped.

"Girl wants to sleep, no more time for me, back to lonesome me go."

She shook her head, but her grandmother's chant was mounting within her senses, and the call to sleep was winning her over. She slumped on her pillow. "What are you?"

The Curmudgeon skulked toward her, looking over the length of her body beneath the sheets of the bed, its claws waving as they ran through the air above her.

"Me made of different things, me made of old things, me not like girl things."

She forced her eyes open to find the creature stooped over her, clicking its claws together as it stared at the sheets where her belly button would be. The blue tendrils on its head let out a crackle as it looked back to her eyes. She let out a long breath, her body going limp as she slid off to sleep on her grandmother's chant. She had one more question, but her lips barely moved, and the words never left her in full form.

Why me?

The Curmudgeon clicked its claws together. Allison felt—knew—its reply, though unspoken as she drifted off.

Me wants fleshy pieces, me wants warm pieces, me wants the making pieces.

It craned its neck to look in her eyes, but she was fast asleep.

***

Though Allison liked her skin pale and unmarked, her notoriety at Walking Canvas began to grow. Her art drew a certain crowd and her uncle entertained a fringe element as it was, so she found herself the subject of a certain underground fame. As long as people left her alone at her drawing board she was content, leaving her wide, incandescent eyes hidden in their unblinking trance behind the black lenses of her sunglasses. Some of the customers thought she was a death cultist, with her plain black clothes and the short curly mass of her black hair, but her hair color was a natural black, like her mother's—not the product of some dye. Some people thought she powdered her face, but her skin was milky by nature, and her pale complexion was amplified by the darkness of her hair and her black clothes. It was Florida, but she didn't care. She moved in her own circle and, in that circle, there was just her, her grandmother, and the Curmudgeon.

She didn't adorn herself, except in two aspects. She developed a fascination for the color red, for the vitality it embodied in boldness of color, and the way in which it contrasted with white and black. It was not a blood fetish, but rather her artistic sensibility, so she used red lipstick as her only cosmetic. Her lips were somewhat thin, so she felt they gave her face some dimension beneath the black circles of her sunglasses.

Her other adornment was some silver jewelry, a pair of slender, silver earrings that hung from her ears like two wisps of hair. Like her red lips, she enjoyed them as a complimentary contrast in color. She didn't buy them. The Curmudgeon brought them to her one night, when the full moon loomed huge in the humid air and storm clouds rumbled in the distance. Her grandmother wasn't feeling well, and had drifted off to sleep on the couch. The old manor house was quiet but for the creak of its dilapidated timbers and the random squeaks of its oak floor. In the absence of her grandmother's low Creole chant, Allison had found herself restless in the night, and when the Curmudgeon came to her, the glow of its eyes appeared somehow brighter, and the blue of its coronal aura more intense. It didn't talk, even though she asked it some questions. It almost seemed nervous, like a child before her, clicking its claws together before the emaciated hollows of its ribcage. Her face fell, but when the creature hunched over and withdrew toward her window, it reached out and opened its spindly fingers to lay the silver pieces in her hand. It bobbed its head, clicked its claws once more, and diffused through her wall into the night.

A few days later she read in the paper that a grave had been dug open in the cemetery outside of town. Some old matriarch was pulled out of the ground, her casket ripped open and the rotted remains dumped on the grass.

Her grandmother asked her where she got the earrings. She lied and said she bought them from one of the bikers at her uncle's club.

***

Allison didn't bother to consider the border of life and death. It never crossed her mind until she caught her grandmother trying to steal her earrings. They argued, and her grandmother relented. Allison agreed not to wear them in the house. It was the way between them, the way they settled their rare differences, for they had nobody else. Allison wasn't one for conversation, and her grandmother spent most of her voice singing or chanting in her broken Creole. Allison wasn't sure if she was happy in her life, but this was something else she chose not to consider. Such a thing would imply a temporal nature to existence and, though she had gleaned only a minimal education while in school, having the Curmudgeon in her life led her to understand the world wasn't limited to what was seen and felt. Her boneview led her to foster a degree of ambivalence to life and death. When she saw that article about the grave robbery, she only shrugged.

Life comes, and life goes. There are other pieces to existence. They were all there, together, under the warm Florida sun.

***

It was her twentieth birthday when she met *him*. His name was Sam Culp, and he spoke with a slow Texas drawl that tended to unnerve people for its vacant tone. He rolled into town and soon had a job as a bouncer at her uncle's biker bar, but his intimidating presence and compulsive attention led her uncle to give him a delicate task. Allison was being pursued by an ardent fan of her artwork, to the point that she became somewhat uneasy coming and going from Walking Canvas. Sam caught the man outside the shop one night, beat him to a bloody pulp, and dumped him at an emergency room, two states away. Her uncle decided to make Sam a security guard just for Walking Canvas which, on most days, meant that Sam sat outside drinking the various herbal teas he enjoyed. Despite the heat, he always wore a tight knit hat pulled over his shaven head. He wasn't one for conversation, but he was always polite. He paid close attention to Allison as she came and went; he even called her 'ma'am' on occasion, which made her blink in confusion behind her glasses.

A week went by before he introduced himself. She already knew his real name from her uncle, but she came to know his other name, the name that summoned her boneview.

He stood by the door one night, holding it open as he waited to lock up behind her. He tipped his head. "Ma'am. I am Gethrix, the All-seeing."

Her eyes widened as she saw through him. The boneview stupor pulled at her, but she had learned to control it over the years. Gethrix was different, though. When she looked at him, she saw something she'd never seen before.

His entire body lit up from within.

***

Her grandmother wasn't well.

A young lawyer came to the manor house one day, summoned by her grandmother's call. It surprised Allison, as she never gave any consideration to how the house's upkeep was financed, or how her Creole grandmother came to inhabit a dilapidated manor house in Florida.

He was an amicable fellow, the lawyer. His name was Christian Hawthorne. For some reason she smiled when he introduced himself. He was a lawyer, but he seemed a little nervous, and though she realized he was quite competent, he had the air of a lost little boy. He sat with her grandmother and talked finances, which held no interest for Allison, so she went outside and sat under one of the sprawling oaks to watch the veils of moss sway in the lazy afternoon air.

After some time her grandmother called her in the house. Christian asked her to sign some papers. She waited until he left before asking her grandmother about the visit.

"He's a nice boy," her grandmother said.

Allison took off her sunglasses. Her grandmother was the only one she allowed to see her eyes. "What's going on?"

Her grandmother took her hand. "Those papers. It's all set."

Allison's face fell. "I don't understand."

Her grandmother stared at her, gazing into her eyes until Allison grew uncomfortable and looked to the floor. "I remember the sunsets on the bayou," her grandmother said with a sigh. "I'd sit with my grandmother when I was little, and we'd stare off into that horizon. She taught me all my songs. I should have taught them to you. Your eyes, they're just like hers."

Allison blinked.

"Look at me," her grandmother said, taking Allison's hands to give them a squeeze. "Look at me like I know you can."

The boneview came, and when it passed, Allison felt the tears run down her cheeks.

"Grandma?"

She laid a hand on Allison's cheek. "It's just the soft pieces that'll go."

Her grandmother refused any treatment. Allison stayed home and took care of her the best she could, but the leukemia was relentless. Allison had a private service, and buried her grandmother in the far corner of the property, beside her parents. Her uncle came. So did Christian. But he was a gentleman, so he left his briefcase in his car.

***

She went back to work at Walking Canvas. Her uncle wanted her to take more time off, but she shrugged away his concern and picked up where she left off. Gethrix kept watch over her, and said little, as was his way. It suited her well.

Christian came to the house one evening, bringing some papers for her to sign. He offered to bring over some Chinese food when he called her that afternoon, to which she stared at the phone for a moment before giving her reply. "Sure. Whatever."

Gethrix looked up from his tea.

She learned things from Christian that she never knew about her grandmother. Christian was like a boy on Christmas morning when he started explaining everything to Allison. He seemed happy to have a valid excuse for visiting her. He told her the law firm had been under order not to disclose anything to her until after her grandmother's death. Such things had little meaning to Allison. She ate some fried rice and studied Christian from behind her glasses. For the first time in her life, she found herself summoning the boneview on her own, and it came to her in a moment. He was a solid creature, she saw. He would have a long and healthy life. No blemishes of any kind, which meant he took care of himself, and possessed an honest soul. She eased in her chair, listening to him as he read through some of the documents in his briefcase, the evening breeze washing through the vacuous living room. She could hear the crickets outside. His voice reminded her of her grandmother's singing, and how it would pacify her. It reminded her as well of her hermetic existence, the lifestyle she had chosen away from people, to avoid the burden of all the things she saw with her boneview. She asked him if he wanted some sweet tea, and he bobbed his head in gratitude. "I'd like that," he said with a smile. "That would be real nice."

She brought him the tea and cut a lemon as he took a sip. Then he told her the history of her family, and she was happy she already saw his nature, or she might have thought different of him. The story started with Allison's grandfather, who came from old Texas oil wealth. Rather than enter the business, he instead took his trust money and delved into university life. He became a respected figure in the world of Mayan antiquities. One day, he had a meeting with some art dealers in New Orleans. He went to a little restaurant away from the city. Her grandmother was a waitress there, and they were taken with each other from first sight. He bought the manor house and they moved there but, soon after, he died of a sudden, massive heart attack. It was a surprise, as he was a sturdy, strapping man. Her grandmother, already pregnant with Allison's mother, was left on her own. The trust was willed to her, and now it came to Allison.

Christian looked to Allison's impassive face, his gaze trying to discern some reaction from the black circles of her sunglasses. "Allison," he said, opening his hands, "you have an estate worth ten million dollars."

***

She sat in her bed one night, waiting for the full moon. Sure enough, the Curmudgeon came to her. She looked to the glowing orbs of its eyes. "My grandmother could see you, right?"

The Curmudgeon drew its hands to its chest and clicked its claws together.

Allison nodded. "I guess I knew that all along."

Me likes her, likes her when she sings, she sings me to sleep, lonely me.

"Can you still hear her?"

The Curmudgeon nodded.

She sings in me-places now, not you-places, not in soft-piece places.

"What do you want from me?"

The Curmudgeon stooped before her, the blue tendrils of light about the bare dome of its skull crackling as the light of its eyes gained intensity.

Me wants to be like warm pieces, me wants to know life in warm pieces.

Allison frowned. She looked at the Curmudgeon with her luminous sea-green eyes. "I'm going to end up like you one day, won't I?"

The Curmudgeon looked to its claws for a moment before meeting her gaze.

Me not know such things; me be, and me not know more than what me be.

She put her head on her pillow and stared at the ceiling. "I hear you on that one."

The creature stared at her, the clustered rows of its teeth rustling against each other, but it said nothing more.

***

She came to work the next day. Most full moon nights she stayed up late to watch the Curmudgeon play its little tricks with the blue light flickering from its head, so she would sleep through the next day, and take off the day after as well. Once she knew about her wealth, and with Christian managing her financial affairs, she was less inclined than ever to get out of bed. It was so peaceful on the property of the manor house. She could stare at the trees and the moss all day, sipping sweet tea as she watched the clouds roll by.

That last meeting with the Curmudgeon left her restless, though, so she came to work. Her uncle was a little surprised, but what caught her off guard was the reaction of Gethrix. He seemed at first perturbed to see her, but over the course of the day he grew aggressive with anyone who even cast an eye on her. She called him aside and asked him to calm down, to which he agreed with some reluctance but, when she asked him if something was wrong, he drew up in all his intimidating bulk and stared down at her.

"I'm here to protect you," he said. "I know you need help. I see it, ma'am."

She stared at him, her face its usual impassive mask. "Sure. Whatever."

She went to dinner with her uncle. She sat in the restaurant with her head down. So many of those people, their bones were already occluded. Too much fat in their diets. It was hard to see that, as it wasn't a direct thing to her boneview, but the poor circulation showed its subtle weakness in the pallor of the bones' ivory glow. She told her uncle she was worried about Culp. He shrugged and said Culp was a little weird, but they dealt with weird people all day between the shop and the bar. He offered to drive her home, but she wanted to stop at the shop to finish a design. She would drive herself home after. Her uncle locked her in the shop.

She sat at her drawing board. The blinds in the front windows were drawn. The only light was the lamp over her desk.

The door of the storage closet across from her desk flew open. Gethrix was there.

She sat up straight. He wasn't wearing his usual denim jacket and pants. Instead he wore leather biker gear, the thick padded kind meant to protect the body when it hit the pavement. A thick, sheepskin-lined collar was belted about his neck, and his eyes gleamed with a cold ferocity. Her boneview erupted in her awareness, and his glow was almost blinding. He pulled off his knit hat and dropped it to the floor, for the first time revealing the shaved dome of his head. A ring of eyes was tattooed about the crown of his skull, joined by curled tendrils of orange and red flame. He pulled a knife from his pocket and pointed it at her, his face turning crimson before his voice burst between his clenched teeth.

"I am Gethrix, the All-seeing! I have come to set you free!"

She bolted from her desk. He grabbed her at once and threw her across the shop. Before she could gain her senses he jerked her upright and tore the glasses from her head. He cursed, words spewing from his mouth in a rapid litany of rage she failed to understand. Then it hit her: the sounds came back from her memory—like the rhythm of her grandmother's chant, but in some other language, full of fury—and then something else hit her. It was his fist, pounding against the side of her head. He hit her once, twice, before throwing her against a wall. She struggled to stand, but he kicked her where she lay before jerking her to her feet once more. He pinned her to the wall and, with the knife clenched in his teeth, proceeded to pound her with his club-like fist. She felt her ribs crack one by one. Her nose flattened with a sickening pop.

She managed to put up a hand, but he seized her wrist, punched her in the face once more, and grabbed her fingers. He gave a quick jerk back, and snapped the bones at her knuckles.

He was just warming up.

She lost track of what was happening. Gravity seemed to use her as its own plaything. Things collided with her: walls, fists, the cash register, a chair. It was only a gray wash of anonymous agony. At some point he stopped, holding her up in his hands before hurling her through the plate glass windows. She hit the ground as a bloody mess, sprawled there on the sidewalk in a pile of shattered glass and limbs. The shop's alarm came alive with blaring sirens and lights. Some part of her told her help would be on the way; that maybe if she just played dead, she could buy enough time—

He took hold of her hair and jerked her head up. She played dead. He nodded and took the knife from his clenched teeth. "I am Gethrix, the All-seeing, and I have come to set you free, I have come to protect you in the only way I know. I beg your mercy in the greater judgment that must come upon me!"

He let go of her hair and let her head crack against the ground. But then he was back, kneeling on her chest and clamping a hand on her forehead. Through the swollen mess of her face she managed to discern the gleaming tip of the knife, descending toward her eyes.

No, no! Help!

She perceived a flash of blue light. Gethrix looked up in sudden surprise, his face bathed in a blue glow. The air crackled; the streetlights glistened on a sweep of claws. The crushing weight of Gethrix's knee left her. He staggered back, clutching his neck, the ragged tatters of his protective collar falling away. Blood poured between his fingers, his eyes bulging before he fell to the ground.

The Curmudgeon stood over her, claws splayed before its glowing eyes. It spun to look down at her. Bright blue tendrils of flame rose in sharp spikes from its bare skull.

Me came, me came for the girl thing, but now me has to go, me go far away.

The streetlights popped and went dark, only to be replaced by the strobe of police and ambulance lights. Sirens wailed about her. Before she lost consciousness she perceived a glimpse of herself, a reflection on the chrome bumper of an ambulance. Her boneview told her all she needed to know.

It would take far more than a beating to kill her.

***

She woke in a hospital bed, cloaked in bandages. A doctor informed

13

her she faced a long and difficult recovery. Her uncle came and, despite his frightening biker appearance, he cried at her bedside. He swore if he ever got his hands on Sam Culp, Sam would never see another sunrise. She lay there, unable to open her eyes, but she felt quite at peace. With her eyes swollen shut and bandaged, there would be no boneview and, with no boneview, no worries. Her world had gone dark, but for once it was peaceful.

After two weeks all the fractures were healed and, despite some lingering soft tissue injuries, she was good as new. The hospital staff was stunned. She wasn't surprised at all. Somehow, she knew, knew it when she stayed conscious through the beating Gethrix had worked on her. It was a beating that could have killed three men twice her size.

Christian came with her uncle the day she was discharged. He had his briefcase with him, but he put it aside to flip open its latches. She frowned in disappointment, but when he turned back to her he had a pair of sunglasses in his hands, the lenses round and black. Her lips rose in gratitude, and he helped her put the glasses on, the mended fingers of her hand still mottled with bruises. He tucked the earpieces in place and even checked to make sure they were straight on her nose. Only then did he tell her that Sam Culp was still in the hospital, clinging to life after half his throat had been ripped out. Her uncle helped her up, congratulating her on defending herself. Everyone appeared to have made the assumption that she snatched a piece of broken glass and slashed Culp. She let it go.

Her uncle offered to have some of his biker friends guard the house until Culp was in jail, but she refused.

If trouble came, she knew the Curmudgeon would be there for her.

***

In the following months she stayed at the manor house. Her uncle bought her a computer, so she could send him designs from the seclusion of her house without having to venture out to Walking Canvas. Instead, she embraced the wonder of the electronic age, and began a regular diet of home improvement deliveries. Christian came by every so often, but soon enough his visits became more regular and, before she knew it, he was there almost every evening. On the weekends she let him sleep over—downstairs, in a guest room. It was his idea, and it made her smile, because she already knew he was a gentleman, but knew as well she could never tell him how she was so certain of that characteristic.

They painted; they planted gardens. She discovered he was quite handy. He had no family, having been raised by nuns in an orphanage. In his teens he worked with several contractors doing simple home repair, but he was a willing learner, so they taught him what they could in the time he worked. He was dedicated, so they gave him whatever hours he could manage as he put himself through one of the state schools to earn his law degree. He was a self made man but, rather than flash that badge with arrogance, he bore it with humility—knowing full well how fortunate he was to have a productive life after such a disadvantageous start.

She hired some contractors to put on a new roof and paint the house. When it was done she was shocked to see what a difference it made just having the house decked in a fresh coat of white paint. In the past she never thought of the house as gloomy, but there was a certain solemnity to the place in its disrepair. At first quaint with the repairs she managed with Christian, it now looked cozy, and she was even less inclined to break from her reclusive tendencies. But such was the serenity of the place that Christian found himself settling in Allison's ways and, for once in her life she could conclude, with some honesty, that she was content.

A year went by, though it felt like one long summer evening. Christian came to her one afternoon and announced he was up for partnership in the law firm. Because of this, and despite herself, she muted her reservations and took him out to dinner to celebrate. He had a taste for smokehouse and pit barbecues, making it not a fancy night out, but they weren't pretentious people, and nobody would make a fuss of her wearing her sunglasses in a restaurant. They ate like royalty, drove back to the house, and took a long walk. They talked but little, having reached a point where they could be comfortable with each other in silence. When the sun settled on the horizon he took her hand, and they exchanged a glance. She smiled, and they walked on.

They shared a bottle of wine, and soon after he fell asleep on the couch. She grew restless in the quiet night, and walked about the house, her mind a tumult of many thoughts. In the end she sat on the edge of the couch and leaned over him, waiting until he woke. He stared at her before reaching up to take off her sunglasses. She closed her eyes. She felt his lips against hers. She looked down at him and blushed, whispering to him a stark confession regarding the sanctity of her loneliness. He held her, and she welcomed the circle of his arms around her, and then she knew it was right.

He moved in that weekend, and a month later they were married, under a trellis they built behind the house. It was a small gathering, with a few of Christian's friends. Her uncle walked her down the aisle, and one of Christian's friends from the orphanage conducted the ceremony.

She wore her grandmother's wedding dress. It was white.

***

15

A year passed. They celebrated their anniversary with a late dinner, at a more formal restaurant. They ate outside, on a veranda overlooking one of the coastal inlets, where she felt comfortable wearing her sunglasses. The waiter was polite, and moved with some practiced grace, even though she saw crippling arthritis in his future. It put a bit of a damper on her appetizer of calamari salad, but when Christian noticed the subtle change in her disposition, she passed it off as being too hungry from skipping lunch. As they watched the sun set over the water, out in the gulf they could see the fins of dolphins break the water every now and then. They reminisced about the last year, something she found surreal, given that for many years she'd all but resolved herself to a solitary existence. She was happy, she was at peace, and when someone cut them off leaving the parking lot, she grinned, knowing at some point down the line of time the driver was going to crack his skull open.

She dozed off on the way home. Christian woke her when the car rolled to a halt in the driveway. They went to bed, but sleep eluded her. They had made their marital bedroom in the master suite of the house, a room in which her grandmother had never ventured. All those years after her grandfather passed her grandmother slept in one of the other bedrooms. Perhaps it was that thought, perhaps it was something else, but Allison found herself walking the hallway in her white sleeping shirt, arms crossed over her chest.

She stopped before her old room and stared at her things. It was one room of the house she hadn't touched in the slow process of renovation, and it looked no different than when she last slept there, before her marriage. She went to her dresser, her gaze falling on the dangling length of her silver earrings. It seemed another life when the Curmudgeon gave them to her and, looking at them now, that life felt like some odd dream that had possessed her for many years. But then she opened the bottom drawer of her dresser and, pulling it out all the way, found the bag taped to the back containing the collection of little skulls the Curmudgeon had brought her when she was young.

She hadn't seen her ethereal friend since the night Gethrix attacked her.

Her skin tingled with the sensation of an unseen gaze. She went to the window, and there was the Curmudgeon, gliding across the lawn behind the house, its pale corona of light flickering along its dimpled hide. Up the wall it clambered and, as she fell back a step, through the wall it came to stand full before her. It shifted about on its bony feet, clicking its claws before its chest as its verdant eyes glowed upon her. Its head bobbed, and the lipless rim of its mouth pulled back as its crowded rows of teeth rustled to produce their beehive whisper.

"Me sees, me sees girl-thing changes, she changes, but not so much."

She watched as it paced back and forth before her, her arms still crossed on her chest. "You've been gone so long," she began, but, for some reason she couldn't identify, she felt a tinge of discomfort before the Curmudgeon. "I never got to thank you for saving me."

The Curmudgeon continued pacing, but waved its claws about its head.

She trembled, feeling a sudden chill. "Where have you been?"

Me sleeps, me sleeps, very tired me gets when soft things me must hurt.

She looked out the window, to the distant graves of her parents and grandmother. From what she could see under the moonlight, nothing was disturbed. "Where do you sleep?"

Me finds forgotten places, me sleeps 'tween thorn and thistle, 'tween vale and vine.

She had another question, but she was hesitant to ask. She drew a breath and, closing her eyes for a moment, found her voice before looking to the Curmudgeon. "Why did you come back to me?"

The Curmudgeon clicked its claws before pointing to her stomach.

Me come for what me wants, me come after long wait, me come for what the making pieces have done.

Her eyes widened as her hands sank to clutch her stomach. The Curmudgeon looked into her eyes, clicked its claws, and diffused through the wall.

She was alone. She looked down, and then she knew. She was pregnant.

***

It took two weeks for her to wrap her head around this new reality and, until she could say the words to herself without breaking into a panic, she said nothing to Christian. Despite her effort the words fell like lead from her lips when she revealed the news to him one evening while they walked about the property. He stopped short, his eyes wide on her, before he swept her off her feet and spun her around. He held her close and wept with joy and, for a moment, seduced by his happiness, she believed all would be well.

The delusion was short lived. Two weeks later she woke to a full moon to find the Curmudgeon at her bedside, clicking its claws before its chest, the emerald spheres of its eyes lit with an intense glow as they fixated on her belly. She pushed up on an elbow, the Curmudgeon's head turning to her at once.

It grows, it grows! Little soft pieces, they grow and knit inside the making place.

She clenched her teeth, protective at once. "Get away from me!" she hissed.

The blue tendrils atop the Curmudgeon's head crackled, its eyes seeming to swell as they hovered in the cavernous sockets. Christian stirred, but the Curmudgeon waved a hand over him, its gaze holding on Allison. She looked to her husband, but he slumped back to a deep sleep. She turned to the creature as she stretched an arm over Christian's defenseless body. "*Please,*" she whispered, "*don't hurt him.*"

The Curmudgeon drew its hand back to its chest and clicked its claws once more.

Girl owes me, owes me for her own soft life, and now me wants to collect.

She clutched a hand to her belly. "No. It's ours."

The Curmudgeon tipped its head, its knees bending until its face came before her.

Me no take it, me no hurt it, me only wants to be in it, me wants to walk in soft pieces again, me wants to know soft life again.

She blinked, understanding at last. All this time, all the years, it had waited for this.

The Curmudgeon bobbed, the tendrils atop its head dancing in amusement.

Girl may see, but girl not so clever as me, me knows more than girl knows.

It tapped a claw against her forehead. She recoiled, but it drew its bony hand back to its chest. It stared at her before snapping toward her, driving her against the headboard. The tendrils atop its head danced once more, but it retreated and, looking at the sheets where her belly hid, clicked its claws in the air over her. Its gaze came back to her, then it withdrew. It skulked away before dissipating through the wall.

***

The next morning, after Christian left for work, she went into her old room and gathered the bag of little skulls and the wispy silver earrings. She went outside, but then hurried back to find her old painting of the Curmudgeon. She tore it in quarters and stuffed it in the bag with the skulls, along with the earrings. With a shovel in hand, she walked to the far corner of the property where her parents and grandmother were buried. When her parents went in the ground a priest came and said some kind of blessing. Even though she had little confidence in such things, she was desperate. She dug a hole between the graves of her parents and buried the bag.

Christian came home early that afternoon, with a security company in tow. They went to work at once, installing cameras and window sensors, as Allison looked on in horror. Her immediate, if paranoid, conclusion was that Christian saw the Curmudgeon and, in his ignorant desire to protect her, had decided to wire the house. As if such things could stop the Curmudgeon!

He pulled her into the kitchen and told her the news.

Sam Culp was on the loose.

***

She never asked about Culp after the attack, and Christian had decided to leave well enough alone, but he opened his briefcase and took out a folder. He flipped it open on the kitchen table and started by describing Culp as a delusional psychopath. Culp was one of three sons born to a poor family living on a homestead on the wide plains of Texas. Sam's parents were founders of something called the Lone Star Templar Knights Militia and, after recruiting some like-minded followers, they armed themselves and set off on a spree of bank robberies. The LSTKM held no reservations for violence, and their brutal rampage across Texas left more than a dozen people dead before Texas Rangers surrounded them. In the ensuing confrontation Culp's parents, his oldest brother — Dallas — and the rest of the militia were killed, along with three Rangers and the twenty hostages Dallas had executed.

The middle sibling, Austin, fled with Sam to Mexico under the protection of the militia's gun dealers. Austin found his way into the drug trade and, when he wasn't running drugs across the border, he was in the jungles, hiding out with Indians of Mayan ancestry. Sam was taken in by the local shaman, and had a regular diet of psychedelic mushrooms to feed his delusions. But Austin led a dangerous life and, when the Federales shot him dead on the banks of the Rio Grande, Sam returned to Texas. Several brutal killings were attributed to Sam, the victims subjected to intense beatings and their eyes cut out before they succumbed to death. Until he attacked Allison, though, there had never been enough evidence to charge or even hold him for his suspected crimes. Despite extensive questioning by prison psychologists, he never disclosed the nature of the odd moniker he had adopted. He was considered a model prisoner.

He was a candidate for parole and work release. Instead, he murdered a guard and escaped.

Allison looked out the window. The evening light fell on the black, round lenses of her sunglasses. The life, the life she'd kept hidden for so long, that she thought was her own private concern, was threatening to devour everything in the very moment she stood on the brink of an existence she'd never considered: *motherhood*. The word drifted through her mind as Christian held her hand and read through police reports guessing at Culp's whereabouts. She knew they would never find him, but he would find her, just as the Curmudgeon could find her. They were both part of a reality—a level of existence—that could drift with impunity through the common world.

One of the security contractors set a ladder against the house. She looked at him, and the boneview came, and she could see the twisted fragments of his cervical vertebrae. She squeezed Christian's hand and tipped her chin to the window. "That man," she said, pointing to the young worker. "Tell him to get off that ladder. He's going to fall."

Christian looked over his shoulder. "I think they know what they're doing."

"Okay." Her shoulders rose in a small shrug. "Whatever."

Christian stared at her. He sat there for several moments until he saw the tears run down her cheeks from behind her sunglasses. He went outside and told the man to get off the ladder. No sooner did the contractor come down than the locks on the ladder gave way and the thing collapsed with a metallic clang. Christian came back to her, standing in the doorway, his wide eyes fixed on her. "How did you know?"

She frowned. The boneview didn't change. It was coming for that man, if not on her lawn on that day, then some other day, some other way perhaps, but it was coming. He could build a bunker forty feet under ground to live in safety, and he would still die of a broken neck. It was a horrible thing to know and, for the first time in her life, she felt helpless. Her forgotten sense of empathy woke from its long slumber, and its burden was unbearable.

She stood, her ivory sundress catching the evening light to glow before her husband.

"Allison?"

"I don't feel well. I'm going to lie down."

It was an obvious lie. They both knew it, and it lingered there, its stench between them. It hurt him, but he didn't know what to say, or even think.

She went upstairs. She curled up in her old bed and cried herself to sleep.

***

Two days passed, two days of wrestling with a difficult decision, but she knew what she had to do. The house was a virtual fortress, so she got in her car and drove to town. She went to an ice cream parlor and bought a cup of vanilla ice cream with rainbow sprinkles. From there she went to the supermarket, bought a loaf of bread, and went to her car, which she left in a far corner of the parking lot. She sat in the car and ate the ice cream. When she was done she waited, her windows rolled down, her elbow propped on the door and her chin resting on her fist. She watched the people in the parking lot, summoning a boneview of every person who went by. So many people, so many fates built into their bones, all part of some unknown, unseen plan waiting for them.

When she tired, she closed her eyes. That was when she heard tires roll up beside her, and the rumble of a large engine. She looked to her side to see a commercial van parked next to her, the engine still running. No one was in the driver's seat. She got out of her car to look into the van. The steering column had been torn open and the wires hung down, some of them twisted together. She swallowed, closing her eyes before turning to find Gethrix looming behind her, his fist cocked and ready.

She held up a hand. "Hey! I won't resist. I'm pregnant."

His eyes narrowed, but his fist held, ready for the strike.

She dropped her hand. "Easy does it, okay? I won't resist. I won't call it. Promise. I'll go with you. You can let me live then, right?"

He lowered his fist, scrutinizing her impassive face. "Okay, ma'am." He reached past her to open the door, offering a hand for her to get in. He waited until she was in to close the door. He walked around the back of the van and hopped in the driver's seat. He glanced at her before putting the van in drive. "You should buckle up, ma'am, being you're pregnant and all."

***

He drove across town, to a neighborhood even the police tried to avoid. It sat beneath the same brilliant Florida sun, but it was dingy in that southern way, with weeds grown out of control and shaded, neglected roofs covered in thick mats of moss. Various sorts of refuse were left lying on unkempt lawns, with the few houses overshadowed by decaying buildings in a tangled mess of confused zoning and misguided development. For a moment she missed her old black clothes and her red lipstick; the Goth look might have allowed her to blend a little better, but with her ivory sundress there was no concealing she was an outsider. Gethrix, on the other hand, in his denims, his knit hat, and his hulking, intimidating presence, seemed right at home.

He pulled behind an old two story building that had a simple, faded sign with one word in peeling white print: ROOMS. He took her by the arm—a firm grasp, but not painful—and led her up a back stairwell to a second story room. He brought her inside and closed the door. It was a small apartment, with a beaten couch beneath a set of windows, a kitchenette, and a back room. A set of blinds hung over the windows, their broken horizontal slats rattling in the warm breeze coming through the open panes. The door had a deadbolt, which was broken. She could tell by the fresh wood on the door where the screws had torn free. She looked to Gethrix, who was standing by the door, his gaze fixed on her.

"Not your place?" she said.

He shook his head. "Took it. Guy who lived here, he was a rapist. Killed him last night. Put the body in the swamp. Gives me time."

"How much time?"

His stare didn't waver. "Enough time, ma'am." He pulled a knife from his pocket, one of those long fan knives, and twirled it around his fingers to free the slender, sharp blade. "I felt it, felt it right here," he said, tapping the blade against his sternum, "when you used your sight today. Drew me in. Way you were using it, I knew you were looking for me, just as much as I was looking for you." He pointed to her belly. "It wants the baby. I know that. Critters, they always want the babies. From women that have the sight, that is."

She used her boneview on him. His body lit up before her, the way it did before, but she studied him this time, discerning an intricate pattern on his bones, one that glowed right through them. His skull was more than just a skull with its aquiline countenance, and the stare of his yellow eyes was both terrible and beautiful. It reminded her of the sun when it set, when the long golden rays found their way between the swaying lengths of Spanish moss. It was a wondrous kind of light, but look at it straight on, and it impaled the eyes.

She blinked. "Do you have a mirror?"

He pointed to the bathroom. "Behind the door. Don't mind the blood on the floor."

She walked across the apartment and opened the door, turning away from the mess on the floor to look at her reflection in the mirror. She closed her eyes, and there was only darkness. She thought of the evening light, of her evenings with Christian at the manor house, and the darkness let up, and she was at peace. Her eyes slid open, and she stared at herself in full, and for the first time in her life she scrutinized her own boneview, and didn't blink it away. She studied everything she could until she was certain, and then she closed the door and walked back to the main room.

Gethrix was waiting. He had pulled a chair from the kitchenette into the middle of the room. It was one of those white plastic outdoor chairs, the kind seen on decks. He pulled off his hat and tossed it on the couch, revealing the circle of eyes about his head. "Whenever you're ready, ma'am. It's best if I get it done before dark. Critters, they get strong at night."

She closed her eyes before reaching up to take off her glasses. She put them in a pocket of her sundress before letting her lids slide open to reveal her luminous, sea green eyes. He straightened at the cast of her gaze, as if he looked on some monster, but he clenched his teeth, and his hand tightened on the knife. She held up a hand to still him. "I want you to know something, Gethrix. I never used it for selfish ends. If anything, the sight took things away from my life, rather than giving me anything. I guess I was a fool, thinking it was all some game for my private entertainment. I should've known better, but I didn't."

"Most people don't get it," he said. "Makes most crazy. But the critters, they always wait. Real old, they are. Different kind of time, they come from. Not meant for us to know about it. They want to be like us, though. Want to cross over, so to say." He shook his head. "Can't have it. Different worlds. Not meant to mix. Don't know why, but that's the way it is. Things get confused. For us, and for the critters. Three kinds of people, there is. Most don't know. Simple for them. Some see the critters, but don't have the sight. Not so simple for them, but the critters leave them be. But the ones with the sight, the critters know it, know they can connect to them. Boundaries get blurred. Those people forget they belong to this world. Get confused. Try to use the sight for their own ends."

"I never did that," she repeated in defense. "I could've opened a shop and made a fortune telling futures."

He shook his head. "Can't have that, ma'am."

She frowned. "Guess I would've met you sooner, right?"

He said nothing, instead pointing the tip of the knife to the eyes circling his head.

"What about you?" she asked. "I know you have a sight. I can see it in you."

He stared at her. "I am Gethrix, the All-seeing. It is mine to act, not to question. I have come to set you free. I have come to protect you in the only way I know. And I beg your mercy in the greater judgment that must come upon me."

She rolled her eyes. "Sure. Whatever."

He waited until she sat in the chair. Her hands constricted on the armrests.

He stood before her. "You won't call it?"

"No." She let her breath go. "I know now that's why you beat me. You had to beat me near to death so I couldn't call it. I know that's the way, because that's your M-O, but I'm doing this for my baby." She licked her lips. "You never had someone cooperate, did you?"

He frowned. "No, ma'am."

"Will it be quick?"

"Yes, ma'am. I know what I'm doing." He reached down to slice off the excess tongue of his leather belt. He offered it to her. "You might want to bite down on that."

23

"Gethrix?"

"Ma'am?"

"I'm trusting you, Gethrix. I'm trusting you with my baby."

He stared down at her. "I am the All-Seeing. It is not mine to save a baby. You did that on your own."

"Okay." She took the piece of belt and bit down. She looked out the windows. Evening was coming, but then Gethrix filled her vision.

It was far worse, and far less, than she thought it would be.

***

She woke in a hospital. She wondered at the pressure on her hand, but realized it was Christian. Her name burst from him the moment she stirred. He kissed her hand as he squeezed it in his grip. Her other hand rose to feel the bandages on her face. She thought to open her eyes, but they were gone. There was only darkness. Her hand sank to her side.

She turned her head to Christian. She asked, and he told her the baby was fine. He hesitated, and then he told her one more thing.

Sam Culp had eluded capture after bringing her to the emergency room. There was no trace of him.

***

She had a daughter. They named her Nina, and she was born one warm evening in the month of June. Allison held her close, so she could smell her, that wonderful baby-sweet smell that's like nothing else in the world. She was healthy, a robust little baby, just as the last use of Allison's boneview foretold. It wasn't an easy telling, and the future was hidden, as Nina had been so tiny then, and devoid of any actual bone. And now that the boneview was gone, the future was open before Allison, and her Nina, in all its glorious mystery.

She asked Christian whom Nina resembled. Allison wanted to use her fingers to face contour Nina, but she was afraid to agitate her with so much touching.

Christian looked to the black lenses of Allison's sunglasses and fought to maintain his composure. "She looks like you, Allison. She's just like her mother."

She took a breath, and asked the all-important question. "What color are her eyes?"

He hesitated. "They're blue, blue like the sky."

Allison smiled, and nuzzled her lips to Nina's forehead. Christian put his arm around Allison's shoulders. They were three, and they were happy.

***

Sometimes, at night, Allison stirs, and sits up in bed. By habit she reaches for her sunglasses and slips them on, but then she waits and, when it comes, she knows she's ready to move. Gethrix may have taken her eyes but, just as he tried to beat her to death and failed, he hadn't taken all her sight. It wasn't her boneview, no, that was gone, but it was something else. It was like looking through cloudy water to a photonegative world, a shadowed bas-relief of ghostly forms. She kept it a secret, and told people—including Christian—it was just the acuity of her hearing that allowed her to navigate her environment so well. Small things were lost to her, but at least she wasn't walking into walls or tumbling down stairs.

But when she stirs at night, she knows all too well what it is that bothers her. She slips from bed and walks to a window, and from there she can discern the full moon, its silvery light beckoning through the tactile plain to illuminate those other realities that hide from the sensations of flesh and bone. She walks down the hall then, to her grandmother's old room, which they refurbished to make into Nina's nursery. Allison sits in a gliding rocker chair and puts her head back as she listens to Nina breathe, so peaceful in her sleep.

And that's when she hears it: a faint click against the window and, when she turns her face to the window, there's a pale blue glow—and in its midst, two faint points of green light. The connection is lost, though, so the wall has become solid to it, and the Curmudgeon is shut out from her, and her Nina. Nevertheless, the beehive voice still comes to her mind.

Lonesome, lonesome me, girl no love me, girl no love me now.

So she frowns and, though the words are lost to her, she hums an old Creole song. The light at the window fades away, and all that remains is the peaceful darkness of a quiet Florida night.

"You know, I did this, back in the army," Eldin said with a chuckle as he rested against the side of the elevator. "Uncle Sam said that where my abilities was best utilized. Now who he to judge me? I guess seein' where they put me, they was sayin' I got no abilities." He shook his head. "So what about you? Why you wheelin' stiffies in the deep dark night?"

The man standing across from Eldin shrugged. "I don't know," he said with a confused look, "but I'm here now."

Eldin laughed. "The man don't even know why he here! Boy, you look like you fell from the sky and hit every branch on the way down. Now, what you say your name was?"

"You can call me John."

"You know, I had a boy worked down here before you, look like you and him could be brothers, like opposite sides of a coin, see. Is that the way it is?"

John shook his head. "No."

Eldin shrugged. "Well . . .okay, you know, whatever, right? He gone, you're here."

John rubbed his forehead. "So it seems."

The elevator bumped to a halt, and the doors opened to reveal a dim corridor. Eldin glanced at the paper in his hand before looking to the gurney between them. "Selma Sawyer?" He grinned, poking the body with a finger. "See that? Don't see that name much no more, Selma. Now I know this here is an old stiffy without even lookin'. So how about that?" he said with a self-congratulatory tone. "And the big men told me I got no ability. Look at that! The stiffies may be dead, but the story still go on."

John stared. "Selma Sawyer," he repeated under his breath.

Eldin snapped his fingers. "I know that tone, so listen up—she *was*, not she *is*," he said, guessing at John's thought. "Don't go weird on your first night, John-boy. Then I got to wait until they find another replacement. I hate to wait. Don't matter, though. Time don't mean nothin' down here. Way I see it, we either dead or soon to be dead, so it don't make no difference anyhow, right? Right and wrong, that's just a waste of time. Take old Selma here. Maybe she was good, maybe she was bad, but one thing for sure now, she dead." He grabbed the side rail of the gurney and tipped his head for John to follow suit. "Stiffy Sawyer's last ride," he said with a push to get the gurney moving. "Goin' to the place where name don't mean nothin', don't mean nothin'," he went on in a singsong and then fell into a hum as they walked the length of the corridor.

The lights flickered as a deep rumble sounded over them. It was a damp corridor, cold— more a tunnel than a corridor, despite the hospital's attempts to mask the age of that old path. It ran beneath the city street in front of the hospital, and beneath the subway line that lay beneath the street, to link to the sub-basement of an abandoned warehouse. The hospital, in its financial decrepitude and physical disrepair, couldn't afford to expand, so space was rented where forgotten city planners had once deemed it necessary to create, in the belly of the urban underworld.

As the corridor opened to the mortuary crypt John looked about in disbelief, to which Eldin simply nodded. "Lots of stiffies, John-boy. Got no family, got no money, and now got no life, so they stay here until the city come and do pick-up." He nodded to himself. "Lots of stiffies, yes sir."

John's eyes played across the little rectangular doors set in the crude concrete walls. His nose began to tingle.

"Natural refrigeration," Eldin said, pointing to their misting breaths as he picked up a clipboard from his small desk. "Always cold down here. Real cold. Well, what we got? Two months of summer, then deep-freeze all year? Ain't like home, John-boy." He chuckled to himself as he noted the morgue's newest admission. "Ain't gettin' warmer here unless Mister Devil-man decides to run up the fires down below, you know what I'm sayin'?"

John stared at him.

"Ah, now don't tell me you one of them Bible types," Eldin said with a sigh. "If you is, well then you be helpin' the Lord do His work, John-boy. He the Creator, we the desecrator; His makin' leaves a mess, we clean up more the less. Now what you say to that?" He shoved John's shoulder before letting out a great booming laugh that reverberated in the cold crypt.

John frowned. "I say we should put her away."

***

"He agreed to this?"

"Said he understood, said he was ready. I don't trust it, Pete."

Pete shrugged and rested his head against the frame of the one-way window to study the man sitting in the little stark room on the other side of the glass. The man—the suspect—appeared quite at peace as he sat in that room, writing on the legal pad Pete had left with him. "You sure about this? You checked?"

"I checked," came the tired reply. "Read him his rights and offered him a phone call. I went through the drill and he just sat there. Then he looks at me, same empty expression, and says he wants to 'write my tale,' and that I should tell you he's doing it freely."

Pete looked to his partner. "'Write my tale?' Who talks like that?"

"This guy does." Pete's partner, Frank, crossed his arms on his chest. He looked at his watch. "Why do these things always happen at night?"

It was an empty question, but it lingered as Frank looked back at their suspect.

"I don't like this," Pete thought aloud.

"That's got to be the tenth time I've heard that," Frank said. He tipped his head to either side before his eyes settled on Pete. "So what are you thinking? Thinking we got something more on our hands?"

"No, but something isn't right."

"That's an understatement. The hospital has no record of him as an employee. We don't have an address for him. His prints pulled up a big fat nothing. Hospital doesn't have any record of an employee past or present with the name on his work badge. They don't know how he got the badge, but he managed to pass himself off as a legitimate employee. Maybe he's got a fetish," Frank said with a shrug. "Hospital said the last guy who worked before him got fired after getting caught messing with some dead hooker. This guy looks like he could be his baby brother, but the necrophile dropped off the face of the earth. No records on him after being fired. No family. Probably dead somewhere." He shook his head. "People are sick. Getting on a dead hooker. That's just plain evil." He fell silent, realizing Pete wasn't listening to him, his forehead wrinkled in thought. "What?"

"What's the chance of a hospital as old as that dump never having an employee by this guy's name? It just doesn't sit right."

"How's that?"

Pete opened his hands. "We have nothing on him, not a single solid trace of his existence. So who is he?"

At that their suspect looked up, peering at them through the mirrored glass as if there was no window at all. Frank leaned away in surprise, but Pete stared at the man, his forehead still furrowed. "He said something to me when we brought him in."

"Said he didn't do it." Frank snorted, turning from the window as their suspect resumed his writing. "Everybody says they didn't do it."

Pete shook his head. "No, it was something he said to me. I mean, he purposely turned to me and said it when I brought him in the room. He said he'd be going before the night was over."

Frank waved it off. "Head games. Where can he go? Nothing to it."

***

The ring of the morgue phone broke the crypt's silence like a crack in glass. Eldin jerked upright in his chair, startled by the sudden racket. He rubbed his eyes before picking up the phone and waved to John as he wiped down a gurney from their latest admission. Eldin kept his voice low, something so astray from his usual boisterous banter that John watched him with an unwavering gaze. After several moments Eldin slammed the phone down and pushed himself from his chair, laughing. "Pork grind tonight, John-boy!" He studied John for a moment before slapping his hands together. "You know, you been workin' here, what, two months? Never seen nor heard you talk about nothin' at home, so I figure either you ain't got one, or the one you got ain't so good. So tonight we get a little show. Let me introduce you to a good friend of mine."

He led John deep into the morgue, back to a corner. There was a walkway hidden in the shadows, which went past the broken warehouse elevators to reveal a crowded knot of rooms. "They was gonna do the slicin' and dicin' here, but they decided to keep it at the hospital. But they left the table, and now I rent it out, for those times when a certain call goes out to certain people in our fine establishment."

John stared at the cold metal table in the abandoned exam room. "Here?" he said in disgust. "Next to all that empty death out there?"

Eldin nudged him with an elbow. "Come on man, think private, see? These rooms even got heat. I got the only key. Ha! Now I got a hotel too! I can give you a share; you don't talk to no one. Man, some of them even let me watch. Maybe you watch too John-boy and put some action in your life!" He let out one of his booming laughs and slapped John on the shoulder.

"This is unreal," John said in disbelief.

Eldin set a mocking eye on him. "Let me tell you somethin', John-boy. You think I'm some know-nothin' reject down here? I been to school, I been to the army, I been around the world, and you know what? It's the *world* made me this way, see? That mess out there told me life don't mean nothin', so I came down here—man, I ran down here. Down here, in the dark, at night, I get to make my own sense of it. Life, people, all that noise, I get to judge it here. Down here, you're in Eldin's world! And who gonna judge me? Nothin' but a bunch of stiffies, and they all be goin' out with the trash."

John looked to him. "You're unreal, too."

Eldin grinned. "No, I'm Eldin. Who the hell are you?"

John was speechless. He watched as Eldin sprayed down the table before opening a draw to produce some fresh bedding supply. John recognized the neatly folded sheets; Eldin had asked him to get them several nights ago. The request stuck with him for the simple reason that

30

they had no need for fresh bedding supply. But then for no apparent reason Eldin let out another booming laugh, shaking his head as he spread out a foam liner and covered it with the sheets. "Make some money tonight, yes sir!"

"Eldin?" a woman's voice called.

"That you Rose?" Eldin threw his hands up. "Come on in!"

John turned as a young woman came up behind him, but she stopped short, her eyes wide on him. She looked with uncertainty to Eldin, but Eldin waved a hand at John. "John-boy's good. So how's my Rose tonight?" he said, but she didn't answer, instead keeping her gaze on John as she walked into the exam room. Eldin laughed again as she passed him. "That's my Rose, smellin' like a fresh cut daisy," he joked and left the room, poking John with an elbow.

John was about to turn and leave when he heard a rustle from the exam room. He stepped into the doorway. Rose had her back to him, but he could see her empty her pocket, the baggy excess of her blue scrubs crinkling across her shoulders. She had short brown hair and, from the visible bulges of the vertebrae up the back of her neck, he could tell she must be quite thin, thinner than even the excess of the scrubs suggested. He had the dim suspicion he'd seen her before, but she showed no recollection of him.

She rolled up the sleeve of her left arm, but feeling his gaze, she glanced over her shoulder and stopped. She had a tourniquet in her right hand and the barrel of a syringe pressed between her lips. Despite that, he looked into her eyes, and was struck by the sadness he saw there, the sad emptiness. She was an ordinary looking woman, yet he believed she had the potential for beauty, but he knew that would never happen, at least not that way, not in that place.

She strapped the tourniquet on her arm and took the syringe from between her lips. "I'm off duty," she said. When it was done a frown played out on her lips, her eyelids drooping as she continued to stare at him. "What's your name again?"

He hesitated, paling at the sight before him. "John."

"You look like an honest man," she said with a sigh. "You shouldn't be here."

"Yeah, you shouldn't be here," another voice agreed.

John spun around, finding himself face to face with one of the night security guards. The guard turned his face to Rose, his eyes gleaming as he grinned at her. "There's my Rose," he said, raising his hands at his sides.

"I'm going away," she said through a delirious grin. "Simon?"

Simon put a meaty hand on John's shoulder and pushed him aside. "You need to talk to Eldin," he said, but his gaze was on Rose. He

31

stepped by John, into the room, as he pulled his belt from his pants. Rose leaned forward to rest on the gurney, her head atop her folded arms. Her eyelids drooped and closed over her glassy gaze as she began to hum a broken tune.

John returned to the crypt, hands clasped over his head. Eldin was at his desk, feet propped on its worn surface. He was chuckling to himself as he counted some ragged bills, a dingy collection of singles. "Now see here, they could go anywhere," he said to John's unspoken question, "but only at Uncle Eldin's are they guaranteed no one ever gonna know. Simon gives me dough, so I hide the know!" His great laugh boomed once again. "And the big army men said I got no skills, but I'm what you call a 'venture capitalist': I see, and then I venture to make some capital!" He clapped his hands and threw his head back with a little howl. "How about that, John-boy?"

John shook his head. "This is unreal," he said, his mind flashing with images of what he left behind him. He dropped his hands and turned to Eldin. "You do know what's happening back there, don't you?"

Eldin's face fell, his gaze rising from the money in his hand. "Oh, come on now, John-boy. Time to grow up. Don't mean nothin' down here, no right or wrong to it. This here is Eldin's world, and it don't belong to no other world. We're in between, you could say."

John's eyes went wide with disbelief. "Do you know what he's doing to her?"

Eldin slapped the money on his desk and stood. "John-boy, now listen here, and listen good. Don't you go all mournin'-the-fallen-angel on me now. Ain't nobody forced her. She come here on her own."

John's nose bunched up in disgust. "Stuffed with drugs."

Eldin leaned on his desk. "I said, she come here on her own. Nothin' more to it, John-boy. That's the way it is, and it ain't mine or yours to ask, so you best leave it alone."

***

Frank opened the door to the observation room, his gaze resting on the cup of coffee in his hand. Pete still leaned on the observation window; their suspect was still writing in the interrogation room. Frank stared at his partner. "You going to stand there all night?"

Pete shook his head.

Frank rolled his eyes. "You spend too much time here. Go home. To your wife, not that waitress you've been going to lately. You know what I'm talking about," he added at Pete's sudden glare. "Go home. That's where you belong."

Pete coughed. "Are you done?"

Frank shrugged. "This psycho's going to run all night with this nonsense."

"Then I'll stay all night," Pete said, his gaze returning to their suspect.

Frank put his coffee down. "Look at me," he ordered, waiting until Pete turned. "You have to go home sooner or later. What you're doing, it's not going to fix anything."

Pete rolled his eyes. "Assuming there's something left to fix."

Frank hesitated, his jaw clenching as he considered his thoughts. "Look, I'm sorry to hear that. I thought you two would last." He frowned, pausing before he cleared his throat. "I still think you should take some time off. Like now, rather than getting tied up with this clown," he said with a tip of his chin to their suspect. "Go. I'll take care of this."

"No." Pete blinked in surprise at the stubbornness of his response. He rubbed his eyes and looked back to the window. "I don't know. There's something—I have to stay until the morning. I want to see what will happen in the morning."

Frank blew out a breath. "The only thing that's going to happen in the morning is shift change," he said, his voice heavy with the cynicism of too many years, too many long nights, and too many cups of harsh coffee.

***

"By yourself tonight?"

John turned from the fresh bedding supply he was spreading to find Rose standing behind him. It took a moment to find his voice. "Time to go away?"

She turned her head to the side, her eyes sinking to the floor. "I watched three old and forgotten people die tonight."

He looked to the crypt. "I know."

"Yeah, really?" she replied with a sharp edge to her voice, her eyes narrowing. "Don't judge me," she said and glanced away, but then frowned and looked back at him. "Well, don't pretend not to judge me. You have an honest gaze, you know. You can't hide it."

He studied her, but then stepped back and just watched, watched and waited. She rubbed her eyes, but the tear that ran down her cheek escaped the rub of her hand. Avoiding him in the vulnerability of her wretched shame she turned from him, then turned from herself by rolling up her sleeve. He said nothing, waiting until she was done. She was mustering resistance; he noticed the dull vacancy wasn't so quick to signal her disembodiment.

"Where do you get it?"

A panicked look seized her, but she blinked it away. "I steal it."

He stiffened. "That's wrong."

"They're dead. They won't miss it." She waved a hand, trying to resist the moral sensibility he inflicted on her awareness. The loosened tourniquet flopped about her arm as her wedding ring glinted under the dim lighting. "They're all vegetables up there in those beds. They're all dead, they just don't know it yet." She swayed on her feet, butting her palms against her temples until she dropped her hands at her sides. She stood that way for a moment longer, and then she seemed to deflate, sinking down to sit on the floor. She rested her back against a leg of the table as she blew out a breath and closed her eyes.

He said nothing.

"I just want to go away, go back, you know?" She slipped the tourniquet from her arm and let it slither between her fingers to the floor. "Stuff doesn't even work anymore," she said with a sigh, but then her face wrinkled in disgust. "Look at me. All this garbage I'm putting inside me—you know what? I hate this body. I want to wreck it, defile it, just like it wasted my life." She sniffed and looked to him, her eyes dilated, her hands dangling over her knees. "My life, the way it was, it was perfect. I didn't take it for granted, and it still went down the toilet."

She pulled at her lips before a frown seized her. "My baby died inside me," she said, glancing at him before her gaze fell to the floor. "He was so close, but maybe it was better he never came into this disgusting world." She laid her hands over her face and collected herself before looking to him. "I wasn't always like *this*. I used to be a good person, John. A clean person."

He stared at her. Her shame was inescapable.

"But that's in a little box in the ground," she said to his silence. "It's just eating me, eating me a little more each day; it's going to eat me until there's nothing left."

"What's this?"

Startled, John turned to find Simon looming behind him. The man's gaze bored into John. "What are you doing?"

Rose pulled herself to her feet, glaring at Simon with disdain. "He didn't do anything," she said in John's defense.

Simon looked to John with mocking eyes. "Get out of here, mortuary boy." He started to unclasp his belt, but John didn't move. They both turned as the mounting revulsion in Rose's stare filled the room. Simon opened his hands. "What?"

She held up a hand to block him from her sight as she hurried away.

Simon stood in shock. He held there, his jaw hanging, until he accepted that she was gone. Then he turned to John, his eyebrows sinking low over his eyes. "What did you do?"

John took a step, but Simon blocked the doorway.

There was no escape.

***

Pete shifted on his feet, his shoulder sore from leaning against the frame of the observation room window. The suspect was still writing his so-called 'tale', writing without pause, page after page. At first, Pete figured it was nothing more than the ramblings of another psycho that had run aground. He'd seen that before, too many times to count, but this suspect was different. Pete had the unsettling impression that despite the man's calm demeanor, despite his lack of resistance when he was arrested, he was nevertheless in some kind of rush.

As much as Pete wanted to know what the man was writing, he couldn't avoid the lingering memory of the suspect's claim that he would be leaving in the morning.

Frank came in with another round of coffee. Pete took his cup and looked back to the window.

***

John saw Rose about the hospital. She would give him a glance, but nothing else. And then, one night, she came back. It was several weeks later, but she came back. Ignoring Eldin, she found her way to the back of the morgue.

"Look, I want to apologize for what happened last time." She crossed her arms on her chest, looking even more gaunt than usual in the hollow expanse of her scrubs.

He wondered if she knew what Simon did to him.

She watched as he spread out some fresh bedding supply. Her eyes widened when she noticed a pile of used linens, balled up in the corner. She looked up to find him staring at her with a hard gaze. Her face paled as she opened her hands before her chest. "I'm, I'm not here for that. I'm not doing that anymore. I, I wanted to tell you that."

He paused to look her full in the eyes. "Then why come down here? For your medication?" he said, curious that she had purposely decided to speak with him before the emptiness came upon her.

She studied him, her gaze wide and unwavering as she pulled at her lips. Her weight shifted on her feet, first toward the door, but then she shifted back. "I came down early to apologize, okay? I'm ending everything else. I'm going to tell Simon when he comes down. No more, it's over. I realized I hit rock bottom, and I have to turn things around. When I heard what Simon did to you. . . look, I feel responsible. So there

35

it is." She took a breath before letting it go with a shrug. "I don't know. I thought we could, thought we could talk—a fresh start. I think I owe you that," she said, fidgeting somewhat in the awkwardness of the moment. She looked down before wrapping her arms about her chest and fixing her gaze on him. "I don't want you to think I'm just, just some—oh, to hell with it." She drew herself up, blinking in embarrassment, but somehow, she seemed more innocent for her unease. "Hi. I'm Rose."

He said nothing.

"So, ah, how'd you end up down here?" Her lips trembled in a nervous little smile, but it soon faded before his stolid expression. Her gaze fell to the floor. "You know, maybe this was a mistake." She turned to leave, but her head sank at the sound of Eldin singing in the outer crypt. She looked up at John, her lips parting, but she stopped short when he opened a hand.

He stared at her, debating what he would say, until his silence began to unnerve her. "I did something," he said, but then he rubbed his forehead and reconsidered his words. "I, well, you could say I was thrown out from the family business."

She let out a breath, her shoulders easing as some of the tension broke. A small, plaintive smile played across her lips. "Thrown out? What—is your family the mob?"

He blinked. "I have to say, I've never heard quite that description before."

"Oh, no offense, it was just a little joke, something my husband would say."

He shook his head. "None taken. It's a fair comment."

"Well, you know, I know it's tough, being on your own," she said with a tip of her head. "My mom, she raised me by herself. She only had me, and I know it was real hard. She worries all the time," she said quietly, her gaze falling to the floor as she rubbed her arms. She stood for a moment, her lips pressed in a tight line before she looked at him. "I think, I think she knows, knows what I've been doing. I'm trying, trying to get better." She licked her lips. "So, the family business, is it something like what you do here?"

He nodded, but clenched his jaw as he was struck by the image of her. An odd sensation welled up within him—something he'd lost, something perhaps she saw in him, driving her need to at once redeem herself in his eyes and convince herself he would even care. It was *compassion*. And the more he studied her, the more it haunted him, with the crypt and its mist of apathy so near. She was a frail, wasting thing; a blue ghost, cold yet wanting, lost among pitiless shadows in a despicable place.

Yes, that's why I'm here. This is what I lost, what I had to find again.

36

He stumbled for words as he realized he stood mute. "The family business . . ."

She shrugged. "What did you do?"

And then it bolted back to him—burst within him—his memory, its images a set of shadows snapping to sharp, glaring focus. He fell back a step, his voice lost. It was very difficult to look at her then, but he understood why—and why he must. He hesitated, stilling her with an open hand when she was about to turn away. "I broke a law, and my father threw me out," he said, his voice coming with an anxious tremor.

She frowned. "Hey, we all make mistakes, right? That's life."

He knew her words were a peace offering, but they hit him like knives as his consciousness bloomed within him and, on its heels, the anxious anticipation of facing himself in full, and earning his redemption. He trembled, trembled with shame before her, struggling to find a way to explain things, to explain the exquisite nature of his crime. But then he rallied, swallowed over a dry throat, and looked at her. "There was a death," he began.

She stared at him. The tension was palpable, her fear an unspoken thing between them, fear born of the sudden realization she might be alone with a killer. She went rigid when he closed and locked the door to the room.

He turned to her. "I had a position of great authority, a position of significant power, and I abused it. I grew restless in the complacency of my authority, and did something for no reason but to show that I could. This power was entrusted to me, but in my vanity I came to think it was in fact mine, because I discovered I could turn it upside down. Yes, yes! It was that way, I came to believe in my arrogance it was mine, that I could do with it what I wished," he said, then lowered his head and closed his eyes. He was quiet for a moment, but then his eyes snapped open with the remainder of his memory to find her befuddled gaze locked on him. "It could not escape my father. I was cast out, exiled, to this vile place, to witness the fallout of what I had done, to remember it in a way I'd never forget." He opened his hands. "I must right the shift, you see, correct the change, and set you right."

She blinked. Her skin tingled. His gaze engulfed her.

He leaned toward her and, despite herself, she was frozen, paralyzed, her wide eyes bulging as they followed his intrusion of her personal space. Close he came, and closer still, close enough to whisper in her ear.

"Rose, there's more to this world than flesh and bone."

He withdrew from her then, standing by the door for a moment before pushing it open.

Her breath came short and tight. "Who—what—"

"This is my tale," he said. "A confession of redemption, and retribution."

"Rose?" Simon called from the outer crypt.

"Come to pluck that flower again, did you now?" Eldin's laughing voice echoed. "She's in the back with John-boy."

John turned, but looked over his shoulder to Rose. "Stay here."

She watched as he walked out, disappearing down the hall toward the crypt.

The morgue rumbled. The bulbs flickered and went dark. Rose fell back, retreating against a wall before sinking to the floor. The rumbling resumed, louder and louder; so loud she covered her head and thought her ears would pop, so intense she thought the subway was coming right down through the crypt's walls, so loud she started screaming just to remind herself she was still alive. The bulbs flashed in the morgue, a blinding bright flash—it burned it was so bright—

And then it was silent, silent and dark, and she thought herself crushed beneath tons of concrete and masonry, but she felt herself breathe, and the air was cold, cold and clear.

She opened her eyes. John was standing over her. With a gasp she recoiled, her feet slipping on the floor as she tried to push herself away. She wrapped her hands over her head, her panic stricken eyes burning from the shadows of her face.

He sank to a crouch before her. "The pleas of your heart are not mute, but it is you who must make them be. Take your life back. Go home." He studied her for a moment, his jaw clenched, before he rested a hand on her stomach. She squirmed, but the warmth of his hand stilled her. He looked into her eyes. "I can not give back what I took from you, but I can promise you a future, if you leave this rotten place." He took his hand from her and stood. "This is my crime, and mine to bear for what I did to you."

She stared at him. Then she bolted, and he was alone.

Satisfied, John walked out to the crypt and sat at Eldin's desk. He waited, waited with eternal patience between two smoldering corpses until Simon's partner found him, and soon enough he was in the company of Detectives West and Fromin.

***

John put his pencil down and looked to the observation window. "I'm done."

Pete jumped, almost asleep before the window. He blinked. He was alone.

"Detective Peter Fromin," the suspect said. "I would like to speak to you for a moment."

38

Pete looked at his watch. It was almost dawn. Almost time for shift change, but that was a distant thought. Like a machine he paced around the divider wall to leave the observation room and enter the holding room, yet he felt as if his awareness lingered behind the glass; that he was watching himself take a seat across the table from this strange person with the inconsequential name.

"What?" Pete said, the hoarseness of his voice betraying his uncertainty.

John stared at him. "It's time for me to go."

Pete stared at him for several heartbeats before he could frame a thought. "You fried two people. Where do you think you're going?"

"It's time for me to go," John repeated, but then leaned forward to peer into Pete's eyes. "Detective Fromin, I know you wish to go home, that you wish to return to something you think you have lost. You won't find it in the cases you work, only reasons to accept defeat."

Pete opened his mouth, but John seized his wrist and the moment his grip clamped down on Pete's skin, Pete's throat closed around his breath. His eyes bulged in shock, but he was frozen in his seat, unable to move. John's eyes narrowed as he let his gaze bore into Pete's eyes. Then he raised a finger to hold Pete's attention, and released his grip. Pete's hand snapped against his chest, but he couldn't move, couldn't breathe, couldn't even think.

John held his narrowed gaze over his raised finger, but then he eased, his hand opening between them. "I can do no more for you, Peter, and for that I apologize. It is a hollow gesture to what you have endured, but I promise you, if you wish it to be, things will be set right. I will see to it." He nodded and took a deep breath. "Now. Time to go."

The light flickered.

Pete looked up. His eyes washed white as the bulb popped and blew.

Frank opened the door to the room. "Pete?"

The suspect slumped in his seat; his head hit the table with a thud. Frank stepped forward. His hand recoiled the moment he touched the man.

John Smith was ice cold.

***

The paperwork lasted for hours, but everything required proper forms. In the end, in a strange way, Pete decided it was the way of people to try to assert some kind of control over mortality by bombarding the uncertainty of its meaning with documentation. Names and papers, papers and names, all to record what was passed, even though it was already meaningless to the living. There were many things, he realized, on which the living wasted their energy— calamitous pitfalls of avoidance and denial generated by regrets and guilt, serving as emotional documentation of things gone by, things lost to time, things tripping people in the merciless march of mortality.

He moved like a zombie. He didn't know what to think.

When the phone call came he found his voice was nearly lost. He hung up the phone with a trembling hand, his bloodshot eyes darting in his head. He looked across his desk, waiting until his partner felt his gaze and looked back to him. "I want to go home," Pete whispered.

Frank stared at him.

"I want to go home. I should be home."

Frank watched as Pete rose from his seat. Frank nodded, waving a hand at the stacks of paperwork. "Don't worry about this. Just go."

Pete swallowed over a dry throat.

Frank watched as Pete slipped his arms into his coat. Frank sipped his coffee and cleared his throat. "You know, your dead friend there, he didn't write anything that whole time," he said as an afterthought. "I sent it down to be looked at. Some kind of symbols, or hieroglyphs, or something. Nobody can make sense of it. Thought you might want to know."

Pete opened his mouth, but said nothing.

Frank waved him off. "Tell Rose I say hello, okay?"

MY OTHER ME

The labels were distasteful, but their potential evolution perhaps more so: stalker and sociopath, sadist and murderer.

Noel sat in his car, alone in the vast, empty expanse of a commuter college parking lot. His knapsack was on the passenger seat and, resting on top, the results from the personality survey he had completed for one of his professors. It was supposed to be an elective assignment for an elective class, a paid exercise for volunteering his time, but those notions were lost. He had considered his misgivings, but he needed the money. When he sat in the computer library to fill out the survey his doubts had resurfaced, as his opinion of his nature wasn't all that positive to begin with. Intuition wouldn't let him down. He deemed himself weird, but the idea of being a threat had never entered his mind.

It was a small comfort. It was a big lie.

He shifted in his seat. Rain pattered on his windshield from the empty darkness above.

***

His mind wandered. An hour passed, maybe more. It was of little importance.

It wasn't easy being a math major. The classes were difficult, the workload was enormous, the international cast of professors was often difficult to understand, and his fellow students formed an eccentric breed. But even in that domain, he was a loner. He'd been drawn to math because he was an abstract thinker, but he didn't see himself fitting within the host of greater mathematical minds. Archimedes, Pythagoras, Leibniz, Newton: they were great classical thinkers—not only mathematicians, but philosophers as well. Noel didn't consider himself a philosopher. Many of those great predecessors were artists as well and, in that regard, Noel felt some kind of connection. But even there, it was a strain. It wasn't the subtle complexity of Nature's intricate patterns and rhythms that drew him, but rather the way things were connected—in a more precise context, the way in which things could be disconnected, to betray the underlying ligatures.

The world was a mystery to him, and he found himself as a greater mystery within the curiosity known as existence. The relativistic sense of his identity as defined by those around him gave a temporal sense of perspective, but that measure only served to reinforce through all its complications the very simple conclusion he'd already reached.

He was weird. There was no getting around it.

He rubbed his face and looked at the survey. How could he explain those results? The last thing he wanted in life—the very last thing—was to draw attention, and now he felt the coming glare of a thousand searchlights of condemnation. Even in the dark seclusion of his car he felt his cheeks warm as he blushed in humiliation. He was quiet, he stayed to himself, and he had no friends. He knew the common, inevitable conclusion to those facts was that he was weird. But the survey, that stupid set of questions that should have been an inconsequential exercise, was going to give him the appearance of something nefarious. His professor would see it, and the can of worms would open from there. There was no faking it, no going back to change his answers. The survey resided on the university's intranet servers, and had closed upon completion to forward to his professor.

All for a few dollars. If only he didn't need the money.

His skin crawled. His heart raced. He slammed a hand on the steering wheel and started the car. He wanted to get drunk; he wanted to die.

Oh no, there's something else you can do.

He slammed his hand on the steering wheel again. "No, that's got me in enough trouble already. Besides, I could get caught."

It's dark. It's late. No one will see. No one will know.

He frowned, debating with himself. His gaze darted about before he nodded. "You know, you're probably right. You usually are."

***

He drove across the university grounds until he came to a set of dorms and, once there, he snaked through the parking lots until he found the unlit corner of his choice, over by Hastings Quad. It was an open lot, so there was no risk of yet another parking ticket he couldn't afford. He turned the headlights off, steered to a stop toward the dorm buildings, and killed the engine. After several moments he opened his knapsack, pulled out a sketchpad and pencil and, leaning the pad against the steering wheel, flipped to a clean page. It was dark, but enough light seeped into the car from a distant lamp pole to provide an amber glow. He slumped in his seat and looked up to the dorm building, his gaze rolling across the windows. A number still shone with light as students worked into the late hours.

Which window is hers? He tapped the pencil's eraser against the sketchpad. She wasn't his girlfriend—such a thing was unknown to him—but she was without a doubt the object of his fancy, his Miss Moonpie. The name came to him as a culmination born of the circumstances around her entry into his life. He saw her walking across campus one day as he ate a pretzel, and he'd followed her ever since. He had no idea who she was, or what she did, although he guessed she was some kind of biology student, as she seemed to frequent the bio buildings. She often walked alone, so he decided she was single, and titled her with 'miss'. He often thought of her at night, when he felt most alone and desperate, so his thoughts of her were painted with the stark light of the moon. As for the 'pie', it was a childish notion, as he found her to be the only palatable thing in his life, even if his obsession with her seemed a rather unsavory thing.

But there he sat and, for a few minutes at least, he forgot about the survey, he forgot about his classes, he forgot about his assignments. Life could be simple; simple the way he thought life should be simple, between a man and a woman of his interest. He couldn't conceive a more common pursuit. In days of old it was a romantic notion for a woman to have a secret admirer. Times had changed, though, and perspectives as well. The survey drew a telling portrait.

He looked to the pad. He'd sketched her before, but there would be no sketch now. He was too tired. Before he knew it his chin sank to his chest, and he fell fast asleep.

***

The next morning he sat up in bed and stared at his bedroom wall before shuffling downstairs. The door to his father's art studio, the Inferno, was closed. It was a sure sign his mother had a bad night, another echo of the stormy relationship between his parents. Even now, with his mother alone, the memories welled up from the abandoned studio like whispering ghosts.

He found her sitting at the kitchen table, staring out the window, her hair disheveled and needing a good wash, her night coat drawn about her thinning frame. Her chin rested in one hand, the cigarette in her other hand a wilted chain of untapped ashes. Two plates were on the table and, between them, a frying pan with some scrambled eggs. An open bag of bread sat next to the pan. It was the usual breakfast, what his mother referred to as the 'psych nurse overnight special.'

He waved a hand to clear the smoke and sat at the side of the table. He looked at her in profile and, as his gaze lingered, she blinked and turned to him. "You came in late," she said, her voice hoarse.

He scooped some eggs onto his plate. "I was doing work in the library."

She looked to her cigarette and with a frown stubbed it on her plate. Another one came out of her pocket, which she lit. Her eyes narrowed as she took a long pull, scrutinizing him as his gaze darted about his eggs. "Is this Friday? You're going to that freak fest tonight, right?"

43

He kept his eyes on his plate, but stopped eating. "Horror convention," he corrected.

She flicked her ashes on the floor. "Maybe you'll meet one of those undead girls."

"They're called Goth girls." He tossed some eggs in his mouth. "And no, probably not."

She stared at him. "Maybe you'll meet one of those Goth guys."

He put his fork down and sat up straight. He stared out the window to the shabby mess of the backyard. His mother had a particular way of freezing him in the past, by heaping his father's sins on his shoulders. He had some odd memories from when he was little, times when he had trouble sleeping, when he would tiptoe down the hall to peer into the Inferno. It seemed his father never slept. Sometimes, Noel saw his father painting his mother—not a likeness on canvas, but painting *her*, before the two of them dissolved in a knot of naked limbs. There were nights, when his mother worked extra hours, that he peered in the door and saw the same scene, but with one of his father's art crowd friends. And then there were those other nights, when his father just sat on a stool, talking to himself.

Noel took a breath before meeting his mother's cold gaze. "I've told you, I'm not like Dad." He stood and put his plate in the sink. "Don't bother waiting up for me."

***

He rode the bus from the commuter parking lot to campus. He sat at the front of the bus as he usually did, so he wouldn't have to look at anyone. His gaze could wander outside the window, over the trees that lined the road. Sometimes, if luck would have it, he would spot his Miss Moonpie walking across the drive from Hastings toward campus. Once, when he was tired from staring at his ceiling during another sleepless night, he stared at her too long. She looked at him, looked right at him and met his gaze. Only then the moment registered, but by the time he thought to look away she lowered her face and hid behind the long trail of her brown hair.

He frowned as he considered that memory. It was such things, he knew, that kept him isolated. If he was normal, he would've talked to her long ago; if she then ignored him, he could move on to someone else. Instead, he stared, he followed, he sketched; he obsessed, and so she became something more in his head than she could ever be in life. He knew he'd aborted all normal possibilities by that process, but that was his nature. Having to deal with someone else, to empathize with another, it just struck him as a needless headache.

44

His ears perked up as he heard someone mention Hastings Quad. He didn't want to be obvious, so he kept his gaze out the window, but he listened to the two students behind him. Late last night, in the deep dark hours, a girl had been attacked while she walked alone. Hit over the head with a rock, knocked out cold but, otherwise, she was okay.

His skin crawled. If someone recalled him parked in the lot, he would be an immediate suspect, and his trail of parking tickets would bear a damning testimony. How could he explain himself? What would he do if the results of his survey came out, and it was pieced together with his being seen and someone being attacked? What if—what if *she*—betrayed him by telling someone she saw him staring at her from the bus that one morning?

He lowered his head and rubbed his face. His heart was pounding. *I didn't do anything. No, I didn't do a thing. I'm harmless.*

***

The day dragged by.

One of his professors tried to loosen up a lecture on double integrals by inviting an open discussion regarding a debate between Leibniz and Newton. The two great mathematicians were at odds in their day, and had confronted each other in a debate to espouse their different beliefs. Newton preferred the clockwork precision of his laws, rooted in his faith of a precise divinity, one that had crafted the universe and its governing laws with the meticulous care of a master craftsman. Newton deduced his laws of motion under the guise of an absolute background reference frame: all motion and energy occurred in respect to that baseline. It simplified the mathematical study of motion, distilling it to a manageable, rudimentary set of laws.

Leibniz, the philosopher, espoused something perhaps more complex, that Nature was a mélange of varying compositions, that it possessed no notion of the absolute. All motion, all energy, all there was of the universe existed only in subjective relation between various observed entities. What Leibniz advocated was a higher math, a higher understanding, one that foreshadowed Einstein's relativity and the shifting states of perspective it entailed. It was troubling, for it defied notions of the Absolute; it challenged the very idea of an Absolute as a reference. The only path to enlightenment, to understanding, was to discard the Absolute. It held an irony that few were willing to embrace.

Both men argued theory. But Newton had the advantage, as his laws of motion predicted the outcomes of direct observation. The Absolute may have been a mathematical conceit, but it served its purpose. Irony had upended itself.

The debate in Noel's class was not to favor one position over the other, but rather to discuss who should be deemed the greater mathematician. It was of little concern for Noel, as he had something more immediate in mind. By that point of the day, he was convinced he was going to be arrested.

***

No one came looking for him. No one questioned him.

Because he was a nobody, he told himself as he sat in a fast food place eating a greasy burger for dinner. Nobody would ask him, because nobody knew him. He was a nobody on that campus, among all those people.

He chewed his burger. He looked out the windows. It had been a gray day and, as the last light faded, it started to rain.

He took a deep breath, and a different thought came to him.

The high grass hides the predator.

He tipped his head. "But I'm not like that," he said as he wiped his mouth.

Sure you are. You just don't know it yet. Look at all the other things we've done. You didn't have the nerve for any of it.

He shook his head. "I'm not a coward."

The silence in his head spoke volumes of condemnation.

He sat there, burger in hand, trying to calm the mounting anxiety in his chest, until the silence was too much to bear. He dumped the remaining burger on its wrapper, stuffed his waste in a garbage pail, and threw the door open as he went out into the rain. He wanted to drink. He wanted to die. He wanted to break everything around him. Coward! Shy, yes, but a coward? Socially inept, without a doubt, but weren't there reasons for that? Damn straight there were!

He got in his car, slammed the door shut, and tore out of the parking lot with spinning wheels. He sped toward the highway, his heart pounding in his chest. He had looked forward to the horror convention with such anticipation, only to have it ruined. Instead of trembling with excitement to watch some goofy movies and watch some strange people, he was locked in his car and locked in his head, his world once again imploding among reverberating whispers of self-recrimination. They came in that other voice of his, those whispers, that unhealthy third person voice in his head that held nothing but condemnation for every action he took and every decision he made.

"I'll show you, I'll show you!" he said between clenched teeth, smacking a hand on the steering wheel. "Screw you! I'll do it! I will!"

He pushed the gas pedal to the floor and watched the speedometer climb. Eighty, ninety, triple digits!

He took a breath. The moment came upon him: affirmation through terror. He closed his eyes and forced his hands open to release the steering wheel. Unguided, unaware, his car rocketed down the highway.

His pulse was a steady sensation, a high throb in the top of his head. Adrenaline surged with the subconscious fear that he could be obliterated at any moment, but the immediacy brought a thrilling, welcome moment of clarity. He transcended his own confines; it was sweet liberation, sweet rapture, the kind he imagined his father must have felt in his last moments on the planet. Noel perceived the two warring voices in his head, stilled as the fear of death uncoiled each heart-pounding moment to eternity. He could sense his own voice, the one that kept him in check, the one that lashed out in frustration in such moments of recklessness, the one that stared at a plate of eggs while his mother heaped her misery on his narrow shoulders. But then he could sense that other voice, the cool, clear voice that whispered subversive thoughts of destruction and dissolution. He had a name for it, a clever dodge, but one that nevertheless compelled him to both confront and accept that other side of his nature.

My other me. In his mathematician's desire for concise definition of terms, and out of the natural desire of the human mind to create order among chaos, the reference had collapsed to its inevitable acronym: Mom. He knew it was an unhealthy connection, perhaps a subconscious act more telling than any personality survey. But when Mom came to him and whispered its darker inclinations, he at least insulated himself from total madness by shortening the name even further, to one of brutish simplicity: Mo.

Mo took care of him, though. Mo could whisper horrible things to him, not unlike his mother, but Mo could push him to do things he would never think of doing. His pursuit of Miss Moonpie came to fill his greater perception of the whole interaction. Mo wanted him to go after her, but he tempered that brash inclination. Where Mo could be impulsive, he was patient and persistent. On the other hand, where he was imbalanced in his rage, Mo could operate with ruthless efficiency.

Like right now, stupid. Open your eyes before you turn yourself into road pizza.

***

He stopped at a twenty-four hour convenience store, his body still swimming in the adrenaline rush of his blind speed trip down the highway. He was too young to buy alcohol, but he knew his way around that. He tripped into a display of small snack bags to send them

47

cascading to the floor. The store's attendant cursed him out, but got down on hands and knees to clean up the mess. With the attendant distracted, Noel slipped away, stashed a bottle of whiskey in his knapsack, and strolled out of the store. Before the attendant knew what was happening Noel was halfway back to the university.

He wanted to drink by Hastings Quad, but his better sense kept him away. He parked in the commuter lot, away from the rows of cars attracted by the convention. So he sat in his car and drank, drank until he was floating in his seat, until his mind was good and numb.

He was ready. Horror Con beckoned.

***

He shuffled about the main lecture hall, its large rooms used as theatres for the convention. He watched several horror movies, wasting the precious money he earned from the personality survey, moving from one room to another to catch the moments he liked best. But even with that, he started to tire of the movies. There were only so many ways to behead someone, only so many ways to impale, crush, maim and kill. Zombie movies had their own flare but, after watching a headless zombie strangle someone with its own eviscerated intestines, everything else seemed rather tame.

With his imagination drenched in gore and his buzz fading, he found himself in his old reality, stranded in the isolation of his mind. He made his way over to the student union, where there were displays of local artists and tables set up for merchandising. Most of the goods were garbage, cheap things made by child laborers in foreign countries with strange names. Some of the people behind the tables were interesting; he always drew a certain pleasure from the guys selling knives, because they kept women in scanty medieval warrior costumes nearby. He was always too nervous to talk to them, and every time the result was the same. The knife guys would catch him staring at some of the pierced belly buttons—and tell him to get lost.

One vendor held his attention, though. There was an old man sitting behind a long table draped in black velvet at the end of the merchant display, where the lighting was somewhat lacking. The dimness helped accentuate the old man's display, as his table was set with various sculptures of hand blown glass sitting atop bases with various colored lights, most of them purple and violet, some amber and fluorescent green. In the middle of the table was a wave tank, one of those psychedelic remnants from the sixties. Noel crouched before the tank and watched the oil slosh with lazy grace inside the slender glass case as the tank tipped one way and then the other. The base, besides having the rocker motor, had a violet light that illuminated the oil in the tank. He was mesmerized but, when he asked the price, his eyes widened. He frowned, but the old man shrugged, and refused to bargain down to Noel's range.

Disappointed, he made his way over to the art displays, but after all the cinematic portrayals of torture and murder, the still portrayals of paintings lacked impact. They weren't like his father's paintings, after all. His old man might have been eccentric, but he knew how to paint. The things he created in the Inferno were masterworks of fear, not for the graphic violations they could depict, but for the expressions of torment and glee exchanged between victims and perpetrators. What made his father's paintings unique was the anarchic displacement of those expressions. It wasn't always the perpetrator relishing wanton acts; it wasn't always the 'victim' in torment. There were depictions of twisted rapture, of victims laughing in ecstasy as they compelled their assailants to debase themselves in despicable violations. It was more than sympathy for the deviant mind; it was empathy for the acts themselves. Life, death, pain, glee: they were bound by emotionless strands of flesh and the ethereal bonds they contained, bonds that transcended human understanding. Unseen ligatures they were, things that defied explanation, things that failed to be confined by variables, constants, and equations.

The world, Noel knew, was not mathematical. Only the tactile realm obeyed what math and science would call 'rational' laws. And the rest, all the rest, it could only fall within its diametric opposite.

He stood before a painting. It was dark, done in shadow, depicting a man gazing in a mirror. The man's reflection was an empty expression, though the eyes were saucer-wide beneath a knotted forehead. The reflection was shadowed by a greater outline, its black form shrouded in a glistening, prickly corona. Its narrow, tapered eyes glowed sinister red.

There was something more to existence than what could be seen, things that led to the madness of Noel's father, to the man's mounting fits of night terrors until he drove his car at triple digit speed into a concrete bridge piling.

Noel knew the truth. The rational world was a deception created by the human mind to comfort human insecurity. The only truth, the ironic truth, was belief in an irrational existence.

He retreated to a shadowy corner, sat on the floor, and stared at the painting as he sipped his whiskey.

***

It was after midnight when he made his way toward the life sciences building where the convention's meet-and-greets were held. There were advertisements for several psychics, and his curiosity was piqued.

He walked across a parking lot, glancing up at the black night sky. The rain had stopped for the moment, but he walked with the hood of his jacket pulled up. There were a few cars in the lot, but it was a lonesome place, cloaked in the heavy silence of the late hour. He paced between the hooded lamps of the lot, the long shadows they cast of his passing form curling beside him in his peripheral vision. Dazed with whiskey, the countless scenes of torture and violence he had watched that night filled his mind. The hairs on the back of his neck rose as waves of chills rolled along his spine. He wondered about the girl who was attacked by Hastings, and if she saw the coming shadow of her attacker. His gaze darted between the hollow sounds of his sneakers on the pavement as he watched his shadow flicker from side to side, moving from the light of one lamp to another. It was disorienting, it was confusing— if one of them was an attacker, would he even notice the man's outline, or would he lose it in the confusion of his own shadows?

Despite his sudden fear that he would find some demon stalking him, he shot a quick glance over either shoulder to dispel the paranoia that he was being hunted. Predatory instinct inverted upon him so that he felt the quickening of the prey, his pace picking up speed as his shoulders bunched up and his head sank down. It was such a vast parking lot, and he was so alone, so vulnerable.

His shadow jumped from his right to his left as he came beneath another lamp, the one he just passed lost behind a tree. His gaze locked on the shadow and, as he stared, it appeared to move closer to him, to press in on him—

He looked, but he was alone. He sucked in a breath. *Mo?*

Turn! Now!

He trembled as he whipped around. The dizziness of the whiskey sent him stumbling, his vision blurring and his hands flailing to keep his balance. The hooded lamp sent his shadow spinning about him, collapsing upon him and, as he watched, the shadow opened its arms.

His throat clamped shut. The world went black.

***

He came to his senses in the lobby of the life sciences building. It was spacious, with rounded enclaves along either side containing comfortable chairs. They were meant for people to sit and discuss philosophy or whatever other nonsense they were studying, but on the night of Horror Con, they served as booths for psychics as they worked their own cons. After the paid sessions broke up the lobby became an open forum for smaller informal conversations, fed by caffeine from the lobby's coffee bar. The crowd had dwindled to a few scattered groups as the hour passed into that netherworld between deep night and early morning.

His gaze lingered before him on a placard set up by the coffee bar, advertising one of the so-called psychics. A man sat there, sipping his coffee, nodding and smiling to several people who walked by him, but his gaze turned to Noel with increasing regularity. For some reason, Noel just stared, stared with his unblinking, emotionless stalker-stare. The man was dressed like one of those armchair pseudo-intellectuals, wearing a tweed blazer over a black turtleneck shirt. After what seemed a very long time the man's face fell, and he walked across the lobby toward Noel.

Noel fumed. Couldn't he be left alone?

The man stopped before Noel but, with him so near, Noel realized the man wasn't looking quite at him, instead looking somewhat to Noel's right. The man nodded. "Hello. Mind if I have a seat?" he said, opening a hand to one of the chairs.

Noel wanted to say no. He wanted to tell this huckster to get lost. But despite himself, he heard something very different come from his mouth.

"You can sit if you want."

Noel looked around. He had the sudden realization it was pitch-dark where he sat. He looked to his side, and saw himself in profile. His mind froze in confusion.

The stranger settled in a chair, looking to the thing that sat beside Noel— looking to Noel, in fact. And then that thing spoke, and Noel heard the voice that used to be his.

"You can call me Mo."

Noel bucked, but he was nothing. He was as shapeless as the displaced shadow he had become, a non-entity in the absence of light.

The man tipped his head. "You can call me Greg."

Noel watched his hand point to the placard. "What happened to Gregor, the Leningrad Luminary?" he heard himself say.

The man glanced over his shoulder before turning back. He waved a hand and smiled. "That's just a front. It's more like Greg, the New Jersey Janitor." He sipped his coffee, his steady gaze holding on Mo's eyes. "Do you have a front?"

Noel bucked in disbelief.

Hey! I want my body back!

He watched his lips curl in a mischievous grin. "Used to. I'm new here, you could say."

Greg's affable smile became a knowing grin. "I see more than that. I'd like to offer you a complimentary reading."

Noel wanted to scream for help. Could Greg sense him, or was it salesmanship?

51

Mo shifted in his seat, turning his head to glance in Noel's direction. The look of amusement in his eyes was almost as disturbing as his assumption of Noel's body. Greg followed Mo's gaze, but Noel stared back at the man, helpless.

Mo cleared his throat, his eyes narrowing as they bored into Greg. "Okay, janitor man. You got me. I'm not what you think. Now what?"

Greg frowned and shook his head. "I'm not here to challenge you. I'm just a psychic with a sense."

"Yeah, right," Mo said, but despite his self-assurance, Greg's calm, confident statement surprised him almost as much as it surprised Noel. Mo shifted in his seat. Some of his swagger faded, but it returned in a heartbeat. He studied Greg before swallowing, the sound almost audible. "So you're a psychic? Okay. Tell me what you see."

Greg opened a hand. "I think you come from a different place."

"Amateur." Mo rolled his shoulders. "I told you that. Try again."

Greg gave him a nod. He sat, his eyes widening before they blinked. "An unseen place."

Mo glanced at the darkness of Noel's banishment. "Shadows."

Greg continued to stare at Noel's body, but it was clear something was bothering him. "Shadows," he repeated under his breath. "Right, shadows. I should tell you something, Mo. You know, I used to live a different life. A very different life." He pulled down the collar of his turtleneck shirt, revealing a dark scar around his neck. "Attempted suicide by hanging. Oxygen deprivation. Oddly enough, it provided clarity. Irony, I guess you could call it, if you look at things from a different perspective."

Mo chuckled.

"I can sense things," Greg repeated. "And what I sense. . ."

Mo's face fell. He raised a finger and waved it in caution.

Greg leaned forward, his elbows on his knees, and glanced to his side to make sure no one could hear him. "These bodies, Mo, they're not what you think. They bleed. They die."

If not for the surreal path of the discussion and his disembodiment, Noel would've collapsed within the delusion of the moment. Instead, he found nothing but a fixed attention on every spoken word. He had nothing else.

Mo sighed in apparent boredom. "What's your point?"

Greg hesitated, his gaze falling to his coffee. He took a sip, his lips drawing to a tight line before he looked back to Mo. "You know, I don't do this psychic thing for fun. I see what I see, and not everything is what it appears to be. Some, uh, 'people' are not what they appear to be. They follow a different rule. I do this to find them, to ask them to be careful. All this," he said, rolling his eyes to the world about them, "it's not what you're used to. It's a different game in the driver's seat. A far different game."

Mo waved him off. "I'll be fine." He waited until Greg walked away to glance toward Noel. "You'll see," Mo whispered. "I'll be just fine."

***

The ceiling of Noel's bedroom was a gray wash in his perception. Mo still had Noel's body, so Noel was left weak and diffused, pooled in a dark corner. Mo lay on the bed, flat on his back, staring at the ceiling.

Mom?

"Don't call me that," Mo said at once. "You have no idea how screwed up that is."

Noel grew anxious, his darkness flitting about the corner of the room. He wondered if Mo had witnessed everything in Noel's life; if he had, in fact, been there all along.

Mo nodded. "Unfortunately, yes."

Were you with my father?

Mo turned to look into Noel's corner. "No. Every person has their own 'other'. From the way things went with your old man, his must have been a real bad ass."

Is that why he killed himself? Is that why he was crazy?

Mo shrugged. "I don't know. It's hard to say. I told you, everyone's different."

Noel hesitated. *Are you going to give me back my body?*

Mo propped himself up on his elbows before looking to Noel. "See, this is where things get all screwed up. You think this is your body, that you possess it. It's just a lump of fertilizer without the spark to make it alive. I'm that spark. For lack of a better term, I guess you could call me, and things like me, the soul. Nobody knows why but, for some reason, we get connected to bodies. Your life, everything around you that you think is so important; it's just a daydream to things like me. We're passive witnesses, most of the time."

Noel hung on every word, but his inevitable desire loomed over their meaning. He wanted his body.

Mo frowned. "Listen to me. What you think of as 'you', that's just an illusion created by the lump of fatty cells in your head. Things like me, we're the only real things. That's what makes people nuts when they perceive our presence, when they hear our thoughts."

But I'm still here.

Mo turned to sit on the edge of the bed. "You're a shadow looking back at yourself. No one can hear you. No one can see you. So, are you even there?" He took a breath, tipping his chin up as his eyes narrowed.

"When this body dies, I move on. There's always some other pile that needs a push."

What about me?

"Ah, the big question." Mo opened his hands. "Do you really want to know?"

Noel thought of what Mo had told him. The answer was there, and it stilled his mind.

Mo nodded. "That's right. You're just a fantasy of your own flesh, nothing more. You think I'm your dream but, in reality, you're the dream. When your body dies, it's lights out for you. The 'hereafter', that's for me."

Noel pooled in the corner, befuddled.

Mo rubbed his face and slumped on the bed. "Get some sleep. Tomorrow's going to be a big day."

***

Noel remained a pool in the corner. Sleep proved elusive. Looking over to his bed and his sleeping body, he wasn't sure he could remember what sleep was. It was like looking into some other life, some other reality. Perspective had played its game with him and, now that it had shifted with such inescapable consequence, the logical side of Noel's mind set about redefining the new parameters of his awareness. Certain sensations, such as the blink of his eyes, the rush of air in his chest, and the sound of his pulse in his ears when he concentrated his thoughts, they were fading to remote memories. It was a bad trend, he knew. Forgetting those things meant forgetting his body; it meant surrendering to his disembodied perspective.

It was bizarre with its frightening immediacy, yet he couldn't debate the certainty of his situation. He wasn't sure what to make of Mo, or if he should believe anything Mo had said. It wasn't necessarily an assumption of Mo as a deceptive aspect of his own personality, but rather the fact that in the past Mo's inclinations often neglected certain aspects of Noel's world. Thinking of it, it made a certain sense. It was a paradigm shift of his awareness, but it possessed a symmetrical character to its nature; and, as with any geometric system, it held a certain logic to its structure.

It wasn't a mirror, or a window, through which his thoughts peered. It was a subjective transition, and it defied the innate notions of divided states of awareness. If what he perceived as his intellect was a fantasy generated by his own flesh, then the perception of existence about his flesh was fantasy as well. Nothing was real, and so everything was real.

Conundrum, or contradiction. It was a puzzle of semantics, ridiculing any reference frames of absolutist structures.

Night and light.

Right and might.

Not just convenient sounds in language, but links—ligatures—creating the impression of opposed ideas.

He was a pool of shadow in the corner, an absence of light. Nothing, but yet something. He didn't tire, and his thoughts rambled in a fractal mess lacking any causal connection. Perhaps, he wondered, his thoughts would form the whisper of a dream, the dreams he used to know as his own, that he knew then as Mo's rambling thoughts in days gone by. And with that, everything began to make sense. He had opened the door for Mo in the abstraction of his thoughts, in the distraction of his obsession, in the emotional constriction of his childhood.

He looked to the bed. Mo rolled over, putting his back to Noel's corner, and snored in peaceful sleep.

***

Time passed.

The house was still. Rain fell through the darkness. It was familiar, yet different.

So some things remain the same. He was alone and desperate in the claustrophobic quiet of night. His thoughts drifted to the one solace he knew, and that was to ponder his Miss Moonpie. With so much stripped from him, she still remained. He could visualize her, visualize her in all her splendor and, in his artistic sensibility, he harmonized with the exquisite composition of her features as he imagined reproducing them on a sketchpad. And since he was only an absence of light, he had no eyes to close, so she took shape within his mind at the same time his sleeping form registered with him.

There was an odd moment then, one that jarred him from his reverie. In the retreat of his mind, his body felt no more real than the representation he crafted of his Miss Moonpie.

Was Mo right? Did Noel exist, or was he just an illusion? What did it mean to be real?

Mo, sleeping with his back to Noel, turned his head. "Hey, dumb ass," he said under his breath. "Do you mind? I'm trying to sleep over here. Stop mumbling in my head."

Rain fell through the darkness. The shadows were black and still.

***

Mo sat on the edge of the bed, rubbing his face against the gray morning light. Rain pounded against the roof above. He shifted about, rolling his shoulders to loosen their cramps, licking his teeth in protest of his pasty morning breath, lifting his toes to stretch the arches of his flat feet: all things that marked the peculiar singularity of the body known as Noel.

Mo dropped his hands and looked to the corner. He stared for some time. "Hey," he whispered at last. "You still there?"

Still here.

Mo tipped his head back. A silent curse formed on his lips. He pushed the body of Noel out of bed, shuffled down the hall to the bathroom, and braced his arms on the edge of the sink. He stared in the mirror. "I bet you think you've had some sort of psychotic break, that you think you're experiencing some kind of acute-phase dissociative personality disorder." He put his hand on the switch for the vanity light and tipped his head to pick out the shadows in the corner of the mirror's reflection. "Accept it. You're not real. I'll show you—now."

He flipped the switch, bathing the room in light. The shadows disappeared.

Still here.

Mo looked into the reflection of Noel's puffy eyes and frowned. As the moments mounted the muscles on his jaw stood out in bands of tension. "Okay. You don't want to accept it? Now we do it the hard way."

Still here.

Mo went to Noel's room, pulled on some clean clothes, and headed downstairs to the kitchen. As usual, his mother was sitting at the table, with the pan of eggs and the opened bag of bread, and the wilted cigarette in hand. She turned her melancholy gaze to him, and Mo played it just the way Noel would have reacted, his head down to avoid her scrutiny. Mo settled in his chair, but Noel found himself drifting, blending with the dim light of the gray morning to bleed across the walls. He looked to his mother, and the tired repetition of the scene, and found it to be a pathetic thing.

Mo cleared his throat at Noel's thought.

His mother flicked her ashes on the floor. "Watch those gore flicks all night?"

Mo bit his lip to maintain his composure. "Yes."

She took a long drag from her cigarette, the way she did when she was contemplating some barb to throw at him. Her watery eyes blinked as she blew out a long trail of smoke. "You watch them alone?"

Mo leaned an elbow on the table as he poked at his eggs with his fork, ignoring her question. "Can I ask you something?"

His mother stared at him. "You need money?"

Mo shook his head. "Remember when I was little, and Dad bought me a hamster?"

She coughed as she fished a cigarette from the pocket of her night coat, the lit one still dangling between her lips. She lit the new one from the old before crushing the butt on her plate. "It was a gerbil. And yeah, I remember the little rat. Escaped. Good riddance."

"I was supposed to clean out the tank," Mo continued, his eyes still on the plate.

Her gaze slid toward him.

Noel fretted, helpless on the wall. He didn't like where Mo was going.

Mo rolled his shoulders and nodded. "I forgot to clean out the tank, and you got so mad, you picked out the droppings and put them in the eggs before I woke up. You let me eat that, that shit omelet, before you were kind enough to tell me what was in it." He looked up to meet his mother's puffy face. "It didn't escape, you know. I was so upset, I killed it."

It was a horrible memory, buried under years of hurt. Noel wanted to let it go.

Mo shrugged. "Yeah, it feels like yesterday."

She blew out a breath. "Grow up. It wasn't supposed to be a pet. You know what your father was up to. Get over yourself."

Mo sat up straight. He put his fork down.

She looked out the window at the morning rain.

Mo snatched the pan and smashed it over her head. Blood erupted from her scalp amid the metallic bong of the pan on her skull. The cigarette flew from her lips. The chair fell back to crash on the floor, her limp body splayed like uncooked dough.

Mo stretched his neck to look past the table at her still form, the pan still clenched in his hand, its dark form hovering where it had shattered her skull. He glanced over his shoulder to stare at the wall. "You have no idea how long I've wanted to do that," he whispered. "So, are you still there?"

The sight of his mother filled Noel's awareness. The moment had exploded with such surprise he found himself numb to its reality. All those years he sat with her, and the humiliation had bred nothing in him but obedience and senility, the hurt of her abuse hanging over him like an amorphous shadow.

Still here.

Mo stamped a foot. He bolted from his chair, knocking it over in his haste. "Don't you get it? How could you be real? How could you sit next to her all this time after what she did and do nothing about it? Who do you think held all the anger and hurt? Me! Go away already!"

Still here—

Mo cursed. He walked over to the body. Her chest rose in a stuttered breath. Mo glanced at the wall, then at the pan in his hand. He clenched his teeth and shook the pan before laying it upside down over her face. He looked to the wall, clenched his fists, and stomped his foot on the pan. When Noel made no response, Mo bashed the pan with his foot again, then kept at it until a wet crack sounded out and his mother's hands and feet gave a sudden twitch. Mo looked down and took a step back. Blood oozed across the floor from beneath the pan.

Noel stared, and then realization hit him. He was watching an exercise of Mo's anger, not his own. He had no anger. He was a shadow. He'd always been a shadow.

Mo threw his hands up at the scene before him. "Shit! Look at this!"

Noel was indifferent. It was Mo's mess to clean.

Mo spun to the wall. "Still there?" he said in disbelief. "What—" he began, but then his eyes widened as he shook a finger in the air. "I get it! You still think you're real. I know what to do. I'll show you once and for all!"

Mo kicked the pan off his mother's shattered face and dragged her body to the bathroom, grunting with effort. He dumped her in the tub, washed his hands, and mopped the kitchen floor. Then he went back upstairs, walked down the hall, and stood outside the Inferno.

During Noel's childhood the Inferno was off limits. There were only those few glimpses he stole during his sleepless nights. Other than that, his father would keep the place locked. After the man splattered himself on the highway, Noel's mother left the door unlocked, since she was usually too drunk to find the key on the nights she wandered into the studio.

Mo pushed the door open. He stepped inside. He looked at the half dozen paintings left after the father's death, all of them in various stages of completion. The theme was consistent, though. All of them had the rudimentary composition of mirrored images.

Mo shook his head. "It must've been some battle," he said under his breath. "If only the old man had known the truth."

***

Noel lost track of time. Time no longer seemed important. He was too busy contemplating his notions of abstraction, absolutism, and relativity to pay much attention to anything. It numbed and occupied his awareness. He didn't think of his mother at all. In the end, the only gift he could claim from her was apathy.

Mo parked outside Hastings, in the usual spot. "Still there?"

It took a moment for Noel to summon the echo.

Mo nodded. He opened the knapsack and pulled out the sketchpad. He leafed through the pages until he found the sketches of her, embellished in Noel's obsession to her doe-eyed magnificence. "Look at her."

So beautiful. . .

"Maybe you didn't pay attention, but I always did. All those times we watched her, you were too out of it to catch the details, but I kept all of them." He looked up from the sketchpad. "See that? Third floor, second window from the left. That's her, and her lights are on. Remember, you stalked her into the building one time, when she was talking to her friends, before that time you blew it by letting her see you on the bus? You followed her up the stairs, but at least you had the sense to keep going so she wouldn't catch on. I remember that, crystal clear. And I remember she's always here on Saturdays. Doing homework, I guess."

Noel didn't understand.

Mo put the pad away. "You think you're real. I'm going to prove once and for all you're not."

Noel wasn't sure if he cared anymore. He was just floating, adrift in his thoughts.

Mo snapped his fingers. "It matters to me. I don't want any doubt lingering in this head of mine." He took a breath. "Miss Moonpie, we shall meet at last."

***

Patience was Noel's virtue, but not an attribute Mo possessed. They waited in the car until Mo slapped a hand on the steering wheel. "Here we go," he said, his eyes narrowing on a car that rolled up to one of the buildings. It was an old car, typical of a student's rolling wreck, but it had a roof placard pinched in the door advertising pizza delivery. Mo rummaged through the knapsack until he found one of the new, sharpened pencils Noel kept for sketching. Mo took it in hand, pulled up his hood, and stepped from the car.

The pizza guy never saw Mo, too concerned with keeping the box of pizza level as he hurried to the door of Miss Moonpie's building. Mo overtook him just before the door, shoving him against the wall before ramming the sharpened pencil point through the man's ear to skewer his brain. His body convulsed before going limp. Mo let him drop, rolled him into the bushes, and picked up the pizza. After that, it was easy to get in. He made his way up to Miss Moonpie's room, buzzed her door, and waited.

"Hello?" her muffled voice said from behind the door.

Mo pulled out the receipt tucked into the lid of the box. "Delivery for three-four-five."

"Sorry, but I didn't order any pizza."

His eyes darted about. "That's what it says here. Are you Mary?"

"No, there's a mistake, I—"

"Look, it's my first day, and the receipt's all wet. Could you take a look?"

There was a pause, but then he heard the latch unlock. She opened the door as far as the chain lock would allow, her face visible in the slit of the door. "Let me see—"

Mo slammed his shoulder into the door. The chain popped loose, the door pounding into her face and throwing her back. Mo spun on his feet and closed the door as he tossed the pizza aside. He pounced, tackling her to the floor before she could gain her senses. She tried to scream, but he punched her hard in the stomach, clamped a hand over her mouth, and looked down the hall of the dorm. It was quiet. They were alone.

Mo froze, Noel's detached fascination at seeing her so close overwhelming Mo's more predatory instincts. He shook it off and, keeping his hand clamped over her mouth, seized her hair and dragged her to her feet. She struggled, her hands clawing at his arm and head, but a good pull of her hair turned her struggle into a solid grip of his forearm.

Noel quaked in the shadows. *Don't hurt her, don't hurt her—don't hurt her!*

"*Shut up,*" Mo growled. "*My* game now."

He led her to the kitchen, punching her in the stomach to knock the wind from her before he flipped the switches by the wall. With his forearm firmly clamped around her throat to hold her in a headlock, he played with the switches until he grew frustrated and turned them off. He dragged her into one of the bedrooms, jerked a desk lamp from its outlet, and went back to the kitchen. He threw her against the refrigerator, her body dropping to the floor as she struggled to catch a breath. He put the lamp down and foraged about until he found a carving knife. The threatening gleam of its point hovered before her eyes as he crouched before her.

Stop it! Don't hurt her!

She cowered, shaking in terror. "Please, *please*—"

Mo smacked an open hand on the refrigerator, the sharp sound driving her rigid against the door. "*Shut up.* Make a sound, make a move, and I'll cut your heart out."

She squeezed her eyes shut. "I didn't do anything, please, I—"

"I said to *shut up,*" Mo repeated, slapping his hand on the door next to her ear. She winced, but he backed away, staring at her down the length of the knife. He plugged the lamp in and tilted its head so the bulb shone straight out. "This isn't about you," he said, turning. "I don't give a shit who you are. It won't matter soon, anyway."

He looked down on her. In the darkness of the kitchen the glare of the lamp behind him threw his shadow across the refrigerator as a looming monstrosity.

Noel's awareness snapped to sudden clarity. Her fear was palpable, growing every mounting moment with her hopeless vulnerability.

Mo tossed the knife in the sink and lunged at her. She fought with him, but he got his hands around her throat, and began to squeeze. "Now you'll see," he forced out through clenched teeth. "Look at her. *Look at her.*"

Her eyes rolled over as she pried at Mo's hands. Her feet flailed on the floor, useless for traction with the thick socks she wore. Veins bulged, her color changed. Beads of Mo's sweat dripped on her cheeks.

Images began to flash through Noel's mind. He remembered sneaking from his room to peek into the Inferno. He remembered eating the fecal omelet, remembered strangling the little gerbil that same day after school. He buried it in the backyard, under one of the overgrown bushes. It was such a mess back there no one ever noticed. He thought of all the times he sketched Miss Moonpie, and he thought of the gerbil, and his father splattered on the highway, and his mother dead in the tub, and the pizza guy with his brain skewered, and his own dispossession of his body. The utter fragility of life collapsed his intellect, overthrew his thoughts, destroyed the apathetic solitude of his shadowed existence.

There was an old man sitting at a table covered in black velvet. The wave tank rocked back and forth, the illuminated oil flowing with gravity in a lazy rush.

He felt like he was falling then, or rather, that he was being sucked down, but the sensation was nevertheless the same, regardless of his perspective, and then—

His mind flashed black, a perfect black, before it flashed white in a violent eruption. Sight exploded before him. There was a high throb in his skull, and he knew the old sensations of thought: the blink of his eyes, the sound of pulse in his ears—the pounding was loud, more intense than he remembered—and the rush of air in his chest, so wanting that rush of air, so absent that precious air—

Breathe. Breathe!

Mo filled his vision, eyes bulging, face red, drool hanging from the lips framing his bared teeth. The image looked frozen, but then Mo blinked, and he threw himself back with a gasp.

Noel slumped on his side, clutching his throat as he sucked in a breath. He coughed, he wheezed, but the air came, and continued to come, and with each rise of his chest and passage of air the pounding in his head eased. His eyes slid shut, and he thought he heard a whisper, but it was faint, and it receded from his awareness, and then a convulsive chill seized him before warmth returned to his trembling limbs. He opened his eyes, but something blocked the light, something like a veil. He swept a hand, and it parted. Silky smooth, it was.

He froze.

Mo was sprawled on the floor before him, his elbows propped beneath him as he lay on his back, panting. "What's your name?"

The whispered reply came in a voice Noel had longed to know. He heard it, heard his name, felt it as it passed across her lips.

Mo slumped back and shot his fists in the air.

Noel recoiled, throwing her body against the refrigerator. Her hair slid across his cheeks, but he tore at it to clear his sight, his heart—her heart—pounding when he looked at her delicate hands. He thrashed about the floor, struggling with a moment of mutual rejection between his intellect and her body, but in the wanting absence of their mutual natures, they bonded.

He clamped her hands on the edge of the counter to pull him to her feet. He swayed there for a moment, her hair sliding over his shoulder. He clamped her eyes shut, his senses overwhelmed as they rebooted to the imprint of her body. Her legs almost gave out, but he leaned on the counter, slid toward the sink, and made it just as the vomit erupted from her mouth.

Mo rose to his feet, coming up behind her to turn on the water. He put a hand on her shoulder—a gentle hand, now that the conflict was over—and steadied her as he cupped his hand beneath the faucet and washed her mouth. He watched as her hand rose to clutch her hair, flipping it across her wrist in a very natural way to get it away from the sink. "That's it," Mo said with a nod of satisfaction. "I knew it would work, I knew it!"

She slapped a hand on the faucet to turn off the water, holding a moment before spitting out the last wash of acrid saliva from her mouth. She rose, swaying on her feet even as her hands clutched at the counter to steady herself. She coughed, and her voice came in a hoarse whisper as Noel drove it from her throat. "I—"she began, but Noel clutched a hand over her mouth at the sound of his thought forming on her lips.

Mo nodded in excitement. "See? You got her. She's all yours now."

Noel squeezed her eyes shut to gather his wits before looking back to Mo. "I don't understand. . ."

Mo held up a hand. "She was here," he said, then, holding up his other hand, "and you were over here. But when she was empty," he meshed his hands together, "you filled her."

Noel trembled. He wanted to peel his—her—skin off. "You, I mean, we, killed her?"

Mo shrugged. "We don't need her. You feel real now, don't you?"

Noel shook her head. His sanity threatened to unravel, but his notions of abstraction rose up within him, and sheltered his fragile intellect. More than that, he was conforming to her body with ever increasing subtlety at each beat of her heart, at each surge of blood feeding the brain that served as the new home of his awareness. He turned to the little window over the kitchen sink and, in the gray afternoon light, picked out her reflection. Her eyes slid shut. "No, no, you said I wasn't real, this isn't real, you said it was *lights out without my body.*"

Mo rubbed her shoulders. "I lied," he said, shrugging off the blunt explanation. "Truth is, I can't imagine being around without you. Actually, I can't be around without you. And you were so obsessed with her. I always had this idea, but it didn't really settle with me until psychic Greg told me about his hanging. See, I drove her out, so you could have her."

Noel stared at the window. He could see her reflection and Mo's reflection—his old reflection—hovering over her. It echoed one of his father's paintings.

Mo leaned over, his chest resting against her back, his chin settling on her shoulder. He put his lips by her ear, the smell of her hair filling his nose. "All those drawings," he whispered, "all that devotion. I couldn't help but feel it, you know. You wanted her so much, craved her, your artist's eye dissecting and digesting every curve, every nuance."

Noel knew the memory and, hearing it in his voice, it was both befuddling and mesmerizing. His eyes slid shut. Fascination usurped his disgust, twenty years of lonely nights culminating to anesthetize his mind against the irrational, surreal experience of being her. His mind tingled, wallowing in the memories of those nights, when she transcended being something so common and cheap as an object of desire. She had been perfection, perfection beyond the rancid reality of his despicable life, perfection beyond paltry notions of gender.

Noel felt Mo's hands on her hips. She tipped her head and eased into him.

Mo circled his arms around her waist. Noel's body had never held a woman. Mo twitched, the excitement blooming within him was so great. He turned her with trembling hands to stare into her gaze. Tears welled up from his eyes. "Yes, so perfect," he whispered, his hands sliding up her arms to brush her hair from her face. "We'll never be apart, never need to know another. It's just us. We're one, as no two could ever be one."

Her eyes slid shut.

Mo closed his eyes. He rested his lips against hers. His pulse pounded in his ears. But something pushed him back then, something that seemed to burn in his belly. He wanted to stay there, to linger on her lips, but the burning pushed him away, pushed him away with what seemed so little force. He dropped his hands from her and opened his eyes, finding her wide gaze waiting from him. She looked down, and he followed her. Her hand was there, clutched around the handle of the knife he had tossed in the sink, and the blade, the long glistening blade, it was *in* him.

They looked at each other.

Noel slid her hand back, and the knife obeyed with remarkable ease. She tipped her head, and the knife went forward once more. There was a tinge of resistance, but then it went on, smooth and soft. The wet warmth of blood enveloped her hand. Mo's eyes narrowed, his lips quivering. He fell back a step, his eyes swelling, as tears flowed down his cheeks.

Noel stepped before Mo and drove her hand out. It wasn't a violent motion, just a smooth, steady traverse of her arm. When the knife went in, Mo faltered. She pulled back and slid the serrated length in one more time.

Mo gasped before his legs gave out, dumping him to the floor. His hands drooped over his chest, but then dropped away to flop on the floor.

Noel knelt beside him. She looked at the knife, looked to Mo, and slid the blade into his belly one last time. She paused before opening her hand to leave the knife in Mo's gut.

"Noel?"

She glanced at her bloody palm before looking back to Mo. "You wanted to set me free, but I can't be free with you." She frowned as his face blanched in death. "Goodbye, Mo."

She sat. She stared at a dead man's body and lost track of time.

But then she closed her eyes and rested her hands on her face. Her fingers trembled at first, but then they eased, and, soon, it was nothing of note. She ran her hands down her body before resting them on her thighs. Her eyes opened.

She walked into the hallway and saw the box of pizza. Her stomach rumbled. She sat on the floor, opened the lid, and was surprised to find the pizza for the most part intact. She took a piece, rested her back against the wall, and took a bite. It was the best food she ever tasted.

Three slices later her friends found her, sitting there in her innocence.

***

Life changed. It started that day in the hospital, when a nurse asked the simplest of questions.

"What's your name?"

There was only one possible answer. "Noelle." The rest flowed from there.

Traumatic amnesia: she heard this phrase several times. It was the perfect front, as she knew nothing of this new life she assumed, of the person she had become. The thing she knew as Noel remained, and was in fact her, but she learned and adapted and in very short order such notions of gender were indeed inconsequential. There was only life, and she was alive. The old times felt like some bad dream, a nightmare from which she had waited to wake with eternal patience. She realized her mathematician's intellect had been crafted with subtle guile to accept the new reality she came to inhabit and the conditions under which it came. It was another exercise in geometry, yet the geometric rules of the irrational were beyond her understanding, and so she accepted them. There were questions in her subconscious, but she buried them, certain that some assumptions of the tactile world defied explanation. They were the mathematical ligatures of nature: pi, natural log, Plank's constant, and so on. Complex numbers, irrational numbers, but fundamental numbers. They were the rules, and mysterious rules they were.

She learned that Miss Moonpie had been a young woman named Claire Lecour. Her parents had some money, and lived in a comfortable house on a large piece of wooded property in an upscale neighborhood. To all accounting, Claire had been a good person, undeserving of losing the right to her body. Noelle sometimes considered that prospect when she lay in bed at night, listening to Claire's mother cry. But this too was something beyond her question. Guilt wasn't an issue, as the crime belonged to Mo, and no one else. She'd been quite content during her short sojourn as a shadow, with the world and the woes it inflicted severed to their own sensory seclusion.

She could sympathize with Claire's parents, and lamented in some measure for their loss. She became an acceptable presence in their life, despite her insistence that they use her adoptive name. They sent her to therapists—understandable for concerned and caring parents—but she knew the conclusion those tinkering fools would have no choice to accept: Claire was gone, and Noelle remained. Claire's father, a respectable businessman and decent fellow of calm demeanor, found the resolve to accept this new incarnation of his daughter. To him, she was still the creature he helped bring into the world, and he refused to abandon her. Claire's mother didn't adapt with such ease to the change. She found it difficult to use this new name for her daughter. It reminded her too much of the madman that took away so much of her daughter's existence, leaving only this stranger behind.

Noelle found a solution for this. It was all abstraction, but she welcomed it. There was peace in abstraction.

She was sitting on a bench on the back porch one evening when the mother came out and sat with her. She took the woman's hand and looked to her. The woman wept at once, but looked to her estranged daughter.

"Please don't hate me," Noelle whispered.

The mother sucked in a breath, a look of horror passing over her. "How could I—"

"You were a good mother once." Noelle waited for the woman to gather herself. "Could you do that for me, too?"

The woman hesitated, but then she sniffed, and opened her arms. Noelle settled into her, and with her head nuzzled to her mother's chest, fell fast asleep in her embrace.

***

One night, as Noelle was in bed staring at the ceiling, a thought occurred to her. She considered the existence of Mo, of her own strange trajectory that had transformed her to be this creature known as Noelle, and wondered what happened to Claire. She remembered that last whisper she heard when taking possession of the body that became her home, and pondered the absence of Claire's whisper since that awful day. Had Claire's intellect been that much less than Noel's, or did the notion of abdicating her body amount to no more than a trivial sacrifice for her? The abstraction nested within Noelle's thoughts, and wouldn't budge. When dawn came she sat on the edge of her bed and looked to her nightstand. There was a delicate gold chain with a cross dangling from the lamp. In the old days, there was no religion in Noel's life. Math, in his opinion, didn't allow for such randomness. Only a sloppy universe would allow for the presence of some mysterious Will operating of Its own accord. But looking at the cross in that moment, she didn't find religion. Instead, in a flash of inspiration, she found absolution of all abstract thought. She need only consider her own mysterious presence to know in full that the apparent irrationality of existence was a guiding Mystery all its own.

She put the chain about her neck. She felt no sense of hypocrisy.

***

Memories fade. They are, after all, nothing more than impressions.

She returned to school. Her parents sent her to a different campus, one within driving range, so she could commute back to the safety of her house and, as Noelle Lecour, she began anew. Her parents registered her as a biology major, but in short order she found herself led astray of biology to courses of increasing mathematical demands, until she told her parents she wanted to become a math major. They seemed troubled by this announcement, but she insisted. They complied, and she performed quite well.

She shunned social life, aside from an occasional study group. During her third semester she found herself the focus of one particular group and, to her surprise, the object of one boy's affection. He was nineteen; younger than her, given the odd hiatus she had experienced. He was polite and sometimes over eager, in that inexperienced way of youth. She missed the signals of a portending sexual advance, though, and one night when they stayed late in the library going over complex derivations, he leaned in and kissed her.

She drew back—was driven back—by some repulsion deep within her she failed to understand. Her head swam as a dim memory woke within her. Claire, at some point, had been engaged to the son of a family friend. Her parents were deeply disappointed when he abandoned her after the attack.

But then something else struck her, a profound emptiness, a penetrating loneliness that resonated within her, that perhaps seeped beyond her skin.

The boy blushed, obliterated in the awkwardness of her silent stare. "I'm sorry."

Her body tingled. She touched her fingers to her lips. "Why did you do that?"

He opened his hands. "I never met someone like you," he said, the words coming out in a hurry. He blushed again, frowning as his gaze fell to his notebook. He tapped the eraser of his pencil on the paper. "I'm sorry. I just, I just thought, well, you know. Damn. I guess I blew it, huh?"

Her mind was blank. She got up and went home.

***

A few days later, on a November Friday of unseasonable warmth, she sat on a bench among rustling red leaves as she chewed a slice of pizza. She brushed the hair from her face before fishing in a pocket of her coat for a rubber band. With the length of her hair secured in a ponytail she looked up to the clear autumn sky, wondering when the cold of winter would arrive. Shrugging at that distant thought, she looked down, only for her gaze to settle on the student union across the campus mall. She sat there, her eyes lingering until the sight registered with her.

Her pizza forgotten, she walked across the mall, missing the ring of a cyclist's bell as she cut before the man. She stopped before the union, her eyes resting on the advertisements posted in the windows. SPOOKFEST REINCARNATED, they claimed. She read on to find out the Halloween festivities hosted at the student union were returning for the weekend. At the bottom of the poster, she found a name.

Psychic Readings, Courtesy of Gregor, the Leningrad Luminary

She fell back a step before running away.

***

Her sense of loneliness refused to dissipate. The holidays came and went, and the cheer and festivities only made her feel all the more distant and isolated. Her parents were concerned, but she allayed their fears by promising them—lying to them—that she was fine. When it came time to register for the next semester, she found herself answering some unknown compulsion to take an art class. Her parents found it odd; in her youth she never exhibited any artistic inclinations.

The day before the semester started her mother took her to the local shopping mall. They strolled about, talking small talk, her mother nudging her toward the upscale fashion stores where she shopped in days of old. They stopped and sat to have some pizza, and her mother smiled when she saw the satisfaction that lit Noelle's eyes while chewing a slice, even as Noelle failed to respond to anything she said.

After some time her mother just stared at her.

Noelle stopped chewing. "What's wrong?"

Her mother gave a little shake of her head. "It's just, well, you never seemed interested in pizza, before."

Noelle looked at the slice in her hand.

"Why do you like it so much now?"

She looked over at the old man behind the counter as he spun a pie. She took a breath and mirrored his motion with a slender finger. "It's circular."

Her mother's lips parted, but she didn't know how to respond.

Before they left they walked by an eccentric, neon lit gift shop, and Noelle came to a stiff halt before the window. Her mother came back to her and followed her wide-eyed gaze.

"What is that?" her mother wondered aloud.

"I have to have it."

"Why do—" her mother began, but before she could finish her question, Noelle was already in the store.

Later that night, when the father came home, he found Noelle in her room, sitting in the dark, staring at her desk. He moved to turn on the light, but she waved a hand for him to stop. He pointed to the desk. "What is that thing?"

She tipped her head as illuminated oil sloshed across her gaze. "It's a wave tank."

"Like, far out," he replied before exchanging a good-humored smile with her. He walked in from the doorway and embraced her, holding her before kissing her forehead. He tipped his head and waited until she looked up at him. "I love you," he said.

He died the next day, on his drive home from work. It was a massive heart attack, the kind that strikes without warning. His foot slipped off the gas pedal, so his car drifted onto the shoulder and bumbled along until it came to a stop in the soft grass. At the funeral Noelle heard some of his friends say the stress of her dorm attack had consumed him but, when she observed him, he had the appearance of someone at peace. She was sad to lose him, but she didn't question his passing.

It was a natural way to go.

***

The snows of winter melted. Warmth returned, and then something changed.

She was sitting in the math library, alone in a study carol on a sunny May afternoon, her empty gaze out the window. Two floors below, students walked about the campus. She was thinking of nothing in particular when her eyes settled on a student walking across the mall. Before she knew what she was doing she dug through her knapsack and opened the sketchpad for her art class. She was given an assignment to draw random things, things that caught her fancy, and keep them in the pad. It was an odd thing for her, as it was such a subjective assignment, quite different from the concrete, defined tasks of her math classes. Yet, for that very reason, she found a special peace to her artwork, as there was no definitive right or wrong.

Her gaze followed the student. She kept watch and, as her hand created a likeness, her blood began to move through her with a vitality she believed she never knew. When she looked at the pad, and saw the wonder of the likeness she rendered, a likeness that had whispered through her hand with such seductive grace, she was swept away on a tide of euphoria that left every nerve buzzing within her.

But soon—far, far too soon—her subject passed out of sight behind a building, and her mood sank, and the sense of loneliness that lurked about her with such gloom returned in full. She frowned, her doe-eyed face beset with sadness until she again studied her sketch, and she was once again amazed—stunned—at what she created.

"Oh wow, you got it, *you got it*," she whispered to herself. "You got her—our Miss Mayday! Yes, that's it, that's what we'll call you."

A shiver ran down her neck.

She trembled.

Her face fell, but then she smiled and, for the first time she could remember, everything felt just right.

It started with a speeding ticket.

Dave had finished a rough day, the engineering firm at which he worked plagued with the madness of looming deadlines and broken budgets. His mind was a dizzying swarm of numbers and three-dimensional projections framed about his obsessive tendencies, so he was never aware of his speed as he flew down the freeway until flashing lights filled his rearview mirror. The trooper was a model of efficiency, his crisp little statements and flat tone deflating any personal sense of urgency within Dave's chest. For all the rebelliousness his subconscious had relished by speeding, his conscious mind fumed at the inescapable tentacles of order that constrained such a petty outburst of his will.

He rolled into his driveway exhausted and exasperated. When he walked in the door of his townhouse he pulled off his tie, went straight to the kitchen, and opened a beer. A therapist once told him that he shouldn't drink, but he forced that memory away. Only after two long gulps did he care to turn around and let the mess of his living room register with his senses.

Snorkel, his cousin Peter, was sprawled on the couch among a mess of water bottles, empty bags of soy chips, and paper wrappers from Ray's Smokey Dogs, the outdoor cafe down the street. It was late in the afternoon, and the sun was still high in the sky, but Snorkel was snoring away, a wet rattle in his throat that escaped between his stubble ringed lips.

Dave was about to kick Snorkel's feet off the coffee table when a young woman came in through the sliding glass doors at the back of the townhouse. She was a curious creature, eccentric in her drifter's lifestyle, much in the vein of Dave's cousin. It was only fitting that she was Snorkel's girlfriend, but her bright eyes and wide smile were always there to welcome Dave when he entered her sight.

She gave him a lazy wave and giggled when she heard Snorkel's snore. She walked over to the couch, her bare feet silent on the carpet. Only a cropped shirt and a peach colored bikini bottom covered her body, leaving most of her lean, tanned frame open for view. Her name was Pixie. When she felt Dave's stare she giggled again, waving her hands by her head to get his attention. "Should we wake him up?"

Dave thought of the ticket. He hated his job, hated the doldrums of his life. He glanced at Pixie's thighs. "Let's get out of here," he said, and with that, kicked Snorkel's feet off the table.

***

An hour later they sat outside Ray's under an umbrella. Dave and Peter each held one of Ray's trademark smoked pork dogs, while Pixie got her usual soy dog. The breeze carried the scent of the Pacific Ocean, drawing Snorkel's head up as his nostrils widened to take it in. "Man, I love that," he said with a sigh. He glanced at Dave. "So you got another speeding ticket?"

Dave nodded as he chewed his dog. "It's a conspiracy. They're after me. I know it."

Pixie shrugged. "I don't believe in driving cars. They make people just like those hot dogs you two eat—processed meat stuffed in a manufactured casing." She raised a finger. "Oil for hay. Everybody should be on horses."

Dave stared at her, but Snorkel bobbed his head in agreement. "Yeah, I like that. And you could pay some homeless dudes to clean up the crap." He sipped his soda and pointed his pork dog at Dave. "Look man, you have to use your head, you know? These guys, they got, like, computers and stuff in all their patrol cars, so you need an advantage."

Dave tapped his forehead. "I already have a plan. I'll slouch in my saddle next time."

Pixie stuck out her tongue before sharing a little laugh with Dave.

Snorkel shook his head. "No, I'm serious. Get yourself a radar jammer."

Dave's face fell. "Why didn't I think of that?" he thought aloud. "Oh, that's right. Because they're illegal, genius."

Pixie nudged his leg with her foot. "Or you could slow down, Mister Type A."

"Slow down? How can I slow down? I can't slow down." Dave shook his head. "Not an option." He regarded her, feeling that tiny tingle in his head that made him want to jump her right there at the table. Her life was so different from his she could've been from another planet, but that only made the ruinous temptation all the more irresistible. Her little sarcastic barbs seemed like open invitations in the innocence of her flirtation, yet it bothered him whenever she prodded him—it reminded him how uptight he could be when life got under his skin.

"I'm not a type A," he said, failing to keep his anxiety in check. "I'm not like those people."

She sipped her iced tea as she rolled her eyes in silent laughter.

Dave looked away, disappointed with himself. He looked over the evening crowd at Ray's, and soon found his attention focused on a little boy several tables over, sitting with his back turned to the table and the mess he left of his meal. He was blowing bubbles, giggling as they shimmered and drifted away on the breeze. The boy glanced at Dave and waved his bubble wand as one of the bubbles popped in the air over his head.

Pixie followed Dave's gaze. "Do you want some bubble juice?" she said with a grin, even as he glared at her. "Even a type A can't help but be happy blowing bubbles."

Snorkel slapped a hand on Dave's shoulder. "Look, we'll go out tonight and get you something for your car. Like, super stealth or something, you know? I know a guy down the way. Met him on the beach. He's got all sorts of stuff. Then we can get some beers and kick back behind the house. We'll watch the stars, or the moon, or something. It's Friday. Enjoy it, man."

Dave opened his hands. "I bought beer the other day."

Snorkel laughed. "You're all out, man. I drank 'em down!"

***

Snorkel led them down the town's main street, walking past the regular shops to find his way to some side streets. They were not the picturesque avenues that led to the wide sandy beaches of the ocean, but rather the cramped, old streets that hearkened back to the days of the town as a quiet fishing village. Snorkel stopped twice, losing his way, but despite Dave's impatience, found his way again, and led them down an alley. He stopped before a rusted metal security door, its dented exterior covered in flaking green paint. It looked more like somebody's back door than a store.

Once inside, Dave understood. It wasn't a store, but one of those underground places, where electronics of dubious or outright illegal manufacture made their way into the country. The 'store' consisted of a single room made to look small with shelves of boxes stacked to the ceiling, marked with brands Dave never encountered in the large chain stores.

The place seemed abandoned until Dave stepped around the corner of a shelf and came face to face with a young man, his exposed, tattoo riddled arms poking through the foam pellets of an open box. He looked up at Dave, his eyes wide before they narrowed in instant hostility. Dave held up a hand, not wanting to fight, but in the beat of his heart and the memory of his day he knew he was all too willing to pound this pony-tailed underworld freak into the floor—until Snorkel came around Dave and the man's face split to a friendly smile. "Toby!" he greeted, rising to thump a fist on Snorkel's shoulder.

Snorkel returned the gesture before pointing to Dave. "Hey, Kim, like, my cousin, he needs some kind of super stealth for high velocity. You know, like a radar jammer, or something."

"Yeah?" Kim studied Dave for a moment before looking to Snorkel. "I

73

don't like him."

Dave opened his mouth, but Pixie came up beside him and squeezed his wrist.

Kim fixed a hungry gaze past Dave. "Hey, Pixie, what's up?" he said to her, but she retreated around the corner, leaving Kim's eyes to settle on Dave. Kim's lips sank to a threatening scowl as he looked down the length of his nose. "He's not one of us," he said in disgust. "Don't like him, don't want to know him."

"Oh, no, he's good," Snorkel said, waving his hand. "Don't let the corporate look fool you. He's as crazy as the rest of us."

Kim settled a hard stare on Dave but, in the end, he relented. "Alright. Follow me."

He snaked his way past them and dug through a large, unmarked shipping package until he pulled out a small black retail box with a red X on the cover. All the print was in characters— Chinese or Japanese, Dave wasn't sure which—but Kim nodded his head with pride when he put the box on an open space of shelf. "This is your baby. Fool proof. But you didn't get it from me, understand?"

Dave stared at the box. "How much?"

Kim smirked beneath his narrowed eyes. "How much you got?"

After some haggling, they agreed on a price which, to no surprise of Dave, was just shy of everything he had. Cleaned of cash, and feeling that he'd been taken, he stood in the doorway, the jammer hidden in a paper bag. He narrowed his eyes against the bright evening sky. Pixie stood on the sidewalk, juggling two small, green rubber balls. She gave him a quick glance and smiled. "You figure out how to juggle yet?"

He watched the nimble work of her hands as her gaze remained in the air. "Sure. I do great until the balls come back down."

She caught the balls, one in each hand, and looked to him. "Hey, you made another joke! That's two for the night. I like that. That's good."

The corner of his mouth rose in a feeble grin. "See, I'm not strung too tight."

She trumped his grin with her wide smile. "Still, one day we'll have to cut those strings."

He blinked. He was at a loss for words, paralyzed as his mind let the unsaid implications of her reply explode in his head. A low laugh bubbled from her at the knot of consternation nesting on his forehead before she rolled her lower lip between her teeth and returned to her juggling. She fell back a step, keeping her eyes on him as the green balls orbited her face.

He made no effort to divert his stare from her, even when she tipped her face to the sun and closed her eyes. He was forced to remember his cousin when Snorkel stepped by him and waved for them to go. Dave stepped out of the doorway and looked back to find Kim standing behind him.

Kim closed his eyes. The words 'FOR RENT' were tattooed across his eyelids. He blinked and waved a splayed hand over his face before closing the door.

"Jackass," Dave said under his breath. He turned to his cousin. "What's with 'Toby'?"

Snorkel pointed to his head. "Like, from TBI. You know, traumatic brain injury."

***

They went home and sat outside until midnight, drinking and talking even as Pixie started to fall asleep against Snorkel's shoulder. Dave's cousin continued to ramble on, stoking Dave's jealousy. He'd give anything to have Pixie, or any other woman of interest, fall asleep against his shoulder. But in his heart, he knew she was right about his personality and, hours after her innocent comment, it still bothered him. He wanted to be more like Snorkel, who had talked him into coming out to California. Five years ago he knew Snorkel as his cousin Peter, a lead engineer at the company where Dave worked. Dave came to learn that the cousin admired for his success was a tyrant to his underlings, a chronic womanizer, and possessed a competitive spirit that knew no bounds. On the other hand, and despite all indications otherwise, Peter was also a local surfer of some renown, and seemed quite at home among that casual, perhaps hedonistic, subculture. That existence of constricted duality ended in a vicious surfing accident that left Peter in the hospital with a drainage tube sticking out of his skull. After a long recuperation he was discharged, and the life he used to know faded like a dream into the ocean's horizon.

The genius for math that once graced Peter's professional life was destroyed, leaving only a shadow of the slacker life he pursued in private. That first year after the accident he was plagued by horrendous headaches, so for several months he lost himself in medical marijuana, at the same time earning his nickname: Dave came home one day to find him floating on his back in the townhouse pool with a fatty sticking out of his mouth, like a snorkel. The joke earned a long series of laughs and stuck, but Peter was, for all purposes, functionally disabled, so Dave took over the townhouse to support him.

As for Pixie, Snorkel met her on the beach one day and, when he found out she had no place to stay, he brought her home. In six months, she never showed an inclination to leave. She grew up on a commune in Montana, and her parents had compelled her to travel so she could learn the mess of the world to appreciate the commune's pastoral lifestyle. Dave worried about her, even about the times before he met her, fearing the world in all its predatory character would devour her, but that same air of innocence he found so seductive seemed to surround her with an impenetrable security buffer. She skated over the life Dave knew, her feet barely touching its surface. She was on a plain he found hard to comprehend, one filled with freedom, with a carefree, detached attitude to the monetary matters that consumed so much of Dave's mind.

He forced his gaze away from her to look up at the stars. Only then did his cousin's disjointed ramblings catch up with him, the meandering paranoia of Snorkel's recent conviction that modern society was in fact a slave state of electronic surveillance.

Dave closed his eyes. "You know you're crazy, don't you?"

Snorkel scratched the stubble on his neck and sipped his beer. "Think what you want, man, but it's all real. You don't see it, because you're still hooked in it. You got to be like me, dude, you know, like free dissociation, you know what I mean?"

Dave blew out a breath. It was statements like that when he remembered the old days when Peter called *him* the lazy slacker. "Why do you talk like that?"

"Like what?"

"Never mind." Dave finished his beer and dropped the bottle into the cooler between them, the bottle splashing in the melted ice. He picked up the radar jammer and opened the box. "Do you think this was worth the money?" he wondered as he flipped through the microscopic print of the multilingual manual.

Snorkel let out a short laugh. "Man, are you for real? There's rays all over the place, dude. What, you got cosmic radiation, you got solar radiation, you got cell phones, you got satellites, you got wireless data nets, you got portable phones—hell, you got the government—dude, forget radar detectors, we need, like, jamming technology built right into us, right into our heads. Now you're talking freedom."

Dave kept his gaze in the manual. "You know, sometimes I forget how hard you hit your head," he said, ignoring the upward flip of his cousin's middle finger. He went through several more pages of the manual, but stopped when one of the large, capitalized caution messages caught his eye. "Hey, look at this. It says not to turn it on in the home environment or to use indoors. What moron would use a radar jammer in their house?"

Snorkel stared at him.

Dave rolled his eyes. "I know, you're thinking if they say not to do it, it's to cover up some other conspiracy."

Snorkel shrugged. "Okay, Mister Know-it-all."

76

Pixie sniffed, opening her eyes to peer past Snorkel's chest and find Dave's gaze. "So?"

Dave stared at her before tossing the manual in the box. "What would that prove?"

Pixie shrugged. "I don't know. Maybe that's the point."

He stared into her eyes and watched as her lips rose in her bright smile. She looked to the stars before returning to Dave, her smile widening when she turned her head and waited for him to follow her gaze to the black sky.

His fantasies whispered to him from the endlessness above them. It was too much to bear. He tucked the jammer under his arm, left them on the patio, grabbed two more beers from the kitchen, and went upstairs to hole up in his bedroom. Chugging through half of the first beer, he paced in the dark, pulling at his short hair as his mind raced in dizzying circles. He was becoming obsessed with Pixie, to the point where he wanted to drown his cousin in the pool to have her all to his own. It wasn't healthy, but it was part of his compulsive personality.

His therapist had told him about that when she suggested he avoid alcohol. She was nice, with a practiced maternal kindness, which had surprised him. He came to her office through a twisted chain of events. His former best friend had bedded Dave's wife and, when Dave saw them in court during the resulting divorce, he attacked them. Not only did it sabotage his divorce, it landed him in court-ordered therapy. It was all a matter of control, more manifestations of those unseen tentacles about his life that were slowly driving him insane. The therapy had soothed him in the short term, until the ironic but inevitable implosion of that process: he started to obsess on his therapist. She tried to counsel him into regular sessions, but he knew the better wisdom was to escape the whole situation.

His cousin's invitation to California couldn't have come at a better time. Dave ran away, rather than deal with the unraveling tendons that held his life and sanity together, in the hope that Peter would set a stable example and create a stable environment. Dave wanted to be good. He wanted to keep his behavior in check. But he knew the truth, that every time he tied his tie a little tighter, every time he pushed himself a little harder, every time the delirious demands of his life sought to squeeze him a little tighter, the more he just wanted to scream *no—no* to all of it, and without a doubt *no* to the foolish notion that he could control himself for any extended period of time. He was crazy, and the more he tried to deny it, the worse he knew he would get. Despite his more level considerations, he came to the unsettling conclusion that the only rational choice remaining on some distant day would be to choose an irrational life.

He thought of Pixie, how good it would feel to hold her. He imagined her eyes, those wondrous embodiments of the endless blue Montana sky, giving up their inner secrets to him. It was intoxicating; it was impossible.

He chugged what was left of his beer and left the bottle on his dresser. He opened the second bottle and chugged it down in one long drought, a raucous burp rumbling from his innards when he was done. He sank to the floor, sitting there with his back against his bed. He knew better than to expect any sleep while actually lying in his bed, not with visions of Pixie running rampant in his head.

His gaze lingered on the box of the radar jammer. He remembered the silly warning, and remembered as well her aimless challenge to defy that warning. With a silent curse he crawled over to the box, took out the jammer, and plugged in his cell phone charger to power it up. It was a small device, and the only indication that its smooth case wasn't empty was the wink of a small red power light. He turned it over in his hands before shrugging and leaving it on his dresser. He crawled back to his bed, slumped on the floor, and rested his head against the side of the mattress.

His blurred gaze fixed on the opaque glass end of the jammer. To his surprise, he felt the anxiety within his chest calm, and the delirium of slurred thoughts in his head whispered away to silence. A long breath slid from his lungs, and he drifted off to sleep.

***

He woke with a start some time later, clutching his pounding temples. The pain was excruciating, a ceaseless pressure behind his eyes that felt as if their orbits would erupt from his skull. He struggled to his feet and staggered through the darkness to his bathroom. Bracing his swaying body against the sink he fumbled through his medicine cabinet for some pills when he felt the strange, unnerving sensation of the pressure migrating from behind his eye to the top of his nose. Blood dripped into the sink. Cursing, he stuffed his nose with a tissue, filled a glass with water, and shuffled back to his bed.

Sitting on the floor once more, and convinced his body simply couldn't handle alcohol like it used to, he tipped his head back to sooth the nosebleed. To his dismay the pressure only intensified, mounting until he ground his teeth in agony and his thoughts faded to one inescapable conclusion: whatever was going on, he had to get it out of his head.

Too dizzy to make his way to the bathroom, he pulled the tissue from his nose and leaned over his water glass, for lack of a better target. He pressed one nostril shut, took a deep breath in his mouth, and blew as

78

hard as he could through the occluded nostril. The pressure soared to piercing agony but, just as he thought he was going to pass out, he felt a definite pop—his eyes bulged, his neck twitched, and he heard a splash from the glass. Blood streamed from his nose, but he groped about, found the tissue, and stuffed it back in his nostril to stop the bleeding. To his relief, the pain subsided.

After several minutes he found his wits and opened his eyes to glance at the glass. It was a red soup of blood, and something stringy, more like cellular tissue than simple mucous, floated in the water.

Disgusted, he pushed the glass away, tipped his head back, and fell asleep once more.

***

He woke with the dawn, not out of any sense of urgency, but more from the pressure in his bladder. He made his way to the bathroom and, as he stood there urinating, his head rolled to the side to catch his disheveled reflection. He wanted to wash out his mouth. His forehead sank as he remembered the headache and nosebleed. The crusted tissue was still stuck in his nose. He pulled it out with care and tossed it in the garbage, and that was when he remembered.

He walked to his bed and reached down for the glass. He looked, blinked, and then threw himself back, his shoulders thudding against the wall as his eyes widened.

"What the—" He shook his head. "No, no, get a grip!"

But the more he stared, the more certain he was of what he saw. He didn't realize his legs had buckled until the floor came up beneath him, but the moment it did, he bolted upright.

The glass was there but, next to it, sitting on the floor, was a little, gray, *man*.

Worse, though its face lacked any features, and in size the whole creature was only as big as Dave's thumb, its face held on him, mesmerizing him, haunting him. It did something odd then, that little gray man. It raised its tiny, mitten-like hand and gave him a rather casual wave *hello*.

Dave blinked. He went rigid, turned on his feet, went in his bathroom, and washed the back of his neck. Too much beer, he told himself. He had to stop drinking.

He walked out of the bathroom. The little gray man was leaning against the glass, arms crossed on its chest. Its featureless face looked up at him, and it shook its head.

Dave went downstairs and found Pixie in the kitchen, cooking some pancakes. She turned and greeted him with her usual welcoming smile, but the minute she looked at him her jaw dropped in alarm. "Oh my God," she said, glancing over her shoulder as she turned to the sink to wet a sheet of paper towel. "What happened to you?"

He looked down, only then realizing his sorry state. He had slept sitting on the floor in his blue boxers and the shirt he wore last night. Bloodstains from his nose had dried on his clothes, leaving a crusted trail of dark splotches. He looked up when she came back to him, standing right before him to wipe the dried blood around his mouth and chin. Perhaps it was the diminutive suggestion of her name, but he never perceived that she was almost his height. Then he thought of the splendid length of her legs, and the shameless presence of that thought, with her standing so close to him, cleaning him, didn't embarrass him, but rather stoked a sense of intimacy he found himself all too willing to entertain.

So he did. He waited until she lowered her hand, and then he kissed her, just a little brush of the lips, boyish in its tentative nature, but a kiss nonetheless.

She didn't recoil. When he pulled back she blinked, but her smile returned. "Do I know you? You look like some guy I know," she added with a glint of mischief in her eyes.

Snorkel staggered into the kitchen, rubbing his face before pushing his hair back. He blinked several times, his blurred gaze darting between Pixie and Dave until he shrugged and slumped in his chair. "Nothing like pancakes in the morning. Good idea, Pix."

Dave sat, across the kitchen table from his cousin. He watched as Snorkel arranged all his medications, checking the labels of each before nodding and starting his daily sort. He looked to Dave several times before tipping his head. "Living through chemistry, dude," he joked under his breath, but there was a certain sadness in his eyes. He leaned an elbow on the table and pointed to the pills in turn. "Like, this one's for seizures, this one's for the chronic pain, this one's so I don't get a clot in my brain, and these tan dudes over here, they're like all different kinds of vitamins, so my brain can fix itself, or something."

Dave watched his cousin scoop up the pills, pop them in his mouth and chase them down with a glass of water Pixie handed him. Looking at the repercussions of Peter's brain injury, Dave couldn't help but think of the little gray visitor he left in his room. He wondered if he would end up like Peter, as some shadow of himself with a ridiculous nickname like Snorkel, while degenerate derelicts like Kim the illegal electronics salesman mocked him with a nickname like Toby.

Pixie put a plate of pancakes on the table. Rather than use a plate, Dave took a pancake and started chewing. It was unlike him. He had a specific plate for eating pancakes, with a well to one side so the syrup would stay put and not make the pancakes soggy. Snorkel didn't notice, too busy devouring his pancakes, but as Pixie stood behind Snorkel and rested her hands on his shoulders, she watched Dave with intense curiosity.

"Don't you want your plate?"

He looked at her, but his gaze fell to her hands, resting on Snorkel's shoulders.

"We're going to the beach for the day," she continued. "Why don't you come along?"

He took a bite of pancake. He thought of her on the beach. He thought of how it felt to have her so close to him, the memory of it mocking its intimacy in that moment. The dark urge to drown his cousin welled up once more.

He blinked, his eyes coming to focus on Pixie's waiting gaze as she retreated to the sink. "I think I'm going back to bed," he said with a tired breath. "I didn't sleep well."

She tipped her head, her lower lip rolling out in a brief pout before she walked by him, brushing his cheek with the back of her hand. The door to the guest room, where she slept, closed behind her.

He looked to his cousin. Snorkel had the small bedroom upstairs.

Why hasn't that ever occurred to me?

Snorkel shrugged. "Man, I can't remember the last time I had a good sleep."

Without a word Dave went back to his room. When he walked in, he had the odd sensation of witnessing the scene from outside his body. There he was, pancake in hand, in his soiled cloths, and there was the little gray man, leaning over the edge of the water glass, scooping up little handfuls of water to moisten its skin. It turned its faceless head, and they stared at each other, almost in a game of chicken, until Dave sank to the floor on all fours. He broke off a tiny piece of pancake in offering, but the little man shook its head. It hopped down from the rim of the glass, held for a moment, then waved its mitten-like hands for Dave to extend his arm.

He hesitated but, in the end, he complied, eased by the innate conviction there was nothing to fear from his little visitor. When he opened his hand on the floor in front of his Lilliputian guest, it clapped its hands together, rubbed them, and reached out to touch his thumb.

Its skin felt moist, slick like a slug, without being sticky.

I'm not a slug.

Dave blinked and jerked his hand back. The thought sounded identical to one of his, but he knew the words had come from *it*. He glanced over his shoulder before closing and locking the door to his room. With that done he hunched before his visitor and, after some thought, rested his hand on the floor once more. "You're telepathic?" he whispered.

It nodded before resting its hands on his thumb. *I'll get better as time goes by.*

Dave's face fell. "What do you mean by that?"

Well, you're not going to abandon me, are you? I'm not just some overgrown booger, you know.

Dave couldn't help but grin. "Right, because talking to my snot would be weird."

The little man tipped its head. *You should have saved that one for her, Mister Sarcasm.*

Dave blinked.

It threw its head back. *You mean you don't get it yet?*

He looked to the glass, his other hand rising to his nose. "Oh shit, I really am talking to an overgrown booger I blew out of my head!"

I had to come out. I couldn't stay in any longer. It lifted a hand and jabbed a thumb to the radar jammer. *The warning message is there for a reason, you know.*

Dave looked to the jammer and took his hand away from the little man to unplug the unit. Only then did he freeze as the import of the man's words struck him. He put the jammer down and turned, staring at the little man, who stood there with arms crossed, tapping a foot. "If the message was there," Dave thought aloud, "and put there for a reason. . ."

The jammer slipped from his hand and fell in the open box.

His mind raced. A little gray man had been living in his head. A radar device forced him out. The people who made the device knew to warn against turning it on indoors, because the radar waves wouldn't be directed away from whoever was in the room with the unit. So somebody knew the waves could knock a little man out of his head that was living in there all along.

I'm taking all this rather calmly.

He shook his head. "That's delusional crap," he said to himself. He looked at the little man and, for lack of a better idea, opened his hand. "Can I call you Gray?"

The little man looked at itself before shrugging.

"So you've been in my head?"

Gray rested its hands on Dave's thumb. *In your brain, to be exact.*

Dave's eyes widened. "How?"

You were born in a hospital. You were immunized. Things like me get passed along in the shots, like a virus. I've always been a part of you, even though I'm not a part of you.

"This is insane." Dave shook his head. "This is every paranoid fear tied in one big knot."

It's not what you think, Gray corrected. *It's rare that a symbiote like me comes out. Most of the time — almost all the time — people never know we're here.*

"Symbiote?" Dave blew out a breath. "You mean parasite."

No, symbiote. Parasites take at the expense of the host. We share. You keep me moist and warm, and I give you something in return.

"A nosebleed?"

Gray shook its little head. *Control. People are wild. We keep people in check.*

Dave's eyes narrowed. "Slave master, is that it? I could squash you, right now."

Why? I'm out of you. You're on your own.

Dave clenched his teeth.

How was the kiss?

Dave pulled his hand away. He sat against the side of his bed, rubbing his forehead before settling his chin in the palm of his hand, his elbow on his knee. He gave Gray a sidelong glance. He chewed on his lip, focusing his thoughts before he slid his leg out to leave his foot by Gray. "If you popped out of me, how come you didn't pop out of Pixie and Snorkel?"

Gray slapped a hand against the side of its head before swiping a hand across its throat.

"Okay, so the TBI Peter had killed his gray. Fine. What about Pixie?"

Gray bent its legs somewhat, then put its hands out and bobbed its knees, as if it were riding a horse.

"Right, she grew up on a commune. She wasn't born in a hospital. She was never, uh, exposed, I guess you would say."

Gray leaned against Dave's foot. *Wherever there's so-called 'Western' medicine, you'll find us living with people. Sometimes I'm not sure — any of us, for that matter — if Western medicine is the way it us because of us, or if we're around because of its practices. I can tell you this, though. The Western world has the rules and structure it has because of us.*

"You sure you want to brag about that?"

Gray held up a hand. *I'm not defending it. It is what it is. I'm no different than you. I'm just another guy, trying to live with the rules.*

Dave put his hands in his lap and stared at the floor. After some time he looked back to Gray. "The kiss was everything I thought it would be."

Gray held its hands to Dave's foot before nodding. *It's all yours.*

"That was you holding me back? All the anger in me, that was all because of you?"

Gray patted a hand on Dave's foot. *I wasn't really aware of it. Our inclination for order is a subconscious thing, mixed in the subconscious thoughts of our hosts. So those things in you, they were both of us.*

Dave shook his head. "I don't get it. If you've been in my head, how do you know about any others like you? Is it the telepathy?"

Gray held up its hands. *I don't know. There seems to be some kind of communal awareness, but it doesn't get cranking without a large group. The opposite of mob mentality — 'group-think' is the phrase for it.*

Dave gave a slow nod, his vacant gaze coming to rest on the back of his door.

Gray reached in the glass of water to wet its hands before rubbing the water over its body.

"You dry up quick, don't you?"

Gray reached for Dave's foot, but then reconsidered. It patted its hands on its head, and then its thought came out. *I'm meant to live in your head, remember. Oh, I did it! No hands! See, I told you I'd get better.*

Dave looked back to his door. A frown settled on his face.

Gray stepped to the side to get a better look at him. *I pop out of your head, and you're having a telepathic exchange with a living snot ball telling you that all the world you know is a conspiracy of little gray guys living in the heads of humanity, and you don't have anything else to ask?*

Dave shook his head. "I don't have to ask. I can feel it already, the freedom."

Gray's head hung.

Dave looked at him; yes, in that moment, he decided Gray was male. Gray came out of his head, after all. He had to be male, because he understood what the kiss meant; or was it just his empathy, after being in Dave's head so many years? "Hey," Dave said, drawing Gray's attention, "now that you're out of me, now that you're free of me, what do you want?"

Gray scratched his head for a moment before clapping his little hands together. *I want to go running, running free, with the wind rushing over me.* He cupped his hands behind his back, striking a meek pose. *I think that's why you got all those speeding tickets.*

The thud of the front door sounded through the house. They were alone.

Dave put his head back and closed his eyes. He told himself he was having a nervous breakdown. He told himself when he woke, Gray would be gone, and everything would be back to the way it was, back to normal.

He thought of Pixie, and the warmth of her hand on his cheek.

***

When he woke he dragged his stiff body off the floor, shed his disgusting clothes, and took a long shower. He took the glass off the floor, washed it out, left it by the sink, but then he reconsidered, filled it

84

with clean water, and put it back on the floor by his bed. There was no sign of Gray. He felt along the side of his nose, and nothing was sore. So it was all in his head, so to speak, he figured, even though the conclusion was somewhat disheartening.

We'll see about that.

He put on a pair of shorts and a shirt, slipped into a pair of sandals, and went downstairs, only to find his cousin passed out on the couch. Pixie was sitting at the kitchen table, drinking a glass of papaya juice, her bare feet up on a chair. "Afternoon meds," she whispered to Dave as he passed behind her to get a roll from the breadbox. "They knock him out cold."

Dave sat across from her, waving a hand for her to relax when she went to put her feet down. He remembered that habit of hers used to bother him, but it seemed such a trivial thing as he sat across from her. "Beach was good?"

She nodded as she sipped her juice. "Nap was good?"

He returned the nod.

They sat still, looking at each other. At first they started to grin, and before long they fought to keep their laughter down as Snorkel snored away. The long light of evening streamed through the patio doors in broad yellow rays. She glanced over her shoulder, the light casting her face in warm tones beneath the short, thick mass of her blond hair. She turned back to him, put her glass down, and took his wrists in her hands. "Let's go."

Before he could say anything she dragged him from the house and walked him down to the beach. The walk took ten minutes. All that time, so close, and he realized it had never crossed his mind to walk to the ocean. It was a splendid Saturday evening, so there were still quite a few people on the wide expanse of sand. The Pacific gleamed under the rosy stretch of the horizon, the white crests of the incoming waves sparkling with the backlight of the sun. There was a cool breeze, but he paid little attention to the shivers that ran across his skin. They walked the beach, close to each other, but he kept his hands in his pockets, wary of creating any seedy perception that he would betray his cousin with such ease. He became aware of how much self control it required with each mounting moment. Temptation reared its head and, unlike those times when he was married, and he and his wife went at each other in aimless arguments fueled by the aimless anger nestled in their brains, he didn't find Temptation's head such a precarious thing to behold. In fact, it was quite seductive—as it should be—and only then did he comprehend something greater than temptation, something that in the absence of control he could at last embrace.

He stopped short and settled his hand on her arm but, not realizing he stopped, she took another step, and so, despite himself, he wound up holding her hand. He looked up as her fingers closed about his. "Tell me about Montana."

She ran a hand through her hair to push it back against the breeze. "Fresh air. Blue skies, blue like you can't see anywhere else. Open space, lots of open space. So big—but it doesn't make you feel small, it makes you feel like you belong."

He opened his mouth, but he didn't know what to say.

She squeezed his hand. "Hey, maybe one day I can tell you more."

"When?"

Her lips curved in her wide smile. "Maybe one day."

"I'm changed, Pixie. I'm not what I thought I was."

She gave him a glance. "We'll see." She walked around him, leading him by his hand. "Come on. Peter's probably wondering what happened to us."

***

When they came back to the townhouse Peter was watching the large screen television hanging on the wall of the living room. He was sipping a beer, watching a documentary about ball lightning, a mysterious meteorological phenomenon that some ascribed to the work of foreign laws of physics or, on a more exotic vein, to foreign levels of intelligence, perhaps extraterrestrial in nature. He seemed to find it amusing, pointing his bottle at the screen as Dave and Pixie sat on either side of him. "Like, some things just are what they are, you know?"

Dave sighed. "I've never seen a tornado. I'd like to see a tornado."

His cousin looked at him. "Dude, where did that come from?"

Dave opened a hand. "I don't know. It just came to me." He shrugged. "I'm still feeling kind of run down. I'm going to turn in."

Pixie gave him a wave, to which he nodded, and he went upstairs. He closed his bedroom door behind him and rested his head against the door. He peered down the length of his nose to find Gray sitting in the glass, arms dangling over the sides, as if it were a miniature hot tub.

"You're back."

Never left. I took a nap under your pillow.

"I took a nap on the floor." Dave closed his eyes for a moment. "Did you dream?"

As a matter of fact, I did, Gray thought, laying a mitten-like hand on his head. *Did you?*

Dave walked across the room and sat on his bed before pulling off his shirt. He held it in his hands for a moment before draping it across the foot of his bed.

Did you dream of her?
"Did you dream of horses?"
Gray looked to him. *Fair enough. I guess we're our own creatures now.*

***

Sunday mornings were special, because they had bacon with breakfast. Snorkel wasn't much of a health food practitioner, but he was paranoid of fats, as he feared they might increase his risk of throwing a clot in his brain and erase some other part of his awareness that wasn't already lost. Dave cleaned up when they were done, while Peter did his medicine allocation for the day and Pixie cleaned her wood flute. It was her routine to play on a street corner in town on Sunday mornings, when the locals who went to church still had a notion of charity in their conscience. If they failed to open their wallets, there was always the morning-walk group, the early-start day tourists, and the locals who wanted to avoid the later day rush for the beach. On an average day she could bring home fifty dollars, enough to cover her expenses for the week. For someone who showed no interest in money, she was shrewd when it came to managing the money she collected. Although Dave provided a roof over her head, she never asked him for a dime.

While cleaning up from breakfast Dave's nose let loose another torrent of blood, which alarmed his cousin. Dave packed his nose and went up to his room. The moment Gray saw him he told Dave it was due to his separation from Dave's brain, and that it was part of the healing process. Nevertheless it left Dave dizzy and exhausted, so he flopped on his bed and soon drifted off to sleep.

***

When he woke it was early afternoon, and he bounded from bed, driven by a sudden frenzy that the weekend was drifting to its end, and nothing but work waited for him in the morning. He groaned and went downstairs to find his cousin and Pixie lounging on the patio; she with her papaya juice, he with a large cup emblazoned with a Ray's Dogs badge. Dave slid open the patio door and put his hands on his hips.
"You two hungry?"
They both shrugged. "We split a soy dog," his cousin said.
Dave looked Peter over. His eyes seemed swollen. "Are you okay?"
Peter opened a hand. "My head. Got a bad one. Haven't had one like this in months."
"You could take a pill."
Pixie pointed at Ray's cup. "I made him some herbal tea. Holistic

87

remedy."

"Yeah, holistic remedy," Peter said under his breath. "I still have a prescription for some leafy holistic stuff."

Pixie frowned. "I thought you were done with that?"

Peter closed his eyes. "I am. Don't want it in my life, and still I have to listen to that stupid nickname, Snorkel."

Dave looked to his cousin in curiosity. "When did that become an objection?"

"What can I tell you? Like, it just came to me now." Peter gazed at both Dave and Pixie. "I got a name, you know."

Pixie smiled and patted his arm. "We love you all the same."

Dave looked up at the blue sky. Their world, he decided, had grown too small. Escape, and its momentary illusion of freedom, would do them well. "Come on," he said, resting his hands on their shoulders. "Let's go for a drive."

***

They cruised up the coast, heading north where the land met the ocean in rising, jagged cliffs, and the ocean greeted the bedrock with foaming white breakwater. Dave had no idea what towns they passed through, and had no care, as he drove with one hand draped over the steering wheel and his other arm perched on the door through the open window. The radio was off. The ocean air blew through the car. The sunroof was open, and warm rays slid over them as the road rose and fell, turned and swerved.

At no particular point he decided he was hungry, and pulled off the highway. He saw a seafood restaurant, and made his decision. He didn't even look at the menu. He ordered crab legs for the table, and told the waitress to just keep bringing them. He gave her his credit card and told her to keep ringing it up. Peter and Pixie stared at him, befuddled. Between the three of them, it was no secret that the house budget was strained, being that Dave's salary and Peter's meager disability checks were the only income to maintain such a premium location.

Pixie leaned toward Dave. "Do you feel okay? Are you sure about this?"

Dave nodded as the first heaping plate of crab legs came to the table. "It's only money."

Peter tipped his head up. "Hey, I forgot to tell you, your retirement fund statement came yesterday."

Dave picked up a crab leg, turning it over as he studied the articulation of the joints. He often let his cousin go through his mail; it gave Peter a sense of the life he used to know before his surfboard cracked his head open.

Dave's face fell as he regarded the exquisite architecture of a leg joint.

Peter smiled. "Dude, you did it, *you hit the mark.*"

Dave said nothing. He wondered if Gray had any bones in his moist little body. Pixie turned to Peter and opened her hands at Dave's silence.

"Like, before the TBI, we had this thing going, to see who could get a hundred thousand stashed away in our retirement funds before we hit thirty-five. I'm out of the game, but Dave here, he did it, just made it in time."

Pixie looked to Dave. "So when's your birthday?"

He was too busy working the leg's joints to answer right away, her voice not registering with him at first. "What? Oh, next week."

She picked up a leg and tapped its claw against Dave's in a mock toast. "Then I guess your Easter egg has a nest egg inside."

He frowned as he cracked the leg open. "This crab was walking around on the bottom of the sea, in what we would call darkness. He probably thought he had it all figured out. Find some food, find a Lady Crab, make some little crabs—it was all good; it was all clear. And then he's scooped up, his body gets pulverized, and we boil him, crack open his legs and pull out the meat." He dipped a piece of meat in the bowl of melted butter and tossed it in his mouth. "Just a thought."

Peter looked at his crab leg. "That's, like, dark."

Pixie shrugged. "We all have our place in the food chain."

Dave swallowed and flagged down the waitress. "A bottle of your best red wine, please."

***

Peter fell asleep on the drive home and, once Dave was sure his cousin was out cold, he pulled over and gestured for Pixie to sit up front with him. She slithered between the front seats in all her long-limbed yoga-nimbleness and sat, studying him as they rolled off on the highway. He said nothing but, when the sun went down and the air grew cold, he closed the windows and sunroof and, in the quiet of the car, it seemed as if they were floating, the car gliding along on its tuned suspension. Perhaps it was the car, perhaps it was the starlit night, perhaps it was the bottle of wine warming his blood but, for whatever reason, the decision that drifted through his mind was not much of a decision at all.

Her hand was resting on her thigh. He put his hand over hers. She looked at him, but he kept his eyes on the road. There was no anxiety, no worry, no cold sweat. He was at peace. Perhaps she sensed it, perhaps not. Whatever the case, she turned her hand to let his fingers mesh with hers.

***

Alone in his room, he moistened a hand towel, scooped Gray out of the water glass, and folded the towel over him. As he held Gray he heard some whispering thoughts in his head, disjointed thoughts that told him Gray was not only sleeping, but dreaming as well. It was fascinating, being able to listen to Gray's subconscious telepathy, but Dave decided to respect his friend's privacy, and hid the towel under the extra pillow on his large bed.

It was late. The morning was going to be difficult. He turned off his alarm.

***

Sleep proved elusive.

He rolled on his back and stared at the ceiling, his thoughts wandering free in the empty white expanse over his head. On a lark he pushed over the pillow beside him to look at the moist towel. "Gray?" he whispered. "Are you awake?"

The corner of the towel flipped over, revealing Gray's mitten-like hand. His featureless head rose and turned to Dave.

"Sorry," Dave said, looking back to the ceiling. "I guess that really is one of the most stupid questions. Unless you could talk in your sleep, that is. You know, sometimes, I think I've always been talking in my sleep."

Is this what you woke me for?

Dave shook his head. "What did you do today?"

Gray sat up and shrugged. *I stared out the window. I took a nap. I played solitaire on your computer. It was very peaceful. It was wonderful. I did exactly what I wanted to do, and nothing else.*

Dave took a breath. "Me, too."

Is that all you wanted to know?

Dave hesitated, watching his thoughts move about the ceiling.

What's bothering you?

Dave let his breath go. "I was eating crab legs tonight, and it sent a few thoughts through my head. Now that we're apart, we can go our own way, do our own thing, and make our own decisions. But there's a certain problem, in that you can't exactly walk out the door to Ray's Dogs, if you wanted to." He looked at Gray. "I don't want you back in my head. I don't want to go back to being angry all the time. I have no idea where I'm going, but for the first time I like the direction."

You don't have to take care of me.

"So you're just going to hide in here? How long can you live on your own?"

Gray opened his hands. *I don't know. I don't care. You need to understand something. You were as much a part of me as I was a part of you. This is kind of an odd thing that we have here. It's rare that a gray comes out. Most often when a person gets disconnected from their gray it's because the gray died. All sorts of things can kill us. Head wounds, like your cousin. Drugs, illegal and legal, can do us in. That's where addiction comes from, by the way. You see, people don't work too well when something bad happens to their gray. You were lucky—I was lucky—that the radar jammer just forced me out, rather than killing me in place.*

Dave closed his eyes. "Do you want to go back?"

Gray crossed his arms. *I can't.*

Dave looked at him.

Once a brain adjusts to not having a gray, there's no going back. The mind creates a new order, sometimes horribly flawed. That's why in most cases it's a bad thing when a gray dies. It's a relationship, between a mind and a gray. That's why we come in during infancy. We grow with our people, and each communion is unique.

Dave frowned.

Do you want me back in your head?

Dave closed his eyes. "No. I was thinking of my cousin, to help him."

Gray nestled in the fold of the towel. *Forget it. It would be a huge mistake.*

***

Peter woke Dave at ten in the morning. For all Peter's apparent slacker calm, the old aspects of his personality lurked just under the surface. Either that, or it was Peter's utter dependency on Dave's income that spurred him to shake Dave awake. "Dude, come on! Get up! They'll fry you, man!"

Dave grumbled and sat up in bed. "Who made you the time police?"

Peter frowned. "Like, back off, alright?"

Dave looked to his cousin. "Headache again?"

"Yeah." Peter shrugged. "I don't know. Maybe it'll pass."

Dave rubbed his face and waited for his cousin to shuffle away. When some semblance of consciousness came to him, he turned in fear to check under the spare pillow. To his relief Gray was still safely tucked away, but he was awake. He propped himself up on his little hands and looked to Dave. *You're going to work?*

Dave let his head hang. "I guess I have to."

How?

Dave looked Gray over and understood at once. "So I can't think the

91

same way I used to, without you in my head?"

Have you been thinking the way you used to?

Dave slumped on his pillow. "Good point." He looked out his windows, contemplating. He licked his lips and made his decision. "Oh well. I guess this was coming sooner or later."

He showered and threw on some clothes.

Pixie was still sleeping. He went out the door.

***

He felt no urgency on the ride to work. He walked in late, waving to the secretaries as he strolled toward the design bays where the engineer teams worked. One of the groups was already huddled around a design table, suffering through a manager's rally speech. As Dave walked by heads turned to track him, eyes widening in disbelief at not only his lateness, but also his appearance. His shorts, t-shirt, sandals, and unshaved jaw were in flagrant violation of the office standards—and yet he did not appear or feel the least bit embarrassed. He was happy he decided to leave Gray at home. He considered taking his little friend in his shirt pocket, but he wondered if having Gray so close would set him at odds against himself. Besides, the moist stain Gray would make on his shirt might foster the odd appearance of Dave lactating away his high-ordered mathematical mind.

The reality of it didn't quite strike him until he dumped himself in his chair. Perhaps it was the somewhat cliché character of the scene as he saw it in his head, perhaps it was the utter and welcome isolation he felt from the wearying reality of his job, or maybe it was the numbing realization of what he was tempting but, whatever the reason, he relished the euphoric anticipation that tingled his nerves at the inevitability of the coming moment.

He didn't have to wait long for his phone to ring. His cubicle, with plexi panels on the upper half of the walls, allowed him to look across the junior members of the design team he chaired. He gazed at his phone. Sure enough, it was the extension for the director of engineering. The man held zero patience for Dave's prior temper tantrums. Dave was protected in the old days when Peter held the director's chair but, after Peter was disabled, his successor made it clear Dave was on a short track to unemployment. Dave propped an elbow on his desk and, after some consideration, decided to satisfy a long held desire. He picked up the phone's handset, held it up, and with some theatrical flare shifted in his seat so that he could shove the handset down the back of his shorts. With the phone in place he hit the angry blinking light of his desk extension and, with a deep calming breath, let his flatulence fly.

Security told him to pack up his personal belongings. He looked over his desk, only to realize what he already knew: there was nothing there for him to take. He stood and started to walk, forgetting the handset in his shorts until the phone leapt off the desk and crashed on the floor. Between his laughter he apologized and pulled the handset from his shorts.

They walked him to the lobby and held the doors for him. *Okay, no hard feelings. Career over. Check!*

He hopped in his car, patted his hands on the steering wheel, and put all those expensive imported horsepower lurking under the hood to work as he floored the pedal and burned several donuts of smoking rubber in the parking lot before tearing off toward the highway.

He glanced at the clock. It was barely noon. Too early, a thought whispered, though he wasn't sure where his intuition was leading him. Instead of the highway he drove about the high-class neighborhoods across the highway from the engineering firm, and watched the expansive lawns and manicured gardens pass by his open window. So much order, he thought, nodding his head in appreciation but, in the wake of that thought came another: it's all so fake. His skin warmed beneath the open sunroof. He ignored the stop signs, being that he was rolling along at only ten miles an hour, but when he was pulled over and given a ticket, he thanked the officer. In the old days he would have argued just to rebel against the emotionless façade of order but, now that he perceived the world around him as a charade of humanity manipulated by little balls of snot nestled in people's heads, suffering society's penalties only reaffirmed his separation from its madness.

He asked the officer, so trim in her immaculate uniform, if she'd ever quit a job.

She asked him if he'd been drinking.

"No," he replied. "But I do have a hundred thousand dollars."

He drove past the restaurants he used to frequent with his coworkers, noting their cars parked outside one of their favored eateries. On a lark he stopped, went in, and, despite their stunned faces, he ordered them a round of drinks, picked up their meal tab, and walked away.

I have a hundred thousand dollars.

He made his way down to the beach, driving along the coastal road until some subconscious inclination drew his gaze down to the clock. It was time. He turned away and, with a little more speed, headed home. It was early afternoon when he parked at the townhouse. He walked around the house row, past the pool, and to the sliding glass doors of his patio. A glass of papaya juice sat on the plastic table by the chairs. He glanced inside, and found his cousin out cold on the couch in front of the television. Afternoon meds; they knock him out. He could see Pixie

standing by the sink, washing her hands. She had her beach clothes on—
the little cropped shirt, the peach colored bikini bottom.

Dave slid the door open.

She spun, somewhat surprised, her mouth open before floating to her
pleasant smile. She held a finger to her lips and hooked a thumb toward
Peter. Dave nodded, slipped out of his sandals, and padded on his bare
feet across the soft living room carpet. He went into the kitchen, watching
as she rested a hip against the sink and rested her hands on her lower
back. "You're early," she whispered with a curious tone.

He closed his eyes and took a deep breath.

"Oh Dave," she said with some alarm, "you got yourself in trouble,
didn't you?"

He let his breath go and opened his eyes. She was right where she
was, waiting by the sink. He paced around the table, fishing in his
pockets to leave his wallet and keys by his chair. He took another step,
and then he was quite close to her. She kept her gaze on him, tipping her
head as she studied him. He could tell she'd gone to the beach; there was
a red glow down the length of her nose and across the curve of her
cheeks. But he saw something else, that mysterious something that was
so alluring the longer he knew her. He hesitated to ascribe it to her
Montana commune upbringing, as it was such a trivial and shallow thing
to do, yet it resonated within his thoughts, for it summoned perceptions
of a world, a life, with a wondrous simplicity he was yet to experience.
And even though his better sense told him his obsessive tendencies were
transforming her to something greater, something more subtle and
elusive than perhaps she could ever be, the work of his inner inclinations
was already complete, and the illusion imprinted upon his emotions. In
her eyes he saw the endless blue sky, in her smile he perceived solace, in
the thick locks of her hair he heard the whispering breezes of open fields,
and the seduction of freedom.

He didn't have to consider what he was doing, because it was already
happening. The moment rose about him, through him, around them both.
He slid his arms around her, held her, and kissed her. She welcomed him,
he could feel it the way her fingers stroked the small of his back, the way
her yoga-nimble body seemed to flow in his embrace. Every nerve
tingled beneath his skin, but at the same time he found himself soothed,
separated from the world and all its nonsense. It had never been this way
with his wife; in the trench warfare of his failed marriage he confused
mindless anger for passion, aimless lust for desire, mutual desperation
for intimacy.

He rested his forehead against hers, his eyes closed as he felt the deep
thud of his heart.

She held him close, trying to calm the nervous tremble of his body.

"Easy," she whispered. "Just relax."

His jaw clenched. "It's just," he began, but reconsidered. "It's been a long time."

"That's okay," she said, her lips brushing against his. "I've been waiting. I can wait a little longer."

"I don't want to wait." He clenched his jaw. "Peter—"

"He's a companion. Look at me," she said, and waited until his eyes opened. "I know, Dave, understand? Peter's broken, but you're not. You're disconnected." She kissed him before retreating from him, her hands trailing down his arms as she stepped back toward her room. She stopped inside the doorway, pulled off her shirt, and let it slide off her arms to the floor. She stood there, half naked, her head to one side, her lips parting.

He stared at her, his long held imagination evolving in full.

"Dave?"

He closed his eyes. It was no longer a matter of wanting, but a matter of necessity.

His feet moved beneath him.

***

His eyes slid open to find the ceiling of her room above him, the blades of the ceiling fan following a lazy spin. It was hard to focus his mind, as it seemed he was in some alternate reality while staring up at the ceiling of her room. He reminded himself it was really his ceiling, a room in his townhouse, as if such petty, absolutist notions of property served for any subjective bearing. His eyes slid shut and a smile crept across his face as he wallowed in the memory of her. He wasn't surprised he fell asleep. It wasn't due to exertion, like the rushed push-pull bedroom aggression with his ex-wife, but rather the solace of satisfaction. Pixie had held him close to her, had kept his eyes full in her gaze, so that in those slow moments with her, there was nothing in the world but her. The more he stared in her eyes, the more conscious he was of being with her, of every sensation coursing through his body. It was inescapable, it was consuming; it was without compare, regardless of his narrow scope of experience.

His eyes opened to the ceiling once more, to the lazy turn of the ceiling fan. It was hypnotic. It only served to remind him how surreal the moment was, the disbelief that this was indeed his life, his house.

He sat up and shook his head to stave the delirium of abstraction. He put his clothes on and opened her door. The view was at once familiar and unfamiliar—his kitchen, but from a new perspective. He leaned against the doorway, bracing himself with his hands as he swooned with the befuddlement that had settled in his life. He shook his head to steady his senses, but it was no use. He felt, in some way, in the only way he could describe, disconnected—

The word rocketed through his thoughts. *Where have I heard that?*

And then he remembered, remembered many things at once in a dizzying spasm of complex connections. Disconnected—it was the word Gray used to describe people who lost their grays—it was the word Pixie used to differentiate him from his cousin. Snorkel— Peter—was *broken.*

Yes, that was the word she used, and he was disconnected. She challenged him to use the radar jammer in the house. She had tempted him all along. What did she say? She wanted to cut his strings. When he told her he was changing, she said she'd see. She said Peter was just a companion. She'd been waiting for Dave. What was she waiting for, why the delay? He had to disconnect. She said she knew, she said she knew before he walked through her door.

She grew up on a commune. She left to see the mess of the world. She left to see the world in all its gray madness.

He remembered Kim, and the man's hostility at the mere sight of Dave, and the tattoo across his eyelids: FOR RENT.

That derelict knows.

Pixie knows.

Does Peter—oh no, no!

The emptiness of the house finally registered in his sight. His eyes widened before darting toward his bedroom. *Peter!*

He ran through the living room and charged up the stairs, only to freeze in his doorway. Peter was on Dave's bed, his back arched high as he slouched over his knees to keep his hand on the inverted glass from Dave's bathroom. Gray was trapped under the glass, his hands balled to fists. He pounded against the glass when he saw Dave.

The radar jammer was smashed on the floor.

Peter looked at Dave, his eyes wide and wild. "Well, look who's here!"

A loud thump sounded from Dave's closet. He looked to his side to see his desk chair wedged under the doorknob. "Pixie?"

"Dave!" her muffled voice called back. "I'm sorry!"

"Shut up!" Peter shouted over her. Gray beat his fists against the glass, and as he did, Peter's eyelids fluttered. He shook his head and waved a finger at Dave. "You've been holding out, man. You've had a little gray dude up here, and you kept it a secret!"

This isn't happening—

Dave opened a hand and took a step into his room. "Peter, calm down, okay?"

"I don't want to calm down! I've been calmed down for two friggin' years! I have to take pills for everything! And the one thing I want the pills to do, they can't do!" Peter rose up, but kept his hand planted on the glass. Gray shoved against the side of the glass, and Peter's eyelids fluttered once more.

Dave waved a hand. "Stop that!"

Peter clapped a palm to his temple, misunderstanding Dave's plea. "I'm not stopping anything! You should've stopped!"

Dave retreated to the doorway, opening his hands. "I didn't do anything."

"Didn't do anything? Didn't do anything?" Peter jabbed a hand to Dave's closet. "You did her, you piece of shit! I can't drive, I can't sleep right; hell, half the time I can't think straight! She was the only thing I had left, and you had to one-up me?"

Dave shook his head. "It wasn't like that—"

"In your ass with your excuses! How many times did I cover for you and your screw-ups? And now you screw with me? Oh, no way, no friggin' way, man."

Pixie pounded on the closet door.

Dave's gaze darted about. "What do you want?"

Peter's forehead knotted as his eyelids fluttered once more. "I, I—" he gasped and pounded a fist against his forehead, his lips separating over his clenched teeth— "I want, I want it back in my head! I can hear it whispering in my head, whispering in the empty places. I want my life back, I want everything back, I want it back, want it back in my head!" His eyes popped open. "You're going to help me."

Dave swallowed. His blood froze in his veins. He remembered what Gray had told him, and now he understood. Even the narrow proximity between Gray and Peter was enough to drive his cousin crazy. And it wasn't just delirium, it was rage; Dave could see the violence waiting in Peter's stare, knew it from having seen it in his mirror so many times in his life. Attacking Peter, trying to wrestle a man possessed with rage, when Dave only felt fear and disillusionment, was a losing proposition.

He could hear Pixie pound on the door. His heart pounded in his chest.

Have to do something—Gray! What do I do?

Gray pressed his head to the glass. *Kim!*

Peter grunted in pain. "That's it, I got it, I got a plan!" He shook his head and pointed to Dave. "You, you're gonna go to Kim. Yeah, he'll know what do!"

Dave opened his hands as his mind cleared. "Kim? He won't even let me in his shop."

Peter's gaze darted about. He looked at Gray before looking to the closet. He jabbed his finger at Dave. "Hey, hey! I'm not an idiot!"

97

Dave pointed to the closet. "He'll open the door for her. He'll listen to her."

"No!" Peter slapped a hand on his head, pulling at his hair as his suspicions ran wild with his paranoia. "You'll, you'll just take her, take her for yourself!"

Dave ground his teeth. "I can't," he said, his thoughts racing. "Listen, I can't leave Gray behind. I'll admit it—I might want her, but I need him. I can't lose him. You see how I kept him safe, right? I'll take Pixie with me to Kim, and you can stay here with Gray."

Peter shifted about as he tried to think, but then nodded. "Right, right. *Mexican stand-off.*" He winced and clenched his teeth again. "Okay. Take her. But listen, disappear with her, and I'll splatter the little dude. *I'll do it.* I got nothin' to lose!"

Dave shook his head and sidestepped to his closet. He kept his eyes on Peter and kicked the chair away. The door flew open under the stomp of Pixie's feet, and the moment she saw daylight, she popped out of the closet and put her back to the wall.

Peter waved to the door. "Go, go—be quick!"

Dave grabbed Pixie's wrist and led her out of the room. They hurried down the stairs and toward the door. Dave, remembering his wallet and keys, had to scramble back and snatch them off the table. He rushed out the door and slammed it shut. Pixie started to dart off but Dave surprised her by grabbing her shoulders and stopping her. "What the hell happened?"

She rolled her eyes. For the first time since meeting her Dave saw a troubled look on her face, and it sickened him. She put her hands on his chest as her knees wobbled with her nerves. "I'm sorry, I'm so sorry," she said quickly, "but I've never seen one alive, out of a person. People on the commune talked about it, but none of them ever saw one, either. I just hoped you had it hidden in your room somewhere and, after, after you fell asleep, I went up, went up to look. I just wanted to look, to get one look at *it.*"

He closed his eyes and rested his forehead against hers.

"I thought Peter was asleep," she continued, her fingers kneading his shirt, "but he must've woke. He went looking for me and found you in my bed and, when he came upstairs looking for me, he found me sitting on your bed. I already had the little thing under the glass—I don't think he saw it at first. He was so hurt, so mad! He grabbed me and, when he saw it, and the moment he put his hand on the glass, he, he went crazy. He stomped on the jammer, smashed it; he grabbed me—grabbed me so tight—and put me in the closet."

"Did you ever tell him about the grays? Does he understand?"

She shook her head. "I think deep down he knew what he'd been missing since the TBI the moment he saw the little thing. I don't know. But I never told him anything about the grays. How could I? Would you have believed me if I told you?"

Dave frowned, his eyes closing as he pushed his forehead against hers and tightened his grip on her shoulders. His eyes popped open to stare into her gaze. It was so similar, and so different, than the way he had stared into her eyes before—

He took her face in his hands and kissed her. "It'll be fine. I got us out the door with one idea, and I already have another."

***

Dave drove to town, too impatient to walk. Pixie sat beside him in the car, her elbow on the door so she could rub her forehead. "I should've seen it coming," she said, glancing at Dave. "I should've seen the changes in him. He's your cousin, and I think because you two are related he's sensitive to your gray's telepathy."

Dave kept his eyes on the road. "You know a lot about this shit, don't you?"

She blinked at the harshness of his tone. "I told you—you wouldn't have believed me."

He ground his teeth. She was right, and he knew it. He pulled into a municipal lot and parked the car before looking at her. "Look, the way I see it, we're on some other side of reality now, Pixie. I don't think there's much I wouldn't believe at this point. So is there anything else I should know?"

She looked to her feet. "Keep driving."

"That's it? Just ditch him?"

She looked back to him. "Ditch who—Gray, or your cousin?"

Dave shook his head. "I just can't walk away. Too much to leave behind."

"All the more reason to keep driving."

"Is this what they taught you on your Montana commune?"

Her gaze fixed out the window, at the ordered world about them. "You don't have to fight this, all this out there," she said, waving a hand to the distance. "You're still thinking about control and order. We have that on our commune, but it's different. These are two different worlds and, as long as they keep their distance, everything's okay. But this, this is crazy. Your cousin is crazy. He'll get us both in big trouble. Nothing good comes of this."

"That sounds like big paranoid conspiracy talk."

She looked to him. "You've been floating in a dream, Dave. You deep-sixed your job. We had a nice roll in the sack. I don't regret

99

anything. But you have to remember, like you just said, we're on the other side of reality. And if you think you can just push back, just laugh at it without *it* pushing back, pushing back hard in all the ways it can, you're not dreaming, you're delusional. You scratch this veneer the wrong way and it'll rip you up like shark's skin. Cops, federal agencies, tax collectors, they'll eat you alive. Your little gray friend may not have told you that, or maybe he doesn't really remember it himself, but there's a definite tolerance limit, and you don't want to cross it."

He closed his eyes. Memories of his therapy sessions whispered in his head. "You know, that makes more sense than anything anyone ever told me." He took her hand and looked to her. "You should have told me, Pix."

"Dave—"

He leaned over and kissed her. "I would've listened to anything you said."

She stared at him, unsure what to say.

"I have to do this." He squeezed her hand. "Besides, when it's all said and done, I have a hundred thousand dollars waiting for us."

***

They walked through town, winding their way through the streets until they stood before the ugly metal door of Kim's shop. Dave knocked, to no avail, but, when Pixie called out a hello, the door opened. Kim's eyebrows settled low over his gaze when he saw Dave, but then he tipped his head and smiled at Pixie. "Hey girl, you need something?"

Dave's eyes narrowed. He wasn't sure why, maybe it was Kim's leering gaze at Pixie, maybe it was Dave's simple conclusion that he despised Kim, but without a single word he shoved Kim back and stepped into the shop. Kim's face bunched up, a litany of profanities streaming from his mouth in a steady slither of his raspy voice. Dave shoved him again, forcing him back by his 'desk', the pile of open, half emptied shipping boxes.

Things changed in a hurry, then. Kim reached in a box and whipped his hand around to level a gun at Dave's forehead. Kim clenched his jaw as he shifted nervously from one foot to the other. "Get lost man! Who the hell do you think you are?"

Dave ignored the gun. Pixie was outside. The door had closed behind him. For some reason, he felt quite calm. "You sold me a radar jammer," he started.

Kim bared his teeth. "I already forgot you! Get lost!"

Dave took a breath. "You sold me a radar jammer, and now I have space for rent," he continued, pointing to his temple.

Kim blinked. His hand started to shake. "Yeah? So? So you know? So what?"

"I need something to put *it* back where it belongs," he lied.

Kim laughed beneath his glare of disdain. He looked over Dave's sloppy clothes and unshaven jaw. "Corporate rat," he said, poking the gun against Dave's forehead. "Gutless little bitch. What's the matter? Can't take it? Like being a weasel, do you? Mule crying because he lost his leading carrot?"

Dave closed his eyes. He could feel the small cold circle of the gun against his forehead. *Such hostility.* He wondered why he felt no fear. It was all surreal. Friday night, he was just another nobody trying to live his life, ignorant to the world around him. Monday afternoon, he was standing in an illegal electronics shop with a gun to his head trying to haggle with some low-life for a renegade device that could help transplant into his cousin's brain the telepathic lump of tissue Dave had blown out of his nose, all of it after he'd held Pixie in a way he never thought possible.

He opened his eyes. "Let me guess. There's no device to put it back, is there?"

Kim's eyes narrowed. "Look man, get lost. You seen the shit, you know how it is, now deal with it, understand? And don't think about calling the cops on me! I got papers for everything. Screw their order, and screw you, you hear me?"

Dave took a breath. He understood why he had to confront Kim. All his life, all the anger, all the aimless rebellion, he'd been fighting something he could never see. And now that he understood it, the anger seemed even more pointless. Pixie was right. He'd been fooling himself these last days, had deceived himself with the euphoria of his careless freedom, with the hopeless concept that he could just drift in the gray morass between the reality of his old life and his new life. It was why he coddled Gray, keeping him like some little pet, keeping him as a subconscious allusion of control, a last gambit to bridge both realities, turning captor to captive.

He heard himself speak. "Pull the trigger."

Clarity through confrontation, prescience while teetering on a precipice: images flashed through him in rapid confluence. He thought of his ex-wife, and the way life had been with her. He thought of the therapist he used to see and, to some extent, the way he obsessed over Pixie in her stead. He thought of his temper tantrums, the fights that embroiled him—both physical and mental—over his life. No wonder his parents didn't talk to him, no wonder they gave up on him. He'd always been the square peg, pounding his head to round off the corners so he could fit into something he couldn't comprehend.

What had Gray said? *Each communion is unique. Subconscious efforts of control. By nature, people are wild.*

The fog receded. Dave understood. He had to choose, one way or the other. He had to disconnect; yes, he had to disconnect. He had to sever his ties, all of them, cut them so there would never be any space for reconsideration or hesitation.

It was almost imperceptible, but he felt a change in pressure against his forehead. Kim's arm was tightening. He was preparing for recoil. It seemed Kim had made his choice, too.

And so Dave made his choice. He knew who he was. There was no going back.

He slapped Kim's hand to the side and seized his wrist before cracking a fist into Kim's face. The gun went off, the discharge deafening in the cramped confines of the little shop, but Dave took little notice. His body seemed to know exactly what to do, now that he let it go. He was over the boxes and on top of Kim in a heartbeat, punching him twice to shatter his nose. He turned and thrust his palm up into the back of Kim's elbow, snapping the joint against its deflection. Kim's hand popped open, the gun fell from his fingers, but Dave flowed into his next move. His forearm slid past Kim's ruined elbow, drawing across Dave's chest before shooting back to ram an elbow into Kim's throat. Kim went limp, his eyes bulging around the bloody mess of his nose as his throat collapsed.

Pixie pushed the door open, holding in the doorway in a low crouch to see Dave grab Kim's shoulders and slam him against the wall. Dave heaved and whipped Kim aside, Kim's extended hand flailing about his maimed elbow before he flopped to the floor amid a mess of boxes. Dave ripped off the flap of a box and stomped it over Kim's face. He emptied the bullets from the gun and, using the gun as a hammer, pounded savage blows on the cardboard shield he held over Kim's head.

"Dave!"

He ignored Pixie, dropping the gun to roll Kim onto his belly. He drove his knee between Kim's shoulders, grabbed Kim's hair and gave a quick, brutal jerk. An awful crunch sounded from Kim's neck as his head bent back, his limbs giving a violent twitch before going limp. Dave took the gun and stood, his chest heaving. He checked his hands for any blood.

Pixie braced her head with her hands. "Dave, what the hell?"

He looked to Kim. "He was going to kill me. I had to."

She slumped in the doorway, shaking her head. "We shouldn't be here, this shouldn't be happening, this is all wrong. . ."

Dave looked into his hands. Of all the violence, all the rage, all the guilt for the hurt he had caused in the blind stumble of his life, he felt nothing now. There was no sense of a crime, only of necessity. She had to understand. It was his action, and full ownership went to him. He felt something, something he couldn't put to words. It was purity and absolution, another confluence of means and ends in a guiltless pirouette. He swallowed, and made his decision. If she didn't understand, he figured she wouldn't have stayed. She might not condone the violence, but he felt she understood the need, and in that, he understood her in a way he never expected.

He let his hands hang at his side. "Pixie. Tell me about Montana."

Her gaze rose to find him. There was a plaintive look on her face. "I want to go home, Dave," she whispered. "I want to go home."

He slid the gun into his shorts and pulled her to her feet. "We're almost there."

"What?" She stopped him with a hand on his chest. "What now?"

He took a deep breath to still his pounding heart. "Peter."

She closed her eyes, her knees weakening until she rested her head on his chest.

He put his arms around her. "We can't leave him like he is. It's not right, for either of them. You know that."

***

He didn't go directly to the townhouse. Instead, he stopped by Ray's.

Pixie turned to him, startled. "What are you doing? I thought we were going to—"

"I'm hungry."

"No, you're crazy."

She didn't quite understand until they finished their soy dogs. He slid the gun from under his shirt, wiped it clean, and hid it in the used foil wrapping of their smoked dogs. He tossed it in one of the garbage pails and returned to his seat to take a sip of Pixie's iced tea. It was evening, and the sun was dropping, its bright light making the subtle shift to long golden rays. He rested his hand over hers, satisfied when she welcomed him in the mesh of their fingers. He studied her with a sidelong glance. "Are you okay?"

She gave him a single nod. "I told you. I heard some stories on the commune."

"Do you think I'm crazy?"

She closed her eyes and took a breath. "Reality is a perception, not an absolute. Every perspective has its own subjective framework, its own logic structure. One man's delusion is another's man's revelation; one man's insanity is another man's genius." She opened her eyes and shrugged. "Either way you look at it, you have to strip it all down before you can build yourself back up."

103

He remembered his thought before he killed Kim. Killing him made even more sense, now, that he considered that thought. Kim held a precious secret, a privileged revelation, and he responded by being a parasite to both sides of that revelation. Killing him wasn't a crime, it wasn't quite a necessity; it was more like an immunological response, inevitable and guiltless.

He turned to Pixie and muttered his thought. "Clarity through confrontation—"

"Wisdom at the edge of reason," she completed. Her warm, welcoming smile returned. "It's a common thought. I've heard similar versions. The words vary, but they're just words. Semantics. The meaning is the same." She squeezed his hand and raised an eyebrow. "Did you think we just rode around on horses on the commune? Being free doesn't mean being ignorant."

He stared at her. "Will you marry me?"

She laughed. "What about Peter?"

"Tell me what I need to do."

Her unblinking gaze held on his eyes. "Do you really want to do this?"

He didn't flinch. "I told you. I need to do this."

"If you insist." She licked her lips. "He's been alone with Gray. We might need a saw."

"Okay." He leaned toward her, even though he feared she might reject him after what happened with Kim. He hesitated a moment, but she didn't recoil, so he kissed her. He opened his eyes and, when their lips separated, her wide smile returned before her eyes slid open. She gave him a little laugh before rolling her lower lip between her teeth. Her blond locks swayed in the breeze as the sun framed her in his sight.

"I love the evening," he whispered. "It's so peaceful."

***

Despite his confidence, he came to the conclusion that he was in fact having the final nervous breakdown he always feared. The world was a joke, order was a parody of hollow inclinations, and grays the washed up comedians in an empty nightclub.

He bought a box saw, and that was when the headache hit him. He knew at once his cousin was up to something, something threatening Gray so much that his telepathic burst found Dave across town. He hurried to the car with Pixie in tow and drove back to the townhouse. She urged him to wait, but he refused to listen.

He came in the door and heard a loud bang. As he sank to the floor he realized it was the crash of the frying pan on his head.

***

He woke sprawled on his side on the kitchen floor, crusted blood flaking from his eyelids. His cheek was wet with drool that seeped from his mouth. His eyes focused to a delirious sight.

Peter was hunched before him, a series of grunts sounding from his throat. He moved, revealing Pixie. She was bound to one of the kitchen chairs with duct tape about her arms and ankles. A single silver strip covered her mouth, but her eyes widened when she saw Dave looking at her.

Peter whipped around, seized the pan from the table, and loomed over Dave. He seemed ready to swing, but when Dave failed to move, Peter eased. He had shaved his head in rough fashion, so that random tufts of stubble dotted the dome of his skull. Above one ear there was a ragged scar, where the drainage tube had exited his skull after the TBI. His eyes were wide and wild, bloodshot beneath the invention on his head. He had inverted a clear plastic cup atop the crown of his skull, trapping Gray beneath and securing the cup with silvery bands of tape running up his temples and beneath his jaw. It was a tight bonnet, so Peter's face bulged in a puffy red distortion of his normal countenance.

Dave looked up, only to find Gray slumped motionless against one side of the cup.

Peter grabbed the collar of Dave's shirt and gave him a rough jerk. "What's with the saw?"

Dave groaned. "What, what are you doing?"

Peter rolled Dave over and slapped him. "What's with the goddamn saw?"

Dave tried to move, but his body felt like uncooked dough, shapeless and without strength. His head drooped to one side. One of Peter's prescription bottles lay on the floor beneath the table, the top missing to reveal the bottle's empty depth.

Peter left him, grabbed the saw from the table and, despite Pixie's writhing efforts, he managed to pull one of her fingers straight to threaten the knuckle with the saw. She squeezed her eyes shut, the chair rocking as she struggled to get free, but Peter put the saw down to give her a vicious back-handed slap. She went still, stunned by the blow. He grabbed the saw and looked to Dave. "No more games! I want it in my head. She told me you killed Kim. Now what am I supposed to do?"

Dave fought to keep his eyes open. He managed to find his voice. "Saw. . ."

Peter stomped a foot on the floor. "I'm not cutting my friggin' head open you idiot! There has to be a better way. How come I can't hear it anymore?"

Dave's eyes rolled in his head. He struggled to think. How many pills had Peter stuffed down his throat?

Peter kicked Dave's leg to get his attention. "Hey! Come on. How do I get it in my head?"

Dave's eyes slid shut. He heard a wet rasp, followed by the rattle of chair legs on the floor. Something warm splashed across his face. He opened his eyes to find Peter standing over him, dangling Pixie's slender pinky to let the blood drip out on Dave's face. He kicked Dave's side and dropped the finger on his face. Pixie was trying to scream, her bellow muted to a hoarse rush beneath the tape as she struggled in the chair. Dave's forehead wrinkled. The finger rolled off his forehead to land on the floor by his ear.

Peter crouched by Dave, tugging at Dave's arm until he had Dave's hand pinned under his bare foot. He grabbed a finger and, before Dave could grasp what had happened to Pixie, he heard another wet rasp and felt his arm jerk. With all the pills Peter had stuffed into him, he hardly felt a thing. Only when Peter dangled Dave's amputated pinky over Dave's face, again sprinkling him with the blood, did Dave understand his finger was just hacked off.

Peter dropped the saw and slapped Dave. "Still with me? I'll keep going!"

Dave choked on his saliva as Peter took the saw and moved toward Pixie.

"Wait, wait—water—"

Peter spun. He shook his head, Gray's drying form rattling around the plastic cup. "What? What about water?"

Dave's arm was wet. No, not wet—blood. He coughed. "It needs water."

Peter grabbed Dave's hair and stared into his blood-speckled face. "Needs water?" His jaw clenched, the constriction of the duct tape bonnet and the pull of gravity turning his bloated face a pale shade of purple. "Needs water, huh? So if it needs water, that means it can dry out—that's it!" He shook his hands on either side of Dave's face. "Dude! *That's friggin' brilliant.* Yes!"

Dave fought to lift his head, but it was no use.

Peter ran from the kitchen and bolted up the stairs. Dave couldn't remember the last time his cousin moved so freely. It only reinforced the reason for his cousin's aggression, every nerve and sinew of his body without a doubt screaming to have a gray back in his head. After a quick tumult upstairs, Peter rushed into the kitchen, a small hair dryer clutched in his hand. Dave had a dim memory of the dryer belonging to one of Peter's former girlfriends; left, he guessed, somewhere in Peter's room beneath the sedimentary mess of clothes accumulated since the TBI.

106

Peter sat at the kitchen table, chuckling to himself as he tore at his duct tape bonnet. The moment he was able he pulled the cup from the tape, closing its open end with his palm before planting the cup on the table. He reached over to plug in the dryer and, when he turned back to the table, his eyes bulged in his head. The dryer whined as he turned it to full power. He grabbed the cup, tilted the edge, and aimed the wide mouth of the dryer into the cup.

Dave shook his head. "Don't, don't do that, please?"

Peter started to laugh. Even with the whine of the dryer, Dave could hear as Gray thrashed about the cup.

Stop! Stop!

Dave lifted his head, but the moment his head left the floor, his neck gave out and his head cracked on the tiles.

The whine of the dryer filled his ears.

Stop, stop!

Pixie went still in her chair, her nostrils flaring as she tried to catch her breath.

Stop. . .

The whine ended. Peter leaned over the table, grinning ear to ear. He glanced at Dave. "You know what? I'm gonna let you watch. You took from me, now I'm gonna take from you."

He slid his hand under the cup before crouching on the floor by Dave. "After all I did for you, you take her from me. You pathetic little bastard. I saved your ass bringing you out here. I gave you another shot at life! And the moment you have the chance to return the favor, you hide it from me and you steal the one thing I have left? You little puke. Your parents were right—I was out of my mind taking pity on you. Now! Watch this."

He lifted the cup and tossed it aside. Gray looked like a piece of driftwood, blanched and brittle. Peter rocked his thumb over Gray with a smooth motion. Gray's little body crackled and collapsed to a pile of dust. Peter glanced at Dave, his manic grin returning, before he hunched over the pile of sparkling dust. He pinched a nostril, and with one long snort, sucked the dust up his nose. Dave managed to lift his bloody hand, but Peter slapped it away as he tipped his head back and continued snorting, his nostrils quivering with the effort. "Get up there," he said between snorts. "Come on, all the way!"

Peter's head snapped to the side. His eyelids fluttered as his eyes rolled over in his head. His hands twitched by his hips. His jaw dropped, the veins on his throat bulging as a wet rattle sounded from his throat.

Gray?

Peter slapped his hands on his head. Blood trickled from his nose.

Dave fought against the rubbery weakness of his muscles to roll onto his side. He balanced with his good hand, his bloody hand resting on the floor before him as if it belonged to someone else. He saw two amputated fingers on the floor where his head had been. He blinked and tried to focus his thoughts. *Gray!*

Help!

Gray!

Help! Get me out of here!

Peter thrashed. His fingers clawed at his scalp, digging so deep his nails drew blood.

Dave! Get me out of here!

Peter turned on his feet, twisting his head side to side. He groaned, his body trembling, before he slammed his head into the kitchen wall. He staggered, only to run from the kitchen and pile head first into a living room wall, breaking the sheetrock. Still on his feet, he shuffled about, went still for a moment, and then charged up the stairs.

Dave grunted and managed to get to his knees. He swayed, blood dripping from his nose as he looked with blurred eyes toward Pixie. Her eyes widened as she looked back at him.

Peter stomped his feet at the top of the stairs.

Pixie motioned with her chin to the saw.

A wave of nausea seized Dave. His stomach bucked, and a mess of half digested soy dog and pills spewed from his mouth onto the floor. He spat his mouth clean and looked up at the steady thud of Peter's feet on the floor. *Gray! Do it!*

Dave! Help me! Dave!

Do it!

Peter gasped. The thumping stopped. Dave looked to the stairs to see Peter come flying down head first, his body flung under Gray's direction. Peter's head hit the railing by the bottom step with an awful clang, his neck snapping as his head whipped to the side under the hurtling mass of his body. He tumbled over the last step to flop motionless on the floor.

Dave coughed and fought to get his good hand on the saw. He crawled to Pixie and cut at the tape binding her. It was slow, and his dexterity lost with the pills in his system, but after cutting several winds of tape Pixie took the saw and cut the rest of the bands. She slid from the chair to sit beside him on the floor, steadying him by wrapping her good hand around his shoulders.

His head drooped forward, his gaze resting in his lap to see the mess of his bloody hand, her bloody hand resting on his thigh. Peter had hacked off both their pinky fingers. He grinned and managed to turn his head, resting his forehead against hers. "Hey," he wheezed, laying his hand over hers. "Look, we're a matching set. I guess we were meant to be together."

She looked at him for a moment and couldn't help but laugh. "Maybe we can use some of those cut strings of yours to put our fingers back on."

"Good one," he said and passed out.

***

When he woke he was on his back on the kitchen floor, but Pixie had stuffed a pillow from the living room couch under his head. She was sitting beside him, his hand in her lap, as she bandaged the stump of his finger. Lengths of surgical tape dangled from her chin, her own wounded hand already bandaged. Her gaze darted to him as he blinked to focus on the ceiling, its detail lost between the darkness outside and the light shining in his face.

"We have a guy on the commune who was a trauma surgeon," she explained. "He was the only medical care I knew growing up. He uses his medical license to order any medicine we need—antibiotics, mostly— over the Internet from Mexican suppliers. He taught us basic field medicine, stuff he learned in the army. He makes a field kit anytime someone goes off the commune."

Dave glanced at his hand as she pulled a piece of tape off her chin and secured a length of gauze. "You sowed me up?"

She nodded. "Best I can. You'd be surprised how the body can recover from some things, as long as you don't get any infections. Antibiotics are magic."

He pushed up on his good hand, his eyes widening before they focused on Peter's still body. "Gray?"

She pulled the last piece of tape from her chin. "Okay, all set." She kissed the top of his hand and smiled. "I think we still have time, if you want to do this. I'll need your help getting him into the tub."

He nodded and rose to his feet, swaying a moment in the lingering wake of the pills Peter had stuffed down his throat. He shook his head, accepting the glass of water Pixie handed him before chugging it down. He nodded again and walked by her to wrap his good arm around Peter's neck and hoist him up. She hooked her arm under Peter's armpit, and together, they managed to drag him upstairs and dump his limp body in the bathtub. Dave stripped off Peter's clothes, and Pixie returned with the saw.

They sat on the edge of the tub, one of Peter's arms dangling over the edge between them. Dave looked to the saw and took it from Pixie's hand. His stomach knotted, but he knew what he had to do. He looked to her. "You should go, Pixie."

"I've seen this before. I'm okay with it."

"No, I mean you should go, as in gone."

109

She looked to him, the hurt plain in her eyes.

"It's my mess, Pix. If they get me, I want to know you're still free."

She leaned over Peter's dangling arm to hug Dave. Her lips brushed by his ear and parted, but she squeezed her eyes shut and said nothing, instead pressing her lips to his temple. She gave him a kiss, but when he opened his mouth to speak, she rested her fingers over his lips to silence him. "Follow me," she whispered. "Now close your eyes, so you don't see me cry."

He heard her bare feet pad across the tiles. She went downstairs. A few minutes passed, and the front door closed. She was gone.

He opened his eyes, looked down at Peter, and kicked the dangling arm into the tub.

***

It took an hour or two for Dave to focus. Gray was his first concern, and after some thought, and a long time staring at the saw with revulsion, Dave came up with a meticulously engineered alternative plan. He rummaged through the house until he found a funnel and a large basin. He moved Peter's body so his head hung back over the edge of the tub, his nostrils pointed straight up to the ceiling. Dave shoved the funnel into one nostril, secured it with duct tape, and then sealed Peter's other nostril, the back of his throat, and his ears with more duct tape and wads of plastic wrap. With that bit of biometric plumbing completed he ran some warm water into the basin, held it over the funnel, and poured it in until the funnel almost overflowed. He waited before rolling Peter over to let the water drain into the tub. Some of it was tinged with blood, so Dave nodded, confident in his plan. He filled the funnel once more, sat on the floor by his cousin's dangling head, and waited. Before long he saw a gray tendril extend from the funnel, its slender length not much different than the way a snail's antenna stalk would swell out from its head. He put a hand by the tendril, and to his relief the tendril wrapped around his finger. Dave held his breath as he gently lifted his hand, the tendril slithering from the funnel like a long gray worm. It wrapped about itself as it dangled from his finger, but he moved with haste to the sink, filled a glass of water, and dunked his finger. The tendril released, and sank as a lump of tissue in the water.

He sat on the toilet and stared in the glass. "Gray?"

The ball remained still.

"Come on, Gray. Come back to me."

The ball wiggled and, to Dave's delight, a hand sprung free. It waved about in the water, and then the ball of tissue wiggled once more before popping open to the shape Dave knew so well. The little head shook before Gray sat up on the bottom of the glass, the featureless face panning about until it settled on Dave.

You got me out?

Dave nodded. "Did you think I'd leave you behind?"

Gray pulled himself up to the edge of the glass. *After all the mess—why don't you hate me?*

Dave shrugged. "I've hated myself long enough. Besides—whatever happened in the past, I wouldn't be here now without having you in front of me."

Gray turned to look at the tub and Peter's opaque, unblinking gaze. *Is now such a great place to be?*

Dave grinned. "I wouldn't have it any other way."

***

Together, they formulated a way to dispose of Peter without raising suspicion. It was gruesome work, but Gray reminded Dave that it had to be done. It took a few bottles of beer for Dave to work up his courage and sedate his innate objections to what he was about to do, but with a dead body in his tub time was a factor, and he set to work. He tore out the carpets of the townhouse room by room and cut them into small sections. Each section was rolled and stuffed with a bagged, amputated body part. He then drove to the town dump and chucked the sections one by one. Bleach kept the odor down in the tub, and kept the drain from clogging with clotted blood. The intestines proved to be a messy detail, but Dave sowed either end of the small intestine shut before removing it and stuffing its ropey length in another bag. The large intestine he hacked free in one length, tied it shut in the middle, and then drained either end into his toilet to flush away the rancid contents.

After two weeks, it was done. The nagging feeling that he was having the mental break he'd feared all his life became a palpable, if not darkly comical, distraction. With his cousin gutted and disposed, he moved on to gut the townhouse: he dragged his furniture out and let the garbage men take it away; he sold Peter's collection of strange paintings to a local art gallery for a token payment. He bought some lengths of pine board, a set of power tools and, during the day, when his neighbors were at work, he went about making some new furniture. Woodwork had always fascinated him in his youth. He remembered the times when his marriage seemed a fight to the death and he would temper his rage by visiting local home stores to figure out how much lumber he might need to build a casket for his wife's body. Even though he never hit his wife, his therapist had found such a consideration to be particularly disturbing.

He fashioned two rough chairs, and was sitting in the stark expanse of his living room one sunny afternoon when there was a knock on his door. He walked to the door and opened it, knowing Gray was upstairs sleeping under his pillow.

A man in a rather cheap suit stood on Dave's doorstep. He had a puffy face, his nose marked by a network of veins that betrayed a history of drinking. He looked about fifty, aged by a rough life. Behind him a plain sedan was parked in front of Dave's house.

"David Fulton?" the man said. He reached in his coat pocket and pulled out a badge. "Detective Henry Pittman. Is this a bad time?"

Dave stared at the man for a moment, realizing how strange he must look, as he stood in his doorway in a shabby shirt and shorts, black work gloves, and an open beer in hand. He shook his head. "Bad time? Oh, I guess not," he replied and walked to the kitchen. "Hey, you want a beer?" he called over his shoulder.

Pittman stepped in, his face bunching up as he looked over the townhouse. Besides the unplugged flat-panel television hanging on the wall, there was nothing left of the furnishings. The two chairs Dave had made sat in the living room, next to a scatter of power tools, scrap wood, and a swept up pile of sawdust. "I'll pass—I'm on duty," Pittman said, tipping his chin to the bottle Dave offered. "Doing a little redecorating?"

Dave settled in one of the chairs and sipped his beer. "Lost my job," he said with a shrug.

"Fired is more like it," the detective said as he walked about the living room, his gaze settling on the power tools. "Been keeping busy?"

"I do my work during the day. These houses have cement block privacy walls. I'm not bothering anyone." Dave shrugged. "Idle hands are not a healthy thing, you know."

Pittman put his hands on his hips. "You're not wondering why I'm here?"

Dave sighed. "Well, actually, I'm kind of in the middle of a nervous breakdown."

"Is that so?" Pittman paced over to the empty chair, rubbing his fingers along one of the arms to see if it was coated with sawdust. "Well, I'll tell you this. There've been some reports of suspicious activity here. Two people lived with you. Your cousin, Peter Fulton, and a female friend of his, known by the name Pixie, correct?"

Dave looked about the empty house. "They left."

The detective studied him. "Left? That's it?"

Dave tapped a gloved finger to his temple. "I'm sure you saw that my cousin was disabled after a traumatic brain injury. Surfing accident. Go figure. He started acting weird, and he just took off on me. The girl, she took off too. I have no idea where my cousin went. She said she was from Oregon, or something like that. I don't know."

Pittman nodded. "So, you're really not curious why I'm here?"

Dave looked him in the eyes and shrugged. "You already asked me that. What difference does it make? I mean, you're already here, right?"

Pittman seemed to find some humor in that, a small grin pulling at the corner of his mouth. "Your cousin has some insurance money coming to him."

"That's nice. I have a hundred thousand dollars. I don't need any money."

Pittman raised a finger. "I know; your retirement funds. You think that'll last?"

"As long as it lasts, it lasts." Dave sipped his beer. "I imagine you want to look around, do the whole investigation thing? Be my guest."

"You don't care about the money, about supporting yourself?"

Dave waved a hand at the townhouse. "Do I look worried?"

Pittman scratched his jaw.

Dave sat up straight, leaning his elbows on the wide arms of his chair. "Let me tell you something. The government prints billions of dollars when it says it needs to, right? That's a lot of paper. Paper comes from trees. So does wood, like the wood for these chairs. But these are real. They'll always have a value, a value I'll know when I plop my lazy ass into one of them. But what is money? You can't really burn it to keep warm, and you can't make a chair out of it. When you think of it, it really isn't useful for anything, except to leverage people against each other, to create an umbrella of control to keep people in line. Trees follow a certain order too, you know. And these two orders, well, they co-exist," he said, putting his beer down to hold his two pointer fingers beside each other. "I've come to the conclusion that our money is printed with a gray-green dye for that reason—green for the order of trees, of natural things, and gray, for that other order, the order that sits like a mist over our lives."

Pittman stared at him. "Are you sure about all that?"

Dave settled back and sipped his beer, a contented smile on his face. "You know, I have to tell you, I think I am."

Pittman looked over the townhouse once more. "Alright then. I guess I'll let you get back to your nervous breakdown. I hope that works out for you. Nice chairs, by the way." He walked to the open front door, but stopped there and turned on his heel. His eyes narrowed on Dave, his lips pressing to a tight line.

Dave took a breath, his expression blank.

The detective walked over to stand before him. He reached inside his suit jacket, his hand holding as his eyes bored into Dave. Then he relented, his face easing as his hand came free to hand Dave a green envelope. "Enjoy your day," he said, and with a nod, left.

Dave tipped his head, looking out his window and waiting until the car pulled away. Only then did he put his beer down and look at the envelope. It was a standard sized mailing envelope, yet it was quite thick. Curiosity nagged him, but he understood when he opened the envelope and pulled out the bundled papers within.

They opened to reveal a map of Montana. His eyes rested on one spot where a red circle was marked. Only then did it occur to him Pixie had left without telling him where to find her.

He looked out his window and grinned. Order beside order.

***

He knew what he had to do, but it took a week to work up his nerve. "You're sure this will work?"

I'm sure. We're like similar poles of a magnet, now.

"Okay." Dave picked up Gray, closed his eyes, and slid Gray into his nostril. His eyes watered, his ears popped, but his nose didn't bleed. Gray was nestled in his sinus, but went no further. Dave drank a glass of water. "Are you good in there?"

I'm good. Onward, my captain!

***

Dave drove north, but he wasn't careless. He dismantled his cell phone and discarded the parts at various rest stops. He kept a wad of cash in the rugged backpack he'd bought, and paid for his gas with good old hard currency, the easiest way to pay without trace among the tentacles of an electronic economy. He left the coast behind him and turned east, his eyes widening at the majestic, snow clad heights of the Rocky Mountains and the beauty of the serpentine highways meandering over the terrain. It was an exotic, consuming experience, the endless ranges of untamed forests and mountains defying any passing comprehension of the world outside society's order. Without any restrictions, due dates, or worries, and his only pressure the anticipation of holding Pixie once more, he took his time, spending nights at numerous inns and lodges to give his mind a better opportunity to absorb this new reality. He continued to live off his cash, careful to be sure he didn't leave any obvious traces of his movements. Soon enough, though, he was rolling down the eastern approaches of the Rockies, and in the distance, he knew the terrain would eventually flatten to the wide plains of the Midwest. But that was farther than he aimed to go, farther than the vacuous depths of his intended Montana, with its average population density of six people per square mile.

Six people! No wonder her commune is out here.

114

He abandoned his car one night at a junkyard, leaving the prestige of its imported sport tuned suspension and smooth flowing horsepower. With the license plates hidden under the driver's seat, he hoped the car would be crushed like all the other vehicles and given over for recycling. It was of little concern, at that point. He already decided to walk the rest of the way.

When he came to the spot marked on the map, he found himself standing on the side of a two-lane road by a mile marker. There was no crossroad, no sign, nothing but rolling green fields that ran into some distant woods, the mountains behind him, and the endless blue sky over him.

He shrugged, sat on the side of the road, and waited.

When evening fell he pitched his tent a good pace away from the road. He lay in the little synthetic dome but, when sleep failed to come, he sat outside, bundled in his sleeping bag against the cold, and watched the sky. With no lights, no distractions, it seemed the stars were close enough to touch, even though the heavens seemed vast and impenetrable around him. He remembered what Pixie had told him, that the sky was so huge it didn't make one feel small, but rather imparted a sense of belonging.

He thought of Gray, nestled in the darkness of his sinus.

"Do you want to see this?"

I see it the way you do. We've been such fools.

***

The clop of a hoof woke him. He opened his eyes. "Pixie!"

She pushed back her wide-brimmed riding hat, hopped down from her saddle, and patted her horse on the neck. She was about to speak, but Dave took her in a tight embrace before cupping her face in his hands. His heart bucked in his chest. He wanted to say it, say it so bad words failed him, so he embraced her once more, and held her beneath that endless blue sky.

She rubbed his shoulders and eased her head back to look in his eyes. "I was starting to worry. I thought something went wrong."

He shook his head. "I had to make sure. I wasn't sure until that detective came, and then I knew. Very slick, by the way."

She shrugged. "I told you. We have our own order."

"So where's the commune?"

She hooked a thumb over her shoulder. "Past those trees." She opened her hands, clad in brown riding gloves, to the land about them. "We own all of this, all this land, but we don't like to advertise it. Goes against the grain of what we're shooting for." She gestured with her eyes

115

to the fields. "So, ready to ride?"

He looked at her horse. It was an attractive buff color, with a black mane and tail. He'd never stood close to a horse, and he found it somewhat of a thrill to have all that grace and strength so near. Pixie took his hand and rested it on the horse's neck, the creature's head bobbing at the touch of his hand. He gazed into the large, dark eyes before turning to Pixie. "Is it yours?"

"Ours," she corrected, tipping her chin toward the commune. "She's the one I like to ride. Her name is Cinnamon."

He stood there, silent as his thoughts gained momentum. "Can I have a horse?"

She grinned. "I don't know, city-boy. Can you ride?"

"I'll be fine." He stepped back. "I'll wait here."

Her eyes narrowed, but then she nodded and gained her saddle. She gave him a wink, and then she was off, standing in her stirrups, her hat bouncing across her shoulders, as Cinnamon sped off toward the distant woods.

He packed up his tent and sleeping bag while he waited but, before long, Pixie came back, going at a trot as she held the reins for another horse, this one a rich, chocolate brown in color. She crossed the road and came to a stop beside him.

"Dave, meet Cocoa. He's a good, sturdy mount."

Dave nodded as he stood and looked the horse in the eye. "There's something I have to tell you, Pix."

She crossed her hands on the pommel of her saddle. "It's Gray, isn't it?" She hesitated, a frown pulling at her lips. "Look, Dave, you can't bring him to the commune. They'll study him. Pick him apart. They won't understand what the three of us went through."

"They won't have to." He stepped back and cupped his hands over his nose. Gray had been so quiet that Dave worried for his little friend. But when Dave started to blow through his nostril, he could feel the pressure behind his eye, and after two good toots of his nose, he felt Gray slither down from his sinus cavity and into his hand. Hiding Gray in his palm, he patted Cocoa's neck before opening his hand by one of the wide, round nostrils. Pixie's lips parted, but faster than she could speak Gray disappeared into Cocoa's nostril. The animal bucked, shaking its head several times. It pranced about them in a close circle, pausing a few times to stomp each hoof in turn. When that was done it stopped short, shook its head once more, and turned to Dave.

Pixie stared at him, stunned. "What did you do?"

Dave smiled. "Oil for hay, remember? This was his dream." He looked to Cocoa and extended an open hand to the field. "What are you waiting for?"

Dave, if I stay in here, I'll forget everything.

"Would that be so bad?"

You have no idea how good this feels.

"To get what you want?" he wondered, glancing at Pixie. "Is it everything you imagined?"

Everything, and more. Oh, hey, you know what? Cinnamon has nice legs.

Dave chuckled as he rested his forehead against Cocoa's neck. "This is why I couldn't leave you behind. For all our differences, we're not that different. Remember, at a certain point, the only rational choice is an irrational existence." He stepped back and patted Cocoa's shoulder. "Embrace it."

Cocoa bowed his head and stomped a hoof. He held, but then took off, charging across the field at a full gallop. He made several passes before calming and trotting back to them, his head held high as he shook his mane. He stopped before Dave, and with some effort Dave managed to gain the saddle. He took the reins and looked to Pixie. "See, I'll ride just fine. I'll even remember to slouch in the saddle if we go too fast, so I don't get a ticket."

She shook her head. "You have it all figured out, don't you?"

He gave her a crooked grin. "We're just two guys trying to live around the rules."

Pixie wrapped her hand in the reins. The empty pinky of her glove bent flat against her knuckle. Her face fell, but then her lips curled in a mischievous grin of her own. She lifted her chin high and winked at Dave, but then took off without warning, laughing over her shoulder.

Dave patted Cocoa's neck and leaned forward in his saddle. "Okay buddy, this is the moment," he whispered in Cocoa's ear. "Put the pedal to the metal!"

Gray bolted beneath him. They gained on Pixie and Cinnamon, and soon Dave's senses were filled with the thudding of hooves, the wind on his face, and the sun in the clear sky. He knew Montana was well above sea level, but as they raced across the rolling green fields, he found himself contemplating elevation in a rather different way. He was floating, floating high above the life he knew, riding on a wild brown horse he would know as Gray.

Madness, amputation, dismemberment; Montana, absolution, disconnection. They were diametric links, opposites tied in a yin-yang push-pull reflection, yet at the same time, in a strange way, they were also interchangeable and indistinguishable labels, meandering beneath those black and white absolutes. Dave perceived them in full and, with them, the character of their inevitable and inseparable union—an amorphous color known as *gray.*

Pixie gave him a glance, her wide smile beckoning.

117

Gray picked up speed.
Serenity flowed through Dave's veins as he neared the woods.
The trees, and their many shadows, waited.

ELMER PHELPS

I'm not what I would consider a 'bad' man. If you would only understand my predilections, I think you would see that I have a sense of morality. It's just that given my predilections—my needs—my moral perspective is perhaps somewhat different from what you would call the 'norm'. I have to feed and, until you overcome your revulsion for that basic reality, you won't understand me.

***

Common wisdom states the obvious truth that there is only one first impression, yet there is a subliminal truth of subtle wisdom that first impressions tinge all things that follow. An early memory, a dramatic moment, an indelible impression, such a thing can imprint itself on the subconscious lens of perception within one's mind, haunting every whispered thought and inclination, lurking in every shadowy corner of dreams and nightmares, hovering over the daytime world as an unseen, and barely perceived, shadow. And even though that memory may have conscious form, the roots of its complexity can delve the deepest parts of awareness to the subconscious core of the mind, mingling with the firmament of self-perception until the two are inseparable, linked in an inescapable cycle of cause and effect.

Elmer's first vivid memory was such a thing, a thing of black leathery wings spreading across his sight in the humid darkness of a summer camp. He woke to the double sting of bat fangs sinking into the back of his neck as he slept on his cot, gleaming yellow eyes peering down at him as pain lanced his body. His senses at once filled with the screams of other children and, as he rolled over, the bat that had assaulted him fluttered over his face before he swatted the thing in terror. His hands seemed to multiply over him, only for him to realize his sister had jumped from her cot to defend him. The bat swooped away, joining its fellows in a chorus of shrieks to escape the camp house through the open skylights. Elmer sank under his sheets, clutching one hand over the bite on his neck and the blood seeping from the wound, his eyes wide with fear.

His sister, one of the house counselors, stood by his bunk, waving a white sheet to get everyone's attention and calm the shouts and cries of frightened children. But when Casey turned, Elmer trembled, for he saw a wound on her neck similar to what he had suffered.

Five were bitten, but only Elmer and Casey had wounds that seeped blood. Over the next few days it was clear by the swelling, the odd coloration, and the short fever they both endured that their wounds were different from the others. There was some concern, and the camp supervisors called Elmer's parents, but no sooner had the symptoms seemed to climax than they subsided, and with stunning speed the wounds withered away, leaving a pair of tiny pale dots where the fangs had punctured skin.

Casey took it in stride. Their parents held the opinion she was of stronger stuff than Elmer, what with his shyness and reclusive nature. Elmer was only ten, but he was inclined to agree. In the end, it was of little importance. He was never able to put his finger on the exact nature of it, but in the months and years that followed, he knew one thing for sure.

Somehow, in some way, he was not the person he was before the bite. Neither, for that matter, was Casey.

***

Casey was five years his elder but, in many ways, she seemed much older. Those years after the incident at camp were marked not only by her transformation to a young woman, but to a thrill seeker as well. Her grades at school soared, even though she never mixed too much with the scholastic crowd. Elmer had no idea who she ran with at night, but he knew well enough her growing habit of sneaking out after dark. Clever in her boldness, she remained a step ahead of everyone around her, so she was never caught, she was never punished, and the corner of her mouth rose in a crooked grin at the vague utterance that followed her in school: *Cassandra Phelps is trouble.* And though she never told Elmer the secrets of what she did on those late nights, she held him in trust. They were siblings, and she would often say they had no one else but each other as allies.

She was always quick to defend Elmer, as he was often bullied for his quiet, reclusive way, and ridiculed for the size of his long nose. Growing up in a small town was a savior in that there was only one school, with all grades in attendance, so she was there for him. On the other hand, growing up in a small town was a curse, as there was no escape into the senile mass of a larger population. The same buffoons that bullied him in his childhood kept it up straight through his teen years. He had no friends. He wasn't smart enough to be in with the brainy kids, he wasn't interested in sports, he wasn't tough, he wasn't artistic, he wasn't stylish, he wasn't witty; he was just pale, shy Elmer. He hated homework, so his lagging grades went nowhere. His only interest lay in the solitude of his walk home and the cramped basement of his parent's house, where he would hole up in comfortable seclusion, stretch out on a couch beneath a blanket, and doze before dinner while watching various nature documentaries. When he turned thirteen Casey was out of school, and that only made things worse. The few friends she knew had some younger siblings, but in Casey's absence they were unwilling to rise to Elmer's defense.

Not that he asked for such sacrifice, or looked in vain for such aid. Deep down, he knew he was on his own. Deep down, he knew he wasn't like anyone else in that school. As the other children bloomed into their teens with the endless vigor of youth, he seemed to wither as the years went on, his pudgy body lengthening but gaining little weight, leaving him a pallid, lanky sliver of milky skin, so unlike Casey and her boundless vivacity. His parents took him to the few doctors in town out of concern for his health, but those 'professionals' only suggested he take more vitamins, and refused to consider anything of greater consequence. Small town; small minds. He took so many vitamins his urine turned fluorescent yellow, and then pale green. He forgot to flush the toilet one time when Casey was home visiting, and she suggested with a laugh that he work for the highway department pissing glow-in-the-dark road lines.

In the years after Casey graduated her visits were always a welcome and wary surprise. Welcome, as he knew they shared a kinship on some level perhaps neither of them completely understood; and wary, as she seemed to be drifting into ever more questionable pursuits in life. She'd gone off to college near the city, and Elmer often wondered if it was the image of the city's bright lights reflecting on the vast body of a great northern lake—just as the college's brochure depicted—that had somehow seduced her but, whatever the cause or the path, there was a growing flippancy in her ghostly gray gaze that both unnerved and thrilled him. She, too, suggested he join a sport to get some sun and strength, but failed to restrain her laughter at the silliness of the thought. It wasn't as condescending as it may have seemed because, with her, he had the ability to laugh at himself, and at the oddity he'd become.

One day, near the end of his senior year, he walked home on a chilly wet day to find Casey's duffel bag dumped in the foyer. He tossed his coat on the couch and dodged through the tight little confines of the house to find her sitting at the kitchen table. She met him with a wide smile and, after they embraced, she opened the refrigerator and popped open two bottles of beer. When he hesitated, worried their father would be upset if he caught Elmer drinking in the afternoons again, Casey waved off his concern and tapped her bottle to his in toast. "Drink up, milk-boy," she said with a tip of her head, and waited until he took his first sip.

He lowered his bottle from his lips. "What's up? Do Mom and Dad—"

Casey slapped a hand on the table, her bottle resting against her lips. She motioned with her eyes to his bottle, waiting until he took it in hand

121

before raising her fist and counting off her fingers: one, two, three, bottoms up! They chugged away until their bottles were empty, Casey slamming her bottle on the table a moment before Elmer. They laughed together as they exchanged a series of raucous burps. Casey reached up to pull her hair back and secure it in a ponytail, letting its brown length hang over her shoulder. "So how's life, Elmer?"

He shrugged. "The same, I guess."

She frowned as she nodded. "Still sucks, huh? I figured as much." She reached behind her to open the refrigerator, tipping her seat back so that she could reach for two more beers. She put them on the table and, to Elmer's surprise, she popped off the caps with her bare fingers. He blinked, his gaze darting to her smiling eyes. "Elmer, I'm going away."

He blinked again. "What, back to graduate school?"

"Screw that. Better. I've been recruited by an enforcement organization."

He coughed. "You're going to work for the FBI?"

She took a breath, studying him as she held her smile, her gray eyes boring into him, the fingers of one hand running through her pony tail. "Sort of," she said at last. "I can't tell you about it. Mom and Dad, either. Rules. I'm going to tell them I'm giving up on organic chemistry to join the field sciences division of a classified enforcement agency. It won't be that big of a lie, actually." She put an elbow on the table and leaned toward him. "I'll get to carry a gun. I'm very excited; it's very exciting."

He rubbed his forehead. "Don't agencies have rules, or something? I mean, you've got two drunk driving charges, there were the fights, and there was that time with the knife—"

She shook her head. "Not important. You'll have to trust me on this, Elmer." She let her gaze bore into him until he squirmed in his seat. "Elmer, you do trust me, don't you?"

He slouched and cleared his throat before nodding.

She mirrored his gesture before snapping her fingers. "Good, that's good." She leaned over in her chair to reach into the refrigerator and take out a plate covered in foil. She put it on the table between them and pulled off the foil to reveal a slab of uncooked cow's liver. The smell met their noses at once, and Elmer swayed in his seat. His mouth filled with saliva. Despite himself, his gaze was drawn, locked, onto that raw pile of organ tissue. It disgusted him, repulsed him in the same way the strip club by the train station and the seedy, seductive secrets within its walls repulsed him, even as the club drew his stare whenever he passed: the more he tried to refute his interest, the more it devoured his imagination.

Temptation.

He had no idea how far forward he was leaning until Casey put her forehead against his to stop his slow nose-dive into the plate. "Are you listening to me?" she whispered.

"I'm listening. Can I have a piece?" he heard himself say.

"That's it. You don't know why, but you want it, don't you?"

He squeezed his eyes shut. Growing up, with his father's meager income from a plumbing factory and his mom's irregular pay as a substitute at school, they had survived on simple dinners. Chicken would come across their table, sometimes pork, but when money permitted his mother would buy some steak from the butcher in town and get it fresh, bringing it home wrapped just then to put it in the refrigerator. Elmer was always convinced he could smell it right through the refrigerator's metal casing, and it would make him restless for a sight of it, a smell of it, maybe, maybe, just a taste, a little taste of it uncooked, still red raw and juicy with the last remnants of diluted blood in the grain of the meat. But he would always get in trouble, because somehow his mother would go for the meat and find a small piece missing, and blame him, even though he never had the nerve to touch the uncooked flesh.

The room spun about him as the memories flashed through him. The trouble stopped after Casey moved out. The conclusion was, at last, inescapable.

Casey had stolen the meat. Why'd she do that?

She snapped her fingers. "You still with me?"

Against all his will, he felt his head bob in an anxious nod.

"Listen to me, listen to every word," Casey continued in a hiss, her eyes meeting his as his lids popped open. "Once a week, you need to eat something raw. I don't care what it is, what it comes from, but you have to eat something raw. Do you understand?"

"Why—"

"Once a week," she interrupted, ignoring him, even as he trembled. "Do that, obey that, and you'll never be sick again, never be tired again. You can be strong, like me, okay? You'd like that, wouldn't you? And the last week you're in school, when one of those jock jerk-offs makes some comment, prove it to yourself by kicking the living shit out of him, you hear me?"

He shook his head and closed his eyes. "What? No! I can't, I'm not—"

She took his face in her hands and forced him to meet her gaze. "Trust me, Elmer. I'm helping you in the best way I know. You have to do this, for your own good. Promise?"

He hesitated, but, in the end, the delirious fantasy of being able to stand up for himself was overwhelming, and he nodded, accepting the solemn oath.

She smiled, brushing the tears from his eyes with her thumbs. She looked at him then, her gaze full of warmth, before she leaned forward to kiss him on the cheek. She held there for a moment, the warmth of her lips on his skin, before she slid away to resume her seat. He rocked forward a bit, flowing into her wake, before his eyes popped open to find her waiting gaze. Her smile returned and, with it, she stood from the table. "Tell Mom and Dad I love them," she said, and backing away from the kitchen, grabbed her bag and went out the door.

He looked at the liver. He devoured it without a second thought.

***

She called later that evening and told whatever lies she planned to tell. Elmer's mother seemed a little disappointed, as she always thought highly of Casey's intellect, and little of her discipline. Elmer's father took it in stride. The old man had been ingrained with a reflexive respect for any organization with an authoritative hierarchy from his time in the army, and the sound of an 'enforcement agency', no matter how vague, sounded officious enough for him. Before the call ended Casey asked to speak to Elmer, and he took the phone and secluded himself upstairs in his bedroom.

"You alone?" her disembodied voice spoke in his ear. It reminded him of when they were little, when they put cups to the wall between their rooms and whispered into each other's ears. Nights were lonely. It had been nice to know she was there with him, in what he came to call the big black empty.

His eyes darted to his closed door. "I'm in my room."

"Good. How was the snack?"

He sat on his bed and pinched the bridge of his nose. "I, I ate all of it."

"Great. Now, listen carefully. You know Gustafson's, at the end of main street?"

"Yeah, the butcher Mom goes to. What about him?"

"I opened an account with him and made an arrangement. Every Friday after school, you stop by and ask for the Cassandra order. Don't say anything to Mom or Dad. I asked old Gustafson to keep his mouth shut, too. The order is for one beef medallion, fresh. You pick it up, take it out with you, go somewhere, and eat the thing."

His mouth flooded with saliva as he pictured the little slab of meat. "Casey—"

"I'll have it all paid for. You just take the order and go. Got it?"

He dropped his hand in his lap and swallowed. "Sure, I guess so."

"Every week. Don't forget, okay? I'll be back soon. Love you, bro."

"Okay."

The line clicked off. He dropped the phone on the bed next to him. His eyes lingered on it for several moments before his gaze came to rest on the wall that separated their bedrooms. Life, he decided, was a strange thing.

Love you too, sis.

***

In the weeks that followed he kept his word and picked up the order every Friday as he walked home from school. Old Gustafson gave him a curious look from beneath the bushy arches of his blond eyebrows, but Elmer nodded his thanks and took the order. He would sit on a bench in the town square and eat the dense red treat of the medallion, quickly learning how best to chew along the bands of meat to get it down without too much of it getting stuck in his teeth. Though he had his doubts of his sister's instructions in the beginning, as time rolled by he was filled with an odd sense of wonder for her apparent wisdom. The changes were slow, but undeniable. His color improved, so that he looked healthy, rather than the milky cadaver he once resembled. Where his day had been a struggle to keep his eyes open, he came to find his body filled with a new energy and, at night, when he slept, instead of tossing and turning he enjoyed several blissful hours devoid of any dreams. His asthma cleared up, and the colds that had afflicted him on a constant basis at last abated.

He was, for all intensive purposes, healthy, something he hadn't known since that summer at camp.

It was such a turn-around his mother was prompted to take him to the doctor, worried that the change, though positive, might be a respite before some proverbial storm. He was examined from head to toe, and to the doctor's consternation—but obvious relief and satisfaction—it was confirmed that Elmer was in fact a normal specimen. When his mother asked the inevitable questions of how and why, the doctor only shrugged. "Teenagers," came his simple explanation. "Short of making a cocoon a teenager is the most mysterious form of life we know of. Strange creatures, indeed."

Elmer blushed, feeling quite foolish as he sat on the exam cot between the doctor and his mother.

Everything seemed to be going well, until the last part of his sister's prophecy came to fulfillment. The harassment Elmer had suffered for so long eased as his condition improved, but it didn't end. To his best guess it had less to do with his improvement than with his suspicion that some of the people who annoyed him overlooked him, the change having altered him enough that they often missed him in the hallway crowds between classes, when it always felt like open season for abuse. All that changed one afternoon, when he went to put his books in his locker before grabbing his jacket for his walk home. It was a Friday, and his mind was filled with anticipation for Gustafson's beef medallion and, after, a cozy afternoon with a documentary about hyenas. Such preoccupation, without a doubt, led to him bumping into one of his tormentors. The response was a shove, something he'd learned to take in stride, so he lowered his head and moved along, in the hope nothing more would follow.

To his disappointment three boys followed him down the hall and out the back door, where the seniors parked their cars. With his head down and his hood up, he never saw it coming until it was too late. The boy he'd bumped into darted around a car, came up on Elmer's side, and threw a punch right into Elmer's jaw.

He staggered and flopped against the side of a car, his hand rising to cradle his jaw. A pair of hands seized him at once and spun him around to slam him against the car. He blinked, and a second punch came, this one straight into his chest. He coughed, but a new realization came to him, something that bewildered him: the punches didn't hurt. He felt their impact, and the surprise of being ambushed, but his senses were intact, and his mind remained sharp, rather than being fogged with pain and the fear it inspired.

He looked the bully in the eye.

He remembered what Casey told him.

His heart pounded in his chest. He had no idea, or care, how or why he came to possess his sudden resilience, but the frustration and anger of being bullied for so many years erupted in his chest like a volcano. He swung his fists and, inept as he was at fighting, the savagery of his attack drove the bully back in surprise. He took several blows, but he continued on, relentless, wild, and when one of his punches split the boy's lip and drew blood, Elmer's eyes bulged in his head as he bared his teeth. That's when several students intervened, piling on Elmer to pull him away as he screamed every obscenity under the sun in red-faced rage. It did little to improve his standing, but the crowd managed to shove him away, and the bully disappeared into the ring of his friends, who were anxious to say the fight wasn't worth it, and they should just let Elmer go. In a heartbeat he went from a victim to get abused to a psycho-weirdo to get shunned. He backed off, shouting curses all the way, until he became aware of himself, embarrassed of himself, and turned to run.

He didn't stop until he made it to Gustafson's.

***

Despite taking several shots to the face, he didn't bruise, he didn't swell, and he didn't bleed. There was some fuss over the matter, but with no serious injuries to show for it, there seemed little incentive to take stock in student accounts of the fight. Aside from the split lip Elmer inflicted, the incident was dismissed as more drama than anything else. His parents weren't happy, and his mother in particular gave him a long talk during dinner around their little kitchen table, to which his father gave a stern nod here and there. In one way, Elmer knew his mother was right, and that he needed to consider what he was doing with his life, as his future seemed aimless. On the other hand, her criticisms washed over him with as little purchase as an autumn breeze, as he knew she had no comprehension about the ways he'd changed.

To be honest, he had little comprehension himself, but he knew it, knew it so deep in his subconscious there was no escaping his new reality.

He hoped Casey would call so he could tell her about it, but for all his restless anticipation, the phone didn't ring for him. He stared at his ceiling in the lonesome night, his mother's words echoing in his head. Graduation was coming. He had no plans for college—not that his grades could take him too far. He had no interest in trade schools. He had no experience working at all, after all the years of being sick and weak. When he looked in the future, something familiar stared back at him. It was the big black empty of his childhood loneliness, only in a more subtle, more consuming, embodiment.

He draped a hand over his chest. His heart thumped away, mindless of its purpose, stupid machine of flesh that it was. He thought of that volcanic outburst the fight had summoned, and how good it felt. Lying there in bed, he wondered where it came from, and where it went, as he only felt a deep lassitude in the cold seep of blood sloshing through his veins.

He let his breath go. Tomorrow would be another day, another tired repeat of his existence.

He turned his head to the wall. There was no whisper to soothe him.

***

Fortune, it seemed, had its own plans for Elmer.

The day before he graduated the phone rang after dinner. He fought not to dive for the receiver in the hope it would be Casey but, when he picked it up, he was greeted by the last voice he would've expected: Big Paul, his father's brother. Elmer's uncle was not in fact a large man, but he had a sense for the world, and his travels in the merchant marine had earned him his nickname. They wouldn't hear from him for months at a time, but then he would visit for a few days before setting off for another post. He lived in the next town over, and kept a house there, a comfortable ranch-style log house on a large tract of forested land in the

Proskoy Wood. He called with an offer for Elmer, as the old woman who managed the house's care had recently passed away, and Paul was wondering if Elmer was interested. Paul offered to pay him, just to live in the house, keep an eye on things, and maintain the property. Paul would even let him use the pickup truck stowed in the garage.

Elmer hesitated, but he knew so little about caring for himself he failed to understand the greater wisdom of his hesitation. All he saw was a way out of town, out of the house, and away from the locals who were staying on after graduation. He would have money, so he could make an arrangement with the butcher in town to maintain his vital supply of meat, and keep his little secret.

His parents liked the idea, as they felt it would compel him to be productive. It wasn't that they neglected their efforts to motivate him, but he expressed little interest, had no hobbies, hid behind his impassive expression, showed little sense of direction, and said even less. His father's theory was that once Elmer had to earn his keep in the world, necessity would make a man out of him. In her own way, Elmer's mother agreed, though she voiced the idea with a more refined choice of words: he was a late developer. Despite their difference in expression, the end result was the same. No sooner did Elmer graduate and say good riddance to school than he packed some clothes and let his father drive him out to Paul's house.

He took his driver's test, and got his license. He was mobile.

He set up an account at the local bank, so he could receive transfers from Paul's account for his stipend. He was funded.

He drove to Gustafson's and canceled the Cassandra account, only to open it at the butcher shop by Paul's house, which happened to be owned by Gustafson as well. So he reinstated the account, and paid for a month's worth ahead of time. He was fed.

A month after graduating, he was set. He sat in Paul's house on a Friday night with his raw beef medallion and watched a documentary about wild dogs in South American slums.

He couldn't have asked for more, he thought.

And that's when the loneliness came back to him. He ate his meat, and wondered where Casey was, and what she was doing. He looked away from the television to the window. Far removed from the road, and all alone in the depths of Proskoy Wood, he never thought to pull the curtains on the long picture window that looked out from the living room to the side of the property. It was cloudy, a night without stars, so the window was an even pane, a dark pool of oil that held his translucent reflection. He looked through that image of himself, sitting, with the medallion in one hand and a bottle of beer in the other hand, into the big black empty beyond.

As shadows have their way, this darkness too began to whisper to him, and so he listened, curious as to what he might hear.

He put the bottle down and cupped his hand to his ear, the meat sitting on his tongue as his jaw went still. He heard Casey's voice, and his lips parted.

He sat for several moments, struck by the emptiness of the house, until his face fell into a forlorn frown. He wondered if she was with someone. Soon after, he wondered what she might be doing with that someone in the dark seclusion of night. And soon after that, perhaps for the very existence of the half-hearted denials in his head, he felt an unsettling suspicion that his attachment to his sister had become something more than it should.

***

The town of Proskoy could be called charming, were it not for its isolation. In generations gone by the town was founded as a way point between the now defunct railroad line that ran through town and the old lumber mills outside town, all of which were closed when vast tracts of Proskoy Wood were taken as a government forestry preserve. Without the rail and without the lumbering jobs, the town slumped into desperation. The only remaining occupations were an empty delirium with the highway department or sitting on a front step waiting for an unemployment check. The young left, the old died, and the middle-aged lingered in the town's senile existence.

That changed when some developers from the distant cities decided to buy up large tracts of the remaining land and sell them as nature retreats for wealthy clients. Taxes went up, developers invested in some of the local businesses, and even though the property owners rarely visited their wooded retreats, they employed the remaining locals to maintain their properties. Proskoy didn't flourish, but found a way to survive, and even though life was simple, and slow, life had nevertheless returned to the dying remnants of Proskoy's downtown.

Elmer came to know the place as summer waned to the varicolored foliage of autumn, and the cooling breeze brought the first whispers of the coming northern snow. Big Paul left detailed instructions as to what Elmer's responsibilities entailed and, despite the commonly held opinion that there was nothing but a lot of empty space between Elmer's ears, he took to his duties with care and made a point to double and triple check everything Paul left for him. After all, if he blew it, he knew the only option was a humiliating trip back to his old bedroom and the small basement to watch his nature documentaries. He had tasted life on his own. It didn't matter to him that he ruined some of his clothes learning to do laundry, or that he realized he had no idea how to cook other than setting a timer on a microwave, but it was important to him that he could move about in a town where nobody knew him and he could leave the embarrassment of his youth behind him. It was a fresh start, a rare opportunity to forge a new first impression between himself and the world around him. It helped that his uncle was known and respected by some of the locals, and Paul had given word that Elmer would be watching the property, so when he introduced himself at the various stores he wasn't met by blank, empty gazes.

In his own shy way, he would offer his hand and bob his head. "I'm Elmer Phelps."

And so, he came into his own.

It comforted him to discover that the few people he had to deal with didn't seem too different than him. Paul's lawn tractor broke down one day, so Elmer loaded it into the pickup bed and brought it to Wilson's garage. Old man Wilson seemed covered in a layer of grime that was as old as Elmer, and he had a small facial tick that caused his left eye to wink repeatedly when he was deep in thought. But he knew his engines—that much became readily evident—fascinating Elmer who stood in silence watching Wilson work on the tractor. The old man started talking, explaining the engine to Elmer. Elmer came by when he could, learning from the old man, and giving him a hand in exchange. Elmer didn't ask for money, but then Wilson didn't offer it, either. They had an understanding, and it was an understanding Elmer found himself forging with other people in town. He sucked up the leaves around Gustafson's butcher shop, so Gustafson gave him an extra steak on Elmer's Friday pickup. He cleaned up the field behind Parson's Diner, so Parson gave him a cup of fresh coffee whenever he decided to go in for a meal.

In his typical way, Elmer felt uncomfortable sitting in the diner, as he sat by himself at the counter, and lacked the confidence to join the conversations of the locals, even though he came to know them at least by name as the weeks went by. But one dreary, rainy day in the middle of September he sat down for his cup of coffee and found himself hooked by a discovery that charmed him from first sight. She greeted him with a smile as she turned from the coffee machine to find Elmer sitting at the counter.

"Oh, hi, there. Can I get you something?"

Elmer studied her. She had straight brown hair, parted on the side, and pulled back in a ponytail. Except for her green eyes she reminded him of Casey, and that was just fine. "Coffee, black."

She nodded and came back to him with a steaming mug of fresh brew. "I'm Samantha."

He breathed in the rich aroma of the steaming coffee. Somehow, the allure of the ground beans, the vapors rising from a hot mug, always outshone the actual taste of the coffee. For a fleeting moment he was puzzled by the sudden emergence of that thought. He blinked and cleared his throat. "Oh, uh, I'm Elmer."

She pointed at him as her eyes went wide. "That's right. You're up at the Phelps place, right in the Proskoy Wood." She hooked a thumb over her shoulder. "Poppa Parson told me about you when I came in this morning. Sort of my first day, I guess."

"Sort of?" He scratched his jaw. "How'd you get more than one?"

She grinned. "Well, you see, I worked, then I quit, then I worked again, then I quit again, kind of going around my college semesters. But I think I've called it quits on the college thing. I don't know. Just doesn't seem right for me." She paused before giving a shrug. "I like it here, anyway. Nice and quiet. Nice people. I like the small town feel, you know?"

"I guess," he said under his breath. He stared at her, his knees trembling to vent his desperation for something to say to keep her before him. "I, I grew up in the next town over, in Fairmont. Small town feel is all I know. It's got some ups and downs."

She leaned on the counter with one hand, her other hand coming to rest on her hip. "I guess every place is like that, right? Me, I grew up in the city, and I thought the same thing, that it's got some ups and downs."

He swallowed over his nervousness, possessed by the acute awareness that aside from his sister, he never had a social conversation with a woman of similar age as he. Only the surreal disbelief of the moment kept him from collapsing into himself and skulking off to the pathetic safety of his reclusive instincts. "I, I've never been to a city. My sister goes to college by the city, on the lake. There's a picture from the brochure, with the lights reflected on the water at night. It, it looks, nice."

Her grin returned. "Hey, everything has its own appeal, right?"

He fidgeted with his mug, his gaze darting about. "So, ah, where'd you grow up?"

Her grin faded to a little frown that fled with a blink of her eyes. "City's a city."

"A town's a town," he echoed.

She tipped her head before nodding in agreement. A sigh escaped her as she stared out the window at the rain. "So how is it up at Phelps' place?"

He sipped his coffee as he considered what to say. "Quiet. Peaceful."

"You know I used to house-sit one of the estates here between semesters. That's how I came across the town. It was nice being alone in a house, but it was a little lonely, too." Her gaze rolled over the locals

131

before returning to him. "Say, you ever get lonely out there?"

He was thankful he was sitting, as his knees turned to jelly. He shifted with a start on his stool, his gaze falling to his mug at the inescapable observation looming between them: aside from the two of them, everybody in town was old enough to be their parents. His heart froze in his chest as he realized what she might be suggesting. He licked his lips and cleared his throat once more. "I, uh, get by, I guess. Things move slow, so I don't feel too lonely," he added, humiliated by the jittery tremor in his voice. "Besides, I have a lot of chores to keep me busy."

"Well, they say nothing good comes from idle hands, right?" she said, turning when Parson called her from inside the kitchen. She looked back to Elmer. "Speaking of which, I guess I have to serve some people." She smiled and stuck her hand out. "Nice to meet you, Elmer. I guess I'll be seeing you around."

He held a small cough before shaking her hand, his stomach dropping as he hoped his palm was not sweaty from nerves. To his relief, she gave his hand a good shake, and there was no twinge of disgust to mar the pleasant smile she held for him. He looked down as she walked off, but he couldn't resist stealing a final glance of her back as she moved down the length of the counter.

He looked to his coffee. He decided he should make regular visits to the diner.

***

He tried hard not to let Samantha fill all his waking thoughts, as he worried he might betray the affliction of his infatuation, and frighten her. His dreams were another matter, being that he had no control over them. The only way to temper the single-minded pursuit of his imagination was to make half-hearted attempts to discredit her. Though he had his doubts—and certainly a grain of disbelief—regarding what he still suspected as her thinly veiled overture that first time he talked to her, he couldn't help but find the little lurking beast of his male ego dwelling upon those simple words that fell from her lips. He sat on the lawn tractor and tried to convince himself that if she made such an overture from their first meeting she had to be of questionable moral character, and the inner voice of his mother's recriminations and his father's propriety fell hard on his senses. Then again, while he was chopping wood, he decided if she was somewhat loose, and perhaps a little aggressive, it could make his life much easier, given the monastic nature of his life, and his complete ignorance in the ways between men and women.

At night he would stare at the ceiling as he lay in the guest room.

There was a ceiling fan over his bed, and he came to hate the thing, even as it made its lazy revolutions to push the air down from the ceiling to warm him. Round and round it went and, the longer he stared at it, so too his thoughts turned round and round, until he sometimes was left with no choice but to stalk about the house and down several beers. The alcohol would still the pounding of his anxious heart and let him plummet to the senile comfort of a dreamless sleep. By the time Halloween rolled around he took the fan down and left it in the garage. In the deep night, there was only a black hole above him. He couldn't see it in the darkness, but he knew it was there. It haunted him, much the way the big black empty haunted him when he would roll over and close his eyes.

He went to Parson's for dinner Halloween night hoping to see Samantha. She was dressed for the holiday, wearing a black leotard under her apron, a beret with pointy black cat ears in her hair, and a black choker that seemed to dance in his gaze as she spoke to him. She gave him her smile, and appeared happy to see him. He talked to her, even as his knees quaked under the counter. At one point, he even made her laugh, though he failed to remember what it was he said the moment he left the diner. It was an evening of pleasant agony.

When he lay down that night to sleep, he looked to his side, in the direction of his old bedroom wall. He closed his eyes, wishing he had a cup to put to the wall, so he could talk to Casey, and she could help him. But as he slipped from consciousness, the image in his head flowed like oil, and Samantha's face went through the subtle yet fluid transformation to assume his sister's countenance. As he stared, her eyes kindled with a yellow light, and her arms snapped out to her sides to unfurl the leathery length of her wings. Her mouth distended, revealing two fangs, and then she launched herself, smothering him in the black veil of her wings. Her fangs slid between his lips to pierce the vital tissues of his body.

He bolted up in bed. Casey's name burst from his lips between panting breaths.

He looked about the room.

He was, of course, alone.

***

Thanksgiving came, and he thought of calling his parents. Following his relocation to Proskoy there were only two occasions when he spoke with them; once when he needed a ride to get his driver's license, and the second time just to say hello. If it bothered him to ask a favor, it pained him to make that second call. Asking the favor reminded him of his infantile ways; the stark moments of empty silence during that second call only served to confirm in his head there was a gulf, a sense of alienation, between he and his parents that defied explanation. They were a certain kind of people, hard-working, regimented in the regularity of Sunday mass, honest in their simple ways. It was such an appraisal that left him with the distinct sense there was no commonality between them and, in the depths of what he believed was his social ineptitude, he found little reason or need to speak with them. It was not disdain, it was not dislike, it was not disrespect; if anything, he knew he held a certain envy and admiration for the clear delineations about their ordered existence, things he knew he lacked. After all, what did he do? He had no real friends, he had an obsession for a waitress who resembled his sister, he ate raw meat every Friday to maintain his health, and his idea of entertainment was to watch nature documentaries with the sound off so he could study the silent language of posture and poise.

Many creatures share the plains, but they are their own creations.

There was the vast, shadowy expanse of the Proskoy Wood and, at night, the big black empty above the land. This gulf lay between he and his parents, between his new life and his old, and the ground was covered with many layers of wilted brown leaves.

He stared at the phone for quite some time. In the end, he put on his coat and drove to Parson's. Samantha was waiting for him.

***

Parson cooked a wild turkey old man Wilson had shot in the woods, and its impressive bulk managed to feed everyone until they sat listless, burdened with their bellies and a pleasant sedation of rich red wine that Parson had saved for just such an occasion. The dinner was hosted right in the diner; Samantha and Parson had pushed together a few tables, set out a tablecloth, and served one course after another. Besides Elmer, Samantha, Parson and his wife, and Wilson, there were a few others in attendance, including Clay—the town sheriff, who took off his hat and insisted on saying grace—along with Gustafson, who wore a dapper blue suit, and his wife, Ingrid, who spoke with a slight Norwegian accent as she conversed most of the evening with Parson's wife, Camille.

It was a pleasant evening, and it left Elmer with a long lost sense of serenity, that these people who were strangers to him a few months ago accepted him into their little social circle. Samantha sat next to him, and had her hair down, its length swaying across her shoulders as she moved. The pleasant agony he knew so well when she was near was dulled by the wine she insisted on pouring in his glass, until she looked at him and giggled as she laid her hands on the reddening glow of his cheeks. "My, my, look at you! I'll drive you home," she said, leaning toward his ear and, when he felt her breath on his ear, he couldn't suppress the silly smile that bloomed on his lips as the alcohol murmured in his veins. Ingrid and Camille whispered to each other, giving him a good natured ribbing while Samantha went with Parson to clean up the table, insisting that no one help.

It was close to midnight when he staggered to the bathroom before returning to the empty diner. Samantha turned off the lights, fished in his coat pocket for the keys to the pickup, and locked up the diner. The sky was a featureless black dome above them and, though their breaths misted in the cold air, the particular heaviness of the air caused her to tip her head back and sniff several times. He heard her say it was going to snow, but all he could think of was the way he draped his arm over her shoulders to steady himself as they walked. She put her arm around his waist, and was unable to suppress her laughter as his lips rose once more in a broad, silly smile.

The next thing he knew the pickup was parked in the driveway, and the cold air summoned him from his slumber to find her standing by the open door. He blinked several times before sliding out of his seat and walking with her to the house. He fumbled with the keys until he had the door unlocked and, when he pushed it open, he turned to find her standing a step behind him, her hands clasped before her as she gazed up at the sky, humming a little melody to herself.

"Samantha?"

She held still as her gaze turned toward him.

"Do, ah, I mean, it's kind of late to be driving, and. . ." He bit his lip, squeezing his eyes shut as he heard himself droning like some drunken moron. He cleared his throat before looking back to her. "Do you want to come in? There, ah, there's an extra bed," he added, unable to suppress the blush that seared his cheeks.

She stared at him for a moment before the corner of her mouth rose in a crooked grin. "Okay."

He watched as she walked by him, her eyes lingering on his as she passed. He struggled to swallow as his mouth went dry. He closed the door and put the keys in his pocket. He found it hard to believe she was standing there in the living room and, for the first time, perhaps for the very reason that she was there, he took in the room. The house was a log cabin, so the walls were dominated by the massive round lengths of the stacked trunks that provided the structure, except where the long window bank ran along one wall. There was a large fireplace, with a slate surround and a black, cast iron screen. A television was nestled in a cabinet beneath the window bank, with several dark green, deeply cushioned couches forming a large U around the heavy slab of a low, oak table. The floor was oak slat, but a wide Persian rug was stretched out

135

beneath the furniture, so the floor wouldn't feel cold to tired feet. There were two end tables separating the couches at their corners, with a bulbous hooded lamp on each. They were connected to timers, and their low wattage bulbs were just enough to give the room a dim glow.

She glanced at him over her shoulder. "Nice place. Is the rest of the house like this?"

He nodded. "I'll show you, if you want."

She stared at him for a moment, noting the steady droop of his eyelids, before she put her hands in the pockets of her coat. "You know, it's late, and you look like you're ready to pass out."

"I'm okay," he blurted, but clenched his jaw, realizing how over-eager he sounded. He rubbed his forehead, unable to look at her. "This, this was a nice night. I don't want it to end."

She held her gaze on him. "Okay."

"Can, ah, can I get you something?"

"Well, you could take my coat."

"Oh, right," he said and shuffled toward her. He took her coat as she slid it off her arms, but stood for a moment before putting it across the back of the couch, for lack of a better idea. He sloughed off his own coat as he walked by her, only to freeze when she took his hand. He started to tremble, his eyes darting about before they met her gaze.

She studied him until her lips parted. "Elmer, everything's fine," she whispered, laying a hand on his cheek.

He shook his head. "I'm just cold." He closed his eyes, but all he saw was Casey.

She tipped her head. "Relax," she said, the word coming in the slow vent of her breath, yet when her fingers traced across his cheek to touch his lips, he all but convulsed and stepped back from her.

He stamped his foot on the floor in humiliation. "I'm sorry."

"Hey, no problem," she assured him. She tipped her head and offered him a little shrug. "There's something kind of nice about it, actually."

He looked around the room in desperation, for anything to escape from himself. His gaze swept across the table to find the phone, only to catch the slow amber blink of its message light. He walked over, picked up the phone, and keyed the menu to see the number of the last call.

"Elmer?"

His hand sank to his side. "My parents called."

She came up beside him. "Is that a bad thing?"

He looked at her. "I'm really confused."

She frowned, but then put her hands on his shoulders and gave him a kiss on the cheek. She leaned back from him, smiling as she rubbed his shoulders. "I think it's better if I just go. Parson's going to want me at the diner for breakfast duty if it doesn't snow. You can call me there, and I'll bring the truck back to pick you up. Okay?"

He nodded. "I'm sorry, Samantha."

She let out a long breath. "Don't be. Like I said, it's kind of nice, rather than some drunken college-dorm horn-dog pawing at me. You and me, I think we'll be just fine," she said, and, with a final show of her smile, squeezed his hand before taking her coat and leaving him.

He stood, alone in the living room, swaying in his half-stupor of alcohol and broken hopes, sinking into the abyss of his frustrated lust. After some time, he blinked and tossed the phone on the couch before slapping his hands on his head. "You let her go," he said under his breath. "How could you let her go? Loser!"

He shuffled to his bedroom and flopped on his bed. He stared at the ceiling, and the black hole where the fan used to be.

And there he lay, until his eyes drooped shut, and consciousness slipped away.

***

He woke to a dull ache in his head, so he held still, sprawled on his back, and refused to open his eyes. He took a breath and rubbed his face as he heard the baseboards creak with the rising heat. His tongue ran along his teeth as he groaned at the taste in his mouth. As his breath seeped from his lungs his hand slid off his face and his head lolled to the side.

"Hey, bro."

He blinked, the muddy mess of his awareness so slow in waking there was no sense of surprise or confusion. He closed his eyes, waited a moment, and then let them open to be sure. No expression came to him, his emotional befuddlement leaving him flaccid and feeble. "Hey there, Casey," he said, his voice hoarse from his dry throat.

She was resting next to him, on her side, one arm folded under her head. She wore a white dress shirt and black slacks. She patted a hand on his stomach as she stared into his eyes, her gray-eyed gaze just as intent as he remembered. Then she smiled and slid over, cuddling up next to him to lay her head on his chest. "I missed you, Elmer."

Her hair slid across her shoulders. A subtle floral scent from whatever shampoo she used crept into his nostrils. He folded his arm to rest his hand on her back, and hold her to him. He closed his eyes, and the big black empty opened before him. Before he knew it he felt his fingers running through her hair, and she nestled her face into his chest with a sleepy moan.

His hand trailed away to drop on the bed.

His breath seeped from him in a long sigh. "I missed you too, Case."

137

***

He woke some time later to find himself alone in bed. He struggled to sit up, his head sore from the wine. He remembered the night before, and Samantha in the living room. Acid rose from his stomach in a nauseating eruption, but he managed to hold it, letting out a raspy cough at the burn in the back of his throat. He rubbed his face and staggered to the window. A fresh snow had fallen, enough to shroud the ground. The sky was heavy and gray. The pickup was missing and, in its place, a dark blue sedan that screamed 'government issue'.

Right. Casey.

He shuffled from the bedroom, down the hallway, and past the living room to find her in the spacious kitchen, cooking some bacon and eggs. The welcome aroma of fresh coffee greeted him. He settled his weight on one of the high stools around the kitchen island and propped his elbow on the island as he settled his cheek in his palm. Casey turned from the stove to give him a sidelong glance, smiling at him as the bacon sizzled before her. His gaze roamed about, taking in the sight of a black vest draped over the stool across from him, a black trench coat hanging on the coat rack by the kitchen door and, on the island itself, a waist belt with a holstered handgun. His face fell as his lips parted, his mind failing to make sense of anything before him.

She turned from the stove and gave him a plate with the bacon and eggs. She grinned and opened her hands as she tipped her head. "Scrambled eggs, cooked dry, and bacon, half raw. Still the way you like it?"

He looked at the plate. It was Friday, time for his order at Gustafson's. He nodded and picked up his fork. "Had some wine last night. Maybe too much. Feeling kind of beat up." He blinked, and for the moment his eyes were closed he beheld the vision of Samantha standing by the door, looking up to the sky and humming to herself. He cleared his throat and shook his head in a failed attempt to dislocate the two realities pressing in on him. "Thanks for breakfast."

"Least I could do." She turned and came back with two cups of coffee, watching as he took his and started drinking at once. "So how's it been here up in Proskoy?"

He nodded. "Good." He froze, his eyes narrowing. "How'd you get in?"

She shrugged, but the old mischief glowed in her eyes. "I picked the lock."

He stared at her, then at the gun, then at his plate. "Right. Good coffee, by the way." He shifted on his stool, dropping his hand from his cheek to pick up his mug and hold it beneath his nose to steam his sinuses. He closed his eyes as he breathed in the steam before settling the mug to look at her, only to find her playing with her hair, running her fingers through the length trailing down her chest. *Same old Casey, I guess.* He waved his fork at her gun. "Is that real?"

"You bet. Just got it, for finishing my first round of training. I'm probationary."

He froze, his gaze darting about the island. "Probation? Do you have a partner or something?"

"Roger," she gave as an answer. "He's not here. I'm on a quick furlough. I can only stay for the day. I have to drive back tomorrow."

"Roger," he echoed. He wasn't sure why, but for some reason he was suddenly annoyed with her. "So who's this Roger guy?"

She ran a finger along the rim of her coffee mug. "I told you. He's my partner. Well, right now, he's my supervisory field agent, but once I clear probation, we'll be formal partners." She rested her chin in the palm of her hand, tipping her head as she tried to look into his eyes. "Have you talked to Mom and Dad?"

He shook his head as he speared a piece of egg with his fork. "No. You?"

She frowned. "I guess I should call later to say hello."

He jabbed his fork to nab a strip of bacon and shove it in his mouth.

She sat up straight and pulled a rubber band off her wrist. When she reached up to smooth her hair back to secure it in a ponytail he turned his hand to point his fork at her.

"Leave it down," he said as he chewed, his gaze never leaving his plate.

Her lips parted as she sat, stilled in the quiet. She put her hands in her lap.

***

They drove to town after breakfast. Casey tried to strike up some conversation, but he found his jaw clamped shut. She asked him what was wrong, but he lied and said it was just his headache from the night before. She seemed to find some humor in that, and laughed as she reminisced about their little drinking bouts after school. She told him he was getting old, since he couldn't hold his own with a little wine. He laughed it off and kept his eyes out the side window. He may have seemed distracted, but his thoughts were quite focused.

Roger. Roger? What the hell? He's probably some kind of asshole.

Figures.

He cleared his throat when he spotted the pickup parked in front of Parson's. He pointed for Casey to pull into the diner's lot as he peered in the windows. Samantha was there. He trembled with nervousness as he felt his life go up in smoke.

He got out of the car without a word and walked toward the diner.

Casey opened her door and stood by the car. "Hey! Elmer?"

He opened the door to the diner and didn't look back.

Casey ducked in the car to kill the engine, closed the door, and hurried after him, pulling up the collar of her trench coat against the cold. Samantha came out from the kitchen and waved hello as Elmer walked up to his usual stool, Casey close on his heels. The diner was empty.

Casey took off her black gloves and offered her hand. "Cassandra Phelps. Casey."

Samantha shook her hand. "Hey, I've heard about you. Samantha Hayes. So how's our friend Elmer doing this morning?"

Casey thumped a fist on his shoulder. "He's always cranky when he's hung-over."

He shook his head. "I don't have a hang-over. It's just a headache."

Samantha grinned. "It's a Thanksgiving turkey hang-over. Let me get you some coffee." She turned, but stopped short to dig a hand in her pocket and produce Elmer's keys for the pickup truck. "Here you go," she said to Elmer as she put the keys in his hand, her fingers giving his hand a little squeeze before she spun on her heel toward the kitchen.

Casey nudged Elmer with her foot as Samantha walked away. When he looked at Casey her eyebrows rose as she gave him a thumbs-up. He felt himself turn ten shades of red embarrassment. Casey put a hand over her mouth to hold her laughter, but couldn't resist jabbing him with her elbow.

Samantha came back with two cups of black coffee. "So how's college life?"

"Oh, I'm not in college," Casey said, she and Samantha looking to Elmer before Casey jabbed him with her elbow once more. She reached into her coat and pulled out a black ID pouch, which she flipped open with a flick of her wrist before stuffing it back in her pocket. "I'm working field enforcement."

Samantha blinked. "Wow. What are you, part of the FBI?"

Casey sat up straight and threw her shoulders back. "Well, ma'am, no—but if I did reveal my role, I would have to kill you," she said, but then grinned and waved her hand. "Sorry. I always wanted to say that. Seriously, though, I can't tell you. Actually, I've already said too much, but I think we're okay here in little old Proskoy."

Samantha's eyes widened. "I hope so. If we're not safe here, the world's really gone down the toilet." She looked between Casey's intent gray eyes and Elmer's downcast gaze and drummed her fingers on the counter. "Okay, well, I have to help in the kitchen. If you need anything, just call."

Casey waited until Samantha was gone to lean into Elmer. "So? Come on, spill," she hissed, reaching over to pinch his arm through his coat.

He pulled his arm away but turned to her. "What, what?" he hissed back, annoyed.

Casey rolled her eyes. "Do I have to spell it out? You know what I'm talking about."

He stared at her before his head shook with his nerves. "I, ah, whatever." He clenched his teeth, his gaze darting to the kitchen and the distant sound of Samantha's voice as she talked with Parson and Camille. He looked back to Casey and summoned his courage. "So what's with this Roger guy?"

She held up a finger. "You're changing the subject."

"No kidding. So what's with this guy?"

Her crooked grin took hold. "He's going to be my partner."

His mouth went dry. He knew that particular tone of her voice. "Did you, ah, you know?"

She tipped her head in confusion. "Of course. On the sly. It's nothing, just fun."

He frowned and looked down at his coffee.

She shook her head. "Seriously, Elmer, you need to relax."

He got up and walked out to the pickup truck.

***

He drove down the street to Gustafson's with Casey sitting next to him in the pickup. He picked up his Friday order and doubled it when he noticed Casey all but salivating as she stared at the meats in the display coolers. Ingrid came out from the back, and despite Elmer's awkwardness, he introduced Casey. As usual Casey out-shined him with little effort and in short order had Ingrid and even straight-faced Gustafson laughing about times back in Fairmont. Ingrid pulled Casey aside and offered her some advice on how to cook the medallions, which Casey heeded with polite attention before thanking her.

They got in the pickup and Elmer drove out of town onto one of the old lumber roads. He followed its winding course into part of the land preserve before finding a place to park. They peered out the windshield to overlook a foam-dappled river coursing down from the higher elevations. They tore into the bag sitting between them, each taking a medallion and holding it in its waxed paper to devour its red mass. They said nothing as they chewed, but as Elmer ate and stared out at the wild hummocks of white water tumbling over the river's rocky bed the oddness of it all struck him. He turned to Casey to find her licking her fingers between wiping her chin with a ripped piece of the paper bag.

"Why are we like this?"

Casey looked at him. Her lips glistened with the slick red juice of the raw meat until she licked them clean. She swallowed and grinned. "Why Elmer, whatever could you mean by that?"

"What's with us and the raw meat?"

She licked her fingers once more, this time in a rather dainty way, before lounging against the door. She drew her loose mane of hair over the buttons of her coat and ran her fingers through its length before looking to him, a surprisingly serious expression on her face. "When was the last time you were sick?"

Her one simple question collapsed his life. *The bat bite? The change?* "I don't get it."

She opened a hand. "Last time you pulled a muscle? Last time you twisted a joint? Come on, you're doing some physical labor now, taking care of Big Paul's place. Ever wake up with sore muscles, sore back, sore anything?"

He laid his hand on his forehead.

She wasn't done. "When was the last time you talked to Mom and Dad? I bet when you moved out, right? You look at the phone, but somehow, someway, you just get this feeling there's this big gulf between you and them like, no matter what you say, no matter what they say, it'll be like doves talking to a wolf, right?"

Snowflakes started to fall. He closed his eyes.

"We're not like other people, bro. We're a breed apart from everyone else, and you know it. That girl at the diner, maybe you're hot for her, but she's like the rest of, well, them," she added with a wave of her hand to the expanse past the hood of the pickup. "And with Mom and Dad, I know it's tough, because I think you understand it already, perceive it on some level maybe you're really not aware of yet, that they're just not going to last like we will. There's some guilt with that." She took his hand. "It'll pass. Look at me."

He sniffed, lowering his hand from his forehead to gaze at her.

She slid across the bench seat of the pickup, moving the empty bag onto the floor as she came up beside him and snaked her arms around him. She kissed his cheek and turned her face into the side of his neck. "I'll always be here for you. I love you, like no one else."

He trembled. He tried to think of Samantha. He felt as if his mind was being torn in two.

Her shoulders bunched up as she shimmied her hips to draw ever tighter against him. "Right now, let's just watch the snow, okay?"

He took a breath, fighting himself until he rested his head against hers. He let himself linger there but, when he closed his eyes, he found the big black empty waiting for him. He sat up straight and put his hands on the wheel. The snow was coming down in force.

"We should go," he said. "This road gets dangerous."

***

They went back to Proskoy, stopping at the diner to get Casey's car. Elmer looked in the windows of the diner, and was relieved to see that Camille was working the counter. If she was at the counter, Samantha had already walked to her apartment in the upstairs of the Parsons' house. He sat in the pickup until Casey had her car cleaned of snow and running, and then took the lead back to the house.

When they got there they went straight in to warm up, sitting at the kitchen island for more coffee. Casey showed Elmer her gun, dropping the clip to show him how the slide worked and then how to load it for firing. He felt the weight of it, and it felt good in his hand, even though he knew it was a toy compared to the hunting rifles and shotguns Big Paul kept locked in the basement. Casey lured him outside for a snowball fight and, before he knew it, it seemed like they were kids again, and they ran after each other in the falling snow until they were soaked to the bone.

They used the two bathrooms to shower, but Casey lingered under the warm water, while Elmer got dressed and threw on a pot of water to cook some pasta. It was the one thing he felt somewhat comfortable preparing on his own. He sat on a stool at the kitchen island as he waited for the pasta and watched the snow outside. He could hear the cold winds moan when Casey finished her shower and turned off the water. He listened to the whine of a blow dryer as he dumped the pasta into a colander in the sink. He called her, but she didn't answer, so he walked down the hall to the bedroom she was using.

He peered inside to see her duffel bag on the floor. Her clothes were spread on the bed to dry. His eyes narrowed when he saw her gun belt on the dresser and, beside it, her wallet, ID pouch, and a slender black case. Curious, but with a wary glance at the closed bathroom door, he walked into the room, taking care to be quiet. He stopped by the dresser and picked up the black case. It flipped open and, inside, he found two odd tools nestled in black velvet. They were chromed, the first a simple hollow tube with polished serrations at one end. The other tool was thinner, and he realized it was sized to fit in the first tool. But unlike the open serrated end, the second tool ended with a tiny ball scoop, its curvature soldered to a braided metal filament that ran through the hollow length of the tool to emerge at the opposite end, where it was soldered to a finger ring. He put his finger in the ring and, when he pulled on the ring, the tiny ball scoop closed on its pinions.

He shook his head, puzzled over the tools, and more so, why she hadn't said anything about them, in contrast to her gun, which she'd been so eager to show off.

The hair dryer went silent.

He put the tools away and closed the case before walking to the bathroom door. He called her name, but when she failed to answer, he knocked on the door, only for it to swing ajar. His gaze rose from the floor as light seeped from the doorway.

She stood by the sink, naked. His heart went still.

She turned and looked at him, but said nothing. She leaned against the sink, bracing her hands behind her. Her hair hung loose about her shoulders. Her skin was still wet from the shower, and her body glistened under the vanity lights. It reminded him of the way her lips had glistened with the juices of the medallions they had consumed.

He felt himself breathe. He met her gaze. He stared until he forced his eyes shut and pulled the door, only to lean against its sturdy wooden mass. He held there, splaying a hand on the door. When he was ready he knocked.

"Elmer?" her voice called through the door.

He traced out her likeness with his finger before grinding his teeth. He tried to overlay the inclinations erupting in his head with visions of Samantha, innocent visions of her sitting beside him at Thanksgiving dinner, of her playfully strutting about in her black leotard for him on Halloween night, of her standing outside his door humming to herself as she stared at the black sky waiting for the snow. But the more he contemplated her and the more he tried to focus on her, the more the visions corroded in his humiliating failures to accept her, to step through himself and welcome the invitations she dangled before him. She couldn't have made it any easier for him without crossing that precarious line of judgment his parents had pounded into him that would label her with a battery of demeaning, dismissive condemnations. Temptation cleaved the knees of his will like a diamond-honed guillotine.

"Elmer, you still there?"

Why couldn't he act? He knew it wasn't for lack of interest, for he knew how his dreams had been lit—illuminated—with a dozen enticing fantasies of the perfect night, the perfect word, the perfect touch. And as that bulled through his consciousness, he at last understood what was in the way. It was the big black empty, and what lurked in its shadows.

And what lurked in its shadows was right on the other side of the door, waiting.

No. . .

He trembled, clawing at his scalp until he found his voice.

"I, ah, I was going to have a beer with dinner. You, you want one?"

Several moments passed before she answered. "I want what you want."

He banged his head on the door. His heart bucked in his chest. Every condemnation in society erupted in his mind, incinerating the last tattered remnants of his will and its barriers in the twists of his life. All the innate reservations, blasphemous visions, and heretical inclinations careened in wild orbit about that one six lettered word he dared not utter, that word that defined what it would be but was so lost in gleaning any hint of the truth of what he felt. It burned, burned within him, burned around him, burned every facet of existence until all was darkness. There was only one little island of reality that remained, and a door across its horizon.

His hand constricted on the knob before he flung the door open. She tensed a bit at the sudden swing of the door, her lips parting as she sucked in a little breath, but she eased, and held her position, just as she had been. Her eyes were wide and wild, wide and waiting, a look that he'd seen so many times in the muted savagery of his nature documentaries—mammalian predators at play, at play to practice their savage hunting skills, at once docile in recognition of their play and eager with the thrill of the tussle.

He thought of all those days walking home from high school, the times he snuck every stare he could at the strip club by the train station. He remembered the thrill, the welcome release, of Casey feeding him that first serving of flesh, and the way the big black empty opened within him soon after. He remembered what she said to him just that afternoon: they were a breed apart. They were different. The rules did not—could not— apply.

His hand was white; his grip was so tight on the doorknob. He looked down at the door saddle. He sucked in a breath, met her gaze, and stepped through. She slapped her hands on the collar of his shirt and yanked him toward her.

He slammed the door shut behind them.

***

He woke to the feeling of her lips on his forehead.

"I have to get moving. Love you, bro."

And then she was gone.

He opened his eyes to find the white ceiling above him. He sniffed at the congestion in his head. He wiped his nose, and when he did, he noticed a few flecks of dried blood.

There was a black hole where the fan used to hang.

***

He was numb for the next few days, trying to make some sense of things. One night, when he couldn't sleep, he went to *that* bathroom and went on a cleaning rampage, bleaching, polishing and scrubbing until it gleamed with the sterility of an operating room.

But he thought of Casey, thought of her all the time and, every time he closed his eyes, every time he so much as blinked, the big black empty was waiting for him. It didn't unnerve him as it did in the past, now that he felt he knew, confronted, and had overcome some of what lurked in its shadows. Rather, it was the increasing, almost omnipresent, dwelling of the big black empty in his conscience that bothered him.

He drove to town one day, taking care to ride the old logging roads the long way around, so he wouldn't have to go past Parson's to park in front of Proskoy Supply, the local general store. He bought a spiral bound notebook and, on a lark, a dictionary and a thesaurus. He didn't remember what a thesaurus was called, so he had to ask for 'that book with the words that are kind of the same,' but, he was so intent in his aim to regain some balance in his life, some of the old reservations and embarrassment crumbled from him.

He drove back to the house, retracing the path he took to town. It wasn't that he was neglecting Samantha; on the contrary, he felt the need to see her mounting with each passing day. But he knew he had to set himself straight, find a new balance—*equilibrium* was the word he decided to use, when flipping through the thesaurus—to solidify his perception of the world. He felt only then would he be able to talk to Samantha, only when he had his perspective established.

He sat at the kitchen island that night staring at the first blank page of the notebook, paging in turn through the dictionary and thesaurus. He wanted to write something for himself that he could read and reflect on, something better than the informal way he talked. So he sat, and stared out at the falling snow. As he tired his mind freed itself, and introspection gained momentum and its own voice and, shortly after midnight, he put pen to paper.

I'm not what I would consider a 'bad' man. If you would only understand my predilections, I think you would see that I have a sense of morality. It's just that given my predilections—my needs—my moral perspective is perhaps somewhat different from what you would call the 'norm'.

He looked out the windows, considering. *Maybe, yes, maybe one day she can read this.*

His gaze fell to the notebook, and he wrote one more sentence, just for her.

I have to feed, and until you overcome your revulsion for that basic reality,

you won't understand me.
He read it over, nodded, and shuffled off to bed.

***

It was the seventh of December when he walked into Parson's. The days since Casey's departure had skipped by him but, when he saw the advent candles on a shelf over the kitchen window, old familiarity filled in the blanks of time. He sat at his usual stool. When Samantha came out of the kitchen holding several plates of hamburgers, her face lit up at the sight of him, and she gave him a quick smile before tipping her head to indicate the waiting table. He glanced over his shoulder, careless of the silly grin on his face, as he watched her bring the plates over to a table down the length of the diner. Three men were seated at the table. They were clean cut, but dressed in casual wear. They were polite, but in a formal, empty sort of way — as if their words of 'please' and 'thank you' came with as little thought as a blink.

His eyes narrowed as he studied them. He knew they weren't locals, which left only the obvious: they were from one of the cities.

Samantha hurried back to him, walking behind him and patting a hand on his shoulder as she returned to her usual place behind the counter. "So, how have you been?"

He was happy to see her, and she seemed happy as well, but he felt obligated to apologize. "Look, Samantha, I don't want you to think—"

She leaned on the counter, her face close to his. "Elmer, it's okay."

He looked at her hands and, rallying himself, he took them in his own. She gave his fingers a welcome squeeze. "I haven't been around because I've been busy up at the house, plowing the driveway and cleaning off the roof and all. But I wanted—well, I thought—maybe, you know, if you want, maybe I could take you out to dinner?"

She looked up from their hands, peering at him from under her eyebrows as her smile grew and her lips opened over her teeth. She studied him for a long moment before she gave his hands another squeeze. "I thought you'd never ask. I'm not working Friday night. Are you free?"

"Now I am," he said, smiling with her. "I know it might not be a surprise, but I thought we'd go to Loggers' Steakhouse. Do you like steak?" he said, unable to hold in his laughter, as they both knew that aside from Parson's, Loggers' was the only other restaurant in town.

The ding of Parson's order bell drew a sigh from her.

Their fingers released as she drew away. She pointed back at him with both hands. "I'll see you Friday, Mister Phelps."

He pointed back at her and stood from his stool. He paid no more notice to the other people in the diner. They were of no consequence to him.

***

He wanted everything to be just right.

He called and made a reservation, even though the skiing crowd wouldn't arrive in the area until the middle of January, when a suitable powder base had built up on the slopes. It was the city people that formed most of the seasonal business for Loggers'; in December, when things were quiet, the well-reputed steakhouse was only open Friday and Saturday nights.

He went in the detached garage set back from the house and stood before the polished gleam of Big Paul's European sedan, a slick black machine with all-wheel drive. Paul left specific instructions that the car was not to be touched except to run the motor once a week to keep the battery in good order, but Elmer was willing to ignore that rule for one night. Besides, ever since the night with Casey, he found himself less and less interested in obeying the dictates of others. He knew what he wanted, what he desired, and he wasn't going to let his old lame ways stop him.

He owned only one dress shirt, the shirt his mother bought him for graduation, when his parents treated him to dinner. There was no party, as he had no friends, and all his grandparents were already resting six feet under. For some reason, the shirt found its way into his clothes when he moved out to Proskoy, and he hung it in his closet in the guest room, knowing it was easier to forget it there rather than have to drive back to Fairmont. But as he buttoned it up after his shower, he let the associations in his head change. No, not the shirt of a pathetic graduation dinner, but the shirt he wore the night he took a woman who was interested in him out to dinner.

He drove to the Parson house, and the couple came out on their front porch after Samantha called down from her window that she was getting her coat. Parson and Camille grinned as they beheld Elmer standing by the sedan. He knew they weren't mocking him. They were happy for him. It made him self-conscious for a moment, wondering how odd he must have seemed when he first came out to Proskoy, but that was another life.

Samantha came down the covered outside stairwell to the upstairs apartment, bundled up in a long wool coat with a furry collar. He could make out a pair of fashionable boots of soft brown leather, with a little heel on them. Her hair was down, the way he liked it.

He almost forgot himself as he stared at her, and moved with a start to open the car door for her. He waved to the Parsons and drove off.

When they walked into Loggers' they were asked to check their coats, something Elmer never encountered before. Samantha whispered in his ear that it was common in better restaurants, so with a little glow of embarrassment on his cheeks he took her coat, doffed his, and checked them in. He turned to see her, and smiled at once. She wore a dark blue dress, tailored with simple but classical lines, with a stiff, upturned collar that hinted at the Oriental influence in its design. The dress ended just below her knees, concealing the tops of her boots. It was so different from anything he saw his sister wear over the years, exuding a femininity that stopped him in his tracks.

Samantha's lips parted in concern at his mute reaction. "Does it look okay?" She glanced down at herself, meshing her fingers against her chest. "It's the best thing I have."

He took her hand. "Samantha, you look wonderful."

She ducked her chin as she grinned.

The maitre d' stepped into their view, surprising them. "This way, please."

They sat at a candlelit table for two in an alcove of large windows that looked out from the hilltop Loggers' dominated. The woods were bare, but the ground was blanketed with snow, and the river that coursed down from the hills ran past the base of Loggers' hilltop, providing a wonderful view. They talked and ate, Samantha's eyes and body language revealing some surprise when Elmer ordered his steak rare and devoured it in the blink of an eye. They had a glass of wine and, at Samantha's insistence, clinked their glasses in toast.

"Since it's like a *real* date," she said with a wink.

He took it in stride, grinning with her. "You might have guessed by now, but I don't get out much."

"You don't say?" she replied with mock surprise. "I hadn't seen you since your sister came to visit. She's back to work?"

He looked out the windows and nodded. "It was just a quick visit."

"So what's this agency she works for?"

He looked back to Samantha and shrugged. "I don't know. She never told me."

"Did she threaten to kill you too?" she said with a soft laugh. "What do you think she does? It's kind of a mystery, don't you think, that she can't even tell her own brother?"

He pursed his lips, for some reason remembering the little tools he found, before he shook it off. "I don't know. Casey's always been kind of out there. But she carries a gun, so whatever it is, I guess it's pretty serious."

The waitress came by and asked if they wanted another glass of wine.

They looked at each other and, with a full meal in their bellies, agreed for one more round. He waited until the waitress left to take Samantha's hand. "I bet it feels good to be on the other side."

She sipped her water. "I've always had to take care of myself, so I've never thought about that. Oh, but this is nice," she added, her gaze panning across the rustic, up-scale antiquity of the restaurant's décor.

He stared at her. He thought of the warmth of her hand. "I've never taken care of anything, so I guess I never thought about it either."

She looked at him. They were silent, with the candle between them. When the waitress returned they were both startled. But as Elmer looked to the waitress to ask for dessert menus, he noticed the three men that were in Parson's the other day. He tipped his chin in their direction and tapped his thumb on Samantha's wrist to gain her attention. "Who are those guys?"

She glanced and shrugged. "I don't know. Not local, that's for sure."

"I know. I could tell by the way they talked to you the other day," he thought aloud, looking back at her when he felt her gaze on him. "You know, not rude, but not really polite either, just. . ." His voice trailed off as he thought of his thesaurus, taking a few seconds to summon a good word. "*Indifferent*, I guess."

"City people," she said as her only explanation before looking out the windows. "Hey, it's starting to snow."

He swallowed. "Do you know what I remember most about Thanksgiving night?"

She looked at him, her eyes filled with sudden unease.

He held up a hand. "No, before that. When you were standing outside, your hands folded before you, your face tipped up to the night sky, as you hummed a little song to yourself." He glanced at the ceiling before taking a breath and meeting her gaze again. He didn't feel like he was lying. No, he wasn't lying. He stared at her. "I think of that, remember that, a lot." He looked out at the snow. "Do you want to go for a walk?"

The waitress came back with the dessert menu. Samantha looked to the woman and waved a hand. "Oh, that's okay, we'll be going now."

Rather than drive somewhere, they decided to walk the woods around Loggers', and enjoy the views from the hillside elevations. It was late, and dark, but the night held the disembodied blue-tinged glow of fresh falling snow, and their breaths misted in the air in crisp white trails of vapor. They saw a deer, and watched until it trotted off. They made their way around the hill until they could look down on the river, its turbulent waters silvery in the twilight. They stood still, huddled shoulder to shoulder, until the snow picked up, and large flakes began to drift down between the black branches of the slumbering trees. She stepped to her side to peer up at an open patch of sky, but kept her gloved hand in his.

"Look at that," she whispered, "it's like it just goes up forever, like looking into the ocean."

He followed her gaze. "I never thought of it that way. I've never seen the ocean, except on TV." He looked to her. "What was that song you hummed?"

She closed her eyes. "A lullaby. My mom used to hum it to me, before she died."

He pressed his lips together as he stood and stared at her. He trembled, but it was the cold, pressing through his coat, and not from within, from his nerves. The reservations were gone. He understood himself then, found the balance he was seeking, the equilibrium he craved. He would live as two beings; he would live as two creatures linked in dichotomous existence. He could be the bat-bitten recluse who feasted on raw meat to maintain his health as he defiled himself in madness with his sister, and he could be a gentle loner who found company with someone perhaps as lonely as he, in a relationship that would be condoned by every aspect of society. It was perfect, almost more than he could ask for, more than he could perceive. And as he looked at her and listened to her humming the old lullaby, his blood surged in his veins with the warmth of serenity. Yes, he would lead two lives, and never the two should meet; never the two to look upon each other, never the two to understand how their over-world and under-world realities were linked through him.

She opened her mouth, her eyes still closed. "Make a wish," she whispered and put out her tongue in wait for a snowflake.

His jaw clenched. The world stilled around him. This was the moment, the moment he dreamed of, the moment he prayed to one day occupy. He stepped toward her, and when she felt him move in the shift of his arm she drew in her tongue and welcomed him with her parted lips.

They drove back to Proskoy Wood in silence. They left deep footprints in the gathering snow, the dried brown leaves crunching far below, as they hurried into the house.

***

Those days leading up to Christmas formed the happiest time of his life.

They spent the weekend after Logger's at the house, walking through the snow laden woods, riding Paul's snowmobiles, retreating to the warmth of the fireplace, and entwining themselves under heavy blankets.

151

When he drove her back to her apartment that Sunday night Parson's wife waved to him as he pulled away.

The empty road rolled past him in the still darkness. He never thought of himself as a thinking person but, sitting in the pickup that night, he couldn't help but think of how his life had changed, and the speed—the finality—with which it had changed. The world seemed brighter when he thought of Samantha and, even though he considered that saccharine thought in relation to his utter lack of experience with women, he felt certain it was more than a case of lust. What he felt for Samantha was something more complex, something he decided to classify as *desire*, with all the subtle implications that went with such a notion. And what had happened with Casey... Casey was his sister and, by that alone, it was something of a different nature, unnatural as it may have been. But as he considered it, he found it hard to even remember that night and the madness that had possessed him, and the abyssal maw of the big black empty that had enveloped him.

No, that wasn't him, that night. The delineation, the division, was clear to him. It couldn't have been him. How could it? What they did, it was unspeakable.

And yet, perhaps inevitable. It had festered for so long, back there in Fairmont.

He came to a stop in the driveway and stepped from the pickup. Snowflakes were falling from the night sky. He stuck his tongue out, and made his wish, even though he put no stock in gods or monsters. There was the world, and that was it. Despite what his parents hoped he would learn those dreary Sunday mornings in church, he decided long ago that life was life, and when it ended, there was only the senile obliteration of death. There was no detached Justice looking down upon the world of men, for if there was, his life would've been much better. Then again, if he had enjoyed the shiny-happy teen life so many people treasured, he wouldn't have run to Proskoy, and he wouldn't have met Samantha. Means and ends, ends and means—there was no point in trying to discern one from the other, or to make any sense of them.

He felt the cool sting of a snowflake on his tongue and opened his eyes.

Yes, for the first time, life is good—and if there is Something out there, thank you.

Proskoy Wood surrounded him, with its depths of mute shadows.

***

He drove out to the diner one evening for dinner and to see Samantha, as had become his routine. The snowfall was almost constant,

152

so the diner was all but empty. It gave them plenty of time to talk, but when Parson came out of the kitchen and figured he'd close up for the night, Samantha held up her hands and asked Elmer to wait. She darted into the kitchen and came back with a white cardboard baker's box wrapped in red and white string. She put it on the counter in front of Elmer and sped by Parson to grab two plates. When she turned to Parson, he shook his head and tossed her the keys to the door instead. He waved goodnight and left them alone.

Elmer looked at the box, but the moment Parson's headlights trailed away she leaned over the counter to take Elmer's face in her hands and kiss him. She was all but bouncing on her feet as she took off her apron and hung it by the coffee machine, sighing with relief when she pulled her hair out of its ponytail. "Come on, open the box!"

He took out his keys to open the little knife he kept on the ring. "What is this?"

She drummed her fingers on the counter in anticipation. "I felt bad the night we went out that we didn't get to have dessert at Loggers', because they have some of the most awesome cakes you can get around here. Well, maybe I didn't feel *too* bad," she added with a glint in her eyes.

He grinned and glanced at her as he opened the box. He sat up straight. "Wow."

She raced around the counter, pulled his coat off, and wrapped her arms around him as she stood behind him. She rested her chin on his shoulder as he looked in the box. "It's called chocolate decadence pie, but it's really a cake. I waited for them to get one ready, because they don't have it all the time unless the place is in full swing. I don't know why they call it pie, but, whatever, it's out of this world. Here," she said, and she moved around him to slice the pie, sinking the knife through the leaves of dark chocolate adorning its top as she felt his arms encircle her. "See, layers and layers," she said, her voice softening as she tried to concentrate. "I know it's a lot—decadent, or indulgent, I guess, but sometimes, why settle? Why settle when you can have everything, right?"

She closed her eyes and let the knife slip from her fingers as his arms tightened around her. His hands slid over her as he buried his face in her neck and the scent of her hair. She muttered his name, but she sank into him as her head rolled back.

Her eyes popped open. "Oh, to hell with it."

She slipped away to turn off the lights in the diner, but came right back to him.

The cake sat on the counter, forgotten.

***

Days passed. Life, as he knew it, was perfect. He spent every moment he had with Samantha, even though her time during the week was pinched by the hours she put in at Parson's. Parson was kind enough to give her the weekend off, and it didn't escape Elmer's perception that Parson and his wife drew a certain delight from fostering Elmer and Samantha.

They were lounging before the fireplace one night in a knot of naked limbs beneath several blankets, their faces turned to the ceiling as a piece of oak crackled away, when she turned to him. "Elmer?"

He hummed a reply, his eyebrows rising, but his eyelids remaining shut.

"Don't you think it's crazy how we found each other?"

"How do you mean?"

She rolled on her side, resting her folded arm on his chest to support her head. "Well, can I confess something first?"

His eyes opened in trepidation. "Uh, I guess so."

She poked his stomach. "It's to the point, so relax, and just listen." She took a breath as she gathered her thoughts. "My childhood, you know, it was a mess. Once my mom died, there was nobody for me. I wound up in an orphanage and got bounced from one foster family to another. I was considered a problem child, and all those poor people, I treated them like crap, because I was so pissed off at the world for being left alone. But there was this nun at the orphanage, and she pulled me aside one time, and I thought, 'Oh great, some friggin' sermon,' but that wasn't it at all. She said things were horrible for her when she was growing up, which surprised me, even though she wasn't one of those to walk around in the penguin suit. Anyway, what she said to me was that sometimes things are tough and, no matter what you believe about life, you have to either find a way to rise above, or sink into it, and let it crush you. It was the first time I thought about the future, and it just kind of hit me, so I started to get my act together."

"What about college?"

"I'm not talking about college. I'm talking about something else. I'm talking about why I'm here in Proskoy, and why I stay here. The Parsons are like family to me. It's peaceful here; I'm peaceful here, even if I get a little lonely sometimes. You know, when you walked in that first day I met you, I just thought it might be nice to have a little roll in the sheets, because it had been a long time since my last good time." She took a breath, lifting her head so that she met his gaze. "But I wasn't expecting, well, this."

He stared at her. "I'm not going anywhere. I can't. You set me free."

It took a moment for her to decipher the apparent incongruence of his words, but when she did, she smiled. She studied him before wiping her eyes. "Good," she said with a nod and rested her head on his chest.

He had the feeling she wanted to be held. He wanted to hold her. He folded his arm around her, resting his hand on her head. She was warm against him, and the vitality of her body was to him a precious thing in the wake of what she said. He stared at the ceiling, and as he did he reached across his chest with his other arm to take her hand in his, and when he did, their fingers clamped shut.

And for some reason he began to fear for her, for himself, for what they shared. He closed his eyes but, when he did, the fear shifted, and took a form he never would've suspected, until it was there in his conscious mind in full, and undeniable.

The oak popped in the heat of the flame. His eyes slid open, but the image lingered.

Casey.

***

He was standing in Gustafson's waiting for his Friday order when the fear ambushed him, tearing through his psyche like a wooden stake. He trembled, his shoulders tightening until his breath was stilled in his chest.

A voice came from behind him. "Hey, bro."

He turned, and fought his trepidation until he peered over his shoulder to convince himself what he heard was real. The moment she registered in his sight, though, he felt himself pulled around to stand before her. The neat little barrier he thought he built in his head exploded and left him stupid and senseless before her, so that only one thought coalesced in his mind, one that did little to sooth him, as he knew it shattered every border and delineation that could exist.

Goddamn, she looks good.

She smiled, standing there in her black trench coat, with her ponytail draped over her shoulder to trail down her chest. She pulled her hands out of her pockets and held them up. "Did you forget me, or something?"

He coughed. "What are you doing here?"

She blinked, stunned. Her lips parted.

Gustafson came over to where Elmer was standing and put the white bag of the standing order on the counter. "Hello there, Casey. Here you go, Elmer."

He reached back and took the bag without a word, his gaze locked on his sister.

A pained look pulled at her face. "Elmer?"

He felt as if his veins had been filled with concrete. He couldn't move.

"I—I wasn't expecting, I didn't know. . ." He clamped his jaw shut. "You, you surprised me." He looked out the window. "Where's your car? How, how did you, how did you get here?"

Her hands sank to her sides. "Roger dropped me off. I thought I'd surprise you."

Roger? He coughed again. *Right, Roger the sure-to-be asshole. Hit a deer, jack-off.*

He blinked. Somehow, the animosity stirred him from his stupor. He stepped forward and hugged his sister. She kissed his cheek and patted her hands on his shoulders as he released her. "I'm sorry, Case, but, ah, I was in my own world I guess, and you just—"

She poked him in the chest. "Like lightning, I am!" she said with a laugh, as if to accept his explanation. She pointed over her shoulder with one black-gloved hand as she ran the fingers of her other hand through the end of her ponytail. "Are you busy, or can you ride with me over to the house?"

Samantha was working. It was coming up on lunch, so she would be busy. There was no way to hide. "Uh, no, no, we can go back."

She hooked her arm in his as they walked out the door to the pickup. "I think you'll like Roger. He's different, like us," she said, grinning when he shot a glance at her. "You'll see," she added. "I'm going to change your life, bro."

His head sank. "My life is just fine."

She gave his arm a little tug to draw his gaze back to her. "That's because you don't know what's out there yet," she said with a wise look in her eyes. "At least not for the two of us. I've been dying to tell you, but I had to clear probation first. That's why Roger's here."

"I don't want to join your agency," he said, stiffening his will. "I don't want to leave Proskoy." He pulled his arm from her as they parted around the hood of the pickup. The doors weren't locked; nobody locked their doors in Proskoy. There was no need. He wasn't sure why he thought of that as he settled in the driver's seat. Casey hopped in the passenger door and slammed it shut on its squeaking hinges. "Casey, I'm not interested."

She opened her hands. "Look, just have an open mind, okay? That's all I ask."

He looked to her. She was playing with her ponytail. Her hair had grown.

She tipped her head at the look in his eyes, and where his gaze lingered. She snapped her fingers, the sound only a dull thud with her gloves on. "Sorry," she said, reaching back to pull the rubber band from her ponytail. She ran her fingers through her hair to loosen it before smiling at him once more. "I forgot you like it down."

He stared at her, trembling in the loose fit of his coat. He squeezed his eyes shut and turned his head forward before opening them. He started the motor, put the truck in gear, and rolled out of the parking lot. When they went past Parson's, he kept his gaze locked ahead, but Casey slid toward him, kissing him on the cheek again as she nestled against him.

"I haven't stopped thinking about you," she said with a sigh, patting her hand on his thigh.

***

They came in the house to find Roger sitting by the fireplace, his legs crossed with one foot dangling over his knee, his arms outstretched across the back of the couch. He had short black hair, a well-defined jaw, and when he gave a polite smile as they came into the living room Elmer could see neat rows of perfect, white teeth. Roger stood, reaching down to close the laptop computer he left open on the table, and put out his hand. "Roger," he said.

Elmer looked at the offered hand. "Elmer Phelps," he said and shook Roger's hand. The man's grip was like a vise, his smile widening when Elmer blinked in surprise. It annoyed Elmer, because he knew Roger's immediate assumption would be that his grip surprised Elmer. On the contrary, it was the thought of Roger's hands having free reign and roam over his sister's bare body that summoned a mix of jealousy and protectiveness so perverse he almost vomited on Roger's crisp white shirt.

Roger took off his black trench coat and draped it over the couch. He ran his hand along his black tie as he looked Elmer over. "So this is the brother I've heard so much about," he said with a nod, resting his hands on his hips.

Elmer pressed his lips in a tight line.

Casey clapped her hands together. "I'll make some coffee."

Elmer stared at Roger. "How'd you get in the house?"

Roger tipped his head back. "Your sister said you wouldn't mind, and the door was unlocked, so. . ." His voice trailed off at the bleak look in Elmer's eyes before his composure returned. He opened a hand and gave a slight bow. "You're absolutely correct. I had no right to enter. Forgive me."

Elmer forced out a breath. They were standing there, across the table from each other. He could sense Roger was waiting for him to sit, a practiced move in deferred authority. Posture and poise. He refused to budge.

Roger licked his lips and gave Elmer a single nod. "You don't like me, do you?"

It was true but, even with Roger's soft, thoughtful tone to the question, the hint of confrontation made Elmer waver. He cleared his throat and stuffed his hands in his pockets.

Casey stepped out from the kitchen, wiping her hands on a dishtowel. "Elmer just takes some time to warm up to people. Right?" He shrugged. "I, I guess so."

Roger opened a hand. "Say, that's good, yes—that's good." He glanced at Casey. "I think the coffee will be ready soon. Why don't we sit down, and make ourselves comfortable?"

Elmer hesitated, but sat down. He kept his coat on.

Roger sat and leaned his elbows on his knees as he looked at Elmer. "That's an astute quality, Elmer, not to warm up to strangers quickly. See, a probing mind, a sensitive mind, will be wary, waiting to learn more of a stranger before judgment is made. Probing minds, minds of substance, are always wary. So, I understand your hesitation. Perhaps, upon first meet, I might not like me either, but that is a relativistic switch on subjectivity we need not concern ourselves with, no?"

"I guess not," Elmer replied. He wished he had his dictionary nearby.

Casey came in with a tray of three steaming mugs of coffee. "Three blacks, order up," she said with cheer, and sat at the end of the same couch as Elmer. "So how are things with Samantha?"

He turned to her. He found it odd that she left an empty space between them on the couch after the way she nestled against him in the pickup. She had let her hair down. She flirted with him, and now that Roger was in the room, she left space between them. It left him in knots, but he was happy she kept her distance. He was confounded.

"Who's this Samantha person?" Roger said.

"A waitress at the diner," Casey said. "She's Elmer's girlfriend."

Roger raised his mug. "Well, bravo, Elmer. Always good to enjoy the riches that surround us, don't you agree?"

Elmer sipped his coffee. He wondered if he could fit his mug down Roger's throat. "I guess so," he said again.

Roger held his mug by his face, breathing the aromatic vapors as he studied Elmer. "Perhaps we should cut to the chase, eh?"

Elmer looked to him.

Roger eased back in the couch, crossing his legs once more as he sipped his coffee. "Your sister and I work for a certain agency, the name of which I shall not repeat at this time. You should know that it is in fact part of the government, and that we do have authority within the federal hierarchy, and extending somewhat past it as well. It is often assumed we work for the FBI, although that is not the case. We are completely 'black' within the government. That is, all our actions, our budget, our identities are all held in the strictest confidentiality. We serve the will and dictate of a very select group of people who would not, and will not, be found on any public registry of any formalized government agency, branch, or directorate. As such, we enjoy a very select set of specialized privileges. Privileges, I should tell you, that are well suited to the highly specialized condition we share, a condition both complicit and implicit with selection for our agency."

Elmer didn't know what to think. His simple, happy little world seemed very far away. The setting sun only served to intensify his sense of dislocation. He stole a quick glance at Casey, only to find her staring at him with her ghostly gray-eyed gaze, a little smile on her lips. He shook his head and looked to Roger. "Why are you telling me all this?"

Roger put his mug on the table. He fixed a steady gaze on Elmer. "When you were a boy you were bitten by a bat."

Elmer froze.

"The same bat that bit your sister."

Elmer closed his eyes.

"You were both infected by an agent that is as rare as is the knowledge concerning its existence. It is not communicable between humans, it is not detectable, but its effect is indelible. While it imparts several rather impressive benefits, it compels those who have been exposed to it to pursue a rather particular appetite, the neglect of which can cause said subject to suffer a steady but marked decline in health and resilience." Roger sipped his coffee. "I believe you know of what I speak, Elmer."

Elmer looked to Casey, but she said nothing.

Roger rubbed his chin before continuing. "We are a breed apart. We only need fulfill our appetite for raw flesh and, in return, we are granted an impermeable immune system, bodies with heightened resistance to physical injury, an extraordinary ability to rapidly heal from all but the most devastating of injuries, and a life span that defies normal human comprehension of mortality. We do not live, we exist."

Elmer looked into his mug with suspicion. It was too bizarre to believe.

Casey nodded. "It's not just words, Elmer. We say we exist, because saying we live inevitably means that we will die. Remember what I told you last time I was here, that Mom and Dad won't last? This is what I was talking about."

Elmer looked out the windows. "So I can't get old?"

Roger smiled with satisfaction. "Not if you feed, no."

"And nobody knows about this?"

Roger tipped his head. "As you can imagine, it is a bit of a secret."

Elmer shifted his gaze upon Casey. "I didn't need to know this."

"Actually, you do," Roger corrected. "We are a precious few. We look out for each other. It has always been this way, because there is no other way possible."

Elmer glanced at Roger, but looked back to Casey. "How, how long have you known?"

She pointed to Roger. "Roger was at the university scouting for recruits when he spotted me one day in a chemistry lab sneaking a raw snack. He filled me in from there. That was right before I came home and told you I was joining the agency."

Elmer closed his eyes. "The day you got me to eat."

He put his mug on the table and stood. Roger kept a steady gaze on him, but Casey stood and put a hand on his arm. "I know it's a lot to get a handle on, Elmer, but this is a good thing. You'll see. Just give it some time, and let it sink in. Don't fight it. Everything will make sense then. Everything," she repeated, squeezing his arm to draw his gaze to her. Her eyes widened to emphasize what she meant, her expression more serious than he'd ever seen.

He zipped his coat. "I have to go," he said under his breath.

Casey moved after him. "Wait, Elmer—"

Roger stood. "No, let him go. He needs time, just like you did."

Elmer stopped in the doorway, fishing in his pocket for the keys. Roger let out a deep breath. "Going to see your Samantha, are you?"

Elmer didn't turn.

"We'll be here for you," Roger added. "Enjoy her, while you can."

Elmer stepped out and closed the door. The frigid air assaulted him. He stood in place for a moment, his head spinning, before he remembered himself and climbed into the pickup. He drove to Parson's and parked, but then he sat for several minutes, unable to move, so befuddled was he. When he found the will to go in he shuffled like a zombie and dumped his weight on his familiar stool, staring into the empty space before him.

Samantha came out from the kitchen, giving him a wink as she brought the plates balanced on her tray to a table at the other side of the diner. He looked her way, and also noticed the three city men once again. They smiled at her with a little more familiarity, one of them even engaging her in some meaningless small talk. *They say there's more snow tonight. Really? Yeah, a few more inches. Well, you be careful driving.*

His eyes bulged in his head. He wondered if he could kill them with the teaspoon on the counter. Was the whole world intent on ripping the innards from every facet of his life?

When Samantha came back she seemed surprised by the ferocity of his gaze and, with a quizzical look, laid her hands over his. "Hey," she whispered, "what's wrong?"

He stared at her, his eyes still bulging. *What's wrong?* Her notion of honest concern only roused a litany of caustic, rabid sarcasm within him. *Let's see. I was bit by a bat from hell, I eat raw meat to live forever, I slept with my sister, and I just found out I'm part of some screwed-up secret society. Hi, I'm Elmer Phelps, you're friendly neighborhood anti-Christ come to take a wrecking ball to your life.*

He forced a swallow and shut his eyes to clear his thoughts. This was, after all, Samantha. She was good. She didn't deserve spillover from the cancerous wreck of his disgusting secrets. If only there was a way, some way, for her to understand. He didn't want to hurt her, and the notion of deceiving her sickened him.

He opened his eyes. "Samantha," he said under his breath.

She put a hand on his cheek. "Talk to me, okay? What happened?"

He blinked. "My, my sister came back."

She forced a smile. "Well, that's good. You two, you're close, right?"

He trembled, the shake of his hands unmistakable as his fingers remained meshed with hers. "My life," he winced. "My, my life is a mess."

She laid her fingers over his lips to quiet him. She leaned over the counter to kiss him, cupping his face in her hands when she withdrew. "Listen to me. You stay right here. I'll be right back." She went into the kitchen and, when she returned, Parson poked his head out from the order window to look at Elmer. Samantha pulled on her coat and led him from his stool out to the pickup. She drove them back to Parson's house, led him up to her apartment, and led him to the couch. She took off his coat, hung it, and came back with a heavy blanket, which she draped over him. She went to her bedroom to change, and then settled next to him, wearing a soft fleece sweatshirt and a comfortable pair of baggy plaid sleeping pants. She pulled off his shoes, and then rested back against the end of the couch, pulling his head to her chest before drawing the blanket over them.

She rubbed his shoulders and lowered her head to kiss his forehead. "Okay now?"

He worked his arms around her and folded his legs on the couch. He nodded against her, his eyes squeezing shut.

"Do you want to talk?"

He shook his head, but then changed his mind. He owed her something. "I haven't told you before, but my family, my life with my sister, it's very complicated."

"Okay," she whispered. She ran her fingers in little circles on his scalp. "You can tell me if you want. You can tell me anything, Elmer. I told you a bit about my past. I haven't exactly walked the straight and narrow. I won't judge you."

He held there, the sensation of her fingers soothing him. "Can, can we

161

just, just stay like this?"

"Of course," she said, and kissed his forehead once more.

He trembled. He tried to focus on her but, the more he did, the more Roger's words whispered with ever increasing truth through the back of his mind. What was he to do? If he denied what he was, if he took Samantha and ran off with her, he would die. If he lied to her and continued on, she would age and die. He couldn't infect her; he couldn't make her like him. Life had spat on him once more, spewing the scorching acid of its hatred for him, but the sense of ethereal wrong implied by such a notion took little purchase in that moment.

There was no space for such a thought, or any other in his head. He was consumed by one thought, and one thought only, that the living, warm flesh that embodied the one person who seemed to care for him would one day be nothing more than dust in his empty grasp.

He held her tighter, tight as he could without hurting her, and turned his face into her.

And so he lay, and wept, as he counted every fading moment.

***

Try as he might, there was no hiding from reality, only a bittersweet respite.

He woke in Samantha's bed, under the quilt, still in his clothes. He rolled on his back and glanced to his side to find her bundled up under the sheets, sleeping with long, slow breaths. He looked to the ceiling, pondered the foul taste in his mouth, and felt his stomach knot as he came to accept what he knew he must do. Hiding at Samantha's was no solution. His plan to keep his two lives walled apart had proved a pathetic failure, and the messy madness of the secret side was threatening to flood over the serene side. There was no choice for him; he had to do something.

He slipped out from under the quilt, taking care not to make a sound, and snuck out of her bedroom to her kitchen. Her apartment in the Parsons' upstairs was comfortable, but somewhat cramped, with the rooms in a line. He was thankful for that as he crept away from her room, knowing with each step there was less chance he would wake her. He left a note on the grocery pad she kept by the refrigerator and, for lack of anything better to write, he kept it short and simple.

Samantha—I have to take care of something. See you later.

He stared at those last three words for a moment, wondering if he should use three different words, but in the end he figured that would sound more like resignation. He had all intentions to see her later. That was the point, after all.

He eased her door shut, went down the stairs, and stepped out to the cold. It was dark, and the sky was clear for a change, the black dome above him pinpointed with countless stars. The moon was a slender, bright crescent. His breath misted before him, hanging in the still air.

He eased into the pickup, started the motor, and rolled away.

He opened the door to the house and found a pale glow coming from the kitchen. He poked his head around the corner and found Roger sitting at the kitchen island with his laptop open before him, his hand resting on his gun where it lay on the island. When he saw Elmer he eased and greeted him with a friendly smile. "How was your evening?"

Elmer stepped past the corner of the foyer. "Good. Where's Casey?"

Roger reached up to pull the chain for the lights on the ceiling fan. When they both squinted against the glare, Roger pulled the chain to turn them off and went to the stove to turn on the dim light under the vent hood. He eased back onto his stool and closed his laptop before offering a hand to the stool opposite for Elmer to sit. "Your sister is sleeping. Do you have trouble sleeping?"

Elmer sat on the stool and unzipped his coat. "Sometimes."

Roger nodded. "That's part of who we are. The longer we exist, the less we need that sleep. It is a horrible waste of time, if you think about it. Did you know that average humans sleep almost a third of their life?"

Elmer shook his head.

Roger held up a finger. "Oddly enough, the government takes roughly a third of the average person's income in various taxes. Perhaps it is a human condition to expect only two thirds of what is available to us, and accept that the remaining third is not to be achieved. That is to say, not without great cost, or risk. Give up sleep, and the human body suffers calamitous side effects. Refuse to pay your taxes, and the government will hunt you down without mercy."

Elmer scratched at the stubble on his jaw.

Roger let out a soft laugh. "I know, odd thoughts for such a late hour. The world sleeps, and here I sit, ruminating, shall I say. But I wish to make a point to you, something that was not quite so easy to discuss before, something I think you may have difficulty appreciating in your sister's presence. I believe, Elmer, that we got off on the wrong foot."

Elmer noticed the pot of coffee. "You could say that," he replied, rising to pour a cup. He turned to Roger, but Roger shook his head. "Look, I'll make this real simple," Elmer said as he returned to his stool. "Whatever you and Casey do with this agency of yours, that's fine. Just leave me out. I'm okay with my life here. You two go your way, and I'll go my way."

Roger drummed his fingers on the island, his gaze holding on Elmer.

"That's the way it's going to be," Elmer insisted. "I'm good with what

I have here."

Roger's gaze wandered over the kitchen. "I see. But let me ask you a few questions, based on what Cassandra has told me, if you will. Tell me, what will happen when your uncle eventually retires, or dies? What will you do to support yourself? What will happen when the Parsons die, and their house is sold?" Roger raised a hand at the bewildered look on Elmer's face. "Forgive me. These are very serious considerations, and you are so young. I'm sure life is comfortable for you now, what with living in the lap of your uncle's good fortune, with the company of people who seem to care for you, and with the affection of your girlfriend. But I ask those questions to help you realize that you live on the surface of a very fragile existence, Elmer, an existence as frail and as translucent as the bubble that it is. Soon—too soon—it will pop beneath you, and the very complacency that is both the curse and comfort of human existence will swallow you."

Elmer shook his head. "No. We'll find a way to make things work."

"Ah, yes, dear Samantha," Roger said, letting her name leave his mouth on the rush of his breath. "What will you tell her when you find out that you are sterile?"

"What?" Elmer looked at Roger in disbelief. "What are you talking about?"

"It's part of our condition," Roger continued. "We believe it is a balancing hand in evolution, in the greater wisdom of natural balance, that we are all sterile, otherwise we would crowd out the planet. You, me, your sister, all of us, we are all sterile."

Elmer backed away from the island. He was nineteen years old. The prospect of children was incomprehensible, too far removed to have entered any notions of his future. He shook his head. "Kids?" In some ways, he still felt like a child himself. "We haven't even talked about kids."

Roger tipped his head. "Very well. Adopt, if you must. No matter. What will you tell them—your dear Samantha, your darling children—when they all waste with age, and you remain young?"

Elmer looked down, at a loss for words.

"You see, Elmer, you are no longer part of the human world. It is only two thirds of what you are, that shabby, frail life humans worry so much about. To you, to us, there is no limit, no end. And with no end, we only need answer to ourselves, only need answer in the perspective of satisfying our desires. There is no other need to consider, and no concern for judgment."

Elmer's eyes snapped up to meet Roger's waiting gaze. He froze, as if a thousand spotlights of condemnation shone on him. Worse, he felt betrayed. *Casey told, had told—*

Roger opened his hands. "Elmer, listen to me. I have one last question for you. If you knew two people, one a sibling, the other not, and lived with them for a thousand years, would you know one better than the other? Would there be any difference between them?"

Elmer fell back a step. He shook his head and put his hands over his ears.

Roger crossed his arms on his chest. "Of course not," he said, answering himself. "These ideas of how we interact, of the boundaries of those interactions, they lose meaning over the span of time, over the length of our existence. Why limit yourself, Elmer? Do you know what we have learned? There is the here and now, and nothing else. I will prove this to you soon enough. There is no judgment, there is no greater presence; there is nothing past the final closure of our eyes, other than senile obliteration. Our time on this planet is precious. We must savor every moment."

There was a familiarity to the thought that struck Elmer like a punch in the chest, except that hearing it from Roger turned Elmer's once comfortable conclusion of the world's mute apathy into a revolting rejection of the world's hidden solace. The difference was time; the difference was having someone in his life. *Samantha.* He squeezed his eyes shut but, when he did, images of Casey flashed through his mind, driving him back until he felt the wall behind him. His eyes popped open, and he found her there before him, wrapped in a blanket, her bare shoulders poking from the warm folds. Her hand snaked out to rest on his chest, and he all but convulsed, his hands snapping up in defense.

He looked away and closed his eyes. "Please," he hissed, "don't, don't do this!"

She took hold of his wrist and led him from the kitchen. He was powerless to stop her, shuffling after her as his mind unraveled. She led him to her room and closed the door behind him. The blanket fell from her in the darkness. She pulled off his coat. She unbuttoned his shirt, and rested her hands on his shoulders. "Elmer?"

He started to whimper.

"I want you to understand," she whispered. "Shouldn't it be us? Don't you remember all those nights when we were young, talking through the wall? We don't need the wall anymore."

He shook his head, and somewhere inside him he found the resolve to deny the whispering madness surrounding him in that impenetrable darkness, in the blind depths of the big black empty. He pulled his shirt around him, pushing her hands away when she tried to stop him. He backed off, feeling his way in the dark, until he found himself in a corner. He slid down against the wall, curling in a fetal ball of denial as he turned his face from the room.

"Elmer?"

He shook his head. "No."

"Elmer?" she said again, the mattress sighing as she sat on the bed. "No!"

"Okay, okay. Nobody's going to touch you. You're safe."

He pulled his legs in tighter and sank further into the corner.

"I'm just going to talk. That's it. All you have to do is listen. Can you do that?"

Silence.

The sheets hissed as she pulled them about her. "It's like when we were little, isn't it, sitting with nothing but the darkness between us? Those are the best memories I have; do you know that? I want you to know, I want to tell you—confess to you, maybe—that I realize my feelings toward you were never quite the way they were supposed to be. It's just, well, you were always this quiet little kid, and the compulsion to protect you pulled at my every nerve and fiber. But at the same time you were a comfort for me, you were a comfort for all the crazy voices that whisper in my head. That's why I talked to you all those nights through the wall, because I needed to hear your voice. You might have thought I was protecting you those years, but you were protecting me just as much. We have an understanding, Elmer. We know each other in ways that other people never get to know each other, and I'm not just talking about what happened the last time we met, but that's what I'm trying to explain to you."

She listened in the darkness. She could hear his short, tight breaths.

"You have to understand what Roger said to you. We're going to live a very long time. All this, all these things around us, all these people around us, they're all going to fade away, but we'll remain. We'll need a safe harbor from the world out there. Who better for us to be with, but each other? Who better to understand us, than each other? Nothing can compare to that, no one can compare to that. I'm not going to ask you to cut things off with Samantha. I'm not going to be selfish that way. But I think, I think maybe we can save a little spot for each other inside, in some special place, don't you think?"

He could hear the wind outside. He wondered if it was snowing. He remembered Samantha standing in the snow, looking to the sky as she hummed her lullaby. His face eased enough for his eyes to open to slits, but there was no escape from the darkness. The images in his head became images in the room. Darkness is the home of Fear, because the searching gaze will fill it with whatever the mind can conjure.

Samantha. If only she wasn't a million miles away.

Casey let out a long breath. "I know this isn't easy, bro. In the end, it'll just be us, and you need to understand that. There won't be anyone left to judge. There'll just be the safety of having each other, and the secrets we hold between us. I trust you more than I trust anyone. And no matter what happens, I want you to know one thing. I love you, Elmer, love you the way no one else can love you, love you in all the idealized ways one should love another."

She fell silent. There was a soft whoosh as her head sank back in her pillow. But then she stirred, rose from the bed, and her bare feet padded across the carpeted floor toward him. She draped a blanket over his shivering form and laid a hand on his head. Her touch lingered for several moments, the pressure of her fingers undulating as she wavered between staying and leaving. In the end she left him and settled back in bed.

There was nothing between them but the still black void.

"Goodnight," she whispered. "I'm here if you need me."

He clamped his hands over his ears. He tried to think of something—anything—to fend off the big black empty gnawing at every pore of his body. His mind flashed with corrupted, carnal visions, sending tremors through his body until every muscle locked, locked in one agonizing contraction he thought would shred every tendon and ligament in one blinding eruption of agony. His fingers clawed at his scalp, the darkness of his eyelids bursting with a kaleidoscopic shimmer of pain.

And then, it was over.

He heard the beat of his heart and, with it, something else, but he caught its rhythm, and through it a sense of peace, a sense of serenity, even as his sister's disembodied gaze washed around him.

"Elmer?" she hissed in the darkness.

He didn't hear her. He couldn't. He hummed Samantha's lullaby, and his body dissolved in a ragged ball as consciousness at last fled his imploding mind.

***

When he woke, he felt a sense of clarity.

But the moment his thoughts stirred from their slumber the creeping dread of night returned to him, and he trembled, working his fingers to the edge of the blanket Casey left on him to pull it just below his eyes. He tightened, peeking past his knuckles and over his shoulder to see the bed empty, the sheets pulled up. Dim light seeped in from the heavy curtains drawn over the window. The door to the hallway was ajar. He held his breath and listened and, beside the steady thump of his pulse in his ears, he heard nothing.

Casey and Roger had left. He was alone.

He pushed up to a shaky stance, clutching the blanket about his shoulders. He crept from the room, looking about to be sure they were gone. He paced to the kitchen and found a note on the island beside an empty mug. The coffee machine was still on, with a pot made and left atop the fading warmth of the hotplate. He looked to the note, and read it without touching the paper.

Elmer—I'll be back in a few days. Love, C

He poured some coffee. He turned around and leaned on the counter, staring out the windows as he held the mug in his hand. The wind moaned outside. His thoughts churned away as he stood there, his arm rising every now and then to bring the mug to his mouth, but soon it was forgotten in his hand.

The storm in his head settled, and from the emotional wreckage several conclusions took shape. His sister had seduced him, manipulated him into a despicable act. Nevertheless, it didn't absolve him from his willingness to partake in the temptation. There was an evil rooted in his life, yellow-eyed and leather-winged, that he had to put to rest. It poisoned everything in him. His feelings for Samantha, and his relationship with her, were in part inseparable from his relationship with his sister, as one bled into the other. He had found comfort from the discomfort with his parents in the shadowed, wooded expanse of Proskoy Wood that lay between their worlds. Problems required definitive action, marked by acts of separation. The deeper a problem, the more definitive the required action. But he had to make a choice.

And then it came to him, that there was in fact no question to his choice.

He put the mug down, picked up the phone, and dialed.

Samantha's welcome voice greeted him. "Hey, you. Where are you? Everything okay?"

"I'm at the house." He closed his eyes. "Everything's going to be just fine. Samantha?"

"What?"

He took a deep breath. "I love you, Samantha Hayes."

She sniffed several times, the phone rustling with her breath.

He waited, his heart stilling in his chest.

"Love you too," she whispered. "Now come back here, you big goofball, okay?"

His head rolled back in relief. "I'll be over in a little bit," he said, and keyed off the phone. He didn't open his eyes until he put the phone back on its charger base. The white ceiling met his gaze. He rolled his shoulders, looked out the windows and, despite the dawning clarity within him, he frowned.

"No," he said under his breath. "You know it's the only way."

With a nod he walked away. He went into Paul's gun locker, took out

the large, black mass of a pump shotgun, and slid the shells home one by
one.

***

He drove to Samantha's apartment, the shotgun tucked behind the
seat of the pickup truck which swayed on the snow-covered road in the
buffeting wind. Despite the worsening weather and the steady snow he
walked with Samantha in the woods behind the Parsons' house, their
hands clasped between them. When the cold bit through their layers of
clothes they returned, and she took out a container of split pea soup and
made tea while the soup simmered on the stove. He was quiet, and
somewhat distant, but when she asked him about Casey, he shook his
head and said things would turn out okay. They ate the soup while
watching a documentary he found, a program discussing several theories
regarding the proposed migratory patterns of pterodactyls in Earth's pre-
history.

The soup done, they huddled under a blanket, the moan of frigid
winds outside drawing them closer together. He was tired from the
madness he endured the night before and, despite—or perhaps because
of—the welcome peacefulness of sitting with Samantha, he found his
eyelids drooping.

She lifted her head from his shoulder and studied him before
whispering his name.

Somewhat startled, he grunted in reply, but she waited until he
turned his face to her.

"How'd you know?" she whispered.

He opened his mouth, but then cleared his throat. He understood
what she wanted to know, so he drew in a breath and hummed her
lullaby. She smiled, even as her eyes welled up, before kissing him and
holding him in a tight embrace.

Later, as he lay awake in her bed, he rested with his eyes closed and
the scent of her hair in his nose as his thoughts plodded through him. He
was exhausted, drained, and yet content, and somehow, despite the
leaden weight of his limbs, he felt at once listless and restless, this
seeming contradiction serving to buoy his consciousness from the
nightmares he was sure rested in wait. His eyes slid open to look upon
the crown of her head as she slept with her back tight against his chest,
the warmth of their bodies joined beneath her blankets and quilt. So it
was he once again found himself in the still darkness of night, and his
voiceless thoughts went by in overlapping visions, a complex language
unto their own.

He pondered many things as the world wandered beneath him

through the vacuum of the big black empty. Yet for all the things he pondered, he found himself returning again and again to the same, simple impressions, subjective and so beyond definitive truth, yet in their own way, achieving a truth he couldn't debate. Roger and Casey proposed that there was life, and that the end of life was obliteration, so there was nothing but the world around them. Lying there with Samantha, as he considered all the reasons, all the endless possibilities that had to be satisfied for them to meet, for them to relate, it baffled him, and moved him to a very different conclusion, deflating the pessimistic disdain his youth had fostered for notions of a greater level of existence. He refused to accept the constrictive idea of fate, but he was moved to consider a different implication for, though he was a stranger to the mysteries of math and the subtleties of probabilistic extrapolations, those endless circumstances that had produced the two singular entities of he and Samantha transcended what a careless world would allow. Could life be so callous, could existence be so shallow, and yet smile on the two of them, to bring their world weary vessels together, in just the right way, in just the right time, so they could commune, and know this feeling between each other? And what was that feeling? Certainly it lived, it existed, and yet it had no tangible form, no physical embodiment; rather, it was more like a ghost, a communal spirit, its presence a whisper in their heads, a tingle in their fingertips, a warmth in their chests.

No, he was moved to accept a different reality, a different subjective choice, one he knew was not original by any means, but one that found its home within him: when that which should not happen by all logical consideration does in fact happen, another causative element must be taken into account. He hesitated to name that element, refused to name that cause, but of one thing he was certain, and that was the utter, undeniable, unavoidable, inescapable, complete failure of the logic Casey and Roger swore as their truth.

Without defiling himself with Casey, he may not have redeemed himself with Samantha. Without the desperation of his youth, he may not treasure the solace he knew in that moment, laying with Samantha under her sheets in the once fearful still of night.

Means and ends, ends and means.

He took a deep breath and closed his eyes. He drew her closer, keeping her safe as they floated in the black waters of his dreams. And beneath the serene, elegant, and sublime beauty of holding her to him, he found a certain clarity of mind, and despite that calm—or again, perhaps due to it—he found the resolve to scheme, to plot, to set careful considerations and plans for bloody mayhem and black murder.

See you in a few days. Love, C

He let his breath go. He drifted off to sleep, certain he would be ready.

***

Christmas came in the form of another cozy dinner at Parson's diner. Samantha wore the choker from Halloween, but she tied a pair of tiny jingle bells to the choker with a length of red yarn. It had a magical effect on him, the bells tinkling every time she laughed, intoxicating him more than the wine he consumed.

After dinner he walked with Samantha back to her apartment, and they exchanged gifts. She gave him a new dress shirt, and he gave her a new winter coat, as the one she wore for every day use was fraying at the seams. They were practical people after all, and not of great means. They afforded themselves one treat, and that was a dinner at Loggers', an anniversary of sorts, but they made a point to stay for dessert and shared a slice of chocolate decadence pie. As they did the first time they walked about the hill on which Loggers' sat, laughing when snow came down in apparent memory of that first dinner. They threw snowballs at each other, chased each other between the trees and, by the time they grew weary of the cold, they couldn't get back to her apartment fast enough. At his request she wore the jingle bell choker to dinner and, by the time they made it to her bedroom, it was the only thing left between them.

Life once again became the happiest time he'd known. But he was careful to keep his senses and, despite all outside notice of his usual ways, he kept a close watch about town, and was ever mindful of the shotgun he kept in the pickup.

He would not be surprised again. Or so he thought.

***

After the last encounter with Casey and Roger, Elmer all but moved in with Samantha. She asked about the shift in where they spent their time, as she found her apartment cramped in comparison to the luxuriant spaciousness of Big Paul's house, but Elmer said he preferred her apartment for its proximity to town and the diner. They could walk everywhere they needed to go and, with the worsening winter weather, not having to worry about driving was a valid argument. But after Christmas he was compelled to return to the house to fulfill his responsibilities, as the property was getting buried under a progressively thicker blanket of snow. So on a Friday morning he swung by Gustafson's to pick up his order, chatted with the amicable butcher and Ingrid, as had become his comfortable custom, and drove out to Proskoy Wood to tend to his chores.

171

It was demanding work. Not only did he have to plow out the long driveway, but he fired up the snow blower to clear a path to the front and back doors, pulled out the ladder to climb up on the roof to clear it of snow, serviced the generator in the shed in case the power lines went down, and ran the snowmobiles to cycle their engines in case all other means of transport were denied by a sudden, heavy snow. By the time evening drew on he knew he was in no mood to drive and, with some remaining miscellaneous chores still waiting to be done, he called Samantha at the diner and told her he would stay overnight. It went against his better judgment to stay, but he brought in the shotgun and kept it on the bed next to him as he slept.

He woke to the smell of fresh coffee. His eyes popped open, and when his hand sprang out for the shotgun, he found only an impression in the quilt.

His blood ran cold.

He rose from bed, pulled on his clothes, and crept from the bedroom to the kitchen. He trembled with anxiety as he peered around the corner of the hall, only to find Roger's waiting stare. Roger greeted Elmer with a hearty welcome, startling Casey as she stood by the coffee machine. She spun on the heel of her boot and gave Elmer a wide smile, her long ponytail sliding across her shoulders. "Hey bro! Merry Christmas!"

Elmer came around the corner, nodding repeatedly with his nerves. "Right, right, Merry Christmas. Uh, you too, Roger."

Roger closed his laptop and rested his hands on the kitchen island. He noted the dart of Elmer's eyes toward the living room and the shotgun left on the coffee table. Roger stuck out his arm and raised a finger to catch Elmer's gaze, then swung his arm back before him to draw in Elmer's attention. "That's not wise to sleep with such a powerful weapon, Elmer. Mistakes can be deadly. Why would you do such a thing?"

Elmer opened his mouth, but stiffened when Casey came up to him and gave him a hug. He gave her a heartless pat on the back as she squeezed him with one arm, a mug of coffee held in her other hand. She gave him a quizzical look as she fanned out to his side, her hand sliding down to the small of his back. He put his hands in his pockets and tipped his chin to the windows. "We, we had a Christmas party, and Clay, the sheriff, he said the wolves range down from the hills some nights this time of year, so I thought I should get in the habit of carrying, just in case."

Casey slipped away to pour him some coffee. "So how was your Christmas?"

He nodded to the mug she handed him. "Nice," he said.

"Sit, will you?" Casey urged before walking past him to the living room.

He settled on a stool, noting his surroundings. Both Roger and Casey were wearing their white dress shirts and black slacks. Their black trench coats were draped over the couch. They both had their gun belts on. Roger's tie was in a neat little knot over the top button of his shirt. The blue agency sedan was parked outside, behind the pickup.

Roger was able to deduce Elmer's darting gaze. "Yes, Elmer, we are here on business."

Elmer pointed to the laptop. "How come you close it when I'm here?"

Roger sat up straight, a slow grin forming on his lips as his eyes narrowed. "Manners, my friend, manners. It is rude to be clicking away when engaged in conversation. Attention should be focused on the person you interact with. Don't you agree?"

"I guess so." Elmer looked back to the laptop. "So what do you have on there?"

Roger crossed his arms on his chest. "I take it you've been thinking about the agency."

"I hope so," Casey said over her shoulder as she rummaged through the pockets of her coat. "Where did I leave it? Aha!"

Elmer ignored her, his gaze lingering on the laptop. "So what do you have on there?"

"Research. The agency has its own secure databases we can access. The laptop has an encrypted wireless connection to a server in the car, which has a further encrypted satellite link. We can bypass the Internet for secure, untraceable browsing. Did you know, for instance, that Proskoy only has one chain of hard phone lines connecting it to the outside world?"

"Why would he care about that?" Casey said as she walked by Roger. Her hand slid across Roger's shoulders and, for a moment, Elmer felt his muscles tighten in subconscious reflex. He wasn't sure if it was the old sense of fraternal protectiveness, or some lingering cancerous form of perverted jealousy, but what he was sure of was a powerful urge he had to lunge at Roger and tear him limb from limb.

He blinked at the flash of rage that passed through him. He shifted on the stool as he calmed himself behind the protective barriers in his mind, barriers formed from his connection with Samantha, the humming lilt of her lullaby, and his disavowal of Roger's beliefs. He tore his gaze from Roger to hide the contempt he was sure seeped from his eyes to watch Casey approach him with a gift in her hand.

She set it down before him and kissed his cheek. "Ho-ho, bro," she said with a laugh.

He stared at the slender, green wrapped box. "I didn't get you anything."

She waved him off and sipped her coffee. "Don't worry about it. Just open it."

Roger held up a hand and looked to Casey. "His meal?"

Casey shook her head and put her mug down. "How could I forget?" She opened the refrigerator and took out a plate with a splendid slab of raw, red meat. Elmer studied it when she put it down before him, as the shape of the cut was something he hadn't seen before. Casey nodded when she saw his hesitation. "Trust me, bro, it's good."

Roger smiled. "Yes, your man Gustafson, he has a good taste."

Elmer looked between them. Eating the raw meat, indulging his need in front of them, was the last thing he wanted to do, but he told himself if he was going to resist them in whatever way he could, he had to remain strong, in every way he knew. He cut a piece off the edge and tossed it in his mouth, and the eruption of saliva almost rushed out between his lips. He trembled; the taste was so exquisite. He had to close his eyes to contain himself as he chewed and let the shredded strands of flesh slide down his throat.

Roger's voice came to him. "I told you, Gustafson surprised me with his good taste."

"Better than I would have thought," Casey agreed. "Now open, open!"

Elmer set his fork down and opened her gift, peeling back the paper to reveal a slender black case. His eyes narrowed as he stared at the case, familiarity returning to him on a wave of suspicion and dread. He opened the case, and his heart sank. Inside he found a pair of delicate metallic tools, identical to the ones he'd found in Casey's possession.

He looked up. "What are these?"

Casey put a hand on his shoulder. "We all get a set, when we're identified by the agency. It's official now, bro. You're part of the club."

Roger pointed to the case. "It's a coring set."

Elmer took a breath. "What's a coring set?"

Casey gave him one of her mischievous smiles. "You're about to find out."

"Put on your shoes," Roger ordered as he stood from his stool. "We're going for a drive. I would assume you're familiar with the estate properties around Proskoy Wood, yes?"

Elmer nodded as he closed the case. His gaze fell on the steak. Drool seeped from the corners of his mouth and dripped onto the island. He wanted to control himself but, staring at the red flesh, he was powerless to resist. In a matter of moments he cut the meat into little cubes that he devoured whole. Casey dropped his boots beside him, but he hardly noticed her as he engorged himself. She took the shotgun and loaded it with the shells that were hidden in her pocket. When she was done she gave the weapon a definitive pump, grinning over the threatening sound.

Elmer looked to her and almost fell off his stool. The last cube of meat slid down his throat and disappeared in the depths of his stomach. The fork clattered from his hand onto the plate. He swayed, his eyelids drooping. Warmth pervaded his limbs; his blood surged through him with a powerful whoosh, as if the raucous mountain river had turned red and channeled itself through his body. His cheeks felt as if they were glowing and, as he stuffed his feet in his boots, he came to the decision that he felt as if he'd downed half a bottle of wine. He wanted to congratulate Gustafson on whatever meat it was, but then he thought of Ingrid. He always liked Ingrid, from the first time he saw her. For a woman a few years older than his mother, he found her attractive.

Good old Ingrid.

He looked up when Casey hooked her arm through his and led him out to the agency car, laughing to herself whenever she glanced at him. She helped him into the back of the car, her ponytail sliding over her shoulder to brush across his face. His eyes rolled over, his hand waving in drunken delight toward her hair like a cat playing with dangling yarn. She pushed him back in the seat and closed the door before settling in the driver's seat. Roger took position in the passenger seat. Elmer slumped back, his hands dropping on either side of him. He felt bloated, but otherwise he was numb with delight.

He heard the clack of keys on Roger's laptop. The car rumbled around him as it worked its way over the snow-draped roads. The rolling, shadowy depths of Proskoy Wood passed by the windows in a blur. The sky was masked with heavy gray clouds. Ingrid had some gray in her hair but, otherwise, she was still blond, as fair as her Nordic roots could allow, and her eyes were very blue, blue as a summer sky.

He chuckled to himself, reveling in his decadent fantasies. Soon enough they changed focus so that his eyes shut as he replayed every intimate moment he'd shared with Samantha.

The car came to a halt. Casey called his name several times before he opened his eyes.

Roger pointed out his window. "That house up there. Do you know this house?"

Elmer nodded. "The Piedmont place. Stock, stockbrokers, or something."

Roger turned to Casey and nodded. "Hit the ignition interrupt and turn the key."

Casey reached under the dash and flipped a switch. When she turned the ignition key, the starter turned over, but the engine failed to fire. She did this three times, the third time letting the starter run for several seconds before Roger held up a hand. He told her to pull the hood release and got out of the car. The hood went up, blocking the view from the windshield, but soon enough Roger's hand emerged and turned in a circle to signal Casey to try the engine again. The starter tried, but failed. Roger came to Casey's window as she powered it down. "That should do," he said. "I'll be back in a few minutes. Gun," he prompted, and took the weapon Casey handed him.

She closed her window and watched him walk off before unclipping her seatbelt and turning in her seat to look at Elmer. She wrapped her arms around the seat as she rested her cheek against the side of the headrest. "How do you feel?"

He blinked several times. "Why, why do I feel drunk?"

She grinned, her gaze boring into him. "If you think we put something in the meat, we didn't. It's the meat itself, Elmer. It's a special cut. Very special. I got it, just for you."

He leaned forward, resting his elbows on his knees as he rubbed his face, trying to make some sense of the muddy wash in his head. He dropped his hands and, when he opened his eyes, he found that Casey's gaze was only a few inches away from him. He cleared his throat. "Did you see Ingrid? I, I like talking to Ingrid, you know. She was nice to me from the day I got here."

Casey's eyes lit with mischief. "You like her, don't you?"

He closed his eyes, blushing as he nodded.

Casey sighed. "Yeah, old Gustafson really loved her. I never knew how much."

He opened his eyes to stare at her. Despite himself, his guard crumbled within him, and life with Samantha seemed a dream that he lost somewhere, a long time ago, aborted when he was a boy, swept away in the beat of leathery wings. There was only one person who was there to protect him all those years. He trembled, trying and failing to rally himself and refute the whispers in his head, but it was impossible with the foggy euphoria of the steak clouding his will.

"Elmer, some things are going to happen today. All the secrets go away. I know you've been resisting it, but today you'll see it all, for everything it is. Are you with me?"

His head rolled forward, his cheek coming to rest on the shoulder of Roger's seat as a stupid, drunken grin pulled at his lips. In that moment, he saw no point in fighting it anymore. Who else could watch him devour raw meat and think nothing of it? Who could he be honest with about the despicable intimacy he'd shared with his sister—except his sister? All the things he knew he had to hide from Samantha, things that he was sure would send her running from him in disgust, could be plain and open with Casey. It was a seduction of a different kind, one less shameful, and yet more insidious, than what she did to him before.

Who am I kidding? It's all a joke; it's all a pack of lies. How long did I dream about this? So what if it's wrong. What is 'wrong' if I never die? She's right. Damn, she's always right.

He shrugged in resignation. Part of him wanted to rip his stomach open and let Gustafson's cursed meat spill on the floor so he could regain his better judgment, but it was too late for that. He gave her a little nod. "Sure. I'm with you."

Her lips parted, her eyes beaming with delight. She grabbed the collar of his coat and pulled him to her.

The hood closed with a bang, startling them. Roger got in the car, looking to Casey as she still held Elmer's collar, her forehead resting against his. "There'll be time enough for that later," Roger said, reaching over his shoulder to lay a hand on Elmer's head and push him back. He kept his gaze on Casey until she turned in her seat before he looked to Elmer. "So then, I take it you're on board with us?"

"He's good," Casey said as she started the car.

"I'm here," Elmer drawled as he wiped his mouth on the back of his hand.

Roger closed his laptop; Elmer closed his eyes. The car started moving again. He heard the distinctive metallic click and clack of weapons being loaded and checked. They were driving up a hill. The Piedmont house was atop a small hill. It was surrounded by a vast expanse of trees, accessible only by the winding length of its drive. Aside from Big Paul's house, it was perhaps the most isolated of the estates. He and Samantha would often fantasize about owning an estate like the Piedmont place. It was quiet and peaceful. Ingrid had once said she liked the Piedmont location when he and Samantha were talking at Gustafson's. Harmless, pleasant small talk. Ingrid was always gracious with small-talk, her presence marked by a calm, earnest demeanor that always made one feel she had a genuine interest in the person she was talking to, no matter how inane the conversation.

"No problem?" he heard Casey say.

He opened his eyes to glance out the window. A car was parked on the side of the drive. A man and a woman were slumped in the front seats, their faces covered in blood.

"No problem," Roger echoed. "The old car-broke-down ploy. Works every time. It's amazing how gullible even trained personnel can be in their misguided sympathy for a motorist stranded in the cold."

Elmer closed his eyes. Were it not for the euphoric fog of the meat, he would've been in full panic. Instead, he shrugged and licked his lips.

Roger glanced over his shoulder. "Are you familiar with the philosophical treatises of Friedrich Nietzsche?"

It took a moment for Elmer to realize the question was directed at him. "What? No."

"I didn't think so. Let me say this. One of his ideas was that the world is here for us to experience its pleasures. Enlightenment, self-actualization and realization, these only come from us having the strength of will to refute the hackneyed reservations handed down from fearful autocrats who sought to control the barbarism of people. But enacting such a belief, a belief we in the agency hold dear, requires a certain material abundance. We have such wealth, Elmer, wealth accumulated and compounded over centuries, wealth you cannot comprehend until you see it in action around you. This exquisite custom fabricated car, our data reserves, our influence within the government— all from the money we hoard, so that we can be unfettered in our timeless lives. Do you understand?"

Elmer hummed a reply. He needed his dictionary.

Roger continued. "One thing about Nietzsche, and that is his endless capacity for quotation. There is of course that little gem that if you look into the abyss, the abyss also looks into you, and that other little gem that God is dead, but my favorite goes as such: 'What is great in man is that he is a bridge, and not an end'." He glanced at Elmer. "You see, Elmer, there is no limit, but ourselves."

"That's a little dense for him right now," Casey said.

"Then just remember this, Elmer," Roger continued. "Never, ever, steal from us."

The car came to a halt. Elmer opened his eyes when the front doors opened, the cold air snapping some sense to his foggy mind. He lifted his head to look out the windshield. Roger and Casey were standing to either side of the car, just ahead of the front bumper, their hands clasped behind their backs. They each held a handgun, the weapons fitted with the fat extensions of silencers.

The door to the house opened, and Elmer blinked in recognition. The person standing there was one of the three city men he saw every now and then in town. In a moment of paranoia he wondered if they were part of the agency, but then he dismissed the thought. If they were, Roger and Casey would've said something.

The man's lips were moving, but Elmer couldn't make out what he was saying.

It didn't seem to matter to Roger and Casey. Their arms snapped forward and they opened fire, riddling the door with bullets that punched through the heavy oak and the man's body with equal ease. Elmer's eyes widened with each shot, the muted *pup-pup-pup* of the silenced handguns almost belying the bloody havoc they wreaked on the man's body as it shuddered and dropped in the doorway. Casey and Roger charged to the open door, Roger flinging it open with one hand as

Casey ducked under his arm and invaded the house. Elmer sat in the car, stunned. He heard several rounds of return fire, the hard pops of weapons without silencers, erupting in a brief wild-west cacophony before the woods were once again silent. He watched with enormous eyes when Casey emerged from the house with a crooked grin. The left shoulder of her trench coat was torn, the fabric puckered outward, and in the gap the red stained mess of her shirt could be seen. Despite the wound, she reached out with her left hand and opened Elmer's door.

Her grin widened to a broad smile. "Don't worry. It's nothing. Come with me."

She grabbed his arm and steadied him as she led him into the house. He looked down in disbelief at the bloody corpse of the man slumped in the doorway. Roger was in the foyer, waiting until they entered to drag the corpse out of the doorway before shutting the door against the cold.

Elmer stopped at the end of the foyer. A living room was to his right. A second body was stretched out on the floor, a neat hole in the man's forehead to explain the spray of red gore on the wall opposite Elmer. Down the hall ahead of him a third body lay slumped across the threshold of a bedroom. To his left, in a reading room with a comfortable looking sofa and a welcome fire, there were three more men, all of them on their knees, their hands atop their heads.

Casey fixed her gun on the three men as Roger walked around them to stand by the fireplace. Roger looked to Elmer and pointed at the men with his gun. "I'm told by your sister that you enjoy watching documentaries on animal behavior."

Elmer nodded. "Posture and poise," he said under his breath.

Roger nodded. "Good. I have a little game for you, Elmer. A matching game. We have three men. One is an FBI field agent, like the others strewn about. One is a senior FBI agent, who believed this was a safe witness protection location and who, I would imagine, is quite baffled by what is happening this moment. The third is a man—not like us, I should tell you—who was contracted by our agency to handle certain financial transactions. In his misguided greed he decided to take a sizable portion of a cash transfer for his own good, a reckless act that landed him in the hands of the FBI before we could get to him. I imagine it was the wild story he told them of his involvement with a mysterious, shadowy, covert government agency that elicited enough interest within the bumbling ranks of investigative bureaucracy to provide him with a witness protection deal. Now, tell me the identity of each man."

Elmer looked them over. The man at the end seemed in his early thirties at most, his face fixed with a stunned expression of disbelief. Elmer pointed him out as the field agent. The man in the middle was older, perhaps in his late forties to early fifties, but there was a hard look in his eyes, with his lips pressed in a tight, stubborn line. Elmer figured him as the senior field agent. The last man was pathetic; a trembling wreck with his eyes squeezed shut so tight that tears ran down his cheeks. This man was undoubtedly the weasel.

Roger nodded. "Very good, very good. If you will, Casey."

Casey raised her arm. She shot the field agent in the head and the senior agent in the chest. Both men flopped onto their backs, blood gurgling in the chest of the senior agent. The weasel cowered as he broke out in sobs, holding his hands up for mercy before Casey shot him in the chest as well.

She turned to Elmer and smiled as she reloaded her gun with a fresh clip.

"If you would be so kind," Roger said to Elmer, pointing at the feet of the weasel. Roger put his hands under the man's armpits and, with Elmer taking the man's feet, they carried him to the dining room, blood pouring from the hole in the man's back. Casey swept the plates and candelabra from the table, letting them clatter to the floor so Roger and Elmer could lay out the body.

Elmer fell back a step, stupefied by the brutality around him.

Roger stood by the head of the body and reached into his coat to pull out his coring kit. Casey followed suit, Elmer remaining motionless until Casey patted her hand against his coat. He reached inside to find the coring kit she gave him. He opened it, looked at the body, and his sense of dread grew to a numbing horror.

Roger pulled a silk cloth from his pocket and wiped his two slender, chromed tools. "It is time for you to understand our closest secret, and our greatest strength, Elmer. As you know, the infectious agent that has caused us to change imparts us with numerous extraordinary benefits, all for the small price of requiring us to eat a regular diet of raw meat. You see, there are certain alterations in the protein metabolism of our bodies, caused by the change, and this is the root of what defines us. Raw beef serves as a fitting meal, but it is not what can give us the greatest benefit. But that is physiological, and now you must learn something that is far beyond known explanation."

Roger leaned over the body and slid the thicker tool with the serrated end into the nose of the corpse. When it would go no farther he stopped and, using the second tool as a fulcrum, turned the first tool several times until it made a slight move deeper into the man's head. "The brain is encased in the formidable protection of the skull. It is not easily accessible except through the sinus cavities, where only a thin tissue layer separates the sinus from the brain. Did you know there is an amoeboid species living in Floridian ponds that if forced into the sinus by a wash of water—say, by diving into a pond—can eat its way through this tissue layer and infest the victim's brain?"

Elmer shook his head. He was growing nauseous. His stomach bucked. But with each mounting moment, he was compelled to accept that it was not revulsion that caused the unruliness of his stomach, but rather a wild hunger that dwarfed any appetite he possessed for raw beef medallions.

Casey put her hand on the back of his neck, her grip tightening to where he couldn't move.

Roger took a breath, licking his lips as saliva seeped from his mouth. "Ah, so sweet the hunger," he whispered to himself as he fitted the slender length of the scooping tool into the hollow shaft of the boring tool. He glanced at Elmer and Casey, his eyes enlarged, as he pushed the scooping tool in until it would go no more. "Watch me, Elmer. See, you stop when you feel resistance. Give the tool one turn, and then pull up on the finger ring. This will give you a measured sample. Casey, recite the rules, if you will."

Casey took a breath. "Never sample more than one core from the same donor. Never sample more than the scooping tool will collect. Never sample without knowledge of the donor's life. Never sample without background research. Never sample from a donor who has suffered severe head trauma."

Elmer blinked. He wanted to run. He wanted the sample. He wanted to die.

Roger withdrew the scooping tool. "And why do we have these rules?"

"Protection against donor memory overlay," Casey replied. She looked at Elmer. "You have to remember this, Elmer, and in a moment, you'll understand it for yourself." She took the scooping tool from his kit and handed it to Roger, followed by her own.

Roger took the samples and, when he was done, returned their tools. He held his own tool and stood up straight. "So tell me, how was Gustafson? He was a stubborn man."

The words hardly registered. Elmer's hand shook as he looked at the tool in his hand, at the little lump of greasy red tissue held in the chromed claw at the end of the tool. And before he could think, before he could stop himself, before whispers of damnation could rally a single utterance, his hand rose and his mouth opened.

His eyes rolled back in his head, his eyelids fluttering. Images flashed through his mind, little spasms shaking his body as he took several short breaths. He saw things, things that were not his memories, memories that came from—

Samples. Donors. Donor imprint overlay. I'm seeing another man's memories!

He swayed, but Casey's firm grip on his neck kept him from falling over.

Gustafson. Ingrid. What did Roger say? Gustafson had 'a' good taste. Casey said she never knew how much Gustafson loved Ingrid. The meat, the meat I ate—it was Gustafson!

He thrashed and threw himself back, slamming against the wall.

He saw Roger and Casey walk into the butcher shop. They asked where Elmer was, and Gustafson said he didn't know. He could feel Gustafson didn't trust Roger. Gustafson knew where Elmer was. Ingrid said so. He could feel the terror in Gustafson's gut. Too late. *Pup, pup.* Roger shot Ingrid in the head and Casey shot Gustafson in the chest. Dying then, bleeding away, and Roger looming over Gustafson as Casey pulled off the butcher's pants. Pain, searing pain, and Roger didn't stop cutting, slicing thick filets out of Gustafson's thigh.

Core him? Casey says.

No, Roger says. *His flesh will tell us enough. Your brother is either with his little girlfriend or at the house.*

Let's go to the house first, Casey says after a moment's hesitation.

Roger looks to her. *I figured you'd say that. Protecting his little tart, even though he shuns you for her? How noble.*

A white ceiling, and thoughts of Ingrid. How peaceful it was, childhood days on a Norwegian shore, fishing in the black depths of fjords.

Elmer's knees gave out. He slid down the wall to hit the floor.

The tissue dissolved in his stomach. The images in his head transformed. If the visions he saw from ingesting Gustafson's flesh were distinct, this new set of visions threatened to blow his eyes out of his head.

Glass towers. Black sedans. A dissolute life of a man with no moral check. Cash for sex from exquisite escorts possessing a mystical beauty that clashes with the ugliness of their trade. No sense of right or wrong, only might and strength of greed. Too much greed. Take the money, the agency will never know. Too much drinking, too much partying. Sloppy work. Calls from the Trade Commission on transaction abnormalities. The money, where's the money? Too many uptight people in cheap government-salary suits asking questions. It's all falling apart, have to run, have to blame, have to make good to get away—that's it, spill the secret, tell the tale, sell out the agency and their weird people, their threats be damned! Take one fat bag of cash as insurance and hide it, hide it somewhere, hide it right under the noses of those fools protecting him. Keep it close, keep it safe, keep that fat bag of cash and all the freedom it delivers!

His eyes popped open. He clawed at his scalp.

Casey in the bathroom: the glisten of wet skin, the length of her hair. There she is, triumphant protector, swatting the screeching bats from him. She's always there, in his dreams, in his shadows, a whisper in the dark, a phantom in his dreams. She is safety, she is power, she is knowledge; she is all that he is not and, rotting in his parent's basement, all that he will never be.

Casey in his bedroom: leaning over him, after a night of blasphemous temptation and ruinous lust. Visions of his parents in mute horror if they ever knew; visions of Samantha running from him, running farther than the world could allow, the big black empty devouring, defiling, defecating the love between them in cynical riots of laughter. All that is good is lost, all that is twisted resplendent in decadent delight.

The world turned upside down.

A fat bag of cash: material excess for freedom. He could take it, take Samantha, and they could run to the ends of the earth, and never be found. All the madness could chase him as much as it wanted and never catch him. It would be deceiving Samantha, it would be protecting her. Sin and altruism in a heady, dizzying cocktail, and when its effervescent delusions popped their last bubble, perhaps truth, perhaps absolution from her, perhaps understanding as she slipped away to mortality.

Samantha!

Casey in his bedroom: standing over him after a night of ruinous temptation and blasphemous lust. *Love you, bro,* she says and lays her lips on his forehead. All bounds and constraints between levels of intimacy are shattered and violated.

Casey leaving him broken in the ruin of her seduction.

Flecks of blood on his nose.

Flecks of blood on my nose. . .

She cored me, she looked into me, she saw my memories, she saw, saw, everything!

She—cored—me!

He coughed and bounced to his feet. Roger and Casey were standing there, their eyelids fluttering over their back-turned eyes. Perhaps it was his inexperience, perhaps it was his outrage, perhaps it was his furious sense of betrayal, but his rage buoyed him up from the madness enveloping him and dispelled the fog in his head. *Monsters, monsters!* He could see the fat bag of cash. He could see the keys for one of the cars parked out back; the weasel had looked at them and often contemplated escape, escape to grab the fat bag of cash.

Move, move! Any second, any second, Roger and Casey could come to their senses.

He bolted from the room to the kitchen and snatched the key ring off the rack by the refrigerator. He ran out the door to find two sedans parked behind the house. He fumbled with the keys, figuring which was the proper key to unlock the door. Seconds ticked by in his head, each an eternity of anxiety and fear. Gustafson and Ingrid, dead. Samantha, he had to get to Samantha. Who knows how many others dead, and the town, his precious Proskoy, smashed from its peaceful slumber.

The door unlocked. He hopped into the car and found a shotgun locked to the dashboard. He fumbled with the keys in his shaking hands until he got the gun loose, then started the car and tore around the house in a fury of spinning tires and rooster tails of snow. He caught a glimpse of Casey looking out the window as he raced by, her hands pressed to the glass, her eyes gorged open in shock. He ignored the insanity of that as he put the window down and slammed on the brakes, the car sliding to a halt next to the dark blue agency sedan. He pumped the shotgun, pointed out the window, and blew out one of the tires before stomping on the gas pedal. The car fishtailed, and he almost went off into the trees, but he worked the steering wheel, got traction, and raced off as Roger came out the front door, his gun trained on Elmer's receding car. Elmer slumped down as two rounds blew through the rear window and out the windshield. The glass occluded in spidery cracks, but he found enough clear glass to see through by one of the windshield wipers and swerved down the winding Piedmont drive, past the sentry car with its two dead field agents, and onto the main road.

He floored the gas pedal and raced through the snow. He had the keys to both cars behind the house. In the snow, even if it had all wheel drive, the custom agency car wouldn't get far, not with a flat tire. He hoped they didn't have a full size spare.

Get the cash. Get Samantha. Tell Clay to call every sheriff in the northern counties.

His mind flashed with memories from the weasel. Before surrendering himself to the FBI, the weasel had come up to Proskoy to an estate one of his clients owned. It was the perfect place to hide the fat bag of cash, right under the nose of his witness security protection, near enough that if he made good on an escape, he could grab the bag and go, go the way Elmer was going.

Familiarity with the old lumber roads from days when he and Samantha would go for a drive saved him a great deal of time. The sun was starting to set. He had no idea how much time had passed, but it struck him that they must have been in the delirium of the weasel's memory for longer than he thought. Night would protect him. In the darkness, without streetlights, the lumber roads around the estates were treacherous. Clay often said some of the estate owners got themselves in accidents because the old roads weren't logged on GPS systems. Elmer hoped that would hold true for data in Roger's laptop.

He sped past a drive and slammed on the brakes, recognizing it as the house where the cash was hidden. The drive was long, disappearing over the mound of a hill. Worse, the drive wasn't plowed, and almost two feet of snow covered its length. The sedan would never make it through and, if he walked to town, Roger and Casey would be on him. If only he had his pickup, it would be simple, but then a different memory hit him.

Snowmobiles.

He grabbed the shotgun, rolled the car into the deep snow at the mouth of the drive to block it off, and slogged the length of the drive to get to the house. The house was wired for security, so he smashed in the front window with the butt of the shotgun in the hope of drawing out Clay and his sheriffs. He clambered through the broken window, went down to the house's wine cellar, and opened the walk-in cold storage past the cellar.

And, despite all reason, despite all rational explanation, and just as he'd seen it, it waited for him, a black duffel bag. He swallowed, his hands shaking as he crouched before the bag and slung the shotgun over his shoulder. The zipper slid open as he pulled it, and his eyes grew the size of serving platters at the stacks of hundred dollar bills crammed in the bag.

He blinked, cursing under his breath, numbed by the sight, and its implications. How could the memory come to him, so vivid, so precise, from an indistinct, tiny lump of brain matter, its structure destroyed the moment it fell in the ravenous acid of his stomach? Roger and Casey disavowed anything beyond the flesh, but he failed to understand how they could, if something as ethereal as a memory could be absorbed from ingesting dead tissue. He didn't want to waste time being philosophical, but crouched before the bag, with the madness at Piedmont fresh in his head, with Casey's manipulations revealed, he couldn't escape the impact of greater implications. He'd come to the conclusion there *was* something beyond flesh and bone, had felt it in so many ways that night his thoughts wandered loose as he lay in bed with Samantha. All those Sundays in his youth sitting in church ignoring everything, and yet it took a horrendous set of abominable acts to finally confirm what he'd so often denied in the misery of his old life and had even tried to rationalize in his time with Samantha: the unavoidable, inescapable, unexplainable acceptance of a reality that defied all rational sense, that was greater than all rational sense. He shook his head, fighting off the befuddling irony that it took lust, temptation, murder, and cannibalism for him to understand something so plain to so many ordinary people—and perhaps those very things were what justified the agency's disavowal of anything beyond the flesh, anything beyond the world. Believing in something greater would necessitate a reckoning, a moment to answer for so many horrible things.

He shook his head once more. He was wasting precious time. He closed the bag, hefted its considerable weight and slung it over his shoulder, and made his way to the kitchen. He rummaged through the cabinets until he found what he was looking for: a set of keys with the soft rubber heads snowmobile makers used to display their emblems.

He went out the back door and made his way to the large storage shed behind the house. He broke out the windows on the shed door with the shotgun, reached inside and unlocked the door, not wanting to waste time with the keys. He turned the latch for the large access door and pulled it up before hopping on one of the snowmobiles. He turned the key, and the gas gauge needle bounced up to indicate a full tank.

He heard the whine of a siren and stiffened. It was far off, yet he hesitated, wanting to be certain nobody was coming up the drive. But then his blood iced, for he heard the distinct pops of handgun fire, the volleys increasing in rapidity until the menacing chatter of an assault rifle echoed through the woods.

Roger. What the hell does he have in the trunk of that car?

Two more bursts sounded out from the distance. There were a few screams, silenced by several more bursts. Then came an explosion and, as Elmer looked in the direction of the drive, he saw a plume of black smoke rise in the darkening sky.

The snowmobile's motor bucked in protest but it started. Without a second's hesitation, Elmer put it in gear and took off through the woods toward town.

***

It took an hour, and even with the abnormal resilience of his body, the bouncing of the snowmobile and the pummeling he took from the duffel bag slamming against his back left him hanging onto the grips in exhaustion by the time he came out of the woods to Proskoy. Darkness had fallen, and the lights were out in town. He brought the snowmobile to a halt, suspicious at once. Roger had made a point of telling him there was only one chain of hard line providing phone access to Proskoy. Elmer could only wonder what mischief Roger might work on the town's electrical supply by use of his laptop. Elmer abandoned the snowmobile and walked toward Parson's diner.

When he came onto the snow-packed street he found many of the town's residents crowded before the sheriff's house, with Clay standing on the front porch trying to calm everyone. Before anyone noticed Elmer he backed off, snuck behind Wilson's garage, and hid the duffel bag in the waste bin. He checked how many rounds he had in the shotgun, reloaded the shells, and walked back to town, searching for Samantha. He wanted to shout her name, run through the crowd, anything to find her as fast as he could but, at the same time, he feared drawing any attention. The fact that he was walking around with a shotgun slung over his shoulder escaped him, but when he noticed several people in town carrying rifles his face fell. His answer came in the demands shouted from the crowd, people desperate to know more about the horror that had befallen their precious little Proskoy, the murder of Gustafson and Ingrid on a quiet morning. People wanted to know why the phones were down, why the power was out, why there were rumors flying around about the fate of Clay's two junior sheriffs sent out to the burglar alarm at the empty Caldwell estate; why, in effect, their sleepy little town was under siege.

Elmer lowered his head in shame and guilt. He pushed his way through the crowd, wondering how it could be so hard to find the only other young person in a town of middle and elder aged people. Time was an inescapable pressure in his head, time for their escape ticking away; time before Clay grabbed him out of suspicion for his absence during the day in a town where everybody kept track of each other.

He came out of the crowd where he went in, only to find a solitary figure standing in the cold on the steps to Parson's diner. He took a step, then two, then broke into a run as Samantha recognized him and called him by name. He charged up the steps to the diner and slapped his arms around her in a clinging, crushing embrace that left her gasping for breath, even as she clutched the back of his coat in her hands.

"I was worried about you," she said, putting her hands on his chest so that she could look him in the face. "Are you okay?"

His lips parted, but he was speechless, struck dumb as he stared into her eyes. And with each passing moment, each mounting moment, a horrible conclusion steadily took form within him. His life was insane, violent, and depraved. He was certain she would never understand and, standing there, he wasn't sure he wanted to burden her with even trying to understand. There was only one thing to do, only one right thing to do, only one fair thing to do. Every fiber within him that craved to hold her was one more reason he knew he had to let her go.

He clenched his teeth, but retreated a step, then two, his hands sliding down to hers.

"Elmer?" Her fingers clutched his to stop him. Her face—her eyes—filled with trepidation, then dread. "What's going on? What's with the gun?"

He squeezed his eyes shut. It hurt to say it, but he knew he had no choice. "I have to, I have to go." He felt her grip tighten, and he forced himself to meet her gaze. "Do you trust me, Samantha?"

She blinked. "Of course! Why—"

He shook his head. "Then you have to let me go."

187

Her mouth opened, and it seemed to him that her face lit with a ghostly glow. But then her eyes narrowed, and her green-eyed gaze glistened as she looked past him, down the length of the street. "Is that who I think it is?"

Elmer looked over his shoulder.

A set of headlights approached, creeping their way down the road, blinding in the darkness of the town without any power for its streetlamps. The car, unseen behind the twin white glare of its lights, came to a halt at the end of the street. The gathered townspeople were bathed in light until the car started moving again, this time swinging in an arc to block the street before coming to a halt and revealing itself as a dark blue sedan.

Elmer kept his gaze on the car, but slid one hand from Samantha's clutch to pull his shotgun free, even as he tugged her toward him.

The car's lights remained on as Roger and Casey opened their doors and stepped from the car.

Clay held up a hand, resting his other hand on his hip holster as he walked to the end of the sheriff house's front porch. "Show me your hands!"

Roger didn't move. "Show me Elmer Phelps."

"Hands on top of your heads!"

Roger and Casey exchanged a glance before Roger looked back to Clay. "Give us Elmer Phelps!"

Samantha came up behind Elmer and, when he felt her against him, he spun on her and shoved her back to the diner. "Inside, inside!" he ordered under his breath, chasing her up the steps.

Clay fired a shot in the air, startling some of the townspeople. The ones who had rifles took their weapons in hand. Clay refused to relent. "Hands on your heads, and get down on your knees! Now!"

Roger looked to Casey and nodded. They sank to their knees, seeming to acquiesce.

Elmer pushed Samantha back into the diner.

Roger and Casey rose once more, this time swinging their assault rifles from their backs to level them on the town.

Clay's jaw dropped as his eyes swelled. He looked around in confusion. His shadow was a long wisp of darkness trailing behind him in the wash of the headlights. The townspeople shifted about, some of them taking a step back, some of the ones with rifles taking aim.

Casey leaned into her weapon.

Elmer shoved Samantha into the diner and dragged her to the floor.

The menacing chatter of the assault rifles tore the night with automatic fire. People screamed and windows shattered as high velocity rounds ripped through flesh and building alike without mercy. Samantha buried her face to the floor in panic, but Elmer scrambled on all fours to one of the window booths and peered out over the sill. Roger and Casey were firing away, their forms illuminated in strobes of yellow muzzle flashes. Roger moved to the back of the car as Casey paced forward, advancing on the town, taking no care for cover when she dumped an empty clip and slapped a fresh one home. She staggered as a rifle round hit her in the chest, but she raised her weapon, and she and Roger let off a deafening hail of fire. Elmer's eyes darted to his side to see old man Wilson ripped apart in the volley, his body crumpling to the snow in a mist of his own blood.

Samantha grabbed his leg. He turned to her, but she screamed when the windows of the diner blew out in an eruption of shattered glass. Elmer rolled out of the booth to the floor, clamped a hand on the back of Samantha's coat, and half dragged her behind the dining counter to huddle beneath the coffee machine. He raised a hand for her to stay put and crawled back to the booth. With care he raised his head to peek out once more. Casey stood halfway between the car and the tangled bodies of the townspeople strewn about the street in bloody clumps. Vapors of warmth coiled into the frigid air from the horrendous wounds left by the assault rifles. Clay was sprawled at the head of the crowd, his gun in the snow beside him, his chest a ragged, crimson mess. Roger had slung his weapon, but stood before the open trunk of the agency car.

The chatter of Casey's gun sent a tremor through Elmer's body. He looked to find her shooting into the windows of the upper stories of the buildings, where some of the townspeople lived. He clutched his shotgun in rage, but at her distance he knew it would be futile to match firepower with her—and Roger. With that thought his gaze darted back to the car to see Roger pull a stubby black weapon from the trunk, its barrel a cavernous maw. A large drum clip hung from the middle of the weapon, which Roger gave a spin before raising the weapon to his shoulder, planting his feet, and taking aim.

The weapon let out a dull *plunk*. A window shattered in the upper floor of the sheriff's house, and then the building shuddered with an explosion, tendrils of flame and ragged debris spurting from the windows. Elmer ducked down and scurried back to find Samantha cringing in a little ball, her hands wrapped over her head. The grenade launcher's *plunk* sounded again, followed by another explosion.

"Elmer!" Roger shouted. "We want the money!"

"You stole from us!" Casey joined in. "After everything I did for you!"

Plunk, plunk, plunk.

Elmer grabbed Samantha and covered her with his body. Three more explosions sounded out, from the buildings around the diner. Elmer's eyes popped open, but the moment he moved another volley of high velocity rounds tore through the diner, showering them with shards of broken drinking glasses and white ceramic dishes from the racks over their heads.

"I know you're in there!" Casey called into the diner. "There's still a chance for you—a chance for us!"

Samantha's eyes opened to narrow slits as she glared at Elmer. "What the hell—"

Elmer put a finger over her lips and shook his head. "Back door," he whispered and pointed. "Come on, come on!"

They crawled along the floor, making their way around the corner into the darkness of the kitchen, its aluminum clad depths shimmering with the yellow fires outside the diner.

Plunk.

They dropped to the floor.

Another explosion, and in the sudden glare of light, Elmer made out Poppa Parson, hiding by his stove with a shotgun trained on them. When he made them out, he raised the weapon and waved them over, but his gaze was fixed on Elmer, burning with rage even as the dirt on his face was streaked with tears. He grabbed Elmer's collar and yanked him under his glare. "My wife was out there!" he yelped in fury. "Camille was out there, and she's gone, she's, she's *dead*. Talk, and talk fast—why do they want you? What did you do?"

Elmer closed his eyes. *What haven't I done?*

Casey called out his name.

Plunk.

Samantha cowered to the floor until she heard the explosion to know she was still alive, but when she lowered her hands from her head and looked up from the floor she found Parson with the barrel of his shotgun pressed to Elmer's cheek, pinning him to the floor. Elmer's shotgun lay across his hand, but his fingers were open. "Poppa, don't—"

Parson looked to her. "Listen to those lunatics out there! They want *him*," he added, pressing the barrel deeper into Elmer's cheek.

Elmer opened his mouth. He had to confess. He needed Parson's help. But before he could utter a single word, they heard the racket of the diner's front door being kicked open. A second later there was a metallic bang from the back of the kitchen before the back door was flung open as well.

They froze, their eyes darting between each other. Parson looked down to Elmer, his jaw grinding away, before he reached over to close Elmer's hand on the shotgun. He glanced at Elmer, nodded, and turned to the back of the diner. Elmer rolled over, motioning for Samantha to get behind him, and crawled toward the order window. He searched about as he rose up on his knees, straining to hear any footfalls that might give away the position of Roger or Casey. He tucked the butt of the shotgun into his shoulder, training the barrel ahead of him as he fought against his fear to peer out the order window.

The diner was a wreck. The town outside was even worse, with fires lighting the night. His breath seeped from his lungs in disbelief, the warm air from his body rising as a condensing mist that caught the light of the fires.

His gaze locked on the glistening vapor coiling before him. His heart stopped. He crammed his eyes closed, afraid to look until he knew he had to, knowing he'd given himself away. He opened his eyes and looked to his side to see Casey standing by the wall, her assault rifle trained on him.

She eyeballed him down the length of the gun. Her lips hung in a sad little frown, her eyes moist. "You did a bad thing, bro. Real bad. It didn't have to be this way."

Elmer hesitated. He wondered if she would shoot him. He knew he had to shoot her.

Their gazes locked. Her eyes began to widen. "Elmer—"

Parson popped up from behind the cutting table and unloaded with his shotgun, the blast slamming into Casey's side and blowing her from her feet. No sooner had the flash of Parson's fire lit the kitchen than Roger let off a concentrated burst from his assault rifle, hammering a hole through Parson's torso. The shotgun fell from Parson's hands as the impacts threw him back against the stove before he slumped dead to the floor. Deafened by the chatter of the assault gun, Elmer never heard the crunch of glass as Casey toppled to the floor, never heard the quick trot of Roger's running feet, never heard the gasp from Samantha. Confused, bewildered, hopelessly out-matched, he shifted about, aiming in the darkness.

Samantha's quaking voice broke the silence. "Elmer?"

He spun and seized still. Samantha was on her feet, but Roger was behind her, and had her back pinned to his chest. His assault rifle dangled from its shoulder sling. His right arm was locked across her chest with his hand planted on her left shoulder, his left arm across her chest with an equally firm grasp on her chin. Her green eyes were vast globes of fear, her hands splayed open at her sides, as Roger glared at Elmer over her shoulder.

Elmer trembled, but his hands tightened on the shotgun.

Roger grinned. "If I pull my arms back, her neck snaps, and she's done. Put the shotgun on the floor, if you would."

Elmer clenched his teeth. He put the shotgun on the floor.

Roger nodded. "That's a good boy, Elmer. Now. I thought we might play a little game. I'm going to ask you a question, and you are going to give me an answer. If you don't, or I don't like your answer, I'll whisper some precious nugget of scandal into dear Samantha's ear. So you see, the game isn't much of a game at all." He glanced at the side of Samantha's head as he pulsed the musculature of his arms to drive a wince from her. "I'm not interested in hurting you, Miss Samantha, but you should know that if I have to, I most certainly will, and I think the slaughter of your once quaint little town will attest to that. Look at Mister Phelps if you will, with all the desperate empathy of your fragile flesh, so that he may understand what's at stake, and not seduce himself with another truly disastrous idea."

Samantha sucked in a breath, her gaze locked on Elmer. Tears ran from her eyes.

Casey staggered around the corner and slumped against the wall. Blood dripped from her mouth as she coughed, her face wracked with pain. Her right hand was inside her black coat, clutching at some unseen wound. Her left hand hung at her side, her gloved fingers wrapped around her handgun. "Elmer," she said before spitting a wad of blood on the floor, "just tell us what you did with the goddamn money."

Roger's eyes flashed. "You're ruining the suspense, Casey!"

Samantha gasped as Roger's arms tightened.

Roger eased somewhat so she could breathe before he smiled on Elmer. "First round. You tell me where the money is, or I whisper into precious Samantha's pretty little ear what we three did today."

Casey coughed, drawing Elmer's gaze before he could speak. She looked into his eyes, looked to Samantha, and the way Samantha's eyes held on Elmer. She pulled her hand from the depths of her coat and stared at the blood dripping between her fingers before clutching the wound once more. Her eyes slid shut before she shook her head and banged it against the wall in frustration, a curse seeping beneath her breath. She raised her weapon hand to wipe her mouth on the back of her glove. "Roger, I need to feed! Bastard got me where the vest didn't protect my side."

"You can satiate yourself soon enough, Cassandra."

Casey coughed again, her shoulders bowling in agony. She squeezed her eyes shut, her lips parting to let a half clotted mass of blood pour from her mouth. She sucked in a breath and shook her head. "I, I can't wait that long. I'm bleeding out. Can't heal fast enough on my own. I need to feed! There's no point to this. We know what we have to do. Let's just do it."

"Patience, Casey, patience!"

Casey's knees quivered and buckled. She slid down the wall to a crouch, leaving a smear of blood behind her. She rested her head against the wall, opening her mouth wide to suck in a breath between her red stained teeth. "Roger, please," she begged before letting out a groan. "Kill her and core him—that was the plan! I'll take a piece of her to heal me."

Samantha whimpered as tears formed rivers down her face.

Elmer glared at Casey.

She gave him a tired look, as if he were still the helpless little boy of his youth. "You took the money so you could run away with *her*? That's it, right? Shit, Elmer, what did you think was going to happen?"

Elmer turned back to Roger. "Let her go. She doesn't know anything. She won't say anything. You can do what you want with me."

Roger sighed. "Oh, Elmer, you know I can't let her go." He held for a moment, then frowned and ripped his arms out to his sides. Samantha's head whipped around, her limbs twitching as an awful snap burst from her neck. Her wide, blank eyes held on Elmer for a moment before she dropped to her knees and, with her body unstrung, she flopped on her face, as if she were a bag of uncooked dough.

Elmer couldn't move. He couldn't breathe. He couldn't even think. His life crumbled around him, fell to ruin in the form of Samantha's broken body.

He stared at her, his face contorted in horror.

The world erupted around him in a flash, then another, then a third, before he understood, before he was ready to recognize the shots ringing in his ears. He didn't flinch; he didn't cower. His gaze was locked on Samantha, but he knew something else was happening, happening to Roger. Roger stood there, looking down at the bloody holes in his lower abdomen. The flashes came again—seven, as Elmer kept count in his delirium—with the last pitching Roger's head up before he crashed to the floor.

Casey gasped. Her arm dropped to her side, the gun with its spent clip slipping from her hand.

Elmer's hands trembled. They wanted to do something, fix something, but there was nothing left to fix. He sank to his knees by Samantha, his hands hovering over her, as if he was afraid to touch her, but then he grabbed the back of her coat and shook her. His lips parted in a silent wail of agony, his breath lost to him.

"Elmer?"

Casey's voice snapped him back to reality. The horror on his face turned to a frightful mask of feral rage. He snatched the shotgun and pointed it at her.

"Wait, wait!" Casey said, shaking her head as she held out a hand. "Listen, listen to me!"

He held still, jaw clenched, glaring at her down the length of the shotgun.

"I, I didn't want it to end this way," Casey forced out. "It wasn't supposed to be like this. I thought I had it all figured out, but I didn't. I'm leaving it up to you."

He held still, silent as a stone.

She closed her eyes. "Damn it Elmer, time is precious! I'm bleeding out. I'd be dead already, if I was normal, but I'm not. My body's not. Look at Samantha! She's still warm. She's still in there. You do the math."

He stared at her. After a long pause his mouth opened, his arms easing to lower the shotgun.

She coughed. "I always tried to protect you. I'm doing it now, doing it for the last time. I saw the way you looked at her. You never looked at me the way you looked at her. Maybe what I did with you was wrong. I don't know. There's so many voices in my head it's hard to keep it straight all the time. Just, just remember, whatever you do, that I did this for you. The rest is up to you now." Her face paled, her shoulders loosening. "I love you, bro," she said, her voice trailing off. Her eyelids drooped over her gray eyes as she stared at him. After several moments her chin sank to her chest. A long breath seeped from her, and then she was still.

Elmer stared at her.

He was alone.

The diner was quiet.

From somewhere deep inside he heard the faint whisper of a thought.

What is great in man is that he is a bridge, and not an end.

He closed his eyes and beat his fists against his temples.

He screamed and, when he opened his eyes, he stared through the ceiling, into the depths of the big black empty, and screamed once more, this time in defiance. He didn't want to entertain Casey's offer, but he knew he had no choice except to follow her lead. There was nothing else to do. Somehow, it would make everything right. Casey always knew how to take care of things.

He started to move.

He stepped over the bodies to rummage about the kitchen until he found Parson's meat cleaver and a large mixing bowl. He dragged the bodies of Parson and Roger to the back of the kitchen to get them out of the way. He put one of Parson's aprons on the floor beneath Samantha's head. He pulled off her clothes, folded them, and put them on the dining counter so they would stay clean. He draped another apron over her bare body to cover her. He knelt beside her, cleaver in hand. He trembled, his muscles tightening in revulsion, in horror and shock, his sanity straining to resist what he knew he must do, his eyes squeezing shut to block the surreal reality from his mind.

But then he forced his eyes open. There was no escape. He had to be strong. He raised his arm high, then his other arm to take the cleaver in both hands, his fingers tightening, his jaw clenching until his face was nearly purple, and then he swung.

The cleaver hit home with an odd sound, a horrible sound: *chok*.

He was panting. He tugged the cleaver free. Not there yet; no, not yet—

Chok.

He screamed, he wept; he spat the acid that boiled from his stomach into his mouth.

Chok. Chok. And then, a loud crack.

Structure is not important. Remember the rules. Never more than the scooping tool can sample. Never core the same person twice.

He twisted the cleaver to open a gap. He stuffed his fingers in, looking away as he pulled at the warm, greasy tissue and dropped it in the mixing bowl. He hummed Samantha's lullaby. Another handful. He thought of her standing in the snow outside the house, humming that lullaby. Another handful. He thought of that night on the slopes outside Logger's, when she caught a snowflake for her wish, and he kissed her.

A final handful.

He covered her head with the apron, took the bowl, found Parson's hand mixer, and stirred up the mess in the bowl until it was smooth and runny. He found the turkey baster, put it in the bowl, and crouched beside Casey before kneeling on the floor. He pulled her head into his lap and rested his hand over her eyes so that her blank gray gaze wouldn't haunt him. He shoved the baster to the back of her mouth and squeezed the bulb.

He waited. His heart beat once, twice.

Her eyelids fluttered, her eyelashes brushing against his palm.

He pulled up another sample and squeezed it down her throat, keeping at it until the bowl was empty. Her hands twitched. Her muscles shook in small tremors. He lifted his hand to see her eyes roll back in her head. He pulled off her coat, balled it up, and stuffed it under her head. He couldn't watch. He clapped his hands over his ears as she began to thrash on the floor, a horrible rattle sounding from her lips.

Donor memory overlay.

He ran from the diner. He ignored the ruin of the town, the slaughter of Proskoy. It wasn't important to him anymore. The Parsons, the Gustafsons, old man Wilson; it was all over, all gone. No matter. He would have everything he wanted. Samantha would understand everything. He wouldn't have to explain a thing. She'd have no choice but to accept it, all of it, understand it, see it with an immediacy that would transcend anything Elmer could put into words. Casey always knew what she was doing.

Despite himself, he had to admit that Roger was right.

What is great in man is that he is a bridge, and not an end.

He understood the meaning of the quote. He had crossed the bridge, and now there was no end in sight. Any notions of borders, or restraint, were so far behind him their existence seemed only a faint, fanciful memory.

He made his way behind Wilson's garage and slung the fat bag of cash over his shoulder. He walked back to the diner. It was the strangest walk of his life. He took that walk so many times, that peaceful stroll with Samantha down the street from the Parsons' house to the diner. It seemed like another world, a flip side of existence.

He shook his head and rolled his shoulders. Perversion. Cannibalism. Mass murder. The thoughts fell from him to be lost in the snow. He remembered the thoughts he considered that night he lay in bed with Samantha. If they made a comforting sense to him then, they came to him now as absolute truths. They had to. There was no other way, no other means to make sense of the madness. Humanity has its notions of comfort and morality, but they are illusions of ignorance. Existence, he decided, was a thing much more complicated, and more subtle, to contemplate. Ends and means dissolve into each other, and morality is just an opinion of incomplete awareness. The only rational path, the only sane path, is one of mute acceptance, because the mind of man is a small thing, for all of its three pounds of eternity.

Little words, big thoughts—a thesaurus of his own creation. He considered such things as he came up the steps to the diner and dropped the bag of cash on the floor by one of the tables.

It was very quiet inside.

A woman stepped around the corner of the kitchen, her empty, bloodshot gaze staring off into space. She looked at him before looking at her gloved hands. She pulled off the gloves and the tight fit of her bulletproof vest to drop them on the floor. Her eyes slid shut, and she stood motionless for several moments before she walked to the sink by the coffee machine. She cleaned the blood from her hands and face, taking several gulps of water from the faucet to wash out her mouth. She gripped the faucet lever to turn off the water before she braced her hands on either side of the sink.

She took a deep breath before turning to face him. "Elmer?"

He studied her, guessing at her unspoken question. "Samantha."

"Yeah," she said with a little laugh, "right." She ran her hands over her face before turning to look at her warped reflection in the aluminum backsplash over the sink. She held for several moments, staring at that reflection, before she seemed certain of herself. She turned around to find his waiting gaze. "I'm Samantha Hayes," she whispered, her hands trembling as she rested them on her cheeks. Her eyes widened over an open smile. "I, I really am Samantha Hayes!"

He stared at her.

Her eyes narrowed. "Elmer," she began, but bit her lip. She looked into her hands, and down the length of her body, a grimace passing across her face before she looked back to him. "Did you, did you really?"

He swallowed. There was no point in trying to hide. He answered with a frown.

"But not after we, we—No. I can see that, I can feel that." She fell silent, her forehead knotting in confusion as she looked down at her hands. She closed her eyes and shook her head before looking to him. "I, I can—I can see some of her memories. You know she did this, did this for us, right?"

"Yes."

She closed her eyes. "I don't know what to think of that."

He shrugged. "Then don't think about it."

She touched her face with her fingers. "This is, this is, *odd*. Why does it make sense?"

"Because you're living it. It makes sense, because it has to. You don't have a choice."

She put her hands on her head. "Old rules, old judgments, I guess they don't work anymore, do they?"

"No, they don't."

She looked at the clothes, her clothes, which he left folded in a neat pile on the counter. She gave him a quick glance before stripping off Casey's clothes, right down to her shoes. She tossed them through the order window into the kitchen, hesitating when she looked at the large red stain on the white shirt. She looked at her side where Parson's shotgun blast had pierced her and, to her surprise, found a series of small, dry vesicles on her skin. After exchanging a curious glance with Elmer she picked at them and, one by one, the skin of the vesicles crumbled away to let a glistening ball of shot fall to the floor, with a dot of fresh, pink skin waiting beneath. It drew a nervous laugh of wonder from her, but then she shivered against the cold, and pulled on her old clothes. Her new body was more fit than her old body, so her clothes were a little loose, but she didn't mind that at all, almost chuckling to herself as she hitched up her sweatpants with her sweatshirt half on. She noticed the rubber bands dangling from her wrist and threw them away.

She finished dressing, pulled on the coat Elmer gave her for Christmas, and let out a sigh of relief. "Now I'm me again," she said with confidence, but then blinked. Her hands rose to find her hair in a ponytail. She hesitated a moment before pulling the rubber band loose and tossing it over her shoulder. She looked at Elmer as she ran her fingers through her hair to smooth it out. She turned to look in the distorted reflection over the sink, running her hands through her hair until she had it parted on the side, the way she had before. She turned back to him. "It's a little longer than I remember."

He watched her with widening eyes. "It's fine."

"I know how much you like my hair," she said, offering him a smile. As strange as everything was, she couldn't help but laugh. She opened her hands and tipped her head back. "So, what do you think?"

He was riveted. All the mannerisms he knew so well, and everything he desired, woven together. Everything right, and everything wrong, all at once.

He remembered the little passage he wrote in his notebook. It occurred to him that he never continued past those first lines.

To understand me, you have to understand my predilections.

He considered his thesaurus, and some of the words he taught himself. He wanted his next thought to have a certain sound, because he thought it was profound, and felt he owed some effort to its impact.

To understand myself, I had to look into the big black empty within me, and see all there was to see, in all the subtle shades in which those things exist. Only in that way can the soul of the one I desire reside in the embodiment of my forbidden lust and not cause my sanity to consume itself in a firestorm of contradictions and conflicts.

For sure, I'm Elmer Phelps.

"Elmer?"

His gaze fell on the fat bag of cash. He cleared his throat and shifted on his feet. He fidgeted with a sudden nervousness that passed as quickly as it seized hold of him. His gaze rested on the table before rising to find her waiting for him. He licked his lips before clearing his throat once more, trying hard not to stammer under the glimmer of amusement in her eyes.

She tipped her chin to the bag. "Is that the money?"

He glanced at the bag and nodded. "Stacks of hundreds." He remembered Roger's subtle threats about their precarious financial security, or more accurately, their utter lack of financial security. "Stacks of hundreds," he repeated. He looked to her. "Samantha, we can go anywhere we want."

"We just need a little steak tartar every now and then, right?"

"From the finest steakhouses," he said with a laugh. "So where should we go?"

Her face fell. "Well, the agency, they'll be looking for the money, right? So we need to go somewhere where people won't ask questions. Some place where the money can last us a really long time. What about South America? We could see the ocean, and it's warm."

"Okay," he said, but noted a troubled look on her face before it turned to an expression of wild excitement. "What is it?"

She grabbed his hands. "It just hit me. How long can we last?"

"I don't know. I guess we'll find out."

"Together?"

He nodded. "Together."

"Then there's one thing I need to know," she whispered. She closed her eyes and leaned into him. When her lips brushed against his she recoiled a bit, but then she came back to him and, as they wrapped their arms about each other, it was no different than before. She rested her forehead against his and drew in a shaky breath. So close together, it was impossible to miss the change in her clearing eyes, their ghostly gray pallor suffused by more green flecks with each passing moment. "Right, I'm sorry, but I had to know. Okay then, together. I just needed to be sure the world wouldn't blow up around us."

He motioned to the windows with his eyes. "Look outside. It already did."

She flicked his forehead and stepped back from him. "Hey, you hungry?"

He glanced to the mess of the kitchen. "Are you serious?"

"Sure," she said, pulling out a chair from the table. She opened a hand and waited for him to sit. "I have a surprise. Not the way I had planned," she said, waving at the disarray of the diner, "but I think you'll like it." She patted his shoulder, holding up a finger as she spun on her heel and went behind the counter.

He looked out through the broken windows.

The sky was dark, a black expanse of featureless clouds obscuring the stars.

A fragment of plate glass from one of the storefronts came loose and shattered on the pavement, the sound lost in the empty night. Fires crackled as the buildings burned, lighting the town in the senile depths of Proskoy Wood.

She returned with a small cardboard baker's box and two forks. "Open it," she said as she settled in the chair next to him.

He opened the box. He couldn't help but grin as he looked to her. "Oh, perfect."

A cool breeze washed through the broken windows to tickle their ankles. They sat at the table, the fat bag of cash on the floor beside them, the town in ruins around them.

"Wait," Samantha said, holding up a finger again, "there's one last thing." She looked over her shoulder at the clutter of broken glasses along the counter before turning back to Elmer. For lack of anything better, she held up her fork and waited for Elmer to mirror her gesture.

"Happy New Year," she said, and with that, clinked his fork before taking his hand. "To new beginnings?" she said with a glint in her green eyes.

He stared at her before he nodded. "Right, to new beginnings."

A large piece of chocolate decadence pie waited for them in the baker's box. They smiled, and their eyes shone upon each other in the moody, flickering glow of society's funerary pyre.

Purity.

At least that's what the villagers called it, or to be more specific, what it sounded like to those not acquainted with their tongue. The word was ancient, passed down for generations, perhaps extending to the time of the step-pyramid builders and their mysterious mountaintop cities. Randal never heard what the exact wording was, or what the translation might be; he had little care for either, even when times were better. But somewhere in those rugged tropical jungles of southern Mexico, in mist clad heights where only the slow Indian chants kept any real record of events, it had a meaning that went past anything he thought he could perceive.

His body shook with convulsions. His skin, becoming more stiff and leathery with every passing breath, pulled across his trembling muscles in waves of agony. Something would have to give. It was an impossible situation. He wanted to scream, but only a hoarse wail registered with his ears. His vocal chords tightened in his throat. His tongue flattened against the top of his mouth, contorting around the plastic tube thrust between his teeth to prevent him from choking. He could taste something, something beyond the bitter flavor of his blood.

It was a moldy taste. It was the taste of bark.

He couldn't open his eyes. Wide leather straps bit into his wrists and ankles as he contorted in the peak of the convulsions. The pain in his side was unbearable. The pressure building inside his abdomen was mounting, mounting—*Christ, let it pop already!*

He slammed his head against the metal table that served as his confinement.

How did it all go so wrong?

It was a pointless thought, but it was a desperate thought as well. He knew the answer, knew it from having seen it in the eyes of those in the past who had the misfortune of crossing his path. The convulsions eased as it came to him. It was a simple thought, and he liked to keep things simple.

It all looks easy until things fall apart.

***

It was supposed to be a simple job.

Don't break the box.

His operational parameters were non-existent. He could do whatever he wanted. The pay was outrageous. Besides, he'd always liked the jungle. The jungle was primitive. The jungle was lawless in one way, ordered in another way. Predators could set the tone. It was perfect.

There was only one condition. The jungle, too, had its delineated borders.

Don't break the box.

He was flying one of those rickety little single-prop planes, a little Cessna type that looked like somebody with a box of toothpicks and a bottle of whiskey built it in a garage. It was most likely a stray AK47 round that hit the engine and took it out. It wasn't important, but when the cockpit filled with smoke and the plane began to lose altitude, all his attention was consumed with trying to find a place to ditch. He was in the mountains. He couldn't see. The wings scraped the treetops, and then the world disintegrated around him in a deafening crack and crash of spars and branches. His body was slammed about as the cockpit tumbled through the various tiers of jungle growth until everything came to a sudden, violent halt in an eruption of water.

The cockpit flooded and sank in a muddy river, taking him with it. That's when he tasted *it*, knew it by taste from having smelled it before. And despite everything else, that was the moment he started to panic.

The box broke.

***

Randal massaged his forehead, trying to quell his lingering headache. The ache only served to remind him of the odd reality before him. He dropped his hand and found his voice.

"How'd you find me?"

Jonah tipped his head back, his eyes hidden behind his sunglasses as he looked up to the brilliant Miami sky. Two plates of hammered Cuban steak and fried plantains sat on their table. The aroma of the steaks, their thin tender length sizzling with exotic seasonings, was a good match to the whiskey in Randal's glass. He swirled the glass, the ice cubes within clanking about.

He didn't expect to see Jonah. His cell phone, the one where he took his work calls, had beeped the night before. He knew the routine. He went to the restaurant at lunch. He ordered two meals. Felix, his handler, would send a contact for a potential employer to sit with him, and terms would be discussed. Simple.

Jonah looked to him and smiled. It was not a friendly smile. "Is it so tough to talk to me?"

Randal shook his head. "Get over yourself. I paid your mother every penny I ever owed, on time and without fail. You know me. Low profile. Not interested in legal problems. Judges, they want explanations."

Jonah leaned over his plate. He waved a hand to waft the aroma of the steak, bobbing his head in appreciation. Instead of eating, he leaned back in his chair and looked to the luxury yachts docked across the inner bay of the city. "Which one is yours?"

Randal blew out a breath. "Okay, so you know about the boat."

"It surprised me. I never pictured you on the water."

"Boating is for idiots. You know what aviators say about floating. Anything you can do when you're dead can't be that hard to do when you're alive."

Jonah's condescending smile returned. "Another philosophical gem."

Randal picked up his fork and pointed it at Jonah before spearing a strip of steak. "I paid for that college degree of yours, so you can take that self-satisfied smirk and shove it up your ass." He tossed the meat in his mouth and kept a steady stare on his son as he chewed.

Jonah leaned on the table with his elbows. He held for a moment, both his and Randal's eyes locked in hidden scrutiny behind the darkened lenses of their sunglasses until Jonah took his off. He narrowed his eyes against the glare of the sun. "I'm in a position to offer you a job."

Randal stopped chewing, his gaze darting about in sudden suspicion. "I thought you were a pharmacist?"

Jonah raised a finger. "Doctorate in pharmacology and biochemistry. I design the medications people get from their doctors."

Randal let out a short laugh. "Then there's nothing to talk about. I don't need a job counting pills." He looked up, his calculating mind derailed by the surprise of being contacted by his son. He took a breath and gathered his wits. "You came to contract me," he thought aloud. "So tell me. How does your world cross paths with anyone in my world?"

"We aren't always well received in the locales where we do field research, despite our investment—"

"Bribes?" Randal guessed, waving his fork at Jonah.

Jonah ignored him. "Despite our investments with the resident population. Even our field research entails installation of significant mobile infrastructure. There is intellectual property as well. All of it needs to be protected."

"Ah, now I see. Security work. Calling on the old man for some muscle?"

"Doctorate in pharmacology and biochemistry," Jonah repeated. "You said yourself I was too smart to get my hands dirty."

Randal's face went still as stone. "There's all kinds of dirt. I've seen them all."

Jonah didn't waver. "We're going off topic. In the circles of contract security you were recommended. I was told to give you a particular word so you would understand."

Randal waved a fork at his son. "And that's it? No terms? I don't work that way. We talk terms, we talk money, we reach an agreement, or we walk away from each other. No exceptions."

Jonah was about to smile, but licked his lips instead. He watched his father loft another slice of meat in his mouth before letting the word fall between them.

"Randy."

Randal stopped short, but then started to laugh. "That son-of-a-bitch."

***

Joe Pendolton stood in the warm tropical sun, wearing nothing but blue cargo shorts and a pair of sandals. His easy grin was in stark contrast to the threatening black bulk of an AK47 assault rifle slung over his shoulder. He waved as Randal peered out the window of a rugged truck that rolled to a stop. Chickens scurried across the road, some of the slower ones getting a shove from Pendolton's foot as he walked over to the truck. Sweat glistened on the bare dome of his head. Like Randal, he recently turned fifty, but had maintained his athletic build. Randal hopped down from the truck cab, conscious in that moment of the strength training he'd foregone over the last year.

He spread his arms to greet Pendolton. "Well, well, as I live and breathe!"

Pendolton mimicked the gesture before slapping his hands on Randal's shoulders. "Randy!" he greeted, using the nickname only he was allowed by Randal to use. "So you finally got your lazy ass off that boat of yours, huh? What've you been doing? Months, and you don't return a single call."

Randal shrugged as he hefted his duffel bag from the back of the truck. He banged his palm on the door of the cab and waited for the driver to pull away. "I was busy."

Pendolton gave him a playful shove. "With what? Blondes? Brunettes?"

Randal couldn't suppress a crooked grin. "Ah, come on, man. Both."

Joe shoved him again before putting an arm around his shoulders. "Still full of shit, just like always," he said with a deep laugh. He waved his other hand to clear the dust kicked up by the truck as he led Randal up the dirt road that ran through the village. "How's your Spanish?"

Randal surveyed the simple, single story buildings on either side of the road. It was clear from the haphazard arrangement of the buildings in respect to the dirt road that the village existed for many years before the road was plowed through its center. He knew that look, the look of 'primitive' people who had no wealth but their pride, reflected in the stolid expressions that met him from the few visible residents. They were descendants of ancient Indians, distinguished by wide, high foreheads above small, dark eyes and pronounced cheekbones. They were distinct, quite different than the Mexicans he used to encounter during some of his previous operations across the Texas border. He looked back to Joe. "My Spanish is fine, don't worry."

Joe tipped his head. "Yeah, well, I won't, because you won't need it, *amigo*. They don't speak it. They use some kind of dialect—Mayan, Incan, whatever. Who the hell knows? Probably hasn't been heard since the friggin' Conquistadors stole their gold and gave them small pox."

"Do we have interpreters?"

Joe gave him a sidelong glance and a mischievous grin. "Yeah, we got somebody."

Randal could tell there was a whole conversation in that comment. "Right."

"Some kooky French chick. Look here," Joe said as he pointed to an abandoned wood frame building. It looked like it might have been a church at some point, with wood plank construction that set it apart from the rest of the stone brick dwellings. Whatever it was, or whoever built it, it was very old, with the wood molded to a dark brown and many of the wall planks crumbling. The roof span sagged, but the small, simple steeple over the crooked door still held a bell, its surface green and pitted with corrosion. A rope hung from the bell's pivot, but it had broken, or been cut, to dangle free over the doorway. "She wasn't the first kook to come out here and get lost, it seems," Joe continued.

Randal blew out a breath. "Missionaries. I guess it didn't take." He looked to Joe. "What's your appraisal of the locals?"

Joe shrugged. "Mountain people. Friggin' primitives. Don't know shit." He turned down a side path, which snaked down a sharp decline into a dense growth of lush green trees. "Do you know where we are?"

Randal frowned. The last plane he boarded was a small cargo plane. No corporate logos. It was a flight that crossed more than geographical lines. There was a pilot and a very serious looking contractor who insisted Randal blindfold himself. It was that, or get off the plane. He had to hand over his personal GPS and satellite phone as well. Under any other conditions, such things were deal-breakers. But with the money he was getting paid, he was willing to accept that things would be different and, so, they were.

Despite that, he hated to admit the truth. "No, I don't know where we are."

Joe threw his head back with a single laugh. "That makes two of us, Randy!" He led them on until he came to a turn in the path and they stopped short. "Here we are, old boy. Welcome to Underlab."

Randal looked down to a building nestled in the steep slope they stood over. It was covered in camouflage tarps, but he could see the modular construction and exposed reinforced ribbing of corrugated walls.

Jonah stood beneath the rain shelter of the building's double doors, his hands on his hips.

***

Randal struggled against the bindings that held him to the metal table. He wanted to open his eyes, but the lids felt as if they were crusted shut. His limbs were trembling, almost quivering. He felt as if his joints would burst in an isometric act of self-destruction.

Something changed then. Another strap came to his perception, pulled down over his forehead before being jacked tight. He pushed his chin up in an effort to wiggle free, but the binding was too tight, and he forgot about the plastic tube in his mouth. It collapsed between his teeth for a moment, and the subconscious urge to break free was replaced in a heartbeat with the instinctual panic to draw air in his lungs. Only then did he realize he couldn't draw air through his nose.

He froze. He remembered the smell — *that* smell — and the word came back to him.

Purity. Yes, that's it.

It was a cohesive thought. He clung to it like a lifeline in the dark.

"Hold still."

Jonah? He croaked as he tried to speak. His thoughts broke. Cohesion was lost.

Something burned, burned like two bolts of lightning across his face.

He screamed, and his eyes popped open. A white ceiling, blurry. Bright lights.

"Marked epidermal expansion. Note increased collagen cross-linking and associated tissue rigidity. Double all dosing levels of elastimer vector injections. Fusion of anatomical orifices. Note need for surgical intervention."

He thrashed. Something had gone horribly wrong.

Don't break the box.

Jonah was there. Jonah would help.

Or would he?

Jonah!

***

206

It started in the Midwest, the so-called heartland.

Her name was Johanna, and Randal met her in high school. There was one night, the only night of high school he thought worth remembering, when he got her alone. She was working late on the senior float for homecoming day. His plan was to set it on fire. She was brilliant, and he was trouble. They had flirted for almost a year, convinced they perfected the little art of the distant glance. Social cliques would not tolerate a 'date' with her, no matter how much he tried to clean up his act or remind people that he was a minister's son. She was the mayor's daughter. Her future glistened with high possibilities. She won the science fair, math competitions, debate trophies, and scholarships to the best schools. He managed to stay out of juvenile detention.

It was wrong in every sense of what wrong could be, so of course it happened. Right there under the float, hot and sweaty and desperate, just like any scandal should be. But that was just the beginning, although it set the tone. She got pregnant. Worse, she insisted on having the baby. It rocked their little town. She missed the very end of her senior year, but studied at home, and still graduated valedictorian. At the insistence of both their parents they got married. She gave birth to a son and named him Jonah. Randal didn't like the name, but he had no say. Johanna's parents watched the boy so that Johanna could pursue her college aspirations.

Randal joined the army, for lack of anything better to do. It could provide income, housing, and an outlet for his destructive tendencies, along with a much-needed dose of discipline. Despite all the whispers around him and Johanna, and with whatever greater power there was as his witness, he did everything he could to keep on the straight and narrow.

It couldn't last, because it was all lies. He hated lies, but he learned that people loved lies. Oddly enough, the more the truth could hurt people, the more they seemed to embrace the lies. Lies were easy. Lies were soothing. Lies said everything was just fine, even when every fiber of instinct knew everything was two seconds short of a train wreck.

Jonah was reading when he was three. He was just like his mother. Johanna had met her future intellectual match. The boy had no idea the illusion of his family was soon to end.

Randal met Joe in the army. They were brothers in spirit. Randal had met his match in debauchery, and decided he'd had enough of the lies. He found there were only a few things he was good at: drinking, fighting, and whoring, and not always in that order. He viewed order with contempt. Order, after all, was just another lie. There was only disorder and, over it, the way people try to play nice with each other. The delirious farce of his marriage taught him that lesson in spades. *Ad infinitum*, Johanna would say. He had something less eloquent, but more pointed to offer in return. He was never much for Latin and the pompous intellectualism it courted.

The divorce was settled as Jonah turned four. He'd just finished memorizing his multiplication tables. He said he felt a need to understand division.

Clever little bastard.

***

Randal brought the duty truck to a halt and rested back in his seat, his hands draped over the steering wheel as he beheld the view before him. Beyond the flat, jungle-green plate of the truck's hood a boulder had been rolled into the road to mark its end. There was little need, as the road ended at a cliff, its sheer precipice dropping hundreds of feet. What made the sight most fascinating was the clouds skimming the valleys beneath him, and he could look across the flat tops of those fluffy white shingles. If he could entertain a notion of whimsy, he could walk off the cliff and stroll across the clouds to the next peak jutting up in the sky.

Jonah turned to him with a smile. "Impressive, isn't it? All the world sits below us."

Randal ignored his son and looked to his left at the long gray building that ran across the flat peak. It was a pre-fab, like Underlab, but at least twice the size. Its roof was decked out with solar panels, covered by automated directional vanes, so the reflective glare of the panels could only be spotted directly overhead. The site was in the middle of some forgotten city of Meso-American antiquity, with skeletal remains of stone brick walls littering the flattened top of the peak. There were some trees, but they were low and gnarled, as if gasping for air. It was not that far from the truth. When Randal stepped from the cab, he braced himself on the door in a moment of dizziness. It would take time to adjust to the altitude.

Jonah walked around the front of the truck and opened a hand to the building. "You've seen Underlab, now you can take a look at Highlab. This is where all the heavy research goes on. The extracts we work with, they only exist in the cells of a few plant species, species that were not known until we came up here."

"Great," Randal said, looking back to the clouds. "Can I smoke them?"

"If you're expecting a goaded response to an infantile remark, you're going to be disappointed."

Randal sighed. "So how'd you find this place?"

"The village in the valley where you were flown in. Some of the

208

extracts from the species here are used in local home remedies. From the chants of shamans to the gossip of traders on the rivers to rumors in the larger towns downstream, the possibility of something remarkable came to us. And so, here we are."

"Chants of shamans," Randal said under his breath. "Do they have doctorates?"

Jonah overlooked the remark. "This is the opposite terminus of your route. You drive from Underlab to Highlab and deliver the packages you've been given. They are not to be opened under any circumstances." He pointed to the double doors at one end of Highlab's building, where three small yellow crates waited, their reinforced resin shells scuffed from abuse. "You need to be most careful with the yellow crates. Inside the crate is a box, and inside the box various products relating to our research. Some of the contents are highly refined and concentrated, and not suited for human exposure."

Randal scratched his chin. "Doesn't look like anybody else has been too careful."

"That's from a prior project," Jonah said quickly to dismiss any concern. "It's very simple. You load the packages, you move the packages, and you deliver the packages. If any locals get in the way, you deal with them in any way you see fit. We prefer discretion, but examples may have to be made, and you have that latitude."

Randal regarded his son. Jonah had learned how to talk around violence with those tired, vague technical expressions corporate enforcers favored. "You've done your homework. Some things don't change. Good boy."

Jonah nodded. "Mister Pendolton was quite forthcoming when it concerned some of your previous exploits."

"I bet." Randal pointed past the building, where a small, single engine plane was anchored at the top of a short, sloped runway. "What's with the rubber-band toy?"

"Emergency transport. We brought it up here in pieces and had it assembled. I wanted a rotary rather than fixed wing but, with the angle of the runway, the plane can achieve a stable glide path by gravity alone. I know you're certified for both types of craft."

Randal scratched his jaw. "What kind of emergency are we talking about?"

Jonah studied his father for several moments before he spoke. "We'll discuss that at a later time. For now, remember there is only one rule: don't break the box."

Randal snorted as he put his hands on his hips. "Don't break the box. Right." He drew in a breath as his gaze was drawn back to the clouds beneath the summit. It was as though he was on another world.

***

Randal bought his boat after his last job. It was a messy job, with a high body count, more than his contractor was prepared to accept. Containment had been breached, and rumors of a murderous white man spread through several villages along that stretch of the Nigerian delta. Oil money or no, word got out. His employer took it in stride—this was the business, after all, but his contractor was most displeased. He decided to lay low by taking a little vacation in Athens. A bomb was left in his hotel room. It was dumb luck that he was down the hall to get some extra towels for his shower.

After some consideration he christened his boat, a fifty-foot trawler, as *Fredo* and registered it to Liberia, the black hole of international ship registry, where all good outlaws logged their papers. His employer secured a spot on a yacht transport, and his new floating home made its way to Miami, where he met up with it after Athens, and found his way to near anonymity. All he had to do was drop some cash to dock for a day when it was time to fuel. His finances ran out of Swiss accounts. He liked the Swiss. They didn't ask questions. It kept things simple.

Despite what he told Jonah, he came to enjoy being on the water. At night he could stretch out on the flybridge and stare up at the stars while little wavelets lapped against the hull. Sometimes he would forego anchoring, and just drift on the water, much in the way he would drift in his thoughts. In his younger days he came to love flying for the moral disconnect with the dirty world beneath him. He remembered those stories of 'bomber morality', the moral disconnect of young men who sat in the plexi-domed nose cones of B-17 bombers as they dropped their tonnage on the civilians beneath them. It was a convenient association for him as he went from job to job, flying in with his fellow mercenaries. Unlike those young bombardiers, he didn't stay in the sky, but he nevertheless followed their lead. The places he went were like islands, fractured locales that could be razed without care for the lives left in waste behind him. He'd step on a plane and fly off to some other place. There was always some other place to go.

As time passed and pragmatism reared its ugly head, his opinion changed. He couldn't stay airborne indefinitely. In all its subtle implications, he had to come down to earth sooner or later. The only compromise was to float. Floating implied equilibrium, a balance of opposed forces. There was the sky above, moody as it could be, passing through its day and night. But there was the ocean beneath and, despite its moods, there was a dimension to its vastness that didn't change. Its depths fell away to darkness, to unplumbed mysteries, where an underworld existed, alien and detached, ambivalent to the chaos above.

On his boat, he found himself nestled between those opposed and yet harmonious realities. They knew nothing of each other, yet they existed side by side.

And so he would lay there at night, naked beneath the black sky, pondering such things.

Simple, and yet not so.

He counted shooting stars.

***

"For a guy who lives on a boat, you're looking a little pale," Joe remarked as they walked a perimeter patrol around Underlab. It was only Randal's second day at the sight, and Joe had already zeroed in his suspicions. "Too much fish, I bet," Joe said with a laugh. "You're turning milk white, just like them."

Randal shrugged. "When in Rome, you know."

"Yeah, well, I heard Athens didn't agree with you."

"Felix told you about that?"

"When your name came up for this, sure he did." Joe wiped a hand over his balding head before snapping his wrist to shake off the beads of sweat. "So what do you think of our lodging?"

Randal opened his hands. While Jonah's research staff slept in cramped cots within the air conditioned comfort of the lab buildings, the security personnel were left to appropriate housing in the village. It was not as aggressive a policy as Randal first thought when hearing of it, as a good portion of the village's residents had departed to neighboring villages when the lab buildings went up. They were given healthy compensation, of course. Randal and Joe shared a crude structure of rough hewn rock, its roof a simple but highly efficient cross lacing of wide tropical fronds that kept them dry during the evening downpours and the heavy clinging mist of the cool mornings. There was a power outlet, at least, fed from the lab.

"We've had worse," Randal said under his breath. "Remember Venezuela?"

Joe snorted. "Those goddamn beetles should have saddles on them." He glanced at Randal. "So what was the story with Nigeria?"

Randal shook his head. "You know how it goes. It went."

Joe nodded. "Just remember this is low profile. Security, that's all. Not engagement."

Two other contractors passed by them, rustling through the undergrowth on the slope above. Randal's eyes narrowed on them, but Joe gave them a little wave. The two men, dressed in green cargo pants and t-shirts, moved along, their hands resting on their AK's. Randal

211

waited for them to pass before lowering his hand from his shoulder holster and the nine-millimeter he kept on the ready. "You know them?"

Joe frowned. "No. They're corporate. Not with us."

"Who is?"

Joe's frown rose to a wide smile as he clapped a hand on Randal's shoulder. "Buddy, Uncle Felix only sent us on this tea party. It's you, me, and a hefty deposit for our accounts."

Randal clenched his teeth, thinking of the little hut they were sharing. He'd known Joe since his army days. He was the closest thing to what Randal could call a friend. If the job went to shit, nobody would have their backs, except the cover they could give each other. Randal liked things simple, but at a certain point there was a difference between simple and selfish. He had to tell his secret because, if it came to it, Joe should know not to worry about him.

"It's working for Jonah, isn't it, that's got you clamped up?" Joe guessed.

Randal scratched his temple. "Part of it."

Joe put a hand on Randal's shoulder and brought him to a halt. "Talk to me. I brought you in because I thought this would be easy money for us, a good way to close out our careers. We're not getting any younger, and even Uncle Felix is thinking about calling it quits. But even if you're not ready to hang it up, I figured this would be a good way to get you back in your game after that Nigerian nightmare. Let you clean up your reputation as a stable operator, an—"

"I'm dying."

Joe stood still, his mouth hanging at the abrupt news. After several moments he seemed to remember that and closed it, his lips pressing to a tight line.

Randal blew out a breath. "It's an inoperable brain tumor. I'm screwed."

***

He was trembling on the metal table, the bindings on his limbs and head seeming to grow tighter with every uncontrollable shudder of his body. The pressure in his side assaulted him with maddening agony. He had no idea how long he was confined, but it seemed an eternity of suffering. He lost count how many times Jonah had hovered in his vision, the blurred sight of him piercing the darkness after the usual searing bolts of pain across his face.

They have to cut my eyelids open so I can see.

He wanted to scream around the tube in his mouth. The light above him grew brighter, and his skin seemed to warm. Flushes of heat washed through him, and the trembling eased, only for him to become aware of something much more disturbing.

He had learned during martial arts training that, even without sight, a mind knows the periphery of the body that encompasses its awareness. It's not only a subconscious imprint of the size and shape of the body, but something more complex, an inner sensitivity to the body's norm, and deviations that upset that perception. It was such a process that could denote the location of bruises, inflammations, swellings—

He thrashed the moment the thought came to him. *The pain in my side. The pain in my right side. My right side is distended. My right side is—is immense!*

He gargled phlegm as he tried to scream. Something prodded his side. He didn't have to look to know what he felt. Somebody was touching him. His eyes darted about.

The nearest person was a white-coated blur off to his right. Far off to his right. In fact, halfway across the room.

"Note induction of secondary stimuli. Note cohesion of neural system. Note residence of primary neural reception in native form."

What the hell?

It was too much. It was insane. He contorted, struggling to scream. Flecks of blood flew in the air. They were black.

***

He sat on his bunk, listening to the rain. It was early. It was his third day on Jonah's job. He took his pills and washed them down with half a bottle of water. It was an experimental treatment, stuff he picked up in Paris on his way home from Athens. Felix gave him the contact of a private pharmaceutical lab that had contracted their services in years gone by. The pills helped, but they were buying time, nothing else.

He stood and walked over to Joe's bunk, poking Joe's stomach with the bottle to wake him. Joe rolled away with a curse, but Randal wouldn't relent. "Hey. Where's this interpreter?"

Joe waved him off. "Walk around," he said, his face buried in his little pillow. "You'll find her."

Randal pulled on his pants, slipped his arms through his holster, and settled a wide brimmed bush hat on his head. He pushed the door open, shoved aside a mottled brown chicken with his foot, and looked out into the morning downpour. Nobody was moving in the village. He figured they would wait for later to tend their rice. Three days, and he was already tired of rice. It fed more people in the world than any other foodstuff, but he never lost his Midwest appetite for meat and potatoes. Chicken over rice, vegetables over rice, beans over rice, shit over rice; he hated rice. Rice reminded him of the sprawling debris that was humanity, that struggling mass of people clinging to a meager existence. In his experience, most of them were rice eaters. As he walked about, he had no idea why those thoughts occurred to him. Maybe it was the tumor, working its subversive roots into some other part of his brain.

He cursed under his breath as he wandered aimlessly through the village. Aside from the occasional chicken and wayward glance from a dark doorway, he could've been on the moon. He felt like a lone survivor. He looked to the trees. Their many layered canopies of foliage were so green that even in the rain they shimmered with an iridescent jade glow. Wild birds broke the silence with their morning calls, sounding out the canopy for warnings.

He leaned against the radiator grill of the duty truck, his gaze darting about. He looked to the old abandoned church and its pathetic steeple with the corroded bell. He tipped his head, his eyes narrowing in curiosity. The pitting on the bell, it was something salt water might do, but not jungle humidity. He started to ponder that thought when his gaze was drawn to the side by a flight of birds. They soared off, lost from sight behind the heights of the surrounding trees. His gaze sank, and that was when he found the cabin.

It was a small structure, like the rest of the dwellings in the village, except this one had a singular form of decoration. Most of the villagers took effort to adorn their mantles with various wild flowers they would find in the surrounding growth, but this doorway had the flowers secured in the middle of the door with some root-twine hanging from a rusty hook. The door was painted blue and, to either side, there were two small circles of wood, one painted red, the other painted green.

Navigational buoys? Why would someone up in the remote mountain jungles decorate their door with little harbor buoys?

His eyebrows furrowed beneath the rim of his hat. He pushed off from the truck and walked to the dwelling. He hesitated a moment to flip off the safety on his handgun before knocking on the door. It swayed inward ever so slightly on its hinges. He waited, but he heard nothing within. Every instinct told him to go, every suspicion told him he was about to step into an ambush, but still he stood there, licking his lips as he weighed his thoughts. He reached across his chest to rest his hand on his gun. His finger was near the trigger. He knew he should go, but then he reached out with his left hand and pushed open the door.

A woman's voice greeted him. *"Bon matin, Monsieur."*

He stepped in from the rain. It was dark but for the light of a single yellow candle resting on a table before him. A woman sat next to the table, her legs crossed to support the book she was reading. She had short hair that grew in loose curls, its black mass cropped tight along the back

214

of her head so that her neck was bare. Her large brown eyes lingered on him as her thin lips formed a smile.

He looked from her to take in the rest of her dwelling. It was the same size as the one he shared with Joe. A bed was off to his left. A metal bracket was fastened to the wall beside the door. A wooden beam rested against the wall. *She secures her door at night. An odd practice, in such a remote area. Have to remember that.* There was a bookcase behind her. She wore a long brown dress that looked like she'd made it herself. It let her blend into the shadows, except for the red kerchief tied loosely about her neck.

She tipped her head as he stared at her in silence. *"Je m'appelle Genevieve. Et tu?"*

He studied her face in the candlelight. He couldn't guess her age. "Randal," he said. *"Parlez-vous Anglais?"* He held up his left hand, his thumb and pointer finger pressed together. *"Je parle Francais un peu,"* he lied, making a point to enunciate, the way a novice would speak an unfamiliar tongue. French was only one of several languages he'd picked up over the years. He knew enough to tell she hadn't been to France in a long time; even in the few words she voiced, he could discern the tonal inflections had lost their domestic sound.

"Un peu? Then we will speak English," she said. She mimicked his hand, but spread her finger and thumb. "I speak more than a little."

"Good." He let the door close behind him. "So you're the interpreter?"

She watched his gaze dart to his right to take in her little stove as the door closed. Only then did his hand sink away from his gun. She tipped her chin to the weapon. "Nine or ten millimeter?"

"Nine. Ten is a hand cannon. I don't need that."

"No Kalashnikov for you?" she said, with a notable Russian inflection on the name of the famous designer of the AK47: *Kalash-nee-koff.*

His eyes narrowed; she either knew Russian, or Jonah's party was not the first group to intrude on the villagers. He listened to the rain outside. Her dwelling was very dry. Her questions were not what he expected. "The AK is devastating, but it's not discreet. Sloppy. Sloppy makes a mess, and a mess is not simple. I prefer simple." He rested his shoulders against the wall behind him. "So you can speak to the locals?"

She closed her book and put it on the table. "We have an understanding. Would you like some tea?"

He hesitated a moment. The shape of her cheekbones complimented the wide gaze of her eyes. He hadn't seen that look in quite some time. He decided to stay. He knew then why Joe gave him a sly look when asked about the interpreter. Joe knew what Randal liked. He tipped his hat back. "A cup of tea would be fine."

"*Alors,*" she said with a smile and opened her hands. She stood and brushed by him, turning once to point at her bed. "I only have one chair. You can sit at the foot of my bed, if you'd like." She stood before her stove, her back to him. Several clicks sounded out before a blue flame popped up beneath the tin kettle on the stove. She glanced over her shoulder when he sat on her bed, the telltale creak of its wood frame giving him away. "You work for the company?"

"Contract security." He waited until she looked back at him. "You work for the company?" he echoed, his suspicions already burning with a hundred questions.

"*Non.* I am under a different agreement as well."

"With who?"

She tilted her head. "That is a secret between me and the trees, *Monsieur.*"

He pointed to the table, where she left her book. A quick glance at the volume when he went to sit on the bed revealed no detail, except it was leather bound, and appeared quite old. "What are you reading?"

"Hunchback," she said. "Victor Hugo. Bong-bong, bong-bong," she added, gesturing as if she were pulling on bell ropes. "Early edition. An heirloom. My father handed it down to me."

Randal, too, had some leather heirlooms from his father when he was young. They healed long ago. "Have you been out here long?"

"*Oui.* Too long," she said with a sigh. "But I am happy here, so I stay."

"What do you do?"

Her dark eyes bored into him. After some time she smiled. "I interpret."

She looked back to the stove when the kettle rumbled and started to let out a sputtering squeal. She poured the steaming water in a mug, dropped in some dried leaves, and then spooned out a syrupy liquid. When she came to him with the mug she looked him in the eye to spot his skepticism. "You Americans prefer your tea in little bags, I know, but here, it is different. This is a local plant that the natives drink. It is the closest thing I've found to a palatable tea. And the syrup is similar to honey, a sap from one of the local tree species growing near Highlab. The natives recommended it to me. It has a unique flavor."

He took the cup. She kept her gaze on him as she retreated the few steps to her chair and sat down. He breathed in the vapors from the cup. It was somewhat sweet, but it had a moldy undertone, almost like the smell of wet bark. "What's this syrup called?"

She rolled her eyes up, her fingers wiggling as she seemed to struggle for a proper word. "This is not an exact translation, but they will not tell me a proper translation, if one even exists." She rested her hands in her lap and looked to him. "They call it Purity."

***

He hid on his boat during those first few weeks of taking the experimental pills he acquired in Paris. A doctor found the little tumor in his head before he left for Nigeria, during the exhaustive physical exam Felix demanded before any job. Randal's doctor urged him not to go to Africa, but Randal doubled his usual 'incentive' payment for the man's discretion and called Felix the moment he left the office. He lied and told Felix he was good to go. He had to go. He was enraged. The world sucked, and he wanted to smack it around like the stupid bitch it was. All the anger that brewed in him during his childhood, all the black hate that had festered while his father whipped him with a belt, all the mindless outrage for the lies he tried to live, and his own failure to be better than the lies with his own son, erupted into his consciousness. He got on a plane knowing he was going to kill people. He wanted to kill people. If he was going to die, somebody else needed to die as well. To the predator, so too the prey. The balance must be maintained.

His mood couldn't have differed more by the time he returned. The tumor was a notion when he left, but by the time he was home floating in the Atlantic on *Fredo* it was an inescapable reality. It came for the most part in the form of headaches, but the pills made things worse. He was exhausted. His body hurt, but not in the ways he knew from being in fights or car accidents. It was an unavoidable ache that seemed to grow from every joint. The doctors in Paris told him the pills they gave him were a mix of traditional medications and their newer, experimental formulas. He stopped taking the traditional pills. He'd rather go out in an eruption of the tumor than waste away in the slow agony of cancer death. To his relief, within days of stopping the old pills he was feeling much better. The headaches remained, but they didn't worsen. He didn't go back to his doctor. As much as he hated lies, he decided to lie to himself, and wrap himself up in the denial that the tumor was in temporary check. It had to be. Naked under the starlight, he knew there was no other option.

His time at sea was not all loneliness. He had a few phone numbers he held onto, professionals he'd found to be well worth their money. Wealth had its privileges, and he did quite well for himself over the years. There were three numbers in Miami he liked to use, but he knew there was just one he wanted to use. Despite what he told Joe, she was the only one to visit his boat, and her visits were few in number.

Her name was Josephine. To call her an escort was not fair. In fact, Randal wasn't quite sure what to call her, if he even cared to classify her.

217

She seemed to be more of a kept woman, but a woman kept by a very select clientele. Unlike his younger days, it wasn't about empty lust and the hollow conquest it entailed. He'd mellowed somewhat with age. He was hesitant to think that he was growing pensive—ironic as that might be—because that would imply accepting the reality that he wasn't the invincible madman he'd been in his twenties.

She would meet him at whatever dock he chose to fuel his trawler. Sunhat, chestnut hair in a ponytail, sundress, sandals—so very pedestrian. Beneath her sunglasses were large brown eyes, with an exquisite almond taper. She was stunning, a necessary requirement for the life she chose, but she possessed something more. She had a way of making him feel relaxed and safe, in a strange form of maternal attentiveness that could give Freud a field day. He knew that was part of the game, but with Josephine the attention felt genuine, and he'd dealt with enough lying eyes in his life to know the difference. On the other hand, they both knew he couldn't tolerate the presence of anyone in his private life for too long. It was a wonderful arrangement.

She was French, born in Marseilles, and had been an aspiring ballerina until she hurt her knee. She was a graceful swimmer. He found it serene just to watch her move. After all the brutality and violence in his life, he found a deep solace in watching the smooth, aquiline flow of her limbs as she moved about the boat. It let him believe he had a sense for finer things, an appreciation for the subtle artistry of nature.

He didn't tell her he was sick. The last time he saw her he made a blunt little statement that he was going away. Their conversations were usually on the short side. She poured him wine to go with the dinner she cooked and asked if she would see him again. It wasn't all business, because she held his hand when he didn't answer. They watched the starlight that evening, resting naked beneath the dark sky, the way he preferred. But when he was tired, he gave her a little kiss on the forehead and went to bed, saying nothing to her. He never pressured or expected sex from her. She held a different meaning for him.

She came to him that night. He woke to find her next to him under the sheets. It wasn't a performance; it was personal. When he brought her back to the docks later the next day things were different. His usual way was to stay up on the flybridge and exchange a simple wave with her as she retreated down the dock. They had an understanding. But that last day he let the dock assistants tie *Fredo* to the dock's cleats. Josephine looked up to him, but he came down from the flybridge and stood before her.

She took off her sunglasses, studying him from beneath the rim of her hat. "Randal?"

He kissed her and then closed her in a tight embrace, holding her for several moments. When he felt her hands on his back he slipped away from her. He tipped his head. "Okay."

She put a hand on his cheek before stepping off the boat. She made to turn as she walked the dock, but she caught herself, and put a hand to her eyes as she picked up her pace.

He motored out into the Atlantic.

He drank some whiskey.

He listened to the dolphins.

It was the only night of many lonely nights that he contemplated putting a gun to his head. He knew desperation. This was different. Desperation was anxious; this was soothing.

She was the closest thing he had. "Okay," he said and wiped his eyes.

He counted the shooting stars.

***

It was a week into the job when Jonah felt comfortable enough, or lonesome enough, to talk to Randal about the research. Randal was sitting in the cockpit of the rickety escape plane tied down next to Highlab, checking over the craft when Jonah appeared by the open passenger door, holding up a clear plastic cup with a bubbly liquid that could only be champagne. His eyes sparkled, and his mouth was open in an excited smile. "Success! Our first success!"

Randal folded the rag in his lap and looked at his son. "Found a bottle opener?"

Jonah lifted his cup before emptying it in one long gulp. "E-V-I," he said, enunciating each letter with care as he ignored Randal's comment. "Elastimer vector injections," he explained. "Revolutionary, revolutionary! Tell me, what's the biggest problem with burn patients, after infection risk?"

Randal thought back to basic training before he shrugged. "Skin grafts?"

Jonah pointed at him, but then waved his hand. "Scarring! Loss of the skin's natural flexibility and its cohesion with underlying tissue structures. We just overcame that problem, right here, *right in that building*," he said, opening a hand to Highlab. "Do you know what this means?" His voice elevated with emotion. "No more scarring. No more surgical adhesions. I won't explain the process of engineered retroviruses and genomic activation but all you need to know is that we did it. We took samples of epidermis wrecked with burns and made it supple as a baby's bottom. We took skin that was hard as wood and made it flow like water!"

Randal hummed as his imagination dwelled on that thought.

"We can reverse it, too. Think of the military applications," Jonah said, guessing at Randal's silence. "Just imagine it, imagine having skin tougher than oak, but with the flexibility and pluck of the skin you had when you were eighteen." He threw his cup and slapped his hands on either side of the door. "Wait for what comes next. This just opens the door; think of it as a precursor, a required dry run to the final goal."

"So what's that, the fountain of youth?"

Jonah laughed. "No. It's about controlling cells and what they do. That's why this is so exciting, because it means we're on the right path. If you can control what cells do, you can make them do anything. Don't forget, we start out as one cell, and that one cell differentiates to provide us with all the very specialized types of cells that compose a mature human form."

"Are you telling me you're growing body parts in there?"

"Think bigger," Jonah said, tipping his head back to catch the sun on his face. He closed his eyes for a moment before looking back to Randal. "I think I found it."

"It? A cure for cancer?"

Jonah leaned against the plane, chuckling. "No, no, not that." He stared at Randal before he continued. "Not the cure for cancer. The cure for, well, everything."

Randal's lips parted. He blinked. He ran a hand through the short, coarse mass of his salt and pepper hair. He didn't know what to say, but a selfish suspicion raced through his mind in a heartbeat. *Does he know I'm sick?*

Jonah looked out to the clouds skating past the peak and gave a single nod. "Right. Celebration's over. I have to get back to work."

"Okay," Randal said as Jonah spun on his heel and walked away. He waited until he was certain Jonah was back by Highlab before flipping open the rag in his lap and looking down at the micro-transmitters he'd smuggled in. It took two days, but he had them all, passing them in his stool after swallowing them before boarding the flight to the lab site. He was well acquainted with the finer arts of smuggling, and knew as well that until somebody figured out how to secure the twenty or so feet of safe, usable cargo space in the human intestinal tract that no installation could be secure. He planted the transmitters in several locations, and continued to plant them, in the end hoping to have audio surveillance of every point he could access. The small digital audio player he packed was obsolete and therefore discreet to an untrained eye, but it doubled as his central receiver. Range was short, but the receiver hidden in the player worked quite well.

It was not to steal secrets. It was to stay informed.

He knew Jonah hadn't told him everything. His son was smarter than that.

***

Two nights later he slipped out from his hut after Joe fell asleep and walked off into the jungle, avoiding the corporate men walking their perimeter. He sat on the bulging root of a massive tree and took his digital player in hand, pressing the play and stop buttons together to access the player's receiver. The track skip buttons allowed him to index through his transmitters. There was nothing of interest, except the bungling efforts of one researcher to get a female comrade into bed. Randal shook his head, turned the player off, and slipped it in a pocket.

The rustle of leaves drew his gaze up and his hand to his gun. Holding still, he surveyed the surrounding jungle, so nebulous in the depths of its foliage. He'd learned how to hunt people in the jungle at night, and it dealt more with sound than sight. He closed his eyes and waited, and heard a distinctive sound, the sound of someone defecating, marked by the flatulence of a Westerner's digestive system coping with the tropical humidity and unfamiliar foods. He moved from the root in the direction of the sound and, sliding his handgun free, took aim ahead as he peered around a tree.

He found Joe standing by a broad-leafed bush, shoveling dirt with his booted foot as he wiped his hands on a leaf. "Hey," Randal whispered, so as not to stun his friend.

Joe spun around, snapping his AK to the ready, before easing up. He still held the gun, but his arms relaxed and his familiar smile returned. "What are you doing out here?"

Randal slid his handgun in its holster as he glanced up to the sky. "Thought I'd watch for some shooting stars." He nodded his chin to the bush. "Those leaves cause a rash."

"Yeah, that's real funny, Mister Wise-ass." Joe stepped away from the bush. "Had to drop a stinker," he said before hooking a thumb toward Underlab. "I don't think the geeks like it when we go in the general latrines there and fire off a twenty-one gun salute. Besides, it's peaceful out here at night." He rested his hands on his AK. "So, did you see our little interpreter walking around?"

Randal shook his head. Since that first time he met Genevieve, he saw her twice outside her hut when he was driving the duty truck back to the village. Both times she invited him in for tea, which he accepted. As usual, he didn't talk much, but then, neither did she. She reminded him of Josephine, reading her book while he sat and stared at the wall, lost in his thoughts.

He blinked, remembering himself. "No, I haven't seen her."

"Watch for the lantern," Joe said. He patted Randal's shoulder. "Sack time for me."

Randal watched him go. He turned on his feet. The debate within him didn't last long. He returned to his root, a good vantage point to monitor the area, and waited. In due order he saw the pale glow of a lantern bobbing through the growth. He stood, and let himself be seen by waving to her. She stopped short and stared at him as he walked to her. She was wearing her brown dress with a gray blanket roll slung across her body.

"You shouldn't walk alone," he said. "It's not safe, with the predators around here."

She smiled at what she took as a dated sense of chivalry. "I'm not afraid."

He took the weight of the lantern from her hand. "I'm talking about the two-legged variety. You don't exactly blend, and you can't always trust these corporate gunslingers to keep themselves in check. Where are you going?"

She raised an eyebrow, studying him for a moment before her smile returned. "I like to walk at night. Do you want to walk with me?"

He held out his arm with the lantern. "Lead on, *Mademoiselle.*"

She turned to him before breaking out in laughter. "*Mademoiselle?* How young do you think I am?"

He shook his head. "Oh, not so fast. Even I know not to discuss a woman's age. I thought you might like it better than if I called you *Madame.*"

She hooked her arm through his and stared at him.

"But if you insist, I wouldn't guess a day over thirty-five."

She laughed again, but this time it was lower, as if she were finding humor in something he knew nothing about. "Ah, *Monsieur* Randal, you flatter me."

He let it go. She kept a hold of his arm. It felt good.

He looked up to the hidden canopies of growth above them.

They walked through the jungle and, before long, even with his experienced sense of direction, he found himself glancing over his shoulders to discern his whereabouts. She continued on, giving no hint of being lost; on the contrary, she seemed to know exactly where she was going, even when she stopped. She would look about, rest a hand on a tree, then nod and continue on. At last they came to a clearing, framed by two towering trees, and he followed her gaze up, where the black void was lit with every star in the night sky.

"*Magnifique, n'est-ce pas?*" she said. When he turned to her she patted his arm before stepping away from him. She let her head hang back and flowed through several lazy pirouettes, her arms out to her sides. "Do you like to watch the sky?"

He caught himself staring at her and looked at his feet before looking back to the sky. He hesitated, but then decided to let his guard down. "I own a boat. At night I like to lie out and count the shooting stars over the ocean."

She came back to him, wrapping her arms over her chest as she kept her gaze to the sky. "Ah, yes, the stars and the sea, both so timeless. The stardust from which we are made, and the water from which we live."

Her voice, with its accent, came to him like music in the night. It reminded him of Josephine and, with that, a marked heaviness weighed on his chest. He looked at Genevieve. When he spoke, the bitter undertone of his voice was unmistakable. "Don't tell me you're one of those New Age types?"

She took her blanket roll off her shoulder and shook her head. "What does this mean, a 'New Age type'? I have not heard this expression before." She looked about the ground, shifting on her feet.

"You can't expect to put a blanket down on a jungle floor at night," he said, turning the shutter on the lantern to put more of the yellow light on the ground. "Look at the ants. They'll swarm you."

She shrugged. "Then I will go where they are not. This is what I always do. I leave them be, and so they leave me." She stopped short when she seemed to find a spot she liked. She glanced at the sky once, turned a bit, and then crouched to undo the blanket. She put aside a leather water bag and a tin cup, then snapped out the blanket and let it sink through the air to the ground. She looked about and picked up a small rock, which she rubbed against a tree before holding it close to her mouth. She whispered something, as if she were talking to the stone, even though her eyes were wandering about the depths of the dark jungle. She pressed two fingers to her lips before pressing them to the stone, and then set it at one corner of the blanket. She repeated this with three other rocks, setting them at the other three corners of the blanket. When she was done she looked his way and opened her hands at her sides. "Now, Monsieur Randal, we may lie down, and watch for your shooting stars. I have something for us to drink to keep warm. The chill will come soon, when the cooler air above us rolls through the jungle and, with it, the morning mists. Will you join me?" she said as she settled down and patted a hand beside her.

He stared at her. "You talk to rocks?"

She studied him for a moment before she gave him that knowing smile of hers. "I told you. I interpret."

He grinned before nodding. "Okay," he said under his breath, closing the shutters on the lantern and joining her. He was a little uneasy sitting on the blanket, as it went against everything he knew about being in a jungle at night. Despite that, or perhaps because of it, he was reminded of something else, and decided to pursue a different course with her. "So tell me, *Madame* Interpreter, how do the natives feel about the research?"

She shrugged as she sat Indian style, her eyes on the stars. "They have many memories over the ages. This is one more. They are very wise when it comes to perspective. They do not like the presence of these outsiders, but they will pass, like so many before them."

"Is that why they took the bribes for their homes?"

She grinned. "Money," she said and looked to him. "They remember the gold that was stolen from them, so very long ago. Money — wealth — it is no different than the seasons. It is here, and then it is gone. Like these outsiders, this money too will lose meaning over time." She gave an absent-minded wave to the distant peak of Highlab. "You have seen the ruins. So much work to make those temples, and now they sit broken and lost, monuments to gods that now sleep forgotten in the jungle. You can hear them snore in the rustle of the leaves at night. But it was not their anger that tore down those temples, it was water, so free when flowing but, in the head of a root, held under pressure, even a delicate seedling can break the strongest stone. The people here have learned the lesson of this over the ages."

"So they don't care about money?"

She looked to the sky. "Stone shapes the earth beneath us. Men shape stone. Time turns them both to dust, but the jungle lives on."

"Right," he said under his breath. He'd seen enough hollow transcendentalism around the world to know that money always won out. He wasn't necessarily proud of his cynicism, but the lies and disorder of the world had taught him to expect nothing less, and to view things with nothing less. "So that's their denial for selling out?"

She observed him with her knowing smile. There was a glint in her eyes under that starlight, as if she were looking on a foolish little boy. "They did not take any money, Randal. They did not leave; they choose not to be seen. They will not be seen until these outsiders leave."

His eyes narrowed as he met her gaze. He wasn't sure what to think of her statement, so he went to his main concern. "They won't resist?"

"No, they will not resist. You have many men with guns. That would be foolish."

"Good," he said with a nod. "Because this is the easiest job I've ever done, and I don't want that to change. By the way, these corporate bozos aren't *my* men." He looked to the sky before leaning over to pick up one of the stones. "So what did you put on the rocks? There's not a single creepy-crawly on this blanket."

"I put nothing on the stones."

He glanced at her.

"You should put it back," she said with a soft singsong to her voice.

He looked away from the edge of the blanket. A column of hearty tropical ants was nearing. He held the stone to his nose to take a whiff, but there was no scent to detect. He waited until the ants were close before returning the stone. To his surprise, the column swerved, without pause or the confused scurry so typical of agitated ants, and plodded around the perimeter of the blanket. Somehow, she had tricked him. It was the only way, but how? There was no trace of a scent on the stone. He sat up straight before looking away from the ants to find her expectant gaze, staring at him down the slender length of her nose. She fascinated him, even if that little smile of hers was starting to annoy him. He met the expression in kind. "So you talk to ants too?"

Her lips parted as she let out a laugh. For someone who'd been with natives in a remote jungle, her teeth were exquisite. She took his hand and gave it a squeeze, and the strength of her grip surprised him. "Ah, *Monsieur* Randal, have I not told you? I interpret."

He patted her forearm and laughed with her. "Okay. Anything else I should know?"

She studied him as her humor quieted, but then her smile returned. Her eyes swelled on him as she rose to her knees, holding a finger up to him as she rolled her lower lip between her teeth. She opened her water bag and poured some water into the tin cup she had brought along, and turned to offer him the cup. "Would you like a drink?"

He looked at the cup. Propped on her knees, her face was above his and, when his gaze rose to meet her eyes, she was framed by the night sky. He recognized the compulsion waking in his chest. He wanted more than a drink. He took the cup and, as he brought it to his lips, he picked up a familiar aroma. He looked back to her, curious. "Purity?"

She took off his hat and ran a hand through his hair, her fingers probing his scalp as they went, her lips parting as her eyes followed her hand. Her eyes met his as her fingers trailed across his neck before her hand sank away. "Drink, Randal."

He would've thought he was crazy, were it not for the certainty in his mind. It wasn't the work of paranoia, or the fear of his secret tumor being known. His face fell. "How. . .?"

She took his hand and raised the cup to his lips, watching as he drank. When the cup was empty she took it from him and shifted to sit Indian style once more. She took his hand and pressed it between her palms, her fingers fanning out to overlap his own. "I think you know more than you wish to believe, my friend Randal. You love the jungle, no? You love it the way so few come to love it. You love it for the mysteries of its various orders, the ones we can see and, more so, the ones we do not see. It is a hard life, the path you follow. It is filled with much anger. But I see how you move through the jungle. You do not move like the others." She held up the sandwich of their hands between them, their fingertips just below the cast of her gaze. "This is the world, the way our hands are held: there is the order we know, the order we see in our dreams, and the order that exists outside of our thoughts. Between them is the madness of the unknown, as they cannot see each other freely. They are separate, but joined, appendages of each other. The natives have a phrase for it, which I best relate as *le chant des ombres*."

The song of shadows. The water felt warm in his stomach.

She lowered her hands and held his gaze. She said nothing.

He felt the world sway beneath him. If he didn't know better, he would have sworn he was on the flybridge of his boat. But there was no ocean, only the jungle, and Genevieve held nothing in common with Josephine, aside from her country of origin.

It was the sensation, he realized, that linked the two realities in his head.

It was the sensation of being adrift, of forgetfulness.

The silence was broken when several birds took flight through the canopy, startling them. Genevieve blinked and pulled her hands back, but her gaze spread in a heartbeat and darted past his left shoulder. In the next heartbeat he turned and whipped his handgun free, taking aim down the length of his arms into the shadows about them.

She cupped a hand over his mouth when his lips parted. She held silent, her hands coming to rest on his shoulders as she turned his aim. "Randal—"

The wailing alarm of Underlab split the silent night. Powerful spotlights, rigged in the trees, snapped on in unison, tearing away the veil of night to bathe the jungle in a harsh white glare. Randal narrowed his eyes against the sudden eruption but, in the moment it took him to regain focus, he saw something he refused to believe, saw someone emerging from the side of a tree—not from behind the tree, but right out of the bark, separating like globules of oil in water to form the unmistakable, four limbed silhouette of a man. The intruder saw him as well, the man's body snapping toward Randal and Genevieve.

Shouts sounded out around them. The alarm rose in pitch through another deafening undulation. The intruder crouched, and then launched.

Randal didn't need to feel Genevieve's clutch of his shoulders. He knew what he had to do. He fired off three quick shots before ducking to the side, swinging his arm back as he turned to shove Genevieve behind him. A shadow flew past them and hit the ground with a heavy thud and a spray of twigs. Randal shifted his footing to keep his body between the downed intruder and Genevieve as he leveled his gun at the intruder's head. Only then did he blink, the sight before him too unreal for his mind to accept.

Randal's immediate assumption was that the intruder was wearing some type of camouflaged leotard. But staring down at the man beneath the pitiless lights, he could see the reality of the situation. The man was naked.

He was dark green, green like the leaves of the trees.

Jonah charged from the jungle to look at the oddity stretched out at Randal's feet. Randal kept his gun trained on the downed intruder. Genevieve's breath slid across his neck as she hid behind him.

The intruder stirred.

Randal clenched his teeth as the monster whipped around. He opened fire, emptying his clip into the monster's forehead. It bucked and swayed with the impact of each round, but failed to go down, until the last round hit and the back of the monster's head exploded in a cloud of black fragments. Only then did Randal hear Jonah's shouts as the monster slumped to its knees and flopped on its back. Too late, Jonah grabbed Randal's arm to stop him. In the rush of Randal's adrenalin he responded by reflex, turning his arm to break the grip and thrust the snout of his gun toward Jonah's face. He held then, his finger hovering over the trigger, his gaze boring into Jonah's eyes. In the next moment he blinked, dumped his empty clip, slapped a fresh one home, and pulled the gun's slide to resume his aim on the monster sprawled on the dirt before him.

The undergrowth rustled with the sound of springing twigs as members of the corporate security team broke into the open, their AK's aimed high until they spotted the downed monster. They drew in close and, even though the monster was still, they kept their weapons trained on its corpse.

Jonah fell back a step before his anger got the best of him. He turned on Randal, his eyes bulging. "You fool! Why did you—"

"What the hell is this thing?" Randal demanded. "Talk to me!"

Jonah stepped past him, standing over the fallen freak as he studied the wounds from Randal's gun. The first three impacts were clear, and testament to Randal's accuracy: one in the stomach, one in the chest to the left of the sternum, and one on the left cheek, just under the eye. Any one of them should have dropped the creature, if not kill it outright, but not only had it survived, it had rallied for another attack. Jonah's anger dissipated to an anxious nod of his head as he waved over his security men. "Bag it and bring it back to Highlab," he ordered. "Very impressive, very impressive!" He turned to the security men and waved a hand across his throat, signaling them to silence Underlab's alarm.

Randal eased as the security men threw a tarp over the monstrosity. "Is this part of your breakthrough? What does this have to do with curing diseases?"

Joe came out of the growth to stand beside Randal and Genevieve, his mouth opening when he looked at the prone, ruined beast before the security men wrapped it up and dragged it away. From the look of it, it was no easy task to drag the body. Joe blinked and looked to Jonah. "What's with Chlorophyll Bill over there?"

Jonah jabbed a finger at Joe to silence him, but he kept his eyes on Randal. "We will talk later. I have too much to do now. When I explain it to you, you'll understand, but not a word now, not a single word!" He reached down to pick up Randal's spent clip and handed it to him before following his security men away from the clearing.

Randal looked down to his gun and the empty clip. He looked over the dirt where the monster had fallen. He understood then why he was being paid so much. He also wished he had a ten instead of a nine millimeter weapon. The extra punch would've served him well.

The spotlights clacked off. The jungle was dark.

Joe looked about, wary of the impenetrable night. "To hell with this," he said under his breath and slapped a hand on Randal's shoulder. "We should be inside."

"I'll follow," Randal said and waited for Joe to leave. He turned to find Genevieve by one of the two large trees framing the clearing, slumped against the might of the trunk. Her eyes were hidden in shadow. He put the empty clip in a pocket and stepped beside her. "Are you okay?"

Her eyes met his. She stood, her hands dangling at her sides, as if she'd seen a ghost.

He holstered his gun. "Genevieve?"

She walked past him to stand in the middle of her blanket and gaze up into the trees. She hesitated a moment before looking back at him. "We should listen to your friend. We should go. We should not be here tonight."

He watched as she tossed her water bag and mug on the blanket to roll it in haste, her face turning up to scan the jungle several times. She flung her blanket roll over her shoulder and backed toward him, grabbing his wrist when their shoulders met. When he held his ground, she looked to him, her grip tightening with the surprising strength she possessed.

He stared at her. "Genevieve, talk to me."

She took a quick breath and blew it out, annoyed at his stubbornness. "*Le chant des ombres,*" she whispered. "Now, we go."

He followed her. He kept his hand on his gun.

***

His eyes popped open. White ceiling, the bright lights. They came into rapid focus, and so too the waves of pain washing through him.

His body constricted on its own, his muscles bunching and pulling until he thought his limbs would tear apart. A wet gurgle erupted from his throat. He was reminded of the tube in his mouth. The bindings on his limbs held him fast, but the binding about his head was a little looser than it had been, and he was able to twist his head in small starts. His body sense returned to him, and the difference stunned him for a moment. The pain, the horrible agony in his side, it was gone, lost, dissipated, alleviated—he had no care for the term, but it was gone. Yet in its wake his senses readjusted to replace the agony with another sensation that almost robbed him of his breath.

I can't feel my legs!

He was cold. He looked at the ceiling. It seemed far away, now that he could see clearly. Was it further, or had he been moved? It was impossible to tell, but he heard footsteps, and voices, and somehow he became certain he was much closer to the squeak of rubber soles on a polished floor than muffled voices behind white masks.

It was pointless, but he struggled against the bindings, and that was when he felt it, the distinct sensation that his legs were not paralyzed, but rather restricted, bound tight, as if he were a babe in a swaddling cloth. He drew in a breath and braced himself before struggling to snap his legs apart. Waves of pain washed through him. He heard the wet rasp of his agony and froze.

The sound hadn't come from him. No, it came from something else, something to his left.

He convulsed.

He heard the rasp. Something erupted then, something like globs of motor oil, dark and syrupy, splattering across the white ceiling. Whatever it was, he wanted to be away from that black slop. He thrashed and wrestled with his bindings.

There was a loud snap.

His head was free!

A piercing alarm sounded out. White coated workers rushed toward him.

He lifted his head. By instinct he looked to his left, where the rasp and disgusting eruption had occurred. It was a matter of threat assessment. White coats dashed before his eyes. Hands grabbed at his limbs.

"Cover his eyes!"

But it was too late. He got the glimpse he wanted. And like most things sought in desperation, he was usurped with horrible regret when he got his glimpse, a glimpse of something disgusting, something unbelievable and, worse, it was staring back at him, it thrashed with him, its cheeks bled where they'd been cut time after time to let the swollen, leathery, dark green lids lift over the blackened, bloodshot eyes, eyes he had looked from—

He went wild. His body bucked with ferocious force. His legs felt as if they would splinter, the binding about them was so great. He heard a horrendous squeal from the thing thrashing on its table to his left, a squeal like nails on a chalkboard and, the more he struggled, the more it convulsed in mindless, excruciating torment.

Hands were fighting to get his head strapped down. That's when it came to him.

His legs weren't bound. They were in that disgusting thing thrashing beside him.

He had been that disgusting thing thrashing beside him.

He had been the painful swelling in *its* side, even when he was still *it*.

But now he was something, something else.

Simple.

Don't break the box.

He screamed, and then he heard a noise, a sickening noise, like the crackling of dried wood before a sharp, tearing sound ripped through the room.

Black fluid burst across the room in a violent spray. He was free.

He screamed, and then someone hammered a needle in his arm.

*** *

The morning after his night in the jungle with Genevieve he sat up in his cot. He hadn't slept more than an hour or two. Joe had waited for him but, when Randal tried to question him, Joe cursed under his breath, clutched his AK to his chest, and huddled in a corner with his eyes on the door. Despite being the closest thing Randal could call a friend, he knew Joe didn't have the stomach for anything too extreme. Randal did the dirty work, and Joe supplied the smiling face. *Chlorophyll Bill.* It was a typical Joe response, a flash of humor to deny his befuddlement. Randal was on his own now. Joe would be useless as an effective asset. Randal gave up and rolled over, dialing through his microphones on his digital player.

Silence.

His stomach sank. Either his bugs had been discovered, or the researchers were locked up in their restricted labs, where he never had the opportunity to plant a bug. He'd fumed about that for some time, had contemplated an escape before realizing that was pointless with the sudden multitude of corporate men marching about the jungle. Trucks brought them in from the town far below in the valley, where their main supply base and airstrip waited as a means to exploit for an escape attempt. He heard the trucks from inside his dwelling, but there were no windows, and so no way to judge how many men were brought up. Besides, if he managed to affect an escape, if he skipped on his job, he would leave Joe in a bind and Felix would have no choice but to liquidate both of them. Felix's business couldn't sustain itself if his operators were known to abandon their posts.

He was trapped.

He left the hut with Joe snoring in the corner and went to the general latrines at Underlab. He took a long shower. With a towel wrapped around his waist he snaked his arms through his holster, picked up his clothes, and went to a sink to shave the stubble on his jaw. When he looked in the mirror, his backbone stiffened into a steel rod.

His hair, salt and pepper the last time he looked, was an even black. He ran his fingers through its thick, wet mass, only to look at his hand and find loose gray hairs. His eyes narrowed as he stared at those shed strands of hair, his memory sparking to remember how Genevieve had run her hand through his hair last night. He'd hoped it was some kind of come-on, but he now knew the truth. And he knew something else as well, that she knew far more than she was telling him.

Le chant des ombres. The song of shadows.

He cursed under his breath. He ground his teeth and stared into the mirror.

It was time to get some answers.

He dressed in a hurry, settled his hat on his head, and walked from Underlab up the slope to the village. He found her hut and knocked on the door as he announced himself. He waited until he heard her slide away the wood beam she used to secure the door. The door opened, half her face emerging from behind the door as she studied him with one eye.

"Can I come in?"

"What do you want?"

He grinned. She behaved as if nothing had happened in the jungle. It was a common mistake in people to act oblivious in the belief it would deny the undeniable. It always failed, at least in Randal's experience. "You know things I can only guess at, Genevieve," he said, making an effort to keep his voice low. "I want you to interpret. For me."

She studied him a little longer before she stepped back and let him in. He noticed a small, smooth stone inside the door, to one side of the threshold. He didn't remember seeing a stone there the last time he was in her dwelling. He looked up to her, knowing his gaze had lingered on the stone long enough for her to notice his scrutiny. He stepped aside as she closed the door behind him, set the beam in its place and leaned her shoulder into the door. "Would you like some tea?"

"What's with the beam?"

She rested her hand on the door as her gaze rested on its heavy planks. "Have you seen the villagers this morning?"

He shrugged. "I never see the locals in the morning."

"You won't see them again." She studied him, dipping her chin to the confusion on his face. "Is this what you want me to interpret?"

He sat at her table and noticed her book, closed and off to the side. "Since you've mentioned it, yeah, I'd like to know where they've run to. But I have something else I'd like to ask." He took off his hat and pointed to his hair. "Some how, some way, you figured out that I'm sick."

She crossed her arms on her chest. After a considerable pause she nodded.

"You noticed my hair last night. No more gray. I feel better than I have in a long time. So I believe I'm getting better, which is not supposed to happen, and then some mutant plant-person attacks us. What do the trees sing about that?"

She frowned. "You outsiders. You think I'm crazy. I thought you were different."

"I am. That's why I'm here asking, instead of blowing you off."

She stepped to the other side of the table and fixed her dark-eyed stare on him. She held on him, unblinking, unwavering, until he blinked and shifted in his seat. No one had lasted so long under her stare, at least not in a long time. She pouted, fingering her lower lip for a moment before she nodded. She put a hand on her book and pushed it in front of him. She pulled her hand back, but motioned with her finger. "Open."

He gave her a look-over before consenting. He flipped open the cover, taking care for the obvious age of the book. There was a title page, with some ornate artwork, the kind that used to adorn books in times long gone. It was indeed an heirloom. He was about to close the book when he noticed the outline of some handwritten letters through the yellowed paper. He glanced at her expectant gaze before he turned the page. He looked at the writing, and translated in his head. *To my darling daughter Genevieve, from your loving father.* Nothing of interest—until his eyes constricted at the antiquated government stamp on the bottom of the page. The hand writing, large and flowing in a way that was common long ago, was done in black ink, but the red ink of the stamp overlapped the lower reach of the letters. The writing pre-dated the stamp. He leaned forward to make sure and, when he was, he read the seal one more time. *Property of Jean-Paul Devalle, Chief Botanist, Academy of Sciences, Paris, appointed 3 April 1866 to His charge, Louis Napoleon III.*

Randal read it twice. He sat up straight. She knew about his tumor. She knew he was more fluent in French than he was willing to divulge. Her father wrote the dedication to her before he had stamped the book.

And if Randal's memory served right, Napoleon III had indeed ruled in France in the later part of the nineteenth century. So if this Devalle was Genevieve's father. . .

He closed his eyes for a moment, then closed the book. He took out his handgun and set it on the table next to the book. He hoped the message was clear as he sat disarmed before her. All guards were down.

"How old are you?"

She was stone still, her gaze unwavering. *"Cent soixante deux."*

"A hundred and sixty two," he translated aloud in an effort to convince himself. "Right."

"You don't believe me."

He ran a hand over his head, stopping when he remembered the change of his hair. His hand sank to the table. *"Au contraire.* The problem is I do believe you. As ridiculous as it sounds to me, I believe you. But I guess with my hair changing color, my tumor in check, some goddamn mutant jungle freak running wild from my son's lab, and a village of people that I think know a hell of lot more than anybody else here, yeah, I guess the only logical choice in the face of all that is to believe you."

She grinned. "It's not easy to let go of what you know."

He felt awkward at once. "I guess you have some experience with that."

She appreciated his little bit of dry wit with a soft laugh.

He looked into her eyes. "Okay. So, what now?"

She stepped back and studied him, chin lifted. "That is for you to decide." She held up a finger as he opened his mouth. "You would ask, 'why me?,' *non*? You are not like the others. There are rhythms, seasons, and tides we do not see. We only feel them, we are their extension, appendages that knit together in patterns of wisdom we are not always meant to understand." She fell back another step and splayed her hands on her chest. "I do not age, I do not tire. This is what I have come to be, because I was afraid to die, like my mother and father, before I could learn all there was to learn of this place. I have learned many things, and I have learned there are many other things I will never learn, but only feel, whispers in the dark. *Le chant des ombres.* Look at me; this body does not age. I am bound to this place, because I could not explain myself if I left. I am a clinging thread to outsiders. I see them and make sense of them to the villagers, and to the other things that dwell here. I am the interpreter, and so no one who comes here understands me. But you, you *Monsieur* Randal, you understand, because I have interpreted you, even if you have not interpreted yourself."

He cocked his head back as he digested what she said. It took a few moments, but the little warning in him that would tell him somebody was crazy remained silent. He figured it was only natural to wonder if he was going crazy. But in the end, he knew he felt quite sane and comfortable. Somehow, with all the weirdness enveloping him since the start of the job, she was the first thing to make sense.

He let his breath go and eyed her book before pointing at its leather cover. "You know, I never tell anyone about it, but I read a lot of old stuff when I'm between jobs. Makes me feel," he shifted in a sudden fit of discomfort, "well, makes me feel like more than the murderous bastard that I am. I've read this book. I've read about this book. There's a theme, of orders in conflict, orders passing through each other. That's why you keep it, right?"

She smiled. She held her hands up by her shoulders and mocked a rope pull. "Bong-bong, bong-bong." She meshed her fingers before her chest and opened her hands. "So then. Can I offer you a cup of tea?"

He stared at her. *Purity*. He thought he was starting to understand. "Does anyone—has anyone—else come to drink your tea?"

She gave a single shake of her head. "No."

He frowned as he tried to consider that, but then shrugged it off and looked back to her. Deep down, he liked the notion of having her to himself, even if it was in an odd way. His frown dissipated to a crooked grin. "A cup of tea would be nice, *Madame* Genevieve."

***

He remembered the first two months after his divorce was finalized. Discharged from the army for fighting, disowned by his family for his dissolute ways, disgraced in his town, he holed up in a welfare hotel outside Cleveland and pissed away what little money he earned bouncing at a nearby strip club. It was a timeless delirium of alcohol and cheap hookers. Joe found him there, had kicked in his door when Randal refused to open it and let him in. Joe had been a slob in the army, relegated to latrine duty on a regular basis for his unkempt appearance and the constant chaotic state of his bunk and locker. But that night, at two in the morning, he stood in Randal's doorway in a three-piece suit and imported leather shoes. It was the kind of attire in a little Midwest town worn as a tacky display of wealth. It was the kind of stuff Johanna's father wore to Sunday mass. The woman in Randal's bed groaned and cursed at Joe's intrusion, but without looking at her Randal put a hand over her face and shoved her on the floor. She grabbed her ratty clothes and scurried past Joe, seeming to know better than to say anything. Joe chuckled as she went by.

Randal squinted to focus against the lights from the parking lot diffusing past Joe's form. "Did you kill a stockbroker or something?"

Joe swung the door shut behind him. "Screw you too, you heathen bastard."

Randal sat up, looking to his side for the bottle of whisky he kept on the nightstand. When he found it empty he whipped it into the bathroom.

Joe shook his head at the sound of shattering glass from the bathroom's shadows. "So how's that family of yours? Got a boy, right?"

Randal raised his hand in the shape of a gun and pointed it at Joe's head. "Bam."

Joe smiled. "It's time to break free, you degenerate shit. It's time I tell you about my family. Did I ever mention my Uncle Felix?"

***

The duty truck rumbled up the road to Highlab. After he had tea with Genevieve some of the Underlab researchers spotted him coming out of her dwelling and waved him over. They gave him a yellow crate, one of the extreme care packages, and told him to take it up to Highlab ASAP. They seemed nervous, but he expected that, given the situation in the jungle the night before with Chlorophyll Bill. The corporate security men were watching him. He glanced at his hut as he walked to the truck. The door was closed. He wondered if Joe was still snoring, or perhaps cowering, in the corner.

The truck labored somewhat as it worked up the serpentine ascent of the road. Randal kept a close eye on the surrounding trees, watching as they lost their height in the increasing altitude. It surprised him how fast the transition was from the towering, lush tropical growth further down to the stunted, stout trees growing near the peak. Such a narrow border it was between those types of growth, between those ordered ecosystems, between subtle shifts in the sliding scale of adaptations. Genevieve's words wandered through his mind, even though he wasn't sure what motivated the recollection, but he let his mental image of her linger in the back of his memories.

One hundred sixty two years old. She looks younger than me. How in hell is that possible? How is any of the crap going on here possible?

He ground his teeth as he rolled to a stop at the end of the road. He looked over at Highlab to see Jonah strolling toward the truck with several security men in tow, their AK's on the ready. Randal frowned at the sight of them, knowing they were next to useless. Such men, their presence was more a matter of comfort than actual security.

He opened his door, but Jonah held up a hand for him to remain in the cab. The security men lingered behind as Jonah walked around the cab and climbed into the passenger seat. Despite looking tired, he had that same air of supreme self-satisfaction he wore when he toasted his success after the first few days Randal was on the job.

"Another triumph?"

Jonah kept his eyes on the passing clouds and rested a hand on the yellow crate. "Yes. But first we need to talk. You saw something last night, something you were not supposed to see. I told you I would talk to you."

Randal bobbed his head. "Forget it. It's not my job to ask questions." He took a breath. "To tell you the truth, I don't want your answers. You have some freaky shit going on up here, and that's your business. I drive the truck. Simple."

Jonah nodded. "Yes, yes, I know, and I know how much you like to keep things simple." He looked at Randal, even as Randal made a point of keeping his gaze out the truck's windshield. "We both know there's nothing simple between us."

"This is business. Nothing more, nothing less. Let's keep it that way."

Jonah patted the yellow crate. "Remember I told you about the EVI, the elastimer vector injection? I was not entirely truthful. That was a side project, a cover, in effect, for what we are really working on."

"Right. The cure for everything."

"Not just that. The cure for *anything*. There's a big difference, you should know."

Randal shrugged. "Okay." He looked to Jonah. "You have a cure for green people?"

Jonah smiled that not-so-complimentary smile of his. He was his mother's son. "I'm working under a great deal of pressure. Time is critical. We've accomplished things I never thought possible. That's not only a result of my running these scientists like slaves, but a fortunate side effect of what we are working on. Do you know how cancer works?"

Randal remained expressionless. "Sure. You get sick. You get lucky, or you die. Simple."

"Simple," Jonah echoed under his breath before shaking his head. "We all start from a single cell. Cells differentiate during embryonic development to make all our organ systems and all the respective cell lines responsible for each of those systems to function. The degree of differentiation is striking; more so when you remember every cell has the instructions for each specialization encoded in its genetic material. Think of cancer as turning back the clock, and a cell forgets what it's supposed to be. Instead it goes off in a new direction, forgetting its proper place. Cell growth is a methodical process. The further back a cell goes, the more aggressive the tumor. Did you know there are documented cases of bowel cancers in men where the tumor cells are so primitive they secrete HCG, the hormone responsible for sustaining pregnancy in women?"

"No, I didn't know that," Randal said, finding that an interesting piece of information, given the things Genevieve had said to him. Somehow, it all seemed to fit. "That's pretty screwed up. Isn't this stem cell stuff you're talking about, getting cells to do what you want, and how to deal with tumors?"

"Ah, that's what many people would think," Jonah said, holding up a finger. "But what we are doing here is completely different. What we are doing here compares to stem cells like the Apollo missions compare to the Wright brothers. All stem cell work requires exhaustive work, much of which is still a mystery, to transform those cells to what you want them to be or, in the case of cancers, replace what is damaged. But what we have here, what we have *here*," he added, patting his hand on the crate once more, "is much more potent. Consider what I just told you about cell clocks and cancer, but extrapolate to a larger degree, beyond one organism. Consider that, more or less, all life is related to varying degrees. Certainly there are unique, differentiating traits, such as the differences between plants and animals, but it is still life and there are many commonalities in cell function between plant and animal.

"We have discovered a compound that enables us to manipulate cell lineage in whatever way we wish. And the key word is *wish*. With one compound, we can alter an entire organism, not just one cell type."

Randal had to replay that in his head to make sure he heard it right.

Jonah continued without pause. "The mind has an imprint of its body, of what it should be, not just objectively, but subjectively — perhaps subconsciously — as well. Our compound allows the mind to tap that reference and fashion the body as it wills it to be. At least, that is our understanding of the process. For now, philosophy and metaphysics will have to trump biochemistry. We have overcome the requisite problems of test subject viability; we only need to hone our ability to weed out the test subject's objective imprint from its subjective imprint."

Randal eyed Jonah, studying him. He had an idea where the conversation was heading.

Jonah nodded. "The man you saw last night, yes. He volunteered to be a test subject. He was a botanist, Randal. The man was a botanist."

"So he turned into a goddamn walking plant?"

"Interference from the subjective imprint in his mind."

"What about the green business? Even I know animals don't make chlorophyll. Where did his cells remember — or wish — to turn him into a plant?"

Jonah smiled again. "The compound we exposed him to is isolated from the cells of an arboreal species which grows only on this one peak. Did you know deforestation wipes out dozens of species before we even get to study them? Who knows what we have lost. But this we have found, and it defies all our understanding. It is nothing short of miraculous. It imparted the genetic knowledge of its photosynthetic ancestry to the tissues of the test subject. He became an entirely new organism to be studied."

Randal shook his head. "This is insane. It drove that guy insane."

"His mental character was not as resilient as we had hoped. That could have been alleviated. His dose was not high enough."

"Dose of what?"

"I should say his dose was not pure enough."

Randal's eyes turned to saucers before he could catch himself.

"You see, I brought you here for a reason," Jonah said with a sigh. "I happened to discover your visit to the pharmaceutical labs when you were in Paris. They form a subsidiary to the parent company I work for. I know why you were there. It's why I brought you here. How do you feel?"

Randal blinked. He didn't want to betray Genevieve, but he had the sinking feeling that had already happened—that Jonah had intended it to happen.

Jonah nodded. "I know. You think that crazy French woman has some kind of mystical knowledge. She's just crazy, and there's nothing special about it, French or not. There are no records to tell us where she came from or what she's doing here or who she is, but she's harmless enough. Except for her tea, that is. You've been drinking it, haven't you?"

Randal pursed his lips.

"The pills you have from Paris, do you know what they are? Micro-doses of the same compound in her tea." Jonah stared at Randal. "You have to let me examine you. I need to know if you're cured, or just stabilized."

Randal turned to Jonah with a menacing glare. "You're not poking around in my head."

Jonah put the box in his lap before slipping out of the cab. He turned to close the door and lingered there until Randal turned to look at him. "This tumor you have, I saw the clinical data they collected on you while you were in Paris. It's an exotic, rare type of cancer, its activation still a mystery. Its cause resides within a single base pair defect for a little known protein coded on a single chromosome—in men, at least. You see, it's sex-linked, carried on the Y chromosome."

Randal simply stared.

Jonah glanced at the box before looking back at Randal. "Time is critical. Nature has reminded me that despite all denials and objections, I am still my father's son."

Randal's lips parted, but he was at a loss for words. He watched his son walk around the front of the truck back toward Highlab. Before he knew what he was doing he opened his door and hopped down from the cab.

Jonah turned back to him. "Don't leave. I'll be bringing back the box for you to take down to Underlab."

Randal took a step, but the security men closed behind Jonah and stared at Randal. He frowned and lowered his head. He felt as if the ground was falling away beneath him. He didn't know what to think, or what to say. His memories on his boat and the time he'd spent with Josephine flooded back to him, washing over the memories of his mindset going into the Nigerian job, and the horrible things he did there. He knew desperation and, though he was sure his son was filled with desperation, he had to admit to himself that in fact he didn't know Jonah from a hole in the wall. He never visited Jonah over the years following the divorce. Johanna had sent a few terse letters telling of Jonah's accomplishments, but Randal always viewed them as snotty little reminders how better their life was without him. Not that she was wrong on that count, but some lingering resentment for his failures always took offense to those letters. He never wrote back. He wondered if that hurt Jonah as much as the belt whippings Randal knew from his own father.

His life was a shamble. The only thing he could with some certainty call an emotional bond was to a French escort who showed him some pity. After his divorce he turned his back on the society he knew, deciding it was nothing more than a pack of lies. Joe was the closest thing he could call a friend, and they didn't talk or see each other unless they were on a job.

But even though his life was a mess, he always enjoyed the jungle. Genevieve was as right about that as she was about his tumor. He understood Jonah's appraisal of her; had things been even a tiny bit different, he would have dismissed her as some crazy hag as well.

He'd formed a different opinion, though.

He looked to the clouds skating past the peak. He was sick of himself, sick of his life.

"Here you go."

Jonah's voice startled him. He turned to find Jonah holding the crate.

"When you brought it up here it only had a stabilizing compound that we developed at Underlab. We do the refining and purification up here at Highlab, because this is where the tree responsible for it grows. It's here now, in the crate, purer than we've ever managed. We need a new test subject, someone with a known problem. This could be history, the cure for everything we know, and everything we will ever encounter. You can be part of that."

Randal took the crate. He stared at it before looking at his son, and was shocked to understand him in a way he never anticipated. "You can't fix everything, Jonah. Some things are meant to die."

"Is that your answer?"

Randal hesitated. "No. It's just one answer." He took a step to the truck, but then looked back to Jonah. "Do you have a woman in your life?"

Jonah blinked in confusion.

"I thought so," Randal said with a sigh. "Look, I won't insult either of us by pretending to give you fatherly advice, but there's something you might want to consider. Being alone isn't all it's cracked up to be. One day, you'll regret always putting yourself first, because you'll find there's no one left around you, and then you'll have to face yourself." He tapped a finger to his temple. "Think about it."

Jonah studied him, his eyes deep and dark. "Don't break the box, Dad."

Randal gave him a final glance and nod and got in the truck. He put the crate on the seat beside him. He looked out the windshield as he turned over the motor. He squinted, peering in the distance where he thought he saw two small, dark objects coming in low toward the peak. He let go of the truck keys and let the engine stall. There was no sound. He wondered if they were birds, but he hadn't seen anything big flying any other day. He looked to his side. Jonah was already well on his way to Highlab.

Randal looked back out the windshield. He had a sinking feeling. Jonah had told him there was no commercial air traffic in the area, the terrain having been deemed too hazardous in the event of an emergency. It was part of what made the location so remote. The research team had to file special requests—that is, bribes—just to get flights into the airstrip down in the valley. But Randal knew the sound of those planes, big four-prop military surplus cargo planes suited for short runways.

The objects were nearing. He could make out the slender lines of wings.

Powered gliders. They were coming straight in.

He started the truck and threw it in reverse.

He just made it to some cover in the trees when the gliders dropped smoke shells on the peak. Chaotic gunfire broke the quiet morning, followed by the sound of explosions.

Randal cursed and stomped on the brakes. Despite the narrow confines of the road, after a few quick spins of the wheel he managed to turn the truck around and speed down the road. He fumbled in his pocket for his digital player, stuffed in an earpiece, and cycled through his microphones. The bugs up at Highlab were all outside, and they picked up the sound of a firefight from their different perspectives. It was impossible to discern what was happening, but it was obvious the peak was being stormed by an armed party, well organized and well supplied.

It reeked of corporate espionage; no government would be inclined to such a risky operation, and no government would even know what Jonah was up to in his labs. Randal had worked enough jobs to know governments were often the last to learn the unsavory details of covert corporate operations.

He reached cold certainty that it was a corporate raid. That was bad. He might get caught in the middle. Worse, the secret of Purity might get out. Whatever it was in exact scientific terms was irrelevant to him, but in a flash he knew one thing for sure, that pharmaceutical profiteers and military researchers would take it and mutate it to something monstrous.

He stomped on the brakes. He had the extract in the crate.

Joe came running up the road toward him.

Randal took a hand off the steering wheel and rested it on his gun, which he pulled out and held in his lap. He watched Joe come beside the driver's door, hands firm on his AK.

"I don't have time to explain," Joe said between breaths. "You got the crate?"

"Is Underlab compromised?"

"You got the crate? Is it next to you?"

"Where's Genevieve?"

Joe shook his head. "What? Come on Randy! Forget that stupid bitch! Is that the goddamn crate?"

Randal's shoulders sagged. Joe was bartering the use of Randal's nickname, and the closeness it implied, for leverage. It was a common thing, when people were ready to turn trust on its head, a way to dispel the rage of the person they are about to betray, or perhaps even draw that person into the betrayal. *Strike one.* He remembered finding Joe defecating in the jungle the night of Chlorophyll Bill. Every smuggler knows there are roughly twenty feet of usable intestinal tract for storage. Joe had used the jungle since starting the job. He must have smuggled parts for something, a GPS of some sort. He'd given away their location. *Strike two.* He hinted he wanted to retire, that he brought in Randal so they could both earn a big fat deposit in their accounts, before Uncle Felix retired. It was another reach for empathy. *Strike three.*

The conclusion was inescapable. Joe was working for someone else, and had sold out the whole operation: Jonah, Purity, Genevieve, and Randal included.

The moment passed. Betrayal turned to anger. Randal angled the gun-hand in his lap and fired. The bullet tore through the thin metal door and went through Joe's right eye before blowing out the side of his head. He staggered and flopped flat on his back.

Joe was the closest thing he'd had to a friend.

Joe had sold him out. After all the disdain and contempt Randal showed the world, he was betrayed by the world he'd created for himself.

Shit. You have to appreciate the irony of that.

Life follows its own order.

Simple.

Randal turned the truck around once more and sped back toward Highlab. Going to Underlab was out of the question. He thought of Genevieve amid the sounds of gunfire below him, but he suspected she knew how to take care of herself. She had survived this long, so he was sure she could survive a bunch of corporate lackeys. Besides, if he was wrong, there was nothing he could do for her. He had a plan, and it wasn't a very good one, but he figured it to be his best option.

He thought of Nigeria. Same, but different. Simple.

The duty truck careened down the road, bursting from the cover of the trees to emerge in the middle of Highlab's chaotic firefight. Both sides turned and sprayed the vehicle with fire, shattering the windows and riddling the driver with bullets before the truck slammed into the boulder at the end of the road. It was all the diversion Randal needed, Joe's corpse filling its final service as the illusion of the truck's driver. Crouched behind a tree, the yellow crate hoisted over his shoulder by its carry strap, Randal took aim and emptied his clip, one kill for each shot, before his predator's sensibility warned him someone would notice his firing position.

He scurried through the undergrowth, keeping an eye on the ruins about Highlab to discern Jonah's corporate men from the black-clad raiding party. The corporate men were trying to hold a perimeter about the lab, but they lacked coordination, and Randal was well aware of their vulnerability along the runway by the escape plane, where the ruins were lost to time. The open expanse left little room for cover between the lab and the downed gliders. He didn't see Jonah, but figured he was safe in the lab. He let it go, his mind filled with more immediate concerns.

Closer to the fight now, he put two rounds in his victims, proximity eliminating the luxury of waiting to confirm a kill. Five men down, and he got hold of an AK, scalped clips from three men, and retreated to the jungle when rounds buzzed by him. Some of the raiding party had caught sight of him, and were in certain pursuit. He picked up his pace, charging through the growth until he ducked behind a tree, stowed the crate beside him, and dropped onto his stomach with the AK trained before him. He rested his cheek on the stock, took sight, and when his pursuers broke through the undergrowth he opened fire. The AK pounded against his shoulder but made quick work of his victims, the potent rounds blowing craters of flesh from their bodies. He fired without care for his ammo, knowing he had clips to spare. When the last body crumpled to the ground he dumped his clip, slapped a fresh one home, and rose.

Something heavy slammed him to the ground.

He wheezed, and at once feared he'd been shot, but the pressure on his back told him otherwise. He tried to roll over but, the moment he moved, a large hand clamped around his neck and hoisted him to his feet, turning him before slamming him against a tree trunk. When his eyes focused, he gasped, finding himself face to face with another one of Jonah's ogres.

It held him, its hand tightening until Randal's eyes bulged, its fist drawing back. Another hand ripped the AK from Randal's grasp, and his gaze darted to the side to see another monster looming beside the tree. Behind its green mass, other shapes were emerging, splitting out of the trees, much the way he'd seen from Chlorophyll Bill, only these monsters were somewhat smaller, but thicker, as if they were older—

The villagers.

He remembered that Genevieve said they choose not to be seen. She was worried that night in the woods when Jonah's test subject had escaped. She was worried because Randal killed him.

She was worried the villagers would forget themselves and take pity on a fallen brother.

He expected the heavy fist to obliterate him. His eyes squeezed shut, but then something took him by surprise. Against all expectation, the fist let him go.

He sank to the ground as he fought to catch his breath, keeping his eyes closed until he heard the leaves rustle around him and the creak and groan of timbers. He opened his eyes at the old familiar sound of gunfire. He was alone, at least to what he could see. The villagers had let him be. There was no time to decide if it was some form of empathy for what the Purity had done for his tumor, or if they knew—in the same way Genevieve seemed to know—that he was different, or if in the wisdom of their age they decided this spasm of violence wasn't their fight, and they would let it silence itself before intervening.

These were not conquistadors with swords, or rivals with spears and clubs.

He grabbed his AK and snaked his way through the growth back to the firefight. A frigid ripple worked its way up his vertebrae at the thought of what lay behind him, of what he might be leaning against each time he braced himself against a tree to take a shot. It was a distant consideration as he neared the firefight, at the high end of the growth past the left corner of Highlab, where the escape plane sat at the end of the runway. When he sank to his belly and crawled to the edge of the growth he was surprised to see the fight diminishing. The raiders were falling back toward their gliders, covering themselves in staggered retreat, but falling back. He looked to his right to find his answer. Two trucks had come up from Underlab, and as he watched a third rolled in, bringing fresh reinforcements. From the wild look in their eyes, they were straight off the fight at Underlab, leaving Randal with the single conclusion that the raid was in the final throes of failure.

He took aim on the gliders, but then relented, his finger slipping away from the trigger. There was no need for him to spill any more blood. He'd already killed twenty men. It was enough for one day. So he watched and, before long, it was over. The gliders, light and already riddled with bullets, served no cover for the raiders. One by one they went down as Jonah's men coordinated their fire. Ten minutes later, the last of the raiders fell dead.

Only then did Jonah emerge from Highlab, walking across the grass to survey the gliders and the black-clad bodies. He shook his head before turning on one of his men and barking away at the man, his finger jabbing back and forth as his anger vented. Randal stayed prone, watching his son at work. He wasn't sure why, but he stayed there for quite some time, observing. Some of the wounded raiders were disarmed and dragged toward Highlab among the wounded corporate men, but there was one serious looking fellow there who motioned for the wounded raiders to be dragged over to him. He had a handgun and, as Randal squinted through the sights of the AK, he knew what the man's job was. He planted a foot on a wounded raider, his lips barely moving as he uttered some questions. He waited a few moments before his arm pulsed with the recoil of the gun, and then he moved on to the next raider, repeating the process.

Randal ground his teeth. He'd done such a thing several times, but what nagged him was the emptiness of the act. He knew for the interrogator it was a heated pursuit for information, despite the outward veneer of calm. But as an observer, Randal was struck by the pointlessness of the exercise, by the futile attempt to make some order of the madness of the raid.

Orders in conflict.

Le chant des ombres.

He should've retrieved the crate and walked over to Jonah. It would've redeemed him in the world of contract security, and Felix as well. It wasn't his place to judge morality; he wasn't paid to decide who should capture the spoils at hand. The crate, with its precious concentrated extract of untold possibilities, should hold no meaning for him. He had no operational parameters, but he did have clearly delineated borders. Don't break the box. Simple. But that all felt so far away as he watched Jonah join the interrogator. He didn't need to hear what they were asking. There was no point. He already knew what he was going to do.

Despite that, the report of the AK still surprised him when it kicked against his shoulder. The interrogator's head snapped to the side, showering Jonah in a bright red spray before the man's body hit the ground.

The rest of Jonah's men stood stock still, dumbfounded. Five of them fell with blood spurting from their chests before they realized they were being attacked. Randal went to full automatic and sprayed out the last of the clip before rolling away into the undergrowth. He worked his way back to the crate, cast it over his shoulder, and tossed the AK with the extra clips.

He walked back to the road, turned toward Highlab, and with his gun in hand strolled out of the jungle. Some of Jonah's men eyed him with clear suspicion, but he ignored them as he walked toward the plane. He glanced at the jungle. The crate stood out like a beacon, even with its weathered and beaten yellow plastic shell. He reached back to pat a hand on the crate before pointing to the plane. In the confusion that followed the firefight, no one noticed.

He looked toward Highlab to find several people tending to Jonah, who had slumped against a wall of Highlab, staring into his bloodied hands as his assistants tried to wipe the smear of brains and blood off his face. His gaze found Randal and held on him, but Jonah seemed incapable of action, still too stunned from having someone's head explode so close to him, and with such surprise.

Randal glanced at some new interrogator who was picking up where the one Randal killed had left off. He looked to his other side to see a line of men approaching the jungle growth in search of the unknown shooter who had killed the lead interrogator. Randal looked past them to the trees. He tipped his head to the plane once more.

The line of men neared the trees.

He was ten paces from the plane.

So close. Don't run, don't run, easy does it.

"Stop!"

It was Jonah. Randal ignored him, opening the passenger door of the plane to put the crate in the cockpit. He walked toward the back of the plane. He looked over his shoulder.

The line of men stepped into the trees.

Screams and gunfire sounded out between the crack and groan of timbers.

Randal ran around the back of the plane and climbed into the cockpit. Shouts rose up around him, but in the eruptions of gunfire it was impossible to make out any words. He started the plane's engine and pulled the release rope for the plane's anchor line. Before he knew it the plane was off at a roll. The cliff face raced toward him. AK fire chattered as Jonah's remaining men fired into the jungle, not understanding the new threat that came to them, goaded by Randal's inference that he was taking the Purity extract away. He was almost laughing with the madness of his plan, half-baked as it was. He had no intention of stealing the extract.

He throttled up, and that's when somebody at last realized he was taking the plane and sprayed it with fire. He ducked as rounds tore through the skin of the plane, but it was the loud clunk that sounded out from the engine that signaled trouble.

He cursed, but it was too late. He buried the throttle, and in the next moment the end of the cliff raced by. The plane dove down, but he pulled on the flight stick, and the plane leveled out.

A second round of fire tore through the plane. The crate bounced off him as if it had been kicked, a puff of foam billowing up from the seat where the crate had rested. The bullet that tore through the plane and hit the crate ricocheted and cracked the windshield. He heard a loud metallic twang and went into a sudden nosedive. Blinded by the spidery mess of the windshield, he struggled with the plane, now like a dead buffalo with paper wings instead of the smooth flying, light aircraft it had been a moment before.

He grappled with the stick, but he couldn't pull up. He was going down.

He cried out in defiance. So much of his improvised plan had worked he was sure he would get away with the rest of it. It all seemed so easy, right up to the point when it all started to fall apart. Steal the plane, fly to some remote place, bury the crate, and make his way out of the jungle. Get a new name, a new life, and disappear. Simple.

The plane shuddered.

He looked out his side window to the rugged jungle beneath him.

Don't break the box.

He made a last pull at the stick, and then something let go. Oily smoke filled the cockpit.

"No!" he said between coughs. "No! Not like this, not like—"

The plane disintegrated around him.

***

He opened his eyes. The familiar panic had dissipated. Past and present linked with each other and merged to a contextual whole. Seeing things in hindsight, understanding them with hindsight, he almost felt foolish for having panicked at the thought of being exposed to the concentrated extract.

He was still strapped to the exam table, but it had been rotated to hold him upright. The confusion was gone, and the madness of his situation as well. His thoughts were in focus before the first blink of his eyes.

"Subject is alert."

His head was strapped tight, so his gaze darted to the side to see one of the researchers typing away before a laptop stand. He closed his eyes, and let the sensations of his new body come to him. It was far different than anything he'd known. His skin felt as if it glowed under the bright lights, and warmth pervaded the underlying tissues of his body. *Photosynthesis.* His joints creaked somewhat as he strained against the bindings, but there was no tightness. In fact, his body flowed with strength, smooth and supple and undeniable. *Elastimer vector injections. How long will they last before I go rigid?* His feet were wet, and somehow it eased the thirst he felt not only in his throat, but through his body as well. He could almost sense the water as slow contractions deep in his legs conveyed the water up to his torso.

It reminded him of something, but he couldn't be sure what it was.

He heard the snap of fingers.

He opened his eyes to find Jonah standing before him, a surgical mask over his face.

Randal held his silence.

Jonah frowned. "Still stubborn as a stump, I see. Fitting, given your present situation, I would guess." He pulled the mask off his face. "In case you were wondering the escape plane had a GPS system hidden in the pilot's seat, which activated the moment you started the engine. I was surprised you didn't consider that, but perhaps it slipped your mind in all the considerations you weighed in betraying me and trying to steal my work."

Randal closed his eyes. He understood what he wanted to remember.

"I thought we had made a connection," Jonah said with a sigh, his voice heavy with disappointment. "We share an unfortunate genetic defect. You could have helped save us both. I held no illusions that you would make an effort for me, being that altruism is a characteristic you never displayed, but in your selfishness I thought you might be willing to entertain some notion of contributing to my work if it meant saving your own life."

Randal took a breath. It was an odd feeling, as it seemed he drew in air over his whole body, imparting a sense of weightlessness. It served as a complimentary dovetail to the heaviness of his new biomass. He felt the water moving through him, and let it drain down his arms to his fingers. His fingertips felt sticky at once.

Oblivious, Jonah rambled on. "You said to me that I can't fix everything, that some things were meant to die. I have no intention of dying, not here, not now, not for a very long time. And if I have to drill a hole in your head, take a hacksaw to your limbs, or roast you in a lumber kiln to do it, I'm going to find out why you have succeeded in an accidental, uncontrolled exposure to an untested extract concentration when all other subjects under very controlled and rigidly rehearsed situations all went insane. So. I will ask one last time. Are you willing to help me, to help your son, and perhaps countless others?"

To Randal, it was another hollow overture of empathy. He wondered if Jonah had found Joe's body. He had no idea how long he'd been in the lab. Perhaps Jonah didn't know, or didn't care, or was too arrogant to think such a ploy might fail.

It wasn't important. He remembered what Genevieve had said to him, that the smallest seedling could use the hydrostatic pressure of its roots to crack the greatest stone. He understood the stickiness in his fingers. It was not a secretion, but rather minute extensions of his flesh, working back along his palm and into the stays that held the straps on his arms. He wasn't sure how long it took, but he held his silence until he felt in some odd extension of his tactile sense every notch and crevice he could find.

Jonah snapped his fingers again. "Is this thing still awake?"

Randal opened his eyes. Jonah was looking at the researcher at Randal's side. The room was empty but for the three of them. Randal looked at his son. He found his voice and, when he heard it, it sounded like the rustle of leaves. It erased any doubt as to what he planned to do.

"Jonah."

Jonah turned to him. "Ah, you still have a voice. Good."

"What would you do with me?"

Jonah took a deep breath and held it for several seconds as his eyes narrowed, scrutinizing Randal. He let his breath go and tipped his head back. "I would do anything, and everything, I could. What would you do with yourself? You know you can't leave this place. The world you knew is lost to you, and you to it. You are as alone as any living creature could be alone. The only hope left for you is to offer yourself up to me. I know how smart you are. I know how you think. I know you understand these things."

Randal closed his eyes. Jonah's words swirled in his head. For some reason, he remembered that night with Genevieve under the stars, and the conversation they shared. Only in that moment did he understand the things she said, and why she had left out her old leather-bound edition of Victor Hugo's Hunchback for him to see. It enveloped his imagination, and then he saw himself, saw himself standing atop a spectacular cathedral, an edifice of man's worship crafted in the boastful pride of craftwork. He looked down from the height of that edifice—that precipice—and beheld the chaos below him, the crossed currents of human inclinations washing about. He saw the misplaced vanity and lust in those who should hold purity for their aspirations. He saw the self-consuming notion of unattainable desire symbolized by a seductive woman of dubious nature. And he saw himself as the hunchback, the monster, presiding over all of it, in the delirium of his madness tugging at his bell ropes so the deafening cacophony of his rage might somehow penetrate his deafness to resonate within the sinews of his body—conveying some message his higher senses were too confused to decipher. Yes, this was how he perceived it in that moment, all of it, the mayhem he called his life, and the thing he'd become, this monster of the summation of his inclinations.

He looked upon his son. He saw what he saw, and knew it well enough from knowing it in himself. Jonah thought he knew everything, and so he knew nothing. For all his intelligence, for all his ambition, when it came to the art of guile, he was still a child, blind to the hidden orders of the world around him, orders Randal now perceived.

He knew what he had to do. It wasn't a decision; it was the natural culmination of so many elements combining in so many intricate ways across time.

And yet, so simple, it was almost uneventful.

In a coordinated isometric contraction he drove the water pooled in his body down his arms, through his hands, and into the dendritic projections he had worked into the crevices of the strap stays. The metal failed under the surge of hydrostatic pressure, and with a great heave of his arms the stays cracked apart. His arms flew out like two pendulums, his fists whipping around and slamming against either side of Jonah's head, shattering his skull and crushing his head flat as if it offered no more resistance than a raw egg. Randal reached down and ripped the straps free of his legs, ignoring the researcher who staggered back in shock as Jonah's body dropped to the floor in a torrent of blood. Randal stepped free of the exam table and the water basin at its base, pulled his fist back, and sent it hurtling to pulverize the researcher's rib cage. The hapless man was flung across the room with the impact, blood spurting from his mouth as his head smacked against the wall.

Randal tore the door to the room off its hinges and threw it aside. He ignored the panic in the lab next to the exam room, swatting aside anyone who got in his way as he smashed down the support columns of Highlab's pre-fab structure. The building groaned around him as he tore his way through its successive chambers, demolishing store rooms, the purification lab, and finally the living quarters, hurtling tiered bunks against walls with panicked researchers still clinging to the blankets they pulled over their heads. At last he threw his shoulder into the outer security door, and after two massive slams of his weight the wall and door gave way to dump him on the ground.

It was dark. The sky was clear. An undulating alarm pierced the night until he heard the deafening crash of the building collapse upon itself behind him. The alarm squawked and went silent; the lights about the building went dark as Highlab's generators failed. Sporadic AK fire flashed in the darkness as security men darted about, searching for this new threat. Randal swatted them with heavy fists when he ran across their path, their bones snapping like toothpicks and their organs rupturing like rotten fruits beneath the weight of his blows. A few stray rounds found their mark on him, but to his relief he felt little pain, and knew the rounds did even less damage.

There was an explosion from the wreckage of Highlab, and he spun to see a ball of flame bloom in the night sky. Security men were backlit by the sudden flash of light, and he took advantage of the moment to pummel several more of them before he caught the glint of headlights coming up the road. He charged to the end of the road and with a heave sent the marker boulder over the edge, where it plummeted to the jungle below with a resounding boom. He turned as the headlights swelled around him and spread his arms in challenge to the truck racing toward him. Several men in the back of the truck stood and fired over the cab, their rounds pounding into him and sending a shudder through his mass, but he held his ground, only to dive to the side as the truck threatened to run him down. In their haste, and with the boulder missing behind him, they had no idea how close they were to the cliff—before they knew it the truck hurtled over the edge and disappeared into the darkness. The sound of screams faded in the darkness before cutting off in a racket of shattered metal and timber.

He took off at a run down the road. He could hear gunfire to his side as he passed the wreckage of Highlab, and between the gunfire he heard the thump of heavy feet charging about the site. There were cries for help, desperate shouts for mercy, but they were silenced one by one between the awful sounds of human forms crackling in violent ruin.

He continued to run, amazed at the tireless energy of his body. He could only guess how much weight he'd gained in his transformation, but he knew he must have gained a density far beyond his human form, as his feet pounded the road and left deep gouges in his wake. As he neared Underlab and the village he heard sounds similar to those around the destruction of Highlab, and knew what he hoped for had come to pass. The villagers, those who had gained the ability to change by will into something like him, had emerged from their hiding in the jungle to reclaim their isolation. It was their score to settle, not his. The secret of Purity would remain a guarded secret. Jonah was correct in judging that Randal had no altruistic allusions, at least by Randal's estimate. But he knew if the secret got out, had he been exposed to the extract when he was the rampaging, predatory psychopath of his youth, he could only imagine the horrific monsters he and men like him could have become. The world would have passed under their brutal dictate, and they the living demons to brutalize humanity for their entertainment.

Perhaps, given that consideration, it was a unique moment of altruism for him. It wasn't important. In one way, Jonah was right. The world was lost to Randal, and he was lost to it. He had nowhere to go.

Except for one place.

He came to a halt in the middle of the village, ignoring the mangled bodies of security men and researchers around him. A fearsome racket of demolition sounded out from the slope that hid Underlab. As he looked about he saw one of the villagers, in form similar as he, charge by and slam itself into the side of a truck. Several security men were thrown from the vehicle as it toppled over, and the villager clambered over the overturned truck to finish its murderous work. Randal looked away at the short flurry of screams before the crunching thumps of the villager's fists silenced the men.

Randal looked to his side, past the abandoned steeple and its old bell to spot Genevieve's hut. He took a step, and to his dismay found his legs going stiff. Jonah's injections were losing their effect, so soon after his escape. He staggered forward, wondering how the villagers remained so nimble.

His suspicion, when it came to him, was so obvious it was of little surprise that it had escaped his consideration.

He stopped before Genevieve's dwelling and tapped a finger on the door, careful not to pound it down in his strength. He was certain she had the door barred. Not that it would stop him from forcing his way in, but terrorizing her was the last thing he wanted to do. She was the only connection left to him in the surreal dissociation of his life. He needed her. He ached to see her. He had to see her, before he feared it would be too late for him.

He splayed a hand on her door and fought to summon his voice. "Genevieve?"

"Tell me your name," she said, bracing herself against her door.

He creaked as he turned to her. "Ran ... dal ..."

An explosion sounded out from Underlab. She opened the door, her lips parting as she stared at him in his new incarnation. She stepped aside and watched as he struggled to move his legs and make his way into her dwelling. Her eyes lingered on him as she closed and barred the door behind him.

She nodded and pushed aside the two guardian stones set beside the door. Some of the stiffness in his limbs was alleviated, leaving him to look in wonder at the stones as he remembered the one she set inside the door the night after Chlorophyll Bill. He looked up to see her retrieve her water bottle before uncapping it and holding it up to his mouth for him to drink. The moment the water washed into him he felt the warmth bloom through his body, and his joints eased at once. He swayed, but caught himself, and rested his back against the wall. "Genevieve," he whispered in his hoarse voice, "I never understood you until now."

She held the water bottle, but rested a tentative hand on his chest, her fingers probing the density of his thickened hide. She looked into his eyes. "You should rest."

"Can't," he forced out. "Go stiff. Why?"

She shook her head. "The villagers, those who can change back and forth, they are ancient to this world. Only they know their secrets, and you see now how they protect them. Do you remember what I told you about the orders of the world? It took them many years to learn not to lose themselves when they change. It is easy to forget our world when the change comes. You know this now. Only they know how to come back, how to remember themselves, how to will their forms as they desire. You have endured the change in days, when it took them generations to master it."

His breath seeped from him in a long wheeze. "No ... back?"

Her face fell before she gave him a single shake of her head.

He creaked as his hand rose. He took care and, to his relief, it was a gentle brush of his fingers on her cheek.

She rested her face in his hand before laying her hand over his.

"No sad," he forced out as her eyes welled up. "Okay with this."

She lifted her leather bottle and poured the rest of the water in his mouth.

There was no swallow to take it in, it simply became one with him. The warmth of the Purity hit him in full this time, and his eyes drooped shut as it carried him away. The easy fluidity of his body returned, and with it he slumped against the wall and let his head tilt back as the mysterious compound did its work. It reminded him of the first seductive detachment of alcohol's blush, the soothing freedom of flight, the serenity of floating beneath the star laden night, when all elements of abstraction found their equilibrium in the senility of Time's tireless tides. Horrors of the past, insecurities of the future, emotional remnants clinging from regrets; all these things did not at once become lost or lose their meaning, but rather their place and perspective altered within him, around him, and became something else, a tidal undulation at the very base of his awareness, where only sleeping thoughts could find their home, where whispers revealed their secrets.

Le chant des ombres.

Ombres, French for shadows. Hombres, Spanish for men. More than a linguistic trick.

He heard it then, felt it inside. Images flashed in his mind through the darkness. He was under a high school float, with Johanna in his arms. He was standing in the middle of a Nigerian village, surrounded by the dead. He was sitting in a cold exam room, feeling far removed as he was told his bleak prognosis. He was lounging on his boat, watching Josephine as she stood on the bow and gazed into the sunset. He was holding Jonah for the first time. He was glaring at Jonah as he stormed out on his family; he was getting towels in an Athens hotel when his room down the hall exploded.

He was watching the stars with Genevieve.

He shot Joe in the head, and watched his one friend drop dead in the midst of his betrayal.

And so, he continued to listen.

The song of shadows.

He opened his eyes. Perception and sight had diverged within him, concepts broken from their semantic relation. Simple, and yet not so.

The day had passed and night returned. His body creaked as he turned to find Genevieve preparing her blanket roll. She slung it across her body and picked up her lamp, but then reconsidered and put the lamp away.

She looked to him. "Will you walk with me, Randal?"

It was a struggle to remember his voice. "Where?"

Her eyes filled with sadness, but a fragile smile pulled at her lips. "I want you to meet my parents."

***

They walked the jungle. It was a clear night. It was still, and a sense of peace filled the darkness, so that he almost felt sleepy as he followed her. Before long she led him to the clearing where they sat the night of Chlorophyll Bill, and then he heard something, something he had not heard before. It was like the song of shadows, but different in an almost inconceivable way, the song bearing a lilt he didn't sense elsewhere.

He stopped, understanding. Once again, he felt like a fool.

She rested a hand on his wrist and pointed to two large trees, the two that framed the clearing, towering up into the night. He remembered the spot before those two trees; it was the same place she put her blanket the night he sat with her. When he looked to the two trees, it was clear to him that they were different, different in a way he could perceive only in that moment.

"They made an extract, even with the limited means they had," she explained. "I was sick, and they wanted to save me. In that time there were no antibiotics. My parents had managed to ingratiate themselves with the villagers in the valley below, and they brought some water with the syrup mixed in. And so, I was healed. I was never sick again. We moved up here, and we were allowed, because the villagers sensed the Purity at work in me. They destroyed our ship, so I could never leave. But my parents were stubborn, and wanted to study this thing that had saved me, and condemned us to this place. They drank their extract and, in time, the change came upon them. The elders led them here. All around us, these are the trees of those who tired of this world, and wanted the solitude of the change, and so forgot how to come back. They live here now, sleeping gods, their dreams whispering in the night. *Le chant des ombres*. And further, high up the peak, are the first who took the change, and the fluid of their body is the source of the Purity, so that no one knows now how they took the change, or if they were ever men to begin with, or if they were the gods themselves of those ruined temples."

He looked down. There was a patch of fresh soil behind him. He looked at Genevieve and found his voice. "For me?"

She nodded. "*Oui, Monsieur* Randal. They made it for you, if you are ready."

He stared at her for some time before lowering his head and stepping by her. He set his feet on the fresh earth, and its loose, cool depth seemed to welcome him. He stood then beneath the night sky and, as he stood and gazed, the world around him seemed to both spin and slow — slowing in the way he perceived the minutia of the surrounding jungle in all its intricacy, and spinning in the way he was able to comprehend it in whole. His body stiffened the longer he looked to the stars, and as he did so he felt the tangled strength of his body order itself in a new way. His toes divided and lengthened, burrowing down to anchor him to the earth. His back stretched and his body thickened as his arms splayed the widening net of his fingers to drink up the warmth of the sun as days came and went. The cool, damp air of the mornings rolled by him, and so too the dew ran down his body, and he drank it up from his pores.

Before he knew it, and at once to his long held anticipation, his intuitions were realized, and he began to embrace a sense of peace he longed to know, perhaps had longed to know in all the turmoil of his former life. It came to him nevertheless and, despite his past, or in some ways he suspected because of his past, his consciousness flowed to this new equilibrium, and embraced it before there was ample opportunity or tangible desire to even contemplate its nature. There was no need. There was a new simplicity he understood, subtle and sublime in its hidden complexity. His roots dug deep down into the earth, and anchored him to the creeping restlessness of the firmament beneath him, steadying him. His body grew tall and straight, so that he had perspective and, as much as he looked over so much around him, he was reminded still of the towering peaks that looked down upon him, and so he knew humility in his wooded might. His many layered canopies of rich jade leaves swayed in the winds, stirred by their currents, and so he knew the tranquility of buoyancy, and the transcendence of weightlessness. And though he was conscious of even the single ant scurrying up the dizzying height of the immensity he became, he was ambivalent to the count of days, though he recognized the change of seasons in the undulating rhythm of the song of shadows.

All these things enmeshed him, and he enmeshed them, and rather than being at odds, or feeling sundered, or wallowing in the antipathy of loneliness, he came to know the opposites of these things, and pondered all things in a different light.

So it was for him, and the years rolled by without count or care.

***

Some things, though, do not change.

Genevieve walked the jungle at night, her blanket roll slung across her body and her lantern bobbing in her hand. She wasn't sure why she carried it; those days of turmoil the last time outsiders came to the village resided now several decades in the past. A few reconnaissance parties had scoured the area in search of any sign of the labs or any of the dozens of people that had formed Jonah's team. The jungle wouldn't tolerate any trace in view, and so, to the frustration of those hard-eyed men, they were left no choice but to abandon their search and look somewhere else. In time, it was forgotten, and no more parties came to look. The villagers who took the change returned one by one, walking back to the village in their naked human form to pull on their clothes, don their hats, and resume the patient tending of their tiered rice gardens. In the following seasons, then, she and the villagers welcomed the solitude they had enjoyed for many years before the turmoil. Unlike the villagers, she had to admit to herself there were certain things she missed—such as the small convenience of gas for cooking, or oil for her lantern.

But these were small concerns and, like the pitted bell in the village, the ship's bell from her voyage with her parents that had brought her across the ocean to the village, those concerns would be a heritage. They held their place, and it was her place to make sense of them.

She was, after all, the Interpreter.

She walked the jungle, and in time found her favored spot, where the jungle canopy opened to reveal the stars above in all their twinkling glory. She looked about before walking to one tree in particular and, with a smile, set out her blanket. She whispered to her guardian stones and set them at the four corners of her blanket before settling down. When a shooting star passed over, she smiled, and let her gaze linger on its trail before she lowered her head and poured some water. The taste, still distinctive after so many years, drew her to lick her lips, and sit in silent contemplation for some time before she shrugged and let out a long sigh.

She opened an old leather-bound volume in her lap and let her fingers trace over the intricate drawing on the title page. It was an old art of a distant age, preface to a timeless tale, one of orders in conflict and convergence. "Bong-bong, bong-bong," she whispered to herself before looking up to the tree under which she sat. "This time, I will read it for you, Monsieur Randal."

The stars shimmered in the sky.

The air was still.

She leaned back against the trunk of the tree and began to read, her soft voice bringing to life the melodious wording of the old French text.

The leaves rustled above her.

About the Author

Roland Allnach, after working twenty years on the night shift in a hospital, has witnessed life from a slightly different angle. He has been working to develop his writing career, drawing creatively from literary classics, history, and mythology. His short stories, one of which was nominated for the Pushcart Prize, have appeared in several publications. His first anthology, 'Remnant', saw publication in 2010. It has since gone on to critical acclaim and placed as a Finalist/Science Fiction in the 2011 National Indie Excellence Awards. 'Oddities & Entities' marks his second stand alone publication.

When not immersed in his imagination, he can be found at his website, www.rolandallnach.com, along with his published stories. Writing aside, his joy in life is the time he spends with his family.